PILLARS
OF
FIRE

"SHAGAN, THE BEST-SELLING AUTHOR OF *VENDETTA,* HAS MINED THE LIBYAN–WEST GERMAN ARMS CONNECTION TO PRODUCE A WHITE-KNUCKLE THRILLER ABOUT IMPENDING NUCLEAR ARMA-GEDDON IN THE MIDDLE EAST. . . . THE ACTION IN SHAGAN'S METICULOUSLY PLOTTED STORY RACES AT BREAKNECK SPEED, FROM BERLIN TO THE SAHARA DESERT TO BALUCHISTAN, UNTIL IT FI-NALLY REACHES AN EXPLOSIVE CLIMAX IN THE ARABIAN SEA. *PILLARS OF FIRE* IS SLAM-BANG ENTERTAINMENT ALL THE WAY. . . ."
—ALA *Booklist*

PILLARS OF FIRE HAS, "AMONG ITS INNU-MERABLE ATTRIBUTES, THE QUALITIES OF ADMONITION AND PROPHECY . . ."
—*Los Angeles Times*

"INTRIGUE AND VIOLENCE AND SUSPENSE . . . LOVE AND PASSION . . . THE AUTHOR OF *THE FORMULA* HAS COME UP WITH ANOTHER FORMULA FOR A BEST-SELLING BOOK."
—*San Diego Union*

(more . . .)

Books by Steve Shagan

Save the Tiger
City of Angels
The Formula
The Circle
The Discovery
Vendetta

STEVE SHAGAN

PILLARS OF FIRE

POCKET BOOKS

New York   London   Toronto   Sydney   Tokyo   Singapore

POCKET BOOKS, a division of Simon & Schuster Inc.
1230 Avenue of the Americas, New York, NY 10020

ISBN: 0-671-68938-X

First Pocket Books paperback printing December 1990

10 9 8 7 6 5 4 3 2 1

POCKET and colophon are registered trademarks of Simon & Schuster Inc.

Printed in the U.S.A.

For the valiant Tiger Flower . . .

It is our right to develop nuclear technology, and when we achieve our goal, 900 million Muslims will share in the fruits of our research . . .

—Dr. I. Q. Khan,
director of Pakistan's
Nuclear Research Center
March 5, 1986

The acquisition of an atomic bomb and delivery system is the legitimate pursuit of the Libyan nation.

—Muammar al-Qaddafi,
November 3, 1987

A nation under siege by terrorists is permitted to use force to preempt or prevent attacks, when no other means is available.

—George Shultz,
January 5, 1986

And when you look into an abyss, the abyss also looks into you.

—FRIEDRICH NIETZSCHE

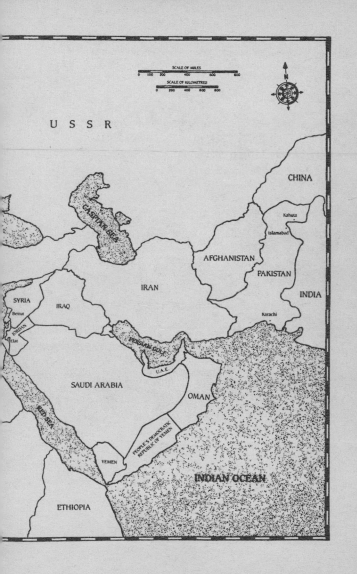

THE
LIBYAN
DESERT

December 6, 1991

PROLOGUE

The eye of God rose majestically, transforming the desert into a surging crimson sea. Shifting sands swirled off the towering dunes and swept across the ridges, wadis, and wild palms of Jarmah. The spring-fed oasis sheltered a communications trailer and the canvas tents housing German technicians and their Libyan assistants. Bedouins of the Siwan tribe hunched over fires, sipping hot tea and eating goat cheese wrapped in freshly baked pita bread. Officers of the Sixteenth Tripoli Brigade sat atop their Soviet-built personnel carriers, smoking French cigarettes and drinking Kenyan coffee.

Isolated from the rest of the camp, a sprawling black goatskin tent was pitched at the edge of the oasis, guarded by thirteen heavily armed young women in leopard-camouflage uniforms.

The tent flap was suddenly pulled aside and the most dangerous man in the world strode out into the desert dawn. He wore a crisp safari suit and polished boots. Mirrored glasses shielded his eyes from the rising sun, and a red-checked kaffiyeh was wound around his head. The charismatic leader of the oil-rich nation smiled and exchanged a few words with the captain of his female bodyguards. Carrying a prayer rug, he crossed a shallow wadi, climbed nimbly up a high dune, and for a moment stood motionless, staring off at the horizon. The vast desert landscape was scarred by an incongruous maze of oil rigs, topped by orange flames burning off excess natural gas. Allah had blessed the people of Libya with immense wealth, and he, Muammar al-Qaddafi, had been entrusted with God's munificence.

Destiny had chosen him to create an Islamic empire stretching from the Atlantic Ocean across the entire North African tier to the Red Sea, and beyond to Pakistan. He, the son of a shepherd, would unite the Arab nations and lead them into Jerusalem. On that great and glorious day, he would be proclaimed the savior of the Arab nation. The Zionists would be consumed by a terrible yellow fire, their cities vaporized, their people baked into the ruins. The plans of twenty-one years were approaching fruition and he had not remained quiescent during these long years of patient waiting. He steadfastly supported revolutionary movements in forty-five countries and had incurred the wrath of the Great Satan. The Americans had challenged him in the Gulf of Sidra, and in April 1986 they had bombed Tripoli and killed his adopted son. Their bombs had been meant for him, but instead murdered the child. They were a cowardly people who relied on sophisticated weapons to do their bidding. But as Allah had ordained, the infidels would be paid back in kind. Their Sixth Fleet would be destroyed and their cities held hostage. The world would soon discover that a superpower had risen in North Africa.

His own nuclear-research center at Tajura would in time produce weapons-grade enriched uranium, but there was no longer any need to wait. His investment in the Pakistani bomb was about to produce a magnificent dividend. The moment of exultation was almost at hand.

The Prince of Islam spread his prayer rug, sank to his knees, faced Mecca, and prayed. After five salaams he rose and nodded to the waiting German technicians.

Dr. Alois Brunner, an aged, sharp-faced German rocket scientist, puffed his way up the steep dune and addressed

4

Qaddafi. "The countdown is in its final moments. Shall I put it on the speaker?"

Qaddafi nodded and removed his reflective glasses. He was about to raise his binoculars when the desert wind sent him a message. He turned and saw them—white-robed Taureg tribesmen astride their camels atop an adjacent dune, motionless, like icons out of another time, waiting to see the fire in the sky. Qaddafi waved to the chief, who flicked his riding stick in acknowledgment.

They had chosen the time of the test launch with great care; unless the patterns had been changed, the American KH-11 spy satellite was not in orbit over Jarmah.

As the amplified countdown proceeded, Qaddafi trained his binoculars on a curious circular formation baked into the skin of the desert.

The ground trembled, and an ominous roar thundered from beneath the desert floor. The circle opened and the huge rocket rose up from its underground silo on a shimmering tail of fire. The German-designed ICBM gained altitude with excruciating reluctance before overcoming gravity and streaking skyward.

Qaddafi watched the fiery tail until it disappeared into the opaque sky.

Minutes later, the transmitter voice announced the touchdown of the dummy warhead on target, six hundred miles to the east.

Qaddafi flicked his mirrored glasses down and glanced off at the far dune. The Tauregs were gone.

BOOK I

RED DESERT

Washington, D.C.
December 23, 1991

CHAPTER ONE

Despite the sudden snowstorm and holiday overload, the Metroliner from New York arrived at Washington's Union Station on time.

Tom Lawford stepped out of the club car onto the dank-smelling underground platform and followed the other passengers up the escalator to the restored Beaux Arts terminal.

As he crossed the cathedral-like white marble concourse, his eyes darted anxiously at the departing passengers. The wiry Asian man with whom he had shared the club car was definitely not following him. The man was hugging a small child and handing a Christmas package to an exotic-looking fashionably dressed woman. Paranoia, Tom thought, shaking his head—paranoia triggered by Hickey's phone call. The passage of time had not changed that tense, sweaty voice. *"Take the noon Metroliner. Steve Garrett will meet you."*

The fact that Hickey had survived all these years was in itself a miracle. John Hickey was a CIA ferret. The Agency funded Hickey and his partner, Steve Garrett, in a private enterprise called Allegiance Research Associates. Their company was one of many proprietary businesses set up by the CIA's Covert Procurement Bureau. While Allegiance Research serviced "straight" clients, its primary function was to handle high-risk situations the Agency chose to distance itself from.

A call from Hickey was tantamount to a summons from the Agency, and as Lawford climbed the ornate staircase, he thought it had come at precisely the right time. They hadn't used him since helping him break the Pentagon purchasing scandal back in the summer of '87 . . . more than four years ago—a long time. But then, disuse was the very essence of deep cover.

The late-afternoon air was cold but not raw. Snowflakes danced in the headlights of moving traffic. The sky was dark blue, but strangely luminous.

Standing underneath the terminal overhang, Lawford stared off at the glowing pristine needle of the Washington Monument and sensed his familiar affection for the old city. It was the nerve center of the greatest power on earth, and yet there was something surreal about the place. Lawford regarded the nation's capital as Hollywood on the Potomac, where fantasy and reality coalesced in Kafkaesque harmony.

From time to time, people waiting for taxis glanced surreptitiously at him. Lawford was accustomed to occasional public recognition. His periodic appearances narrating segments of a popular late-night TV news program had lent him a vague celebrity. His true fame had been achieved in print journalism, but no one connected bylines with faces.

A sudden sharp squeal of brakes pulled him out of his reverie. The passenger door of a black 1991 two-seat Jaguar flew open and Steve Garrett curled his thin lips into something that resembled a smile.

"Sorry I'm late."

Lawford studied Garrett's chalky skin, watery brown eyes, and shabby overcoat.

"Anything wrong?" Garrett asked.

"You don't seem to go with a Jaguar," Lawford replied, corkscrewing his six feet into the low-slung car.

"You're right. This English glitz belongs to Hickey."

Easing the powerful car away from the curb, Garrett turned the wipers up a notch. The blades beat furiously back and forth across the curved glass, but the light snowfall continued to pile up at the base of the windshield.

"Goddamn wipers are useless."

Tom blew on his hands. "How about some heat?"

"It's busted," Garrett said as he slid the window down and spit a thick lump of phlegm. "There's a flask of brandy in the glove compartment," he added. "Help yourself."

Lawford found the silver flask atop some documents, unscrewed the cap, and took a long pull.

"That's better," he sighed, feeling the brandy warming his chest. "How about you?"

"No, thanks. I've got a bleeding ulcer."

Tom took another swallow, capped the flask, and asked, "Where's Hickey?"

"I don't know. He called me a few hours ago and told me to pick you up. . . . Funny, isn't it?"

"What's that?"

"I'm his partner. I handle the money. I take care of the books. But he doesn't trust me—I mean, the way longtime friends should trust one another."

"I wouldn't take it personally. Hickey doesn't trust anyone."

The luminosity had seeped out of the sky and the night had turned black. The headlights of oncoming traffic flared into the tinted windshield.

"Hold on!" Garrett suddenly shouted, spinning the wheel and swerving dangerously off Louisiana onto Delaware Avenue. The sharpness of the move slammed Lawford against the door.

"There's a black Mercedes been tailing me," Garrett said, fiddling with the knob controlling the windshield wipers.

"Try the deicer," Tom suggested.

"Are you kidding?" Garrett replied sarcastically, his eyes darting up to the rearview mirror. "Let me have a touch of that brandy."

"What about your ulcer?"

"Fuck it."

Tilting his head back, Garrett swallowed the brandy and wiped his mouth with the back of his hand.

The traffic thinned and they picked up speed, heading west on Pennsylvania.

"Looks like I lost that goddamn Mercedes."

"Suppose they're working a three-car tail?"

Garrett eyed Lawford with undisguised disdain. "Fucking journalists always looking for something that isn't there."

"And sometimes finding it." Tom smiled. "Where are we going?"

"A CIA safe house in Georgetown."

"Then what?"

"You wait for Hickey's call."

They reached Wisconsin Avenue and entered the heart of Georgetown. The colonial streets were crowded with college students and last-minute Christmas shoppers.

"Seems like a lot of action for a Monday night," Tom said.

"Kids are out of school," Garrett grumbled. "Most of them are either Arabs or Chinks. I don't know what the hell they've got to do with Christmas."

"You're the last true liberal in Washington."

"I'll take their money, if that's what you mean."

"Now you're talking like a conservative."

"Lay off, Tom."

Turn-of-the-century streetlamps glowed softly along Dumbarton Street. The frosted windows of town houses were decorated with Christmas lights, and the sweet aroma of woodsmoke permeated the air. Halfway down the stately street, Garrett turned abruptly into the driveway of a two-story clapboard house.

"The duty agent is Larry Dutton," Garrett explained. "He's big and black, used to play linebacker for the Eagles. He'll show you around. Relax until Hickey calls."

"Thanks for the lift."

Garrett nodded, and shifted into reverse. The Jaguar's wheels tossed up a spray of snow as it spun around and headed north.

* * *

Larry Dutton was a pleasant-looking giant who walked with a slight limp. He showed Lawford into the living room, where a crackling fire blazed in a huge fireplace.

"I've got one going in the study upstairs too." Dutton paused and asked, "You hungry?"

"No, thanks. I had a snack on the train."

"Well, if you get thirsty, there's a bar upstairs in the study. The guest bedroom is on your left at the top of the stairs. You need anything, just holler. The phones are debugged daily."

Lawford entered the bedroom and hung his bag in the closet. He knew the room was wired. Dutton's assurance to the contrary only confirmed the presence of bugs. In the Agency, assurance and deception were synonymous.

The book-lined study was spacious, with a large bay window facing the street. Tom walked around the bar and poured himself some vodka over ice. Taking a sip, he stared at the flames in the used-brick fireplace and thought about Hickey and that long-ago summer of '68 on the Laotian run.

Lawford had been a foreign correspondent for Reuters, and Hickey was ostensibly transporting refugees in the twin-engine Cessna he flew for Capital Air Transport. In point of fact, they were both working for the Agency, running opium out of Laos into Thailand. Thai dealers converted the raw opium into morphine bricks, which were shipped to Sicily and transformed into heroin. The opium proceeds were used to purchase AK-47 assault rifles for the Laotian tribesmen. The covert operation was designed to arm and train a battalion of tribesmen to interdict North Vietnamese troops moving south along the Mekong River.

The clandestine mission proved to be an absurdity, since no amount of urging could convince the Laotians to leave their jungle villages, much less engage North Vietnamese regulars. But in spite of the apathetic tribesmen, Lawford and Hickey continued to follow their orders. They exported opium and imported weapons. They bribed territorial warlords, armed the tribesmen, and in general raised a lot of hell.

In those days, Vientiane, the capital of Laos, was a hotbed of spies, gunrunners, and dope peddlers. Private clubs were stocked with Scotch, vodka, American cigarettes, and exotic-looking Thai hookers. The Laotian dope run had been like a surreal Disneyland ride. Lawford thought that Francis Coppola had caught the essence of it in *Apocalypse Now*.

But there was nothing surreal about that steamy jungle morning when the Huey chopper crashed in a ball of fire. Lawford's shoulder was dislocated, and his right hand smashed. The pilot's neck was broken, and the flames already cooking him were licking at Tom's feet. The Laotian tribesmen stood in a circle, motionless, grinning, waiting for the flames to roast the trapped American. Hickey burst through the circle of tribesmen and suffered third-degree burns on both arms pulling Lawford out of the wreckage only seconds before the big Huey exploded.

Sipping his drink, Tom thought about the fractured prisms of remembered time. The events in Laos seemed to have happened yesterday, but to someone else, and in another lifetime.

Taking a small bottle of aspirin out of his pocket, he popped three tablets and chased them down with vodka. The combination had proved to be an effective antidote for the chronic arthritic pain that radiated out of the nape of his neck and ran down his left arm, balling up in his left wrist. The pain struck at moments of tension, or if he spent too much time at the typewriter. His doctor had advised him to live with the painful condition and avoid surgical intervention.

Alone in the safe house, he felt like a character in Beckett's *Waiting for Godot*. Waiting for what? He was staring at fifty; disconnected and drifting. All the excitement and romance of life seemed to be rooted in the past. His marriage was mired in apathy and indifference. Even his work was no longer challenging. The exhilaration that used to accompany a complex piece of investigative journalism was missing. The spiritual emptiness had become profound after his twin brother's death. But Tom wasn't afraid of death—it was the sameness of life that haunted him. He desperately missed that primal sense of purpose that carried with it both discovery and jeopardy; but maybe that kind of singular resolve was a youthful illusion. He remembered somebody saying that after forty, in order to survive, a man had to become Machiavelli.

He turned and caught a startling glimpse of his reflection in the mirror over the bar. The deep gray eyes seemed to be receding in their sockets, and the classic high cheekbones and chiseled patrician features had assumed a hard, severe edge. It was the face of a stranger.

The phone rang sharply, startling him.

"Tom?"

"Yeah?"

"Hickey. You upstairs?"

"In the study."

"Kill the lights. Walk over to the window—take a look at the street."

"What am I looking for?"

"A black Mercedes with its motor running."

"Hold on."

The snowfall seemed somewhat heavier, and large flakes flickered in the glowing streetlamps. The cobblestones and sidewalks were blanketed in a mantle of white purity. The cars were parked in their driveways. The street was tranquil and deserted, and reminded Lawford of a Currier & Ives winter scene. Returning to the bar, Tom picked up the receiver. "Nothing—no Mercedes. It looks like a Christmas card."

"That fucking Garrett must be on something." Hickey sighed. "Okay. Meet me at Starke's. Fifteen minutes. Table's in your name."

"Fifteen minutes?"

"Hell, you can walk it in ten."

The ubiquitous Larry Dutton was waiting at the front door. The big man gave Lawford a pair of rubber overshoes and helped him on with his overcoat. He then handed him a key and a card.

"Key to the front door and the phone number."

"I won't be long."

"Well, just in case."

"Thanks."

15

Lawford reached the sidewalk and took his time pulling on his gloves and adjusting his cashmere scarf. The snow brought back vivid flashes of his childhood and a small village in eastern Maine. As he walked toward Wisconsin Avenue, he thought of powdery drifts, and snowball fights with his brother, and pretty girls with flushed cheeks and the crisp, clean smell of winter.

CHAPTER TWO

Starke's was jammed with an animated crowd of upscale Washingtonians enjoying that cozy intimate hour before dinner. The Jets and Lions were the Monday Night Football attraction on the TV set perched above the bar.

The large oblong café throbbed with a narcissistic din that reverberated between the white tile floor and the green copper ceiling.

Seated at a table catty-corner in the rear section of the oak-paneled room, Lawford thanked the young waitress who brought him his second vodka martini. The waitresses were students from Georgetown University who worked part-time to help with their tuition. Tom admired the grace with which they moved through the narrow spaces between the crowded tables, balancing trays of drinks, hamburgers, and fried clams.

Hickey was characteristically late, but Tom wasn't concerned. Punctuality had never been Hickey's strong suit. Through a long, angled mirror Tom noticed the reflected image of a man with Arabic features standing at the bar, staring up at the televised football game with hypnotic intensity, as if his life depended upon the outcome of every play.

The sudden loud laughter of a striking young woman diverted Lawford's attention. The dark-haired girl was at an adjacent table on the other side of the narrow aisle. She had prominent cheekbones and the cold, delicately carved beauty of a high-fashion model. Sharing her table was a thin, handsome man whose movements were decidedly feminine. An expensive-looking 35mm camera rested atop their table. The woman tossed her straight black hair, lit a cigarette, and stared directly at Tom. Their eyes locked for a brief moment before she looked away. He had no way of knowing that he had just been the subject of six exposures of high-speed infrared film. He hadn't thought past her modellike beauty, and never questioned why she had attracted his attention, or why the expensive camera was out of its case, with its lens cap off.

Hickey came into Starke's out of a gust of windblown snow. He carried an alligator-skin attaché case and, with his free hand, removed his snap-brim hat and brushed the melting snowflakes from his trench coat. Tom smiled, thinking that Hickey's wardrobe gave him the classic look of a gumshoe in an old Warner Brothers film.

Spotting Lawford, Hickey made his way through the narrow space between the tables. His hair had turned gray, but his pug nose and ruddy complexion lent him a boyish look, and the inevitable middle-age paunch had not yet circled his waist.

The old comrades shook hands and embraced.

"You look great, kid," Hickey said warmly.

"You too." Tom nodded.

Hickey placed his attaché case on a vacant chair, draped his coat over it, and sat down. He took a tin of dark cigarillos out of his pocket and offered one to Tom.

"No, thanks. I'm trying to quit."

"That's what my current lady says on those rare occasions when I feel sexy."

Hickey lit the cigarillo and wiped some sweat from his upper lip. "A lot of great-looking snapper in here," he noted, and with a magician's sleight of hand grabbed Lawford's drink and drained it.

"Help yourself," Tom said, smiling.

"What's a vodka martini between old gunrunners?"

"Dope peddlers."

"That too, baby . . . that too."

Hickey's conversation was easy and congenial, but his tense black eyes constantly swept the nearby tables and his fingertips nervously drummed the tabletop. He caught the arm of a passing waitress. "Is this your table?"

The girl nodded.

"Here's ten bucks in advance."

"In advance of what?"

"Fast service. Let's have two more very dry vodka martinis. Have him make them with Absolut." He glanced at Tom. "Swedes make superior vodka."

"Will there be anything else?"

"Give us a side dish of those big green Spanish olives. You know, the ones stuffed with pimiento, and see if you can find out the score."

"What score?"

"The football game."

"I'll be right back."

Hickey crushed out the cigarillo and asked, "How's Claudia?"

"She's fine."

"You two okay?"

"Comme ci, comme ça."

"What's wrong?"

Tom shrugged. "Atrophy. Everything important has long since been said. It's no one's fault—it's just the years."

"Well, you can't expect permanence. Nothing lasts. Everything wears out. Your eyes. Your ears. Your cock. Your ticker. Everything." A sudden smile appeared on the puckish Irish face. "God damn, it's good to be with you, boy. I've seen you on the tube, but it's not the same. I'll bet you're still quite a cowboy."

"My cowboy days are long over, if they ever existed."

"Bullshit. You're a tough cookie. You've seen the shark more than once."

The waitress served their drinks and green olives, and said, "The Jets are leading seventeen to three in the third quarter."

Breaking into a wide grin, Hickey took out a wad of money, peeled off a twenty-dollar bill, and stuffed it in the waitress's apron pocket.

"What's this for?"

"Christmas."

"Well, thanks." She smiled, somewhat startled. "Thanks a lot."

She hurried off and Hickey raised his glass. "I've got a major bet on the Jets. Cheers, old boy."

They clicked glasses and sipped their drinks.

"What have you been up to?" Tom asked.

"This and that."

"What was that business about the black Mercedes?"

"A Steve Garrett fantasy. He's a good guy, but I've got to keep him indoors."

"Pretty fancy car, that Jag."

"The Agency's been good to me." Hickey shrugged. "What the hell, I only use the Jag for straight clients and chasing pussy."

"In the Washington I remember, a man didn't need fancy wheels."

"Hey, if I had your looks, kiddo, I'd have bought a Toyota."

Hickey sipped the drink, and sighed with pleasure. "Ah . . . they make a great fucking martini." His eyes cruised the room, then settled on Tom, and in a somber voice he said, "I was sorry to hear about your brother. It must have been brutal to watch him waste away like that."

"I never left him. We weren't close, but when I knew he was sick, I tried to make up for the gaps. He died holding my hand."

"That counts for something. That counts for plenty."

"Jack was a talented composer, but went his own way and did his own thing. I could have helped him, but we just never connected."

"You can't blame yourself. That's the way it is."

"It's the way things have become. There was a time when family was everything."

"Never having had any, I wouldn't know," Hickey said, and lit a fresh cigarillo. "You know"—he spoke through the smoke—"I'll be goddamned if you still don't look like a matinee idol."

"Cut the crap, Hickey. I look like hell and you know it."

"We should all look like that. You remember my second wife, Dottie—the redhead, the tall one with the great ass?"

"Vaguely."

"Vaguely? What the hell do you mean, 'vaguely'? Dottie used to walk down the Senate corridor and the nation's business came to a halt. Come on, Tom, you remember her—big tits, narrow waist, and that marble ass."

"It's starting to come back . . ."

"Ahh, fuck you. Anyway, we're lying in bed one night and Dottie says, 'Your friend Tom Lawford reminds me of Gregory Peck. I think he's very sexy in a reserved sort of way.' We had just made love and she's talking about you. Don't be modest. The ladies were always taken with you."

"You've had more action accidentally than I've had on purpose."

"Wrong. Even in the fucking jungle, those sloe-eyed Laotian mooks wanted a piece of you."

"Well, we were exotic . . . white men dropping out of the skies with Swiss francs and opium—and we were young."

"Yeah . . ." Hickey sighed. "We were young. You realize we only need eight more years to make it into the next century?"

"I hadn't thought about it."

"It's an achievement, Tom. Believe me. The Dark Angel's been busy." He paused. "You remember Alex Nickel?"

"Heard about him, but I never met him."

"Hell of an agent, but a pussy junkie. He got killed chasing squirrel."

"Killed?" Tom asked incredulously.

"Yeah . . . Alex was stationed in London, Christmas eighty-eight. He had the hots for this Dutch model in New York. A real piece of Danish—I'm talking about major pussy. Anyway, she phones Alex and turns him inside and out—tells him she's got the night reserved for him." Hickey sipped his martini. "It's just before Christmas. Alex has got to get a plane that afternoon. So he books himself on Pan

Am to New York. The plane blows up over Scotland. Terrorist bomb."

Tom shook his head in dismay. "Jesus Christ . . ."

"The Dark Angel is a cutie pie," Hickey said, crushing out the cigarillo. He stared at Tom for a moment, then leaned across the table and said, "The Admiral has something for you."

Tom felt a thin curl of excitement wind its way through his chest. "What about?"

"I don't know. But as one old dope peddler to another, be careful. The Admiral's full of curves and so's his deputy, Manfredi."

"You told me the Agency's been good to you."

"As far as money goes, but they don't play it straight— I'm on an assignment now that . . ." His voice trailed off.

"That what?"

"Nothing." Hickey drained the martini and sucked on the olive. "Hell of a thing about Alex. I had to cover his presence on that doomed flight with a bullshit story. He was married at the time."

"I wonder who the Dutch model went to bed with that night?"

"What's the difference?"

"There's a difference."

"Yeah . . . well, not to Alex." Hickey rose and indicated his attaché case. "Keep your eye on this, old buddy. I've got to pee—the bladder is not what it used to be. Order another round and a basket of fried clams."

Squeezing through the crowded tables, Hickey disappeared into a corridor leading to the rest rooms. Lawford ordered the drinks and clams and watched the waitress weave her way up to the bar. The football game was still on, but its most attentive fan was no longer watching. The Arab was gone. The striking dark-haired model seated nearby was engaged in an intense discussion with the gay photographer. Tom noticed that the expensive 35mm camera was back in its case.

He shook one of Hickey's cigarillos out of the pack and thought better of it for a few seconds before lighting it. Inhaling deeply, he wondered what the Admiral had in

22

mind for him and what exactly it was that Hickey had been trying to tell him.

The waitress fought her way back to the table and served the drinks. "Clams will be right up." She smiled. "And tell your friend the Jets just scored."

She turned, dropped her tray, and screamed.

Swaying in the alcove, dark arterial blood spouting from his slashed throat, Hickey clutched at the dripping mass of lacerated flesh. His clothes were soaked with blood, and a bright red smear stained the white tile floor behind him.

The waitress's screams were joined by a chorus of shrieking and panicky shouts. It was an aria of terror. Chairs were overturned. Glasses smashed against the tile floor. The crowd at the bar erupted, some fleeing headlong out into the night, others moving around the room aimlessly, in shocked slow motion.

Hickey took two steps and sprawled across a table, splattering his blood over the horrified patrons. The maître d' was on the phone. There were cries of, *"What happened?"* *"Someone's been knifed!"* A woman sobbed, *"Dear God . . . dear God . . ."*

In contrast to the chaos, Tom saw the striking model and the gay photographer walk calmly toward the front door. People slipped and fell, crashing into one another. The bartender jumped up on the bar and shouted for order, but his voice only added to the hysteria. Tom picked up Hickey's attaché case and walked deliberately toward the blood-soaked table where Hickey had fallen.

Hickey's cheek rested against the surface of the table. His eyes were open. A crimson bubble had formed at the raw, gaping hole in his throat. His lips were pursed. He reminded Lawford of a fish that had been gutted while still alive. The shocked bystanders neither moved nor spoke as Tom gently closed Hickey's eyes.

CHAPTER THREE

Carrying the attaché case, his head down against the sleeting snow, Lawford crossed Wisconsin at M Street. Witnessing sudden death had a way of slowing one's reflexes, and he had acted by rote, by the manual: if an agent is down, collect his effects and leave. Do not linger. Do not bear witness. Leave, and notify the duty officer as soon as possible.

It had happened fast, very fast, professionally fast. Tom wished that he had mentioned the Arab to Hickey. A highly trained assassin needed only a few seconds to slip behind a man, tilt the victim's head up, and dig the cutting edge of a straight razor across the throat, rupturing the artery. He should have said something about the Arab's profound interest in a meaningless football game. There had been a time when he might have picked up a signal, a sign—something that indicated the presence of an assassin.

Hearing the distant wail of a siren, he thought the paramedics could have saved themselves the trouble. Nothing more could be done for Hickey. The Metro Homicide Division would have temporary charge of the case, but the

24

CIA would claim Hickey's body and assume custodial rights to his effects. It was not inconceivable that Hickey had been taken out by the Agency. The Admiral might have permitted Hickey to become an "oversight." But why? Hickey's loyalty was impeccable. No, that was paranoia. Still . . . there were precedents.

An icy chill gripped Tom and he shivered from head to toe. His salt-and-pepper hair was soaked. Trudging through the snow, he thought of the irony of Hickey's winning his football bet, a bet he would never collect, but Hickey had a way of accumulating debtors. Tom's own long-standing debt to Hickey loomed larger now in death than it had in life. He owed the dead man some answers, but he would have to think and act with precision. He would have to recall details, arrangements, bits and pieces of conversation and actions. He thought of the striking-looking model. Her table had been positioned so that she faced Hickey in those last horrifying seconds when he swayed in the alcove, blood gushing between his fingers, and yet she hadn't screamed or reacted in any way. She had calmly gathered up her things and left. Had she anticipated the killing?

A rising anger seeped into Tom's consciousness. And in that moment, in the snow of Georgetown, he knew that wherever the trail led, whatever the risk, the debt would be paid.

In the shadowy light of the foyer, Larry Dutton thought that Lawford had aged a decade in the past hour. The journalist's handsome face was pinched and his color was ashen. Dutton helped him off with his overcoat and brought him a towel. Tom dried his hair, kicked off his loafers, and pulled the wet socks from his feet. He sat on the bottom step of the staircase and rubbed some circulation into his icy toes. "Who's the duty officer at Langley?" he asked.

"Everett Stallings."

"Ring him up. Tell him that John Hickey went down at Starke's. His throat was slit and the carotid artery slashed. He bled to death, not more than twenty-five minutes ago."

The big man was speechless, and took a long moment to find his voice. "I think you should speak to Stallings."

Tom tossed the towel back to Dutton and got to his feet. "Just do what I tell you. Have Stallings notify Steve Garrett, and when you get a chance, I could use some dry socks and hot coffee. And, Larry, I've got to open this attaché case."

Picking up the case, Tom went into the study and stopped to warm himself at the fireplace. He stared hypnotically into the flames and conjured up Hickey's sweaty voice: *"I saved you from roasting in that chopper, but you let them kill me."* Tears welled up in his eyes as he crossed the wide room and placed the attaché case on the desk.

Dutton came in carrying an ice pick and a hammer. "Stallings is anxious to talk to you," the big man said.

"Later. Let's get this open."

"Okay. Hold it steady," Dutton said, indicating the case. "Just have to bust the spindle."

He inserted the needlelike point of the pick into the center lock opening and brought the hammer down on the handle of the pick. He repeated the action on the lever locks, and they sprang open.

"There you go."

"Thanks. Stick around."

"I better get Stallings back."

Dutton left, and Tom opened the case tentatively and stared at its disparate contents: a holstered .45 automatic, a tin of cigarillos, a green file folder, a videocassette, and an audiocassette.

Tom lit one of Hickey's cigarillos, inhaled, and placed it in an ashtray decorated with a decal of Bill Casey, the long-dead CIA director.

The single sheet of paper inside the green folder was an Allegiance Research work order dated 12/16/91, and itemized:

CLIENT:
    Lisa Gessler. West German citizen. Passport # NR-G-6852063.

SUBJECT:
    Client requests surveillance of: Heinrich Dieter Mueller. West German citizen. Client suspects Mueller of industrial

espionage concerning secret mold patents of Topf A.G., Wiesbaden, FRG. Mueller on Topf board of directors. Client has reason to believe Mueller selling Topf's patents to certain competing American companies.

Mueller due to arrive Dulles Int'l. via Lufthansa Flight # 256—ETA, 2:15 P.M., EST—12/20/91. Client furnished recent photograph of Mueller.

COMMENTS:

Accepted assignment. Payment to be made in West German marks.

Tom found the grainy black-and-white photograph in a sleeve of the attaché case. Mueller was square-jawed, hard-eyed, and severe lines of age crisscrossed his cheeks.

Drawing hard on the cigarillo, Tom leaned back contemplatively. Who was Heinrich Mueller? Lisa Gessler? Topf A.G.?

Dutton came in carrying a mug of coffee and a pair of brown wool socks. "There's a slug of brandy in that. Be careful, it's hot."

Taking the dry socks, Tom asked, "Have you got something we can play this audiocassette on?"

"Yeah."

Dutton started to leave, hesitated, and said, "I gather you and Hickey were close."

"He saved my life." Tom paused. "A long time ago."

Dutton nodded imperceptibly and left.

Tom slipped the socks on and studied the photograph of Heinrich Mueller, sensing a vague recognition. Had he seen this hard Teutonic face somewhere before? If so, where? When?

The brandy-laced coffee warmed him, and, almost defiantly, he lit another of Hickey's cigarillos. One thing was certain: Heinrich Dieter Mueller looked old enough to have been around during the rise and fall of the Third Reich. Whether Mueller had a Nazi past or not was an open question. Lisa Gessler was another wild card. There was no shortage of private-detective agencies in West Germany. Why had Fräulein Gessler hired Hickey's company to tail Mueller? The German connection suggested a CIA involvement. Lisa Gessler might have contacted Hickey on behalf of the Agency. The industrial-espionage gambit was probably a cover. The whole thing bore the telltale signs of a clandestine operation originating in the Agency's Covert Action Bureau, and undoubtedly connected to Hickey's murder. He remembered Hickey's guarded comment about his current assignment and the Agency not playing it straight.

Dutton entered and placed a small Sony recorder on the desk. He waved his hand, dispersing a cloud of cigarillo smoke, and inserted the cassette into the machine. "You want privacy?"

"No. Stick around."

Dutton activated the Sony and a few feet of gray leader rolled by before the tape emitted a high sonic electronic signal, followed by the now eerie sound of Hickey's voice. *"This is side one. The reverse side has not been used. This side should be treated with suppressors and high-frequency lasers. The quality sucks, but I hope to get something. I'm in heavy traffic on Mass Avenue following the Pakistani embassy limo which is ID'd on videocassette. Mueller is inside the limo with a Pakistani diplomat."*

A burst of static swallowed Hickey's voice and a grating dissonance remained constant.

Dutton and Lawford stared at the revolving tape with total concentration, hoping the static would clear. The slow-motion tape revolutions and the anticipation of hearing another word were excruciating. Tom drew hard on the cigarillo, sipped his coffee, and felt the old nerve pain beginning to throb at the nape of his neck. The logs in the fireplace crackled occasionally but the men were oblivious of everything but the hissing dissonance of the tape. The minutes dragged by. Then suddenly, for a split second, the word *"marriage"* broke through the static. Tom played the tape back and forth, passing over the word half a dozen times before resuming the tape's forward motion.

Watching the grooved knobs of the revolving cassette, the men sensed Hickey's spirit hovering in the room. It was as if the dead man's voice was embedded in the tape, struggling to be heard. The grating sound cleared, and the word *"sentry"* sounded for an instant before drowning in heavy static. Once again Tom ran the tape back and forth. Satisfied the word was indeed "sentry," he pressed the Play button. The dissonance continued for a long time before one final revolution spit out the word *"Qaddafi."* It was clear, defined, and unmistakable. The tape ran out and Dutton extracted the cassette.

"Jesus Christ," he muttered. "Germans, Pakistanis, 'marriage,' 'sentry,' and 'Qaddafi'—what the fuck does it all mean?"

"It means Agency. Did you notice any physical difference between the first two words and 'Qaddafi'?"

"I thought the words 'marriage' and 'sentry' were cut off. Clipped. It seemed to me 'Qaddafi' played longer."

Tom nodded. "Let's play the videocassette."

Dutton turned on the television set and the VCR, selected Channel 3, and inserted the cassette. He then handed the remote control to Lawford. "You can freeze-frame and zoom."

The large screen flickered for a second or two before displaying a black-and-white data card:

DATE: 12/20/91.   TIME: 3:40 P.M., EST.
SUBJECT: Heinrich D. Mueller arrived via Lufthansa # 256, nonstop Frankfurt to Dulles. Flight delayed eighty-five minutes.

The data card dissolved and soft chromatic colors seeped into the screen. The camera panned down and held on a tall, gaunt man wearing a dark coat, a white silk scarf, and a black fedora. Heinrich Mueller was closely followed by a skycap pushing a dolly holding two suitcases. Both men were coming toward camera at a slight angle. From the composition of the shot, Tom guessed that Hickey had been shooting from inside a van parked close to the curb. Despite Mueller's advanced age, he walked erectly and with authority.

A gleaming black limousine waited at curbside. Its trunk was open and a uniformed chauffeur stood at attention at the rear passenger door while the bags were loaded. Mueller got into the limousine. The chauffeur tipped the skycap, then went back behind the wheel. A traffic cop held up the other cars as he waved the limousine away from the curb.

The camera zoomed in on the limousine's rear license plate. The red-white-and-blue plate had the word "Diplomat" at its top and "EP486" at its center. At the bottom, in smaller print, an inscription read: "Issued by the U.S. Department of State."

The TV screen went dark for a few seconds before displaying a wide shot of the limousine turning into the driveway of a gabled three-story building. A gleaming bronze plaque affixed to the door read: "Embassy of the Islamic Republic of Pakistan." The camera cut to a long shot of a well-dressed Arabic-looking man greeting Mueller at the embassy's door. The shot played for less than five seconds. Reversing the tape, Tom froze the frame and zoomed in on the man in the doorway.

"Let's mark this frame for a lift."

"Okay."

"Can you run off a copy of this tape?"

"No problem," Dutton said, and ejected the cassette.

Tom returned to the desk and reviewed his notations: Lisa Gessler, H. D. Mueller, Topf A.G., Pakistani embassy, then the words "marriage," "sentry," and "Qaddafi."

He had no idea what it all added up to, only that the Agency was somehow involved and that two facts were immutable: the case was international and lethal.

Sipping the brandy-laced coffee, he studied the photograph of Mueller. The nagging sensation of familiarity persisted. Where the hell had he seen this leathery face? The press? TV? Somewhere in the mass media? A story he had written? He had, many years ago, interviewed Albert Speer, the Reich Minister of Industry, but could not remember anything that related to Mueller.

Dutton came in carrying a large manila envelope. "Audio and video copies."

"Thanks."

"Any ideas?" Dutton asked.

"One or two." Tom nodded. "See if you can get Stallings for me."

Dutton picked up the receiver and punched a fifteen-digit code. Lawford placed the original audio- and videocassettes in the attaché case.

"Stallings," Dutton said, handing the receiver to Tom.

"Sorry I couldn't get to you sooner," Tom said, "but it's been a—"

"No apologies," Stallings interrupted. "We're very grateful for your care, concern, and professional action." Stallings' voice walked on water. "Collecting Hickey's effects and notifying us was absolutely by the book and crucial."

Everett Stallings was seated at a long table in the third-floor conference room at CIA headquarters in Langley, Virginia. Opposite him was Albert Manfredi, deputy director of the Covert Section. Manfredi wore a small headset wired to the phone and listened intently to the conversation. Stallings continued his praiseworthy comments for another minute or so before Tom asked, "Have you notified Steve Garrett?"

"The moment we got the call. He identified the body for Metro Homicide before we assumed custody."

"Where is Hickey now?"

"He was cremated, and since there are no relatives, we simply—"

"Wait a minute," Tom interrupted. "Are you telling me that in an hour or so it's over? Hickey never lived so he never died? He didn't exist? Use them and lose them. Is that what you're telling me?"

Stallings' steel-rimmed glasses caught the light, and his cheeks turned scarlet. Manfredi motioned him to remain calm. Stallings sighed heavily and in a warm, friendly tone said, "I know how close you two fellows were and I'm—"

"How would you know?" Tom cut in angrily. "You're a duty officer; to you, agents are names in green computer lights. How the hell would you know how I feel?"

Dutton listened apprehensively, wishing Lawford would cool it. It was bad form for an agent to antagonize a technocrat like Stallings.

"It's very late," Stallings said soothingly. "You've got to be exhausted. Hang on to Hickey's personal effects. Get some rest. We'll send a car for you tomorrow." He paused before sinking the hook. "I want you to know the Agency had absolutely nothing to do with Hickey's last case. As I said, I know you two—"

"Don't patronize me!" Tom shouted. "And don't insult

me! This was Agency! And Hickey was a friend of mine, so don't fuck around with me."

Manfredi put his index finger to his lips, cautioning Stallings to silence.

"Do the names Lisa Gessler and Heinrich Mueller ring any bells?" Tom continued sarcastically. "Does a West German company called Topf A.G. sound familiar? How about Pakistan? Qaddafi? Are you still telling me that this was not an Agency action? Because if you are, I'll phone a colleague of mine, Ed Kramer over at the *Post,* and let his readers decide. It's up to you."

Manfredi's hand shot out and cupped the receiver. "Tell him."

Stallings' voice lost its charm and he spoke in a cold monotone. "Hickey's last assignment originated in State Department Intelligence. Their request was transferred to this bureau and personally approved by the Admiral."

"That's more like it," Tom said calmly. "I'm coming over to see you, and I'm hungry, and it's going to be a long night, so order a pizza and some sandwiches and plenty of coffee. Alert the fax unit and sound engineers—I'm bringing a video- and audiocassette that require some expert attention." Tom hung up and glanced at Dutton. "You mind driving me out to Langley?"

"Just keep me out of it."

"No problem."

In the third-floor conference room, Manfredi glanced at Stallings and said, "We better wake the Admiral."

CHAPTER FOUR

The conference room was softly lit by recessed ceiling lights, and the soundless tension was reminiscent of the ominous silence common to hospital waiting rooms. The table was littered with the crusty remnants of pizza and assorted sandwiches, and the aroma of freshly brewed coffee mingled with the residual odor of tobacco.

Albert Manfredi chewed on a dead cigar, his penetrating black eyes fixed on a slice of dried pizza.

Everett Stallings repeatedly cleaned the lenses of his steel-rimmed glasses.

Lawford stood at the window, staring at the snow-covered pine trees bordering the CIA headquarters at Langley. He knew the silence in the soundproofed room was deceptive—in point of fact, the building seethed with the ongoing business of intelligence collection and analysis. Photo labs, satellite enhancement, cipher sections, communication and computer centers throbbed with activity. State-of-the-art electronic equipment was staffed by highly skilled, dedicated men and women, some of whom were, at the moment, working on the material contained in Hickey's video- and audiocassettes. The photograph of Mueller had been faxed to Inspector Hans Lehmans, chief of West German Federal Police in Wiesbaden, for ID and background. Also faxed were Lisa Gessler's passport number and a request for background on Topf A.G. A close shot of the Arabic-looking man who had greeted Mueller at the Pakistani embassy had been lifted from the videotape, and faxed to Mossad in Tel Aviv and to Interpol's computer bank in Brussels. The audiotape was in the hands of the Agency's sound engineers and would be subjected to static suppressors and ultrahigh-frequency lasers.

The events surrounding Hickey's murder framed a lethal puzzle that defied comprehension; but one fact had emerged during the past hour: Tom Lawford, the seldom-used deep-cover agent, had suddenly been endowed with clout. All of his demands had been acted upon without question or hesitation. The source of his newly acquired muscle could only be attributed to the Admiral's intervention, of that Lawford was positive. No one else had the authority to activate expensive and intricate technical processes on an emergency basis.

The buzzer sounded and Stallings pressed a button releasing the door lock. A uniformed security guard entered with an Oriental woman who held three red file folders. "Just in," she said, and handed them to Manfredi.

Manfredi slid a file across the table to Lawford and gave one to Stallings. They read the fax sheet in silence.

Response to Manfredi request: CIA fax # 61376. Contents classified per request 12/23/91. Fax transmitted 08:45 GMT. Wiesbaden, Federal Republic of Germany.

SUBJECT: Heinrich Dieter Mueller:
   The detailed history of subject is on file in United States Dept. of Justice—Special Section. Brief sketch follows:
   H. D. Mueller—born in Bremerhaven, Germany, 10/24/10. Citizen of Federal Republic of Germany—passport # NR-A-3399628, issued in Frankfurt 3/6/88. Valid to 3/5/92.
   Mueller is subdirector of STS Aktiengesdschaft (Space Transport Systems), 19 Friedrichstrasse, Berlin. Subject is

rocket scientist and surviving member of WWII Peenemünde group that developed V-1 and V-2 rockets. Group included Rudolph, Brunner, Diehl, and Von Braun. Mueller appointed liaison (3/43) with SS Chief Heinrich Himmler, and provided slave labor for V-2 assembly factory at Nordhausen. Mueller created the 'Dora' concentration camp adjacent to Nordhausen V-2 assembly factory. Conditions were brutal, many thousands died. In March 1945 Von Braun negotiated scientists' surrender to American Seventh Army and immediate recruitment into the U.S. space program, thereby evading war-crime indictments. Operation code-named 'Paperclip.' Mueller deported from U.S. in '79, returned to Munich, and joined STS rocket group under supervision of CEO Dr. Fritz Kleiser. Alois Brunner and Walter Diehl also associated with STS. For background details, consult: Robert Stein at U.S. Justice Dept., Office of Special Investigations.

(End One)

Part 2

Lisa Gessler common German name but have no record of woman with that name holding passport # NR-G-6852063. Suspect's passport is a forgery.

(End Two)

Part 3

Topf Werksgeschaft—foundry and machine-tool and die company located in Wiesbaden. No apparent connection to STS or Heinrich Mueller.

I remain at your service.

The palpable silence in the room was broken by the loud buzz of the door lock. A silver-haired woman carrying a folder followed the security guard into the conference room. She waited for their attention before saying, "I think it would be simpler if I just read this."

Manfredi nodded.

She read aloud from the sheet inside the file. "The word that sounded like 'marriage' was cut off. The complete word is 'maraging.' I'll spell it: m-a-r-a-g-i-n-g. It's a rare alloy used in the manufacture of atomic weapons. The word sounding like 'sentry' is actually 'centrifuge,' spelled c-e-n-t-r-i-f-u-g-e. This indicates a highly sophisticated method of separating plutonium isotopes from a pool of enriched uranium. 'Qadaffi' is Qaddafi." She glanced up. "I think we all know who he is."

CHAPTER FIVE

Wearing the distinctive purple berets of the elite Special
Forces, two soldiers followed General Dado Harel through
the floodlit Jaffa Gate into the Old City. The soldiers held
their Galil assault rifles at the ready, fingers curled around
the triggers, eyes darting from shuttered windows to domed
rooftops. The General's bodyguards were edgy in the maze
of narrow alleys and nameless streets. After three thousand
years, Jerusalem had not yet realized the blessings of peace.

No single square kilometer on earth had suffered so long
and diverse a bloodspill. It was a place where legend was
more durable than fact. Here, King Solomon had built the
First Temple. Here, the Son of God had risen from the dead.
Here, Muhammad flew up to heaven on a winged steed.
Here, ideas of the great prophets Jeremiah and Isaiah had
changed the thinking of half the world. The old city of King
David was like a seductive courtesan whose favors were
transitory and whose price was paid in blood.

The General always experienced a schizophrenic sensation of fascination and dread in this biblical enclave. He had

tasted both victory and defeat inside these massive walls. In May 1948, during the Jordanian siege of the Old City, he had run messages in the beleaguered Jewish quarter, dodging shells and bullets, racing from cellar to cellar, command post to command post, carrying a few bullets, a canteen of water, an ampoule of morphine. He had told the Haganah commander that he was fifteen, but in truth Dado could not remember his birthdate or recall the identity of his parents. He spoke fluent German but did not know from whom he had learned the language. Dado Harel was a child of the Holocaust.

In March 1945, elements of the British Second Army liberated the Bergen-Belsen death camp; a young British officer found a scabrous, skeletal child sitting trancelike in a lime-sprinkled trench of cadavers.

Dado was nursed back to health in a refugee center, then transferred to a detention center on Cyprus. Fourteen months later, he arrived in Palestine illegally, in a small boat that beached itself in a cove north of Haifa. Having taken the name of a passenger who had died during the voyage, he volunteered for service with the embryonic Jewish Defense Force and was assigned to the Jerusalem front. After months of futile combat, the ragtag defenders abandoned the Jewish quarter to the victorious Jordanian Forces.

He remembered stumbling up out of the smoking ruins of the synagogue into an incredibly bright blue summer sky, and filing out of the Old City behind a line of beaten men. Although still a child, he marveled at the incongruity of surrender on such a spectacular day. Jerusalem had once again laughed at her favorite victims.

In the ensuing four decades, Dado had risen to the very pinnacle of Israel's armed forces. He had survived five wars and countless clandestine operations, and yet he sensed a certain apprehension in this old enclave—as if he were an intruder, a tolerated visitor whose presence was framed in borrowed time.

Feeling the first drops of rain as he passed the magnificent Cathedral of St. James, Dado entered the Mea Shearim enclave of the ultraorthodox Jewish sect. Bearded men wearing long black coats and wide-brimmed black hats eyed the General and the two soldiers warily.

Dado regarded the Zealots with sad disdain. Although some of them were survivors of the East European ghettos and Nazi killing centers, they neither recognized the State of Israel nor permitted their sons and daughters to serve in its armed forces. They stoned secular Jews for attending the cinema on Sabbath, and wielded a political power far beyond their numbers. They had very nearly turned a democracy into a theocracy.

Their psychic survival depended solely on their belief that their unforgiving god Yahweh would protect and preserve them until that glorious day when the prophet Elijah would appear and lead the faithful into the gates of paradise. Only then would the holy men recognize the State of Israel.

Dado followed a group of Zealots into the great plaza of the Western Wall. Floodlights illuminated the massive remnant of the Second Temple. Soldiers patrolled the high parapet protecting the swaying, chanting worshipers below.

Standing at the rear of the plaza, Dado cursed them softly. He could not understand their unswerving faith. Had they forgotten Yahweh's magic soap trick? Yid soap, a pfennig a bar, fresh from Auschwitz—or would you prefer another flavor, fräulein? From Treblinka? Ravensbrück? Dachau? From what wellspring of faith came such unshakable belief and such immunity to history? Didn't they know that Elijah had in fact appeared—in 1941? The Great Prophet had worn a black uniform and called himself Eichmann and led the children of Yahweh into the gates of hell. And inscribed above those hellgates were the German words *"Arbeit Macht Frei"*—work will make you free. The words were seared into Dado's soul, immutable, like the purple numerals tattooed on his forearm.

The General watched them swaying to their ancient metronome, knowing that 2,500 miles away, in the northeast corner of Pakistan, centrifuges and plutonium isotopes were beating to the deadly rhythm of another metronome. The Muslim bomb was on the griddle, and deep in the Libyan desert the killers of Peenemünde and Nordhausen were installing their V-5 rockets for Qaddafi. The men on the Rhine were still dreaming of "final solutions." The Pakistani bomb perched atop the Nazi rockets would finally put an end to the Zealots and their sacred wall.

Dado felt a slow ball of heat rise up in his throat, choking him, flushing his face with anger. Whatever the cost, whatever the risks, the nuclear sun would not fall into this plaza. He, the child of hellfires, would protect and preserve the faithful. Ah, Dado, he thought, you son of a bitch, you fucking hypocrite. On that fateful June day in 1967, you smashed St. Stephen's Gate and led the charge that liberated this sacred place, and you pressed your lips to the stones and whispered a prayer to some mythical God. And you come here now to see the Zealots, to be certain they still exist. Even though they represented everything he despised, their presence was symbolically important to him. They had survived the Diaspora, the pogroms, and, in the end, Yahweh's magic soap trick. And he would protect them. And they would pray and wait for Elijah into the midnight of time.

The General turned the collar of his green parka up against the cold rain, and, followed by the soldiers, made his way toward the Arab quarter.

Khalidi's restaurant was a family treasure passed from one generation to the next. Its customers were a fairly even mix of Jews and Arabs. There was an unspoken but tacit agreement among the warring factions that Khalidi's was to be spared the political strife that plagued the Muslim quarter of the Old City. The restaurant was famous for its hummus—chickpea paste—grilled chops, and homemade pita bread. The place was warm and clean, and its dozen tables were covered with fine linen.

Zev Berger was seated at a rear table with his back to the wall. His bifocals were pushed down on his nose as he read the Jerusalem *Post*. Berger was fifty-two, but his portly figure, melancholy eyes, sagging cheeks, and gray hair added ten years to his appearance. He was a Rhodes Scholar, a student of Eastern religions, a master linguist, and a practitioner of the twin arts of silence and patience. Berger was also the chief of Mossad, Israeli Intelligence, a position he had held for ten years.

Pouring some more wine, he ordered another dish of hummus. Tension was causing him to overeat. The imminent meeting with General Harel triggered a rush of anxiety.

Although he had worked with Dado on a variety of critical intelligence operations, their relationship was founded on mutual distrust. Out of fear and prudence, Berger had committed the General's dossier to memory.

In October 1973 General Harel had been in command of the southern sector on the Golan Heights when eight hundred Syrian T-72 tanks pushed to within three kilometers of the Bnot Yaakov Bridge—the gateway to the Galilee. Dado's son, Dani, was a crew member in one of twelve remaining Israeli tanks. The General ordered the tanks to dig in and make a suicidal stand. Dani was killed along with the others. But their tanks had blunted the Syrian spearhead and saved the Galilee. The General loved Dani with all his heart but never doubted the correctness of his order.

After Dani's death, Dado's wife, Avital, suffered a breakdown and retreated into the arms of the Zealots, seeking absolution for some imagined sin. But Dado never looked back; he moved on from one clandestine operation to the next—planning, plotting, rolling over the opposition with the inexorable ruthlessness of a live grenade.

Sipping his wine, Berger thought Harel was the stuff that military juntas were made of, and since its inception in '83, he had feared the growing power of the General's secret strike force.

The portly intelligence chief tore a piece of fresh pita bread, dipped it into the hummus, and saw Dado's big frame fill the narrow doorway. The blond hair was streaked with gray, but the strong features were well-formed, the dark blue eyes alert and penetrating. The General's Aryan looks could have served as a model for an SS recruitment poster—one of life's small ironies, Berger mused.

Dado sat down opposite Berger and ordered a cognac. "You look well, Yanush," he said, using Berger's nickname. "Sorry I'm late. I had to visit Avital."

"How is she?"

"She prays for Dani's soul and mine."

"Perhaps you should go with her to temple."

"That's one burlesque too many. Besides, I have it on good authority that Yahweh is at the moment in Vienna, having tea with Waldheim."

"Ah, Dado . . . leave it—leave the faithful to their Messiah. You're in Jerusalem: turn the other cheek."

The waiter placed a bottle of Hennessy on the table. Dado poured a hefty shot and tossed it down.

"You said there was news from Erika."

"She confirmed a V-5 rocket test launch supervised by Dr. Alois Brunner. We've already leaked it to the press."

"And the launch site?"

Berger shook his head. "Only Qaddafi and Kleiser know, and perhaps the chief of Libyan Intelligence. Even the German rocket scientists are unaware of the location. They're flown across the desert at night from Tripoli. But perhaps this ploy of yours will produce some results."

Berger scanned the room and slid the folded Jerusalem *Post* across the table. Dado turned the pages and saw the black-and-white photograph tucked into its fold. Pouring another cognac, he studied the picture of Hickey and Lawford seated at a table in Starke's Café.

"Narda snapped that picture moments before Hickey was murdered," Berger explained. "The assassin was run by a Libyan control officer named Abu Nawaf Hasi. Manfredi faxed Hasi's picture to us. Lawford left the café with Hickey's effects, one of which was a videocassette showing Hasi greeting Mueller at the door of the Pakistani embassy. The shot was a lucky one, and Lawford was astute to have had it enlarged."

Dado tapped the photograph with his finger. "Lawford hasn't changed much."

"I didn't realize you knew him personally."

"You know everything."

"Not true, Dado."

"Almost true." The General smiled, folding the paper and handing it back to Berger. "I was ordered by the Chief of Staff to permit Lawford entry to our command post on the Golan in October 1973. He arrived the night of the eighth, when the whole fucking Syrian Army converged at Kuneitra. Lawford was very brave. He ran from position to position under heavy fire, speaking into his tape machine, recording the battle. After the truce, we spent some time together. There was a sense of strength in the man, but he seemed dispirited."

"I've researched his articles," Berger said. "I find nothing to indicate any partiality to the State of Israel."

"That's why he's perfect for the job. Lawford has the credentials and he's publicly neutral. But most important, he now has a cause. His longtime friend was murdered, and he will soon discover that he requires our assistance to avenge Hickey's death. Trust me, Yanush. Lawford will be the drop that fills our gluss."

CHAPTER SIX

Tom Lawford and Deputy Attorney General Robert Stein were in the small projection room on the fourth floor of the Justice building. Stein was a veteran attorney in charge of the Office of Special Investigations—the section of the Justice Department his colleagues affectionately referred to as the "Dustbin." Stein spent his working hours meticulously sifting through the genocidal debris of the Nazi epoch, seeking out the mass murderers who had found sanctuary in the U.S. space program. He had compiled extensive files on the German rocket scientists, and almost single-handedly caused the expulsion of Heinrich Dieter Mueller from the United States.

Only on rare occasions was Stein called upon to furnish information to individuals outside the department. War criminals were not as popular as mafiosi or Colombian drug overlords. So it was with considerable enthusiasm that Stein welcomed the interest of the distinguished journalist Tom Lawford. They had spent the better part of the morning watching documentary footage and newsreel film pertaining to the activities of the rocket scientists, from the inception of the V-1 rocket base at Peenemünde, Germany, in 1936. The footage had been horrific—the development and introduction of V-1 and V-2 rockets were drenched in the blood of slave labor.

Stein was past sixty, but he moved like a boxer, up on his toes, pacing, his hands in motion accenting his words. "There you have it. Mueller, Diehl, Rudolph, Brunner, Von Braun—pioneers of the V-2, the world's first ballistic missile against which there was no defense. The one-ton warhead came down out of the atmosphere at thirty times the speed of sound, exploding on London and Amsterdam with devastating results." Stein stopped pacing and faced Lawford. "Once Von Braun shifted operations from Peenemünde to Nordhausen, the scientists were in the extermination business. Mueller set up Camp Dora adjacent to Nordhausen's assembly tunnels. Thirty-five thousand men died in those tunnels. A worker at Nordhausen was not permitted to survive. There could be no witnesses to identify the location of the secret underground assembly plant. You saw the hangings—the bodies twisting from cranes right in front of Mueller's office. When I nailed that prick, he blamed Himmler's SS killer squads. The fact that Mueller, Brunner, and Von Braun were themselves high officers in the SS was never mentioned. It was Von Braun who kept badgering Himmler for more slaves."

"As I remember, Von Braun enjoyed a fine press in America," Lawford said.

"He was a mass murderer and we embraced him," Stein replied. "In seventy-six, before his death, Von Braun confessed to me—in my office. I have it on tape. He admitted that conditions at Nordhausen/Dora were unspeakable."

"How did these bastards get clearance to enter the U.S.?"

"Secretary of War Patterson and Secretary of State Acheson, along with key people in the Pentagon, designed the whole scam and called it 'Operation Paperclip.' Records were altered and in some cases shredded. The Pentagon bureaucrats believed Von Braun's group was critical to our survival. The floodgates really opened in forty-five, forty-six, and forty-seven. The monsters were not only admitted, they were rewarded with lucrative contracts. Murder had become an acceptable scientific virtue. It was only after the Saturn 5 launch in 1969 that my section was permitted to go after them. A man had to walk on the moon before we got religion." The phone rang. Stein picked it up, turned to Tom and said, "It's for you."

"Who is it?"

"A woman with a thick southern accent."

"Hi theah, Mr. Lawford. This is Mary Jo Flannigan." She spoke with a curious inflection, as if every sentence ended in a question mark. "I'm Admiral Dwinell's executive secretary. The Admiral and Deputy Director Manfredi would like to see you."

CHAPTER SEVEN

Admiral Clarke Dwinell's stately Tudor mansion was perched atop a hillrise overlooking fifteen acres in the exclusive Washington suburb of Kenwood, Maryland. The snow-covered grounds were ringed by a forest of tall pines and protected from intruders by sophisticated alarm systems and twenty-four-hour shifts of security guards.

Lawford and Manfredi were seated in the oak-paneled study waiting for the Admiral to conclude his phone conversation.

Dwinell was sixty-eight, but his face was remarkably unlined, and his eyes were bright and alert. He was an excellent tennis player and kept himself in superb condition. His pleasantly bland features masked a ruthless intelligence and the remorseless objectivity of a professional hit man. His sensitive post in government was a matter of choice and challenge. Dwinell was American aristocracy whose ancestors had defended the port of Boston against the British. The Admiral had been a Rhodes Scholar, was a graduate of Annapolis, and had commanded a battle group in the Pacific theater during World War Two.

He had chaired the Joint Chiefs of Staff and was responsible for reorganizing the intelligence apparatus into a single combined command. He never addressed the press, and believed that truly great leaders maintained a very low profile. He was barely known to the American people and remained a man of mystery even to those in government. The Admiral reported to only one man—the President of the United States.

Upon assuming personal control of the Agency's Covert Section, the Admiral had immersed himself in the dark netherworld of spies and counterspies, of secret bank drafts, dummy companies, arms dealers, assassins, document forgers, safe houses, cryptography, bugs, wires, moles, drops, gunrunners, and drug dealers.

Lawford always felt uneasy around the Admiral. There was something ominous in those friendly gray eyes, something tricky.

The Admiral ended his phone conversation with a touch of feigned charm. "You can sleep on it, Charles. Absolutely. You have my word." He paused. "Anytime."

He hung up and glanced at his deputy director. "The senator from North Dakota."

Manfredi nodded but did not comment.

The Admiral rose and walked to the large picture window and stared off at the distant snow-capped hills. "I had delayed seeing you until you had met with Stein and absorbed some of the background material." He turned and faced Lawford. "We're here to discuss why Hickey was killed, and the critical role you can play in not only avenging his death but also perhaps helping to avoid a nuclear holocaust that would incinerate half the world and render the surviving half uninhabitable. There is nothing in your past activities on our behalf that equals the importance of this assignment."

Tom felt a sudden surge of anger at the Admiral's flag-waving speech. "Spare me the patriotic rhetoric." His voice was tense and his words terse. "That horseshit would have worked years ago. Not anymore. I'm not here to serve you or the state or the free world. I couldn't care less if the whole planet decided to fall through the black hole. I'm here because a man who saved my life—who risked everything for me—was butchered almost in front of my eyes. I'm carrying a huge debt, and I'm going to try to pay it off. So just lay the facts down and leave the national anthem out of this."

The Admiral stared at him for a moment, then nodded. "I understand your grief and your anger and your motives. So I'll do my best to stick to the facts."

He relit his pipe, blew a cloud of blue-gray smoke toward the ceiling, and sat on the edge of his desk. "We know the identity of the control officer who ordered Hickey's murder. He's the man who greeted Mueller at the door of the Pakistani embassy. Mossad has an extensive file on him. His name is Abu Hasi. He's a full colonel in Libyan Counterintelligence. We believe he had Hickey hit in order to prevent further surveillance of Heinrich Mueller or his associates in STS."

"What exactly is STS?"

"Space Transport Systems. It's a West German company founded by a Dr. Fritz Kleiser in 1979. The STS group has designed a modern version of the old World War Two Nazi V-2 rocket, ostensibly to launch weather and telecommunication satellites. Kleiser recruited a few of the surviving Nazi scientists, along with talented young physicists and engineers. Kleiser openly admits that Qaddafi has financed STS and granted them a test range and operational facility somewhere in the Libyan Sahara. But recent intelligence data suggest the true purpose of STS is not satellite placement, but rather the development of a long-range V-5 ICBM capable of carrying a nuclear warhead."

"What about the West German authorities?"

"Unfortunately there is nothing in West German export law to prevent the shipping of rockets designed and intended for peaceful space exploration."

"Nice," Lawford said sarcastically. "That's what they claimed back in eighty-nine about the poison-gas shipments to Qaddafi."

"Only initially," Manfredi interjected. "Once we furnished the proof, they acted."

"They acted after the story broke," Tom countered.

"True, but we had conclusive proof," Manfredi said. "The dead dogs—near the plant. Our KH-11 satellite had photographed the bodies of wild desert dogs lying in close proximity to what Qaddafi termed a pharmaceutical plant."

"Unfortunately in this STS matter, our proof is inconclusive," the Admiral explained. "There's been a leak to the German press, as yet unconfirmed, of a recent successful rocket-launch test in the deep Sahara. An aging Vela satellite picked up a heat flash, but failed to pinpoint the exact location. All of which indicates an underground silo." The Admiral went around behind his desk. "In my view, Hickey's murder not only tends to confirm that the STS operation is military in nature but also tends to support Mossad's allegations of a secret and long-standing nuclear alliance between Libya and Pakistan." The Admiral sat down wearily. "If it's true, we're all facing an apocalyptic nightmare."

Shaking his head in disbelief, Tom said, "I don't understand the lingering doubt—the 'if' in your analysis. Mueller was traveling on a Pakistani diplomatic passport and was obviously under the protection of a Libyan intelligence officer. Hickey's audiotape carried the words 'centrifuge' and 'maraging'—critical elements in the manufacture of nuclear weapons. It's no secret that Pakistan has a huge, operational nuclear-enrichment facility at Kahuta in northeast Pakistan. I researched a story on that plant for the *Times* ten years ago. Hickey's tape concludes with the name Qadaffi. How can there still be any doubt that Mossad is right—that a nuclear alliance of some kind exists between those two Muslim nations? I don't understand your equivocation. Who are you trying to protect?"

"You asked me to spare you flag-waving speeches. I ask you to spare me your quick journalistic conclusions. Pakistan is an ally of sorts on the subcontinent. We've supported its various regimes with billions of dollars. I don't want that aid cut off by Congress. Besides which, we still lack conclusive proof of a Libyan-Pakistani nuclear alliance. What we do know is that STS is testing ICBM's somewhere in the deep Sahara—and we have Mossad's file on the alleged nuclear alliance." The Admiral tapped a thick blood-red file. "It's all in here—and you can study it at your leisure. But basically, the Israelis make the case that in early 1979, Qaddafi agreed to finance the Pakistani nuclear-research center at Kahuta. The project has, over the years, according to Mossad, cost Qaddafi in excess of five billion dollars. In return for which he is to receive nuclear warheads. The production of those warheads is only a screwdriver away."

"And those warheads," Lawford said, "will be fitted to the STS long-range missiles."

"Correct." The Admiral nodded.

"How close is Pakistan to testing the bomb?"

"We believe a zero-yield, undetectable laboratory test is imminent."

"Zero-yield?" Tom asked, surprised.

"It's achieved by the use of Flash X-ray machines. They're supersecret, state-of-the-art. Swedish-made. They shoot pictures at one-millionth of a second and photograph the inner core of a nuclear detonation in a laboratory. We know that Pakistan has acquired one or more of these machines."

"So they can test a nuclear bomb without detection by satellite," Tom said.

"Right. No radiation. No heat flash."

"What we're talking about here," the Admiral continued, "is Qaddafi armed with nuclear warheads and a delivery system. This places the Sixth Fleet in jeopardy, along with the Suez Canal and every major city in western Europe. But clearly Israel is the primary target."

"You think Qaddafi would actually use the bomb?"

"Yes. I do. It's a mistake to believe that because a state has an insane leader with insane goals, it lacks the competency to carry them out. Remember, a fanatic enjoys the advantage of choosing the means and the moment. The fanatic has no moral problems, only technical ones."

"Well, the Israelis have never hesitated to act in the past. They'll sure as hell hit that Libyan rocket base."

"*If* they can locate it in time," Manfredi replied.

"We need your help, Tom," the Admiral said quietly.

"To do what?"

"Locate that Libyan launch site—remember, these bastards ordered Hickey's murder."

"Me?" Lawford asked incredulously. "If the satellites can't find it and Mossad can't find it, how can I?"

"You happen to be uniquely qualified for this assignment," the Admiral said. "The director of STS, Fritz

Kleiser, has been under relentless attack from the European press, and despite all his denials, he's been repeatedly accused of building an offensive missile site somewhere in the Libyan desert. Ever since the poison-gas scandal, the German government has become supersensitive to STS's Libyan connection. The German press has tried to infiltrate STS's infrastructure without success. But Kleiser is very aware of his vulnerability to public exposure. Those reports of a recent V-5 test conducted by one of Kleiser's close associates, Dr. Alois Brunner, have placed STS on the front burner. We have good reason to believe Kleiser would welcome a favorable article by a renowned Pulitzer Prize–winning journalist."

"When you say 'good reason,' just how good is it?"

"The best. Mossad has a deep-cover agent inside STS. The agent believes Kleiser would jump at the chance to have an in-depth wire-service story with your byline."

"Even if he didn't," Manfredi interjected, "we could muscle him with *Nightside.* You could threaten to do a TV segment—interview his employees, his bankers, the West German scientific community, the former Nazis in his employ like Brunner, Mueller, and Diehl. If Kleiser refused to be interviewed and you taped a segment around him, he'd be guilty by omission. What you fellows call an 'ambush' interview. *Sixty Minutes* does it all the time."

"That won't be necessary," the Admiral said. "We don't have to threaten Kleiser. We'll manage to sell him a print-media piece—words and photographs by Tom Lawford; an Associated Press wire pickup will give him a worldwide audience of one billion readers. This proposed article represents a unique opportunity for Kleiser to take the heat off his Libyan operations. I'm certain you can penetrate the STS infrastructure by holding out the carrot of a favorable piece."

"You've already made the pitch, haven't you?"

"Look, Tom," the Admiral said soothingly, "if Mossad is right, if Pakistan is about to supply Qaddafi with nuclear warheads, half the world may be vaporized. You're quite right. The Israelis aren't going to sit still and wait for the apocalypse. Yes, we've established contact with Kleiser. He's been supplied with copies of your recent articles, and videotapes of your *Nightside* segments. He knows that you're objective and fair. Once you meet with him, you'll reinforce the fact that you're perfectly willing to tell the world his side of the story."

"An interview with Kleiser won't give us the location of the V-5 launch site in Libya."

"I think it will. Once you have Kleiser's confidence, you'll demand to visit the Libyan base, without which your story is incomplete. And since he maintains that his operations in Libya are solely for commercial space exploration, how can he refuse to show you the launch site without arousing your suspicions?" The Admiral leaned on the back of his chair and shrugged. "You will, of course, guarantee him that if he objects, for whatever reason, you will not reveal the location of the launch site in the article. But you must see it for yourself. Every major journalist at one time or another has respected his source's need for confidentiality. Kleiser knows that. It'll work, Tom, trust me."

"The same way Hickey trusted you?"

"I resent that!" the Admiral snapped. "I loved that crazy bastard. And I don't throw my people to the wolves!"

Tom thought the Admiral had reacted too fast, and with uncharacteristic anger.

After a tense pause the Admiral calmly asked, "Are you in or out?"

"I'm in, but for my own reasons."

The Admiral shot Manfredi a quick look and the deputy director said, "This isn't a cowboy operation. You'll be walking on water all the way."

"I get the picture, and I'll give it my best shot."

"That's good enough for me," the Admiral said. "For the record, Marco Bonini in Rome will be assigning you to write the article."

Tom shook his head and smiled. "Another illusion shattered. Marco Bonini. . . . I thought I was unique. I'd never have guessed you had an AP bureau chief in your pocket. How much does he know?"

"Enough to play out the charade for Kleiser. You're going to write the piece and Bonini will put it on the wire. He's already contacted Kleiser on a normal, legitimate basis. I'm glad you're with us, but I want no misunderstandings. This is a high-risk assignment. You're not allowed any mistakes. If Kleiser or his Libyan security people get onto you . . ." The Admiral shrugged.

"Your only hole card is Mossad," Manfredi said. "But they have their own interests."

"Who's my Mossad contact?"

The Admiral nodded to Manfredi, who strode to the hall doors, opened them, and motioned to someone waiting in the anteroom.

A tall, shapely girl with fine features framed by shiny black hair entered the study. Lawford stared at her in stunned silence. She was the striking model-type who had been in Starke's Café the night Hickey was murdered.

CHAPTER EIGHT

They were seated at a window table upstairs at Chadwick's under the protective eyes of strategically placed Agency operatives. Outside, the night was moonless, and the running lights of small boats shimmered off the Potomac. Narda Simone spoke English with a slight Israeli accent and used her slender fingers as accents to her words. The candlelight highlighted the vivid topaz spokes in her expressive brown eyes. She wore no wedding band but Tom had an instinctive feeling that she was spoken for. She stared out the window at the white lights of a large moored pleasure boat and wistfully said, "It reminds me of the marina at Haifa."

"I've never been there."

"It's quite beautiful." She lit a cigarette and studied him for a moment. His light gray eyes reflected a curious warmth that played intriguingly against his handsome but coldly chiseled features.

"I'm going to be candid with you," she said. "There were certain things I couldn't mention in the presence of Manfredi and the Admiral. What I have to say now is not pleasant, and were it up to me, I would not discuss any of it; but I have been ordered to inform you of certain facts. This is not a matter of trust or fraternity. This is a matter of your survival—and that's very important to us."

"Us?"

"The State of Israel," she said quickly, and continued. "My government has been aware of the Libyan-Pakistani nuclear alliance since 1979. When we learned of the Nazi rocket scientists' involvement, the matter was given top priority. We have supplied a steady stream of data to your Agency— bits and pieces of intelligence that indicated the existence of this alliance. Admiral Dwinell remained interested, but neutral."

"How could he remain neutral once Qaddafi was involved?"

She shrugged. "We believe the Pakistani involvement is very distressing to your government. Also, whenever we Israelis mention a Nazi connection, we're considered to be paranoid. In any case, it's been the Admiral's view that while our facts pointed toward a nuclear conspiracy, we lacked conclusive proof. When we learned of Mueller's plans to visit Washington, we notified the Agency."

"And the Admiral was suddenly interested," Tom said.

"Well, after all, here was a deported German rocket scientist, an admitted war criminal, traveling back to the U.S. on a Pakistani diplomatic passport. Whom would he see? What was he up to? It was a firsthand opportunity for the Agency to confirm our own fears."

"So the Admiral ordered a surveillance unit set up through Hickey's Allegiance Research company, and you and Manfredi devised the cover story. You became Lisa Gessler, and you fed Hickey that stuff about Mueller selling secrets belonging to Topf A.G."

"Industrial espionage seemed a reasonable cover story."

"Why the Topf company?"

She shrugged and crisscrossed the glowing end of her cigarette in the ashtray, then glanced up at him with an odd, melancholy look. "The use of Topf appealed to my superior's macabre sense of humor. Topf designed and produced the giant double crematorium at Auschwitz." She sighed. "In any case, I assumed that Hickey had been advised of the extreme risks involved."

Tom felt a small icy circle beginning to form in his chest. "Manfredi said the danger to Hickey was minimal."

"In our view the risks were grave," she replied firmly. "I warned Manfredi that Mueller was protected by a team of Libyan assassins housed in the Pakistani embassy, and anyone found to be tracking Mueller would be in jeopardy."

"You're saying that Manfredi never passed that on to Hickey."

"It seems obvious that he either withheld it or the Admiral declined to act on our information. We tried to protect Hickey. We followed him to Starke's, but . . ." She paused. "It happened very fast. Your friend was a guinea pig. I suspect the Admiral had alerted the Pakistanis and their Libyan assassins to the fact that Mueller was under surveillance. The trap was baited, and if Hickey was hit, it meant—"

"They didn't want Mueller followed," Tom interrupted, "and that Kleiser's STS group were key players in the Libyan-Pakistani nuclear conspiracy. And in order to get that proof, they hung Hickey out to die."

She nodded. Tom sipped his wine and she could see the barely suppressed rage in his eyes and the tautness of his mouth.

"Why did you tell me this?" he asked.

"You had every right to know. I hope you will be equally forthright with us."

"Who, exactly, is 'us'?"

"I'm working with Mossad, but I report directly to General Dado Harel. I believe you know him."

"A long time ago. I lost an eardrum in your October '73 war."

"It was not *our* war," she blurted with a flash of anger. "We were attacked on our holiest of days by Egypt, Syria, Iraq, and Jordan."

"I know. I was there."

"Well, people tend to forget. We've been at war for almost fifty years and the world has made monsters of us. What other nation in history has won all its wars and surrendered all its victories?"

"You can spare me the politics. I don't give a damn about any of it."

A sudden gust of wind rattled the big window facing the Potomac. "I'm sorry—"

"It's okay." He sighed. "Tell me, how is the General?"

"He's well," she said with a trace of sadness.

Tom now knew to whom she belonged.

"I have to ask you this and I hope you will . . ." She hesitated. "We have to know the extent of your cooperation."

"My instructions are to cooperate fully with your government on the Libyan-STS situation," he said. "If I locate the rocket launch site, I'm to inform your people immediately. I get the impression that an Israeli air strike on any Libyan military target will not produce tears in Washington."

"And what of Pakistan?"

"That's a different situation. The Admiral wants intelligence data on their Kahuta nuclear-research center, but he will not tolerate an Israeli attack on Pakistan."

"Why would he even be concerned? We lack the technical capability to launch such an air strike. It's fifty-two hundred miles round trip from Tel Aviv to Kahuta."

Tom thought she knew the mileage a little too fast, but he shrugged and smiled. "I just work here. You wanted the truth and I'm giving it to you. One-hundred-percent cooperation on Libya. But if I uncover any Israeli plans to hit Kahuta, I inform the Admiral at once."

"I appreciate your honesty."

They fell silent as the waiter served their dinners and refilled their wineglasses. "Careful," he cautioned, "plate's hot. *Bon appétit.*"

"Go ahead, start," Tom said.

"In a moment." She took a sip of wine and said, "You will be given a first-class ticket to Frankfurt, with connecting flight to Berlin. It's Pan American all the way. You arrive Thursday, January 16. You will take a taxi to the Kempinski Hotel, where you will be contacted by a German woman named Erika Sperling. She's your 'inside' connection. Needless to say, we are deeply grateful to you."

"Don't be. I'm not doing this for Israel."

"Your motives are your own. All I'm trying to tell you is that you're not alone."

CHAPTER NINE

General Dado Harel drove the Volvo in low gear, climbing the steep hill up toward the Golan plateau. Far below, the entire Galilee was a verdant windblown carpet. A cool wind rushed into the open car windows and played gentle games with the tips of Narda's hair. Although still feeling the lingering fatigue of the long flight from Washington to Tel Aviv, she had begun working with Dado almost immediately upon her return.

The Volvo reached the summit and rattled across the wooden slats of the Bnot Yaakov Bridge. Close to the bridge, the rusted hulk of a Sherman tank rested atop a marble slab inscribed with names of the fallen Israeli soldiers who had halted the Syrian armor on October 7, 1973—among them the name of Dani Harel.

They drove in silence, following the military jeep toward the distant snow-capped peak of Mount Hermon. The single-lane asphalt road sliced through golden fields of winter wheat, and flocks of sheep grazed on the slopes of grassy hillocks.

There was nothing on either side of the road to suggest

that the greatest tank battle since World War Two had raged over this pastoral land. The truce line between Israel and Syria was only ten kilometers north, but there was no evidence of military bases, tank parks, or airfields.

Narda studied Dado for a moment. His blue eyes seemed to have faded, and dark circles of fatigue rimmed them. His blond hair was fast turning to gray. God knows what he was planning. God knows what details were stored in that computerlike brain. She loved him but despaired of an enduring relationship. He was haunted by ghosts, and still inextricably involved with his wife, Avital. Although she had slipped away into the arcane mysticism of Zealotry, Avital nevertheless represented a living, breathing connection to their dead son.

Narda closed her eyes, thinking it was a nation of dead sons, lost causes, and endless intrigues. She wondered what had happened to the Dream. Her father's generation had planted millions of trees, filled the swamps, cultivated the stony fields, and built a Jewish state that would be the light unto all nations; but the people of the book had become a nation of warriors. Surrounded. Beleaguered. Damned and cursed by all.

After the death of her brother in Lebanon, Narda had volunteered for service with Dado's Special Forces Division, and in the ensuing years she had placed herself in jeopardy more often than front-line soldiers. Her life, her talents, her will, were dedicated to the restoration of the Dream.

The sudden piercing scream came from far off and overwhelmed them in seconds; the lone F-16 jet fighter howled thirty feet above the Volvo. Imprinted on its sand-and-green-camouflaged wings was the solid dark blue Star of David. They watched it arc up, bank sharply, and streak west toward the Mediterranean.

"Those kids are always practicing," Dado said.

"Yes, but why do they practice on us?"

Dado shrugged. "How often do they get a chance to scare hell out of a general?"

The car radio crackled in a burst of Hebrew being transmitted from military headquarters in Tel Aviv. Narda answered, reporting their position to be six kilometers east of the Druse village of Madjal Shams.

The lead jeep picked up speed and Dado accelerated. They could now discern the nests of antennae and revolving radar scoops atop Mount Hermon. The sophisticated listening devices penetrated into Damascus, forty miles to the north.

They came out of a sharp turn into a mountain pass and entered Madjal Shams. White stone houses with Moorish arches and lacy balconies lined the street. Old men in dark suits and red fezzes played backgammon under shaded terraces.

Women thronged around the open stalls of a fruit market, and radios played romantic Arab songs. The Azizz cinema marquee advertised an old Clint Eastwood film.

The Druse were a tribal people scattered throughout the Middle East and fiercely loyal to the country in which they lived. The Israeli Druse served in all branches of the armed forces and had fought with distinction in five wars.

Following the lead jeep, Dado turned into a narrow tree-lined street and parked in front of a two-story ocher-colored house belonging to the village mukhtar.

The men were seated on an Oriental rug in the center of a domed living room. The mukhtar's wife and eldest daughter served courses of hummus, fried sardines, grilled St. Peter's fish, lamb chops, and garlic spinach.

The group included General Arik Carmil, chief of Air Force Intelligence and Strategic Planning; Zev Berger, chief of Mossad; Matty Alon, chief of Naval Intelligence; Uri Erez, chief of Naval Commandos; and General Dado Harel. The house and Druse village had been chosen for the meeting for the sole purpose of avoiding the omnipresent Israeli press.

According to custom, Narda ate her lunch in an anteroom with the women of the house. Afterward she joined the men in the spacious study with its French windows that afforded a spectacular view of the Galilee.

Stepping out onto the small balcony, Dado signaled to the purple-bereted soldiers waiting below, motioning "ten minutes" with his hands. He came back inside and stood in the center of the room. "Only seven people are aware of this proposed operation," he began. "The Prime Minister, Zev Berger, Narda Simone, myself, the director of the CIA, Admiral Dwinell, his deputy, Albert Manfredi, and an American journalist, Tom Lawford." Pausing for a moment, he continued in a solemn tone. "We cannot afford any leaks. All of you remember the press leak just twelve hours before the raid on the Baghdad reactor. It was due only to the skill of our pilots that we escaped detection and disaster. What I say here remains with us."

There was a moment of silence before Berger asked, "What of the Americans? What can we do if they choose to break the code of silence?"

"Their knowledge is limited to the phase of action devoted to locating the German missile base in Libya. Nothing more. The Prime Minister has authorized my Special Operations Unit to undertake the location and destruction of the missile site and other crucial targets in Libya. Remember, this mission consists of two operations: the Libyan phase is code-named 'Red Desert'—there is as yet no code or plan for the Pakistani phase. You have been briefed on the Libyan-Pakistani connection. Pakistani nuclear warheads will soon be delivered to Qaddafi. Professor Newman has stated that three Hiroshima-size bombs will destroy our country. We have managed, thanks to Yanush"—he used the Mossad chief's nickname—"to penetrate Dr. Kleiser's so-called Space Transport Systems. We also have an agent in place inside the Kahuta nuclear complex in Pakistan. The Americans will cooperate one hundred percent on Libya but not on Pakistan. Kahuta remains a problem."

Dado crossed to the desk, lit a cigarette, and addressed the Air Force chief. "Arik, you are to begin at once to plan and train for a long-range mission over Libya. I am speaking of a massive strike: the terrorist training camps at Sidi Barani, the new poison-gas plant at Bin Gashir, the military command center in Tripoli, oil refineries, tank parks, airfields, and the small nuclear reactor at Tajura. And you, Uri," he addressed the chief of Naval Commandos, "you will prepare landings at Benghazi to destroy the communications center prior to the air strike." He then turned to the

Naval Intelligence chief. "Matty, you will provide support for the landings and subsequent withdrawal of the sea commandos. We will also require support-fire systems from missile boats and helicopter rescue ships. Yanush will provide overall target intelligence, including satellite photographs. Narda will act as project coordinator. The entire operation has to be lightning fast. No more than fifteen minutes—air, sea, and land."

"It costs a fortune to prepare and train for a mission of this size," Air Force General Carmil complained. "I have no budget for such a mission."

"Narda will see to the transfer of all necessary funds."

"This isn't an antiterrorist strike," Carmil persisted. "You're talking about a major operation: varied ordnance, radar avoidance, combined-forces logistics, refueling tankers, rendezvous points over the Mediterranean, meteorology, air-to-ground communication, Hawkeye E-2's, and E-3 electronic jammers, routes in and out, time over target, counterstrike potential, and—"

"Hold it, Arik," Dado interrupted. "For now, in this moment, all you're required to do is design a mission profile. When that's accomplished I'll meet with you on specifics."

"How much time do I have?"

"One week."

"What of the rocket site? The Libyan desert isn't Tel Aviv. You have to pinpoint that site."

"We'll find it. We meet in seven days in the War Room."

The men rose and Berger spoke. "I have a question. Even if we locate the rocket base and take it out, it's still a Band-Aid on a cancer."

The room fell silent.

"In what way?" Dado asked calmly.

"Pakistan's production of nuclear weapons will continue no matter what happens in Libya. What's to prevent them from giving a twenty-kiloton bomb to Syria? Or to the Saudis? Or to Iran? Or Iraq? Or even Egypt? The Libyan air strike will buy us some time, but Kahuta is the head of the snake, and so long as it remains in operation, our national survival is in jeopardy."

Air Force General Carmil spoke before Dado could reply.

"I want all of you to understand that an air strike on northeast Pakistan is beyond the capability of our F-16's and F-15's."

A grim silence enveloped the sunny room. Dado stared at the hard-eyed men facing him. They were men who had withstood the terrible compression of recent history, of five wars and endless terror. Their courage and determination had permitted the tiny nation to survive in a sea of hatred. They were neither politicians, nor poets, nor philosophers. They were warriors, and one did not create fictions with such men.

"You're right, Yanush," Dado agreed. "Kahuta is the head of the snake. But for the moment, I can only say you must leave that problem with me. Concentrate on Libya. We have a long list of grievances to settle with Colonel Qaddafi. This is the darkest operation we've ever undertaken. There will be no written memoranda. Narda will supply codes for phone conversations."

When the meeting broke up, Berger took Dado aside and said, "My agent inside STS informed me that Dr. Alois Brunner, the German scientist who conducted the recent V-5 test launch in Libya, has returned to Hamburg. I thought that perhaps Penelope should pay him a visit."

"It can only help. Go ahead, Yanush."

As they crossed the Bnot Yaakov Bridge and descended the serpentine hillside to the shoreline of Galilee, Narda said, "That shifty son of a bitch, Berger, was trying to find out how you intend to deal with Kahuta."

Dado tousled her hair and smiled. "Forget about it, Narda. Look there, at the Sea of Galilee, where the water breaks on the sandbar. The place where Christ walked on water. He was a true savior. The greatest of all Jews. He taught us how to rise from the dead."

CHAPTER TEN

Alois Brunner stood just inside the forward cabin of the public ferry. The motor launch was crowded with commuters, and its engine strained as it chugged across Lake Alster toward the Uhlenhurst landing. The dark gray winter sky blanketing Hamburg failed to dampen Brunner's spirits. His fellow passengers envied him his deep tan, and an elderly woman neighbor had asked him if he'd been skiing in Austria. He said he had. She then inquired as to the health of Brunner's sickly wife. He replied cordially, explaining that Frau Brunner was still in Switzerland at the clinic, and, excusing himself politely, he left the cabin.

Up on the foredeck, he took deep breaths of the cold air. He had been too long in Libya. The Sahara was a hellish environment: filthy Arabs, scorpions, sand flies, burning daytime heat and frigid nights. After the successful V-5 launch he had flown from Tripoli to Munich and reported to Mueller. Unfortunately, Dr. Kleiser was in Berlin and could not receive his report first-hand. The vigilant and aggressive German press had once again attacked the STS enterprise. Someone inside STS had leaked the news of the successful

launch, and while the report was unconfirmed by any
satellite evidence, it nevertheless created problems for Dr.
Kleiser. The U.S. State Department had formally protested
to the Bonn government. The Israelis had been strangely
quiet, but they had other problems to deal with. If matters
remained calm for another month, Qaddafi would finish the
Zionist state once and for all. The Soviets were another
matter; they had officially complained that German ballistic missiles violated the surrender terms of 1945. While
these problems were not his to solve, the negative press
worried Brunner, but Dr. Kleiser was a master propagandist and would undoubtedly deal with the corporate-image
problem.

All in all, things were proceeding quite well, in more ways
than one. Brunner had spent the night with his nineteen-
year-old mistress, a student at the University of Hamburg.
He took care of her tuition and expenses, and did not fool
himself that it was his lovemaking prowess that kept Fräulein Kluge's cozy smile on her face. She had flattered him
shamelessly, saying that his deep tan and blue eyes made
him irresistible. He presented her with a gold bracelet he
had bought in the Tripoli bazaar, and she had shrieked in
delight, hugging and kissing him—and they made plans to
attend the opera Saturday night.

The throb of the engine decreased and the conductor
announced "Uhlenhurst." Brunner departed with the first
group of passengers, moving quickly to avoid his inquisitive
neighbor.

As he walked past the stately lakeside homes, Brunner
marveled as always at the faithful restoration of the luxuri-
ous lakefront section, all of which had been consumed by
fire in the great British air raids of November 1944. He
opened the low gate at 38 Schöne Aussicht. The gabled
two-story house had increased tenfold in value since he
bought it in 1962. His wife had tended to the flowers and
gardened until her terminal illness made further physical
activity impossible.

The stout, gray-haired housekeeper greeted him at the
door and told him that the package he'd been expecting
from Berlin had arrived that afternoon by special messenger
and was on his desk.

Brunner's study was cluttered, but comfortable. A large picture window faced the street and the lake. He glanced at the thick beige-and-red STS package resting on his desk. A brown string was tied vertically and laterally around the package and knotted at the center. He knew the packet contained nozzle propulsion blueprints for his inspection. He pressed an intercom button and the maid answered. *"Ja, Herr Doktor?"*

"Tee, bitte."

Brunner sat down, picked up the package, and pulled the bow string.

His face exploded in a bright yellow flash.

His arms were torn from their sockets and hurled through the picture window.

The concussion rings moved out, collapsing the walls, sending the second-floor bedroom furniture crashing down into the flaming rubble of the study.

Seated behind the wheel of a van parked directly across from Brunner's house, a pleasant-looking middle-aged blond woman chewed the last of her egg-salad sandwich before switching the ignition on and pulling away from the curb.

CHAPTER ELEVEN

The connecting flight from Frankfurt to Berlin arrived at Tegel Airport in the French sector at 11:35 A.M. The flight wasn't crowded and the luggage was on the carousel in a matter of minutes. Lawford picked up his suitcase and proceeded to customs control. The young officer examined his passport with a cursory glance before handing it back with a smiling, "Welcome to Berlin."

Stepping outside the terminal, Tom felt the instant raw bite of frigid air. But unlike Washington, he was dressed for the cold: fur-lined boots, wool sweater, heavy camel overcoat, and Soviet-style fur hat with earflaps. He hailed a taxi, and placing his bag up front with the driver, said, "Kempinski Hotel."

He settled back in the soft leather, feeling the heady, almost stoned sensation that accompanied jet lag. The long flight had given him ample time to reflect on events that had transpired since his arrival in Washington. The thought that Hickey had been used as bait was chilling; but then, expedience and pragmatism were the bookends of the Admiral's conscience. Lawford now owed the Agency nothing. His only allegiance was to Hickey. He would try to infiltrate the Muslim-Nazi alliance, and as long as it served his purpose, he would cooperate with the Israelis.

The Berlin sky was gunmetal gray, and sporadic gusts of snowflakes danced in the wind. They crossed a steel span over frozen Lake Havel and picked up the six-lane expressway.

Tom was familiar with the divided city, having covered various news events over the years. He preferred East Berlin to the West. What remained of prewar Berlin was in the East: the magnificent Pergamon Museum, the Brandenburg Gate, the Unter Den Linden, the Brecht-Weill Theater, and that sliver of the old Adlon Hotel. There were, too, some of the Third Reich's more infamous buildings still standing: the Luftwaffe headquarters, the Reich Ministry of Propaganda, and the innocuous mustard-colored building of Adolf Eichmann's notorious Genocide Section IVB4.

Noticing a copy of the *International Herald Tribune* tucked into the taxi's jump seat, Tom picked it up, glanced at the front page and suddenly grew interested. There was a photograph of a man identified as Dr. Alois Brunner, who had been blown to pieces in his Hamburg home. The police suspected a leftist terrorist group. The accompanying article went on to say that Brunner was a former Nazi rocket scientist who currently had been serving as an executive with a West German company called Space Transport Systems. The balance of the piece was a capsulized background on STS and its chief executive officer, Dr. Fritz Kleiser. Tom wondered who had hit Brunner and how it related to his own mission, but he felt no sympathy for the murdered rocket scientist. He recalled the grainy SS film of Brunner and Mueller at Nordhausen staring at the bodies of slave-labor inmates twisting on wires suspended from a crane.

The Mercedes taxi turned right into Fasanenstrasse and pulled up in front of the Kempinski. Tom tipped the driver generously and followed a bellman to the front desk. The check-in procedure was fast and efficient and the assistant manager escorted him to his fifth-floor room.

The small suite was at the far end of the floor and faced Fasanenstrasse. From the sitting-room window Tom could see the tristar Mercedes symbol revolving atop the Europa Center office building; and to the east, the ominous watch-towers just beyond the wall dividing the city. He thanked the assistant manager and closed the door, grateful to be alone.

The pain at the nape of his neck was beginning to throb and snake its way down his left arm. He took a pilsner beer from the mini-bar and popped three aspirin, chasing them with the beer. Lacking the energy to unpack, he drew the window drapes, stripped off his clothes, pulled the coverlet down on the king-size bed, and crawled between the linen sheets.

The residue of previous occupants hung in the air: a trace of cigar smoke, and the faint aroma of perfume.

Closing his eyes, Tom thought of his last conversation with his wife. He had told Claudia that he was going to Europe on assignment and if she needed anything to call his business manager. They had chatted for a long time and he'd asked how her work was proceeding. Claudia was a fine writer and potentially a brilliant poet. Her lyrical poems were etched with strange colors and startling images and emotions that touched the soul, but she never trusted her own talent. He had hung up, missing her and sensing the futility of trying to escape the past. What the hell had happened to them? He recalled an old Spanish proverb: "With love, time passes; with time, love passes."

He felt himself slowly easing past the edge of awareness into a somnambulant state. Faces and images began to flash like quick cuts in a film: the dark tunnels at Nordhausen, the topaz in Narda Simone's striking eyes, the Admiral's crafty smile and his cold-eyed deputy, Manfredi, Robert Stein's pugilistic features flushed with rage, and the limping black giant, Larry Dutton, and the watery-eyed, ulcer-ridden Steve Garrett, and the impassive Arab assassin watching the football game, and Mueller, and Brunner. And Hickey, wide-eyed, hands clutching at the dripping mass of violated flesh.

They flared and died, phantom forms in a long chain stretching back to the Laotian jungle. Mercifully, the images faded and he slipped into the dark void of sleep.

CHAPTER TWELVE

Dr. Fritz Kleiser peered out of the tinted glass window that enclosed his penthouse suite atop the Europa Center. Over six feet tall, Kleiser was an athletic-looking man in his late fifties. His dark, brooding eyes and imperious demeanor belonged to another Germany—to the Germany of nobility and Prussian aristocracy. He wore his expensive clothes like a uniform and seldom varied the combination: dark Savile Row suits and gleaming black Italian shoes, tailored blue shirts, and maroon silk ties.

Ever since he could remember, he had worshiped those German scientists whose genius had given the world its space technology. When the American government expelled the German rocket scientists in 1980, Kleiser recruited them into his fledgling Space Transportation Systems. He floated a public stock issue, gathered millions of marks, and built rocket-assembly plants in Munich and Stuttgart.

Offering lucrative contracts, he hired graduate students of Munich's University Space Technology Institute to supplement the aging veteran scientists.

Himself a physicist, Kleiser believed that the simplistic

propulsion systems of the old V-1 and V-2 rockets could be augmented by clusters of coaxial rocket boosters capable of placing communication and spy satellites in orbit at a fraction of the cost of U.S. and Soviet missiles. Although liquid-fueled and requiring a lengthy prelaunch procedure, his improved V-5 could also carry a one-ton nuclear or conventional warhead over a thousand miles.

Kleiser had found eager potential customers in Saudi Arabia, Iraq, Libya, and Syria. In the end, he chose the joint venture with Colonel Qaddafi; it was a decision based solely on money. The Libyan dictator advanced STS close to a billion dollars and provided a test range, base facilities, underground silo, and control rooms. The floodtide of Qaddafi's dollars had enabled Kleiser to purchase sophisticated equipment from the giants of German industry: Telefunken, Siemens, Daimler-Benz, and Merck. The sensitive material was then shipped to Libya via Blankurt-Becker A.G. in Zurich.

Kleiser knew that Pakistani nuclear warheads would eventually be riding atop the V-5, and for whom those warheads were intended; but the apocalyptic consequences were irrelevant. If Qaddafi acquired nuclear warheads from Pakistan, STS was not legally responsible for the misuse of its V-5 rocket by a client. Kleiser was a businessman, not a moralist, and had little regard for either Arab or Jew. Although he thought Hitler a madman, he nevertheless agreed with the Nazi doctrine of racial purity, and if his rockets took off from Libya and devastated Israel, so be it. The world would certainly be better served if Arab and Jew exterminated one another. They were both Semites, *untermenschen,* and deserved their endless bloodspill.

He had, of course, taken great pains to be discreet and maintain the image of a space-exploration company whose aims and goals were strictly peaceful. But in the face of the almost daily revelations of German participation in Libyan and Iraqi poison-gas- and biological-warfare-manufacturing plants, Kleiser's posture of innocent space exploration had become increasingly difficult to maintain. The press had caused indictments to be filed against some of his colleagues at Imhausen Chemie, IBI Engineering, and Ruchstoff Einfuhr. The journalists were in a race to scoop one another

73

on the scandalous violations of Germany's lax export laws by a variety of heretofore respected industrial consortiums. Even the right-wing magazine *Der Spiegel* had raised questions about STS's true intentions in Libya. Although the sensational headlines were based on innuendo and gossip, they had caused stressful moments for the West German government, and the attacks continued unabated. Fortunately, the United States had not yet formally accused STS of any wrongdoing. A third-world country, even Libya, could not be denied a cheap satellite telecommunications system. Still, as the delivery of a Pakistani nuclear warhead to Qaddafi drew near, the threat of revelation increased.

He needed time, another month, six weeks at the outside, and his goal would be achieved. He would receive his final payment of seven hundred million dollars from Qaddafi, and would have sufficient capital to become a major player in the space business. He would, of course, disclaim any knowledge of a Libyan-launched nuclear attack on Israel. Nuclear war in the Middle East had been predicted for years and would come as no surprise. The world could hardly blame STS. All he required was time and luck. He sighed, thinking there were such things in life as good luck and bad luck. The recent V-5 test launch conducted by Brunner had been letter perfect, but unfortunately there had been a leak—unconfirmed but nevertheless triggering a firestorm of protest that swept across the pages of the world press. And Brunner had been brutally murdered in Hamburg.

Kleiser's fingers drummed the desktop. Brunner . . . Brunner could have been hit by the KGB, the CIA, or Mossad. It was not inconceivable that Abu Hasi, the Libyan control officer, had a hand in Brunner's demise. After all, Brunner had conducted the test, there had been the leak, and Hasi suspected all of the STS hierarchy. Hasi basically despised all Westerners, and was obsessed with suspicions and imaginary enemies. Kleiser would soon have to speak with Hasi. One had to control these Arabs.

In any event, the killing of Brunner was an unmistakable warning. And while his employees in the Libyan desert were out of harm's way, he would take immediate steps to increase the security at the Munich and Stuttgart assembly plants. It was imperative to maintain calm and order. Order was the purest of all art forms. The most abstract mathematical equations demanded order. In this case, order depended on a creditable public image. The key was in place. He needed only to turn it. He leaned forward and pressed a button on the speaker console.

"Yes?"

"Has Lawford arrived?"

"The concierge confirmed his arrival."

"See to it, Erika."

CHAPTER THIRTEEN

Lawford woke up feeling totally disoriented, and it took a moment for his surroundings to register. The digital clock on the night table read 8:26 P.M. He had slept for almost eight hours and still felt woozy, but the pain in his left shoulder had subsided.

He got to his feet, stretched, and opened the curtains. The maze of twinkling lights in West Berlin was in sharp contrast to the paucity of lights in the eastern section of the divided city. The Mercedes tristar symbol glowed in blue neon as it slowly revolved over the Europa Center. Directly across the street, the small restored synagogue, with its illuminated Star of David, made a case for the German conscience. The dark brown structure had been destroyed by Nazi thugs on Kristallnacht in November 1938.

Tom suddenly felt warm and claustrophobic. He adjusted the temperature control and heard the hiss as the heat sensor cut off. He needed some fresh air, and something to eat. Dressing slowly, he wondered about the fate of the restored synagogue's missing congregation.

The lobby was sparsely populated and piano music

drifted in from the bar. A few smartly dressed couples crossed the lobby to the famous Kempinski restaurant, but Tom had a craving for American junk food, and the concierge recommended the Pariser Café on Meineckstrasse.

The Kurfürstendamm was alive with nocturnal action—pimps, peddlers, and hashish pushers worked the doorways of cafés and subway kiosks. Flashing orange bulbs advertised sex bars—Mirelle's, Triangle, Ilona's—and a startling series of neon figures engaging in pornographic acts blinked over the Adam and Eve Club. Tom thought that if the Wall ever came down, the austere dignity of East Berlin would be lost in the exchange of freedom for sleaze.

The Pariser Café was a garden restaurant, enclosed and heated in the winter; its tightly bunched tables were occupied by a lively crowd of young people. The current hit single by Whitney Houston played on stereo speakers and underscored the chatter, laughter, and cozy ambience. Uniformed waiters carrying trays of food and beer moved quickly from the kitchen to the garden tables.

Tom sipped his beer, then reluctantly lit a cigarette, vowing that once this assignment was over he would swear off the weed forever. He noticed a very pretty girl seated opposite a handsome boy at an adjacent table. They held hands and seemed to be deeply involved with each other, but from time to time the girl glanced shyly at Tom. Kids, he thought; never having had any of his own, he regarded them as a species apart.

The music changed from soft rock to a romantic ballad by Aznavour, and the French lyrics reminded him of Claudia and Paris. He could trace the crack in their marriage back to the summer of '83, to that first week in August when the doctor confirmed that Claudia was pregnant. That same week he flew off to Beirut and became a reluctant celebrity.

It had been the time in Beirut when kidnapping journalists was fashionable. The Hezbollah terrorists had been tipped off to Lawford's presence in the city, and the trap was sprung on Rue Verdun in Muslim West Beirut. A black van roared out of an alley, swerved, and blocked the sedan in which Tom was a passenger. Grabbing his driver's AK-47, he dropped three of the masked terrorists as they leapt out of the van. Tom was a superb marksman with the Soviet-made machine gun, having had years of experience with the weapon in the Laotian jungles.

It had been half a minute of hell. Thirty seconds of acrid smoke, bursts of rapid fire, bodies falling like rag dolls, and the screech of tires as the sedan careened around the van and streaked across the Green Line into the safety of East Beirut. The televised and published reports of the thwarted kidnap attempt had made him an instant media star, but the incident and the time in Lebanon cost him dearly. Claudia lost the baby, and the inner glow that had warmed their marriage for years was extinguished. His escapade in Beirut had been one adventure too many for her, and Tom always suspected that the baby had been aborted.

He crushed the cigarette out and sighed heavily, wondering what it was he was seeking here in this fateful city. Revenge for Hickey? Yes—but there was something more profound than vengeance. He had to rediscover a sense of purpose before the tide of moroseness carried him to that desolate place where everything was an encore.

After dinner, he walked a brisk mile to Budapesterstrasse, stopping for a moment at the familiar site of the legendary Berlin Zoo. He'd written a travel piece some years ago in which he described the zoo's star-crossed history. The Berlin Zoo had been the bizarre site of a last desperate stand by fanatical SS troops against five Soviet armored divisions. Tom was always struck by the irony of Hitler's thousand-year Reich ending ignominiously in the Zoo.

He stared at the grim gray concrete facade and wondered about that last battle—tanks, rockets, shells, automatic weapons, animals running wild, and Wagner's *Götterdämmerung* blaring from loudspeakers. He shivered in the sharp cold air and, promising himself a visit, resumed walking.

Some twenty minutes later, he found himself in the once-elegant but now-deserted Potsdammer Platz section. He strolled past the majestic facades of abandoned prewar Italian, Spanish, and French embassies, whose interiors were burned-out shells. The foreign embassies were now located in Bonn, and these ghostly relics of Belle Epoche Berlin had remained unoccupied for almost half a century. The journalist in him was intrigued by the secrets those ruined salons held.

The wail of a siren and flashing blue light of a speeding police van pulled him out of his reverie. Absorbed in his thoughts, he had been unaware of the dark solitude enveloping this desolate area. Except for the occasional rumble of elevated trains traveling on the S-Bahn, it was ominously quiet. Picking up his pace, he crossed a dimly lit boulevard under the S-Bahn and walked alongside a long row of abandoned, boarded-up tenements. There were no pedestrians, no cars, no signs of life.

The only sounds were his own footsteps echoing off the cobblestones. He began to feel a growing sense of foreboding. He was unarmed, in a strange city, pursuing a lethal conspiracy, and had foolishly wandered into a deserted no-man's-land.

Turning abruptly, he started back toward Budapest-erstrasse. His breath vaporized in the cold as he half-walked and half-ran toward the diagonal street bisecting the elevated S-Bahn.

He was less than two hundred feet from the corner when he saw the Mercedes coming slowly toward him.

The big sedan showed no lights.

He felt the first icy trickle of adrenaline leak into his chest cavity as he heard the rattle of an approaching train.

These were professionals. They made no mistakes. Hickey had been cut down in a matter of seconds. Whoever was in that Mercedes was armed with automatic weapons. They'd wait for the train to thunder past. The noise would cover the high chatter of their machine guns.

He glanced at the tenements, but their doors were sealed. There was no cover. No place to hide. The rumble of the elevated train was closer. His temple throbbed and icy beads of sweat oozed out of his forehead and trickled down his cheeks. He began to run, but it was too late.

Swerving suddenly, its rear tires smoking against the cobblestones, the blacked-out Mercedes veered across the traffic lane, jumped the sidewalk, and screeched to a halt facing him. The train thundered directly overhead.

He clenched his fists and his body tensed, anticipating the searing heat of the slugs.

The high beams hit him full in the face, blinding him . . . holding him, paralyzed, in place. The doors flew open and two men with guns drawn motioned him to raise his hands.

"Passport!" the big one with the rimless glasses ordered.

"I don't have it," Tom rasped. "I gave it to the concierge at the Kempinski."

"Turn. Hands against the wall."

The thin, wiry man patted him down and removed his wallet. The two men glanced at the New York State driver's license and the glassine envelope displaying his social-security card. Opening the small card case, the wiry man removed Lawford's CBS pass and green Reuters press card.

While the big man held the gun on him, the wiry man went back to the Mercedes and made two brief telephone calls. After what seemed an eternity, he returned.

"This is the crossing point of hashish from East to West. What were you doing here, Mr. Lawford?"

"Reminiscing," Tom answered sheepishly.

"Come, we'll drop you back to the Kempinski. Your hotel room is a safer place for reminiscing."

CHAPTER FOURTEEN

The sprawling Kahuta Nuclear Research Center was situated in the scruffy foothills of northeast Pakistan twenty-five kilometers from the twin cities of Islamabad and Rawalpindi. The five levels of working infrastructure were below ground; only the protective concrete cupola, air-filtration plant, military barracks, and parking area were visible. The complex was ringed by an electrified fence topped with layers of barbed wire. Tall watchtowers equipped with powerful carbon-arc lights illuminated the perimeter fence. Paratroopers of the elite Third Brigade patrolled the compound. Strategically placed Crotale surface-to-air missiles bristled skyward and flights of American-made F-16's patrolled the skies eastward to India. Army tanks blocked the roads leading in and out of Kahuta. Private and military vehicles were forbidden entry to the village without a pass stamped by the chief of State Security.

The director of Kahuta was the distinguished Pakistani metallurgist Farheed Shah.

Shah had dedicated his life to the achievement of a single

goal—the development of a Pakistani nuclear bomb. He regarded the Kahuta facility as the shining symbol of Pakistan's emerging scientific excellence, and he moved through its labyrinthian corridors with an almost spiritual joy, as if he were chief curator of a wondrous treasure-filled museum. There was only one exception to his enthrallment with the site. He dreaded the fifth level, where U-239 plutonium isotope, the deadliest of toxins, was stored in lead coffins. Named after the God of Hell, plutonium served only one purpose, to detonate an atomic or hydrogen bomb, and its presence had always unnerved him. The slightest leak of the lethal isotope could render the entire northern province uninhabitable forever.

It was therefore with trepidation that Shah glanced nervously at the clock in the fifth-level machine shop as he waited for Dr. Jamil Tukhali to complete his thorough but futile inspection of the Swedish-made Flash X-ray machine. The highly complex, top-secret X-ray machine was capable of seeing through a thick core of steel and photographing a nuclear-triggered explosion at a fraction of a second.

Shah regarded Tukhali as a rare jewel, a gift of Allah, a genius born to primitive parents in the rebellious tribal province of Baluchistan. That Tukhali had overcome a poverty-stricken, tragic childhood and risen to the highest ranks of Kahuta's team of nuclear physicists was a stunning achievement. Shah treated the handsome young physicist as if he were his own son. Tukhali feigned an attitude of respect and admiration for the portly director, but in truth he considered Shah to be a benevolent dictator, a man of modest scientific talent, gifted only in matters of organization and industrial espionage.

Shah had been responsible for smuggling the blueprints for the gas-centrifuge enrichment process out of the top-secret NATO plant at Almelo in the Netherlands. The director had also worked closely with Qaddafi in obtaining a continuous supply of raw yellow-cake uranium, but his greatest coup had been the acquisition of the X-ray machines, which were barred from export by the Swedish government. Unfortunately, a mysterious press leak crippled Shah's startling achievement. Upon confirmation of the story, the Swedish Prime Minister ordered the manufacturer to withhold the operating manuals, without which the state-of-the-art machines were useless.

Shah wiped some beads of perspiration from his upper lip as he watched Dr. Tukhali's fingers trace the X-ray machine's circuitry once more before finally waving his arms in surrender. "It's no use. I've had my team on this problem for months; perhaps with more time . . ." Tukhali's voice trailed off.

"We'll have the operating manuals very soon, my boy."

"Forgive me, sir, but I've heard that for almost two years."

"But not from me." Shah smiled. "Come, let's get some air."

Leaving the machine shop, they walked past the copper-lined chambers stacked with the ominous lead coffins containing the deadly U-239 plutonium isotope.

As they approached the elevator, Shah said, "I'll never forget the day those X-ray machines arrived at the dock in Karachi. President Zia personally congratulated me. Of course, we had no way of predicting that the Swedes would withhold the operating manuals. But," he went on as the elevator door opened, "with patience everything is possible."

They got off the elevator on Level One and walked along the reactor hall past white-clad technicians operating banks of computers that monitored the reactor.

Climbing a circular steel staircase, they stepped out onto the observation deck.

The unobstructed sight before them was enthralling.

The reactor soared two hundred feet up to the protective dome of the cupola. Uranium fuel rods, arranged in perfect symmetry, were submerged in a reservoir of celery-colored heavy water. A layer of thorium blanketed the reactor core, adding to the constant neutron bombardment enriching the uranium. Powerful pumps pushed radioactive water through miles of pipes made of pedigreed steel that connected to thousands of whirling gas centrifuges.

The great reactor hall always reminded Tukhali of a sinister science-fiction cathedral bubbling with the alchemy of doom.

Theoretically the plant could produce three hundred

kilograms of enriched uranium, enough to assemble twenty Hiroshima-size bombs a year, but in practice, the Kahuta facility yielded less than fifty kilograms of weapons-grade uranium. Only those centrifuges whose rotary parts were fabricated with a specially hardened, maraging steel remained operative for long periods of time.

"A pity," Shah commented. "We've never been able to produce at full capacity." He paused. "But despite the problems, we have made great progress."

Dr. Tukhali nodded solemnly. "All that remains is the test."

"Come, let's have a cup of tea."

"I'm sorry, sir, but I don't have time. I have an engagement in Pindi this evening."

"Ah—good for you, my boy. I'll walk you to the car."

"It's not necessary."

"I insist." Shah smiled. "I need the fresh air, and I have a confidential matter to discuss with you. A matter of great importance."

Twenty miles west of Kahuta, in the old section of Rawalpindi, the Makasiqor Club was a secular oasis in the otherwise harsh Islamic state. The private restaurant was reserved for the power elite of Pakistan.

Salim Bashira was seated at a rear table set into the concave arch of the wall. He sipped his chilled Russian vodka and checked his gold Patek Philippe watch—8:45 P.M. Dr. Tukhali was late and Bashira was concerned. The brilliant young physicist was usually punctual. Bashira's heavily lidded eyes narrowed as he peered into the semidarkness and snapped his fingers at the waiter. The man hurried over, and Bashira ordered another vodka and some naan bread with sweet pickles and chilies.

Salim Bashira had been born in Bombay of Persian parentage. His father was in the import-export business and early on recognized that his son had a genius for dealing with the complexities and intricacies of international trade. The young Bashira excelled at the University of Bombay and completed his studies at Oxford. Afterward he returned to Bombay and took over his ailing father's business. His father had died in 1947 and his mother six months later.

Bashira sold the business and migrated to Karachi, Pakistan, where in less than a decade he had built a worldwide shipping empire. His fleet of freighters and tankers flew the convenient flags of Panama, Cyprus, and Liberia, taking advantage of their anonymity and tax laws, and his network of shipping agents spanned four continents.

Bashira's personal fortune was rumored to be close to a billion dollars. He owned choice real estate in Rawalpindi and Lahore, but his home was a magnificent seaside villa in the exclusive Karachi suburb of Clifton. His lavish parties were attended by influential people in the military and government. Over the years, he had performed many favors for the state: much of the critical hardware at Kahuta, including the Flash X-ray machines, had been smuggled and shipped from North America and western Europe on Bashira's ships. He worked closely with the director, Farheed Shah, and the godfather of Pakistan's nuclear program, Dr. I. Q. Khan.

Most of Pakistan's eight-billion-dollar opium crop was transported on Bashira's ships sailing from Karachi to Palermo, where it was refined into heroin and transshipped to Amsterdam. Bashira never participated in the profits of the opium trade. Deducting only operating expenses, he turned the profits over to the appropriate government officials. His largess was predicated on maintaining easy access to the country's power structure.

The waiter set down the tray of hors d'oeuvres and another shot glass of chilled vodka. Bashira bit off a piece of chili, sipped the vodka, and chased the hot-cold combination with the sweet pickles. As he chewed the naan bread, he thought that over the years he had managed many things, but none so challenging, none so dangerous, and none so rewarding as the secret he had harbored most of his adult life. Salim Bashira was an Israeli agent. His mother had been a Jew and instilled in him the ancient faith inscribed in the Holy Scrolls of the Torah. On her deathbed she had sworn him to serve the survivors of the Holocaust and to do everything in his power to help preserve the State of Israel.

In April 1954, while on a business trip to Hamburg, he arranged a meeting with the Israeli consul general and offered his services to Mossad. He had, over the years, passed critical intelligence data to Jerusalem. It was Bashira who had alerted Mossad when one of his ships had transported the Swedish Flash X-ray machines. The subsequent press leak and pressure on the Swedish government not to supply the critical operating manuals were the direct result of Bashira's tip.

He had first encountered Dr. Tukhali at a reception in the house of Director Shah. The young physicist had drunk too much palm wine and cornered Bashira. Tukhali spoke with quiet rage about the government's ruthless suppression of the Baluchistani people. Bashira commiserated, but did not probe or press. He did, however, offer to help rebuild Tukhali's destroyed village. After all, he was a man of considerable wealth who contributed to numerous charities, so why not to a worthy cause in the province of Baluchistan?

He subsequently visited the ravaged village and arranged to finance its restoration, as well as the construction of a desperately needed hospital.

Several months later he invited Tukhali to a weekend party at his seaside villa. It was nearly three A.M. when Bashira asked his inebriated guest to take a stroll along the beach. Deftly steering the conversation toward politics, he commented on the lack of freedom and opportunity for those unfortunate citizens of Baluchistan and other tribal districts. His words unleashed another flood of pent-up hatred and frustration. Tukhali revealed that he had often thought of sabotaging Pakistan's nuclear showpiece as an act of vengeance, but had decided it was impossible. There were security guards and informers everywhere. Armed revolution was the only course to take, but it had to come from the people, and it required money. The wily shipping tycoon caught the unmistakable aroma of greed rising out of Tukhali's revolutionary fervor, and decided to take a chance on the young physicist. Bashira suggested that certain interested parties were willing to pay large sums of money for information regarding the Kahuta nuclear facility.

Six weeks later he opened a numbered account for Tukhali at the Bank of Alfin A.G. in Luxembourg. After each meeting, he supplied Tukhali with an updated bank statement and maintained the charade that it was all for the Cause.

"Sorry to be late."

Tukhali's voice came out of the dimness and startled Bashira. He rose quickly and shook hands. "Sit down, please, Jamil. I was worried about you."

"I must replace my car. I had to drive in low gear all the way."

"Disgraceful. Pick out a new car; I'll see to the cost. Nothing ostentatious, though—a Toyota, or perhaps a Fiat." Bashira signaled to the waiter, who hurried over to the table. "What would you like?"

"Iced tea with absinthe," Tukhali replied.

The waiter left and Tukhali lit an American cigarette, inhaling deeply before leaning across the low table. His jet-black eyes shone with fervor and his high cheekbones and long, thin nose reminded Bashira of a pharaonic mask. "Director Shah arrives at the Madelaine Hotel in Paris next Thursday. Sometime during that weekend a Swedish agent will transfer the Flash X-ray operating manuals."

"I assure you, Jamil," Bashira said quietly, "this information will translate into a significant addition in your account."

"Any risks I've undertaken have been for the Cause."

"No doubt," Bashira readily agreed.

"Time is running out," Tukhali said. "Qaddafi only waits for us to deliver the warheads."

For the benefit of those at nearby tables, Bashira threw his head back and laughed as if Tukhali had said something outrageously funny, and still smiling, asked, "How much time?"

"Once we have those X-ray manuals, we can conduct a zero-yield test explosion almost immediately."

"Can't the warheads be shipped without the test?"

"Of course, but without a test there's no guarantee of detonation. If you were Qaddafi, would you accept warheads that had not been tested?"

"It's not a valid comparison. Qaddafi is a mystic, as was Hitler. Men like that are unpredictable and capable of anything."

CHAPTER FIFTEEN

The Communication Command Center was buried far below the surface of Israel Defense Forces Headquarters in central Tel Aviv. The lights in the soundproof theater were dimmed for General Arik Carmil's briefing. The Air Force Intelligence chief stood in front of a projection screen displaying computerized pictures of various Libyan targets. The pictures were projected from the brain of a huge supercomputer, named Yuval-15 after its inventor, Dr. Yuval Newman, director of Technion. The computer was operated by a young officer attached to Special Operations Division. Seated alongside the officer, Narda Simone made copious notes. Leaning against the wall, sipping coffee, General Dado Harel listened intently to the briefing.

The photographic target information referred to by Carmil had been obtained by night-seeing drones launched from Israeli picket ships off the coast of Libya. The film was then transferred to magnetic tape and reduced to algorithmic equations and fed into the computer, which translated the Algol into geographic images. Carmil pinpointed strategic targets along the Libyan coast from Tripoli to Benghazi, and south to the oil fields at Al Kufra.

His words were precise, clipped, and typical of veteran combat pilots trained to measure their words while flying at twice the speed of sound.

The gaunt, dark-eyed Air Force chief concluded with an overview of the mission profile and a status report of preparations, including the battle plan for interservice attack points. "We can be ready in three weeks," Carmil said. "All we require is the location of that Libyan V-5 launch site. The film of the coastal targets has been transferred to our flight simulators. My wing commanders are already flying simulated combat missions. They will soon be familiar with every building, tree, and swimming pool from Tripoli to Benghazi."

Dado turned to the computer operator. "Let's have a look at Kahuta."

Instantly a computerized map appeared on the large projection screen. The geo-image displayed two routes from Israel to Pakistan. The overland route traversed Jordan, Iraq, Iran, and, eventually, Pakistan. The overwater route stretched from Israel's port of Eilat, south over the Red Sea to the Gulf of Aden, and east into the Arabian Sea to a point off the Pakistani port city of Karachi.

"As you can see," Carmil said, "the distance and obstacles are formidable, and the location of Kahuta in the northeast corner compounds the problem." Using a pointer, he continued. "The overland route is out of the question. Our flight-attack groups and tanker craft would have to invade the airspace and radar-defense systems of Jordan, Iraq, Iran, and finally Pakistan itself. A round-trip distance of fifty-two hundred miles flying over hostile territory and rendezvousing four times with refueling tankers."

"Why four times?"

"Even with extended-range fuel cells, drop tanks, and modest bomb load, our F-15's and F-16's would have to refuel twice each way, over a landscape honeycombed with radar and missiles. It's not possible, Dado."

"And the route over water?"

"No better. If the attack force left the Negev and flew south to the Gulf of Aden, and on toward the Arabian Sea, that first six-hundred-mile leg is sandwiched between Egyptian and Saudi radar, and even if by some miracle the attack force and its support craft remained undetected, they would still have to fly one thousand miles over the entire south-north axis of Pakistan in order to reach Kahuta, here." The pointer rested on a red spot below the twin cities of Rawalpindi and Islamabad. "The flight group would be at the very edge of India and the Soviet Union."

Carmil spoke to the officer operating the computer. "Let me have Kahuta and surrounding area."

The electronic map dissolved and re-formed into a detailed square area of northeast Pakistan.

"A strike on Kahuta from India would be child's play," Carmil continued. "It's only an eight-minute flight from the Indian air base at Amritsar to Kahuta. Twenty seconds over target and the Islamic bomb would be history. If we could fly from any Indian base west of Delhi, it would be a simple matter."

"India will cooperate in matters of intelligence only," Dado replied. "They have three times refused to cooperate in launching an air strike."

"Well then"—Carmil shrugged—"Kahuta is a threat we must try to live with."

"Concentrate on Libya," Dado ordered. "Leave Pakistan to me."

The men shook hands and General Carmil said, "I assume the Prime Minister knows what's going on."

"You don't think I would organize an adventure of this magnitude on my own?"

"I do. And you would." Carmil smiled, then started to leave, stopped, and as an afterthought said, "One of my wing commanders, an ace, a brilliant pilot, claims he saw a lion in the Arava."

Carmil was not a man to create bizarre jokes, and his black agate eyes were serious.

"A lion?" Dado asked incredulously.

"Yoni was on a routine training flight when he saw this male lion in the Wadi Musa ravine."

"There have been no lions in the Holy Land since the time of ancient Judah, since the Romans brought them for their games."

"Yoni swears he saw an African lion with a great dark mane."

"From the cockpit of an F-16, shadows and shapes assume strange forms," Dado said. "But in Yaweh's Promised Land, who knows? Perhaps Yoni saw the last lion of Judah."

"Perhaps." Carmil nodded.

Dado and Narda rode the elevator up to the surface level, and as they crossed the headquarters' compound she bombarded him with a myriad of procedural details yet to be dealt with. He answered her questions with alacrity. She always marveled at the vast amount of disparate and complex information he routinely handled.

He accompanied her to a jeep driven by a green-bereted Druse soldier. Narda climbed in and Dado said, "Tell Zichroni to organize a meeting with all branches in ten days. And then you will—"

"I know very well what I have to do," she interrupted, and cautioned, "Take care with Berger."

There was nothing in the low-ceilinged room to suggest that it was the office of the chief of Israeli Intelligence. There were several battered file cabinets, a cracked leather sofa, four folding chairs, and two grimy windows that overlooked a helicopter pad. The sole contemporary accoutrement was a streamlined phone console resting on the cigarette-scarred oak desk.

Looking disheveled, as always, Berger munched on a half-eaten roll between puffs of a cigarette.

"You look tired, my friend," Berger said.

"It's the light."

Berger indicated a pile of reports on his desk. "The war continues. Five PLO guerrillas killed trying to infiltrate by sea at Nahariyah. Another squad of three crossed from their West Bank state and shot up a busload of tourists. And from Egypt, with whom we enjoy peace, six Katusha rockets were fired into Beersheba, and from Lebanon, four killers captured at the Metullah fence."

Berger's rundown of the continuing terrorist attacks was a subtle rebuke at Dado for having endorsed the ceding of

Gaza and a section of the West Bank to the PLO. "It's bad," Berger added, "it comes from all sides."

"Let them come. Let them do their worst. The terrorists keep the nation united."

Berger rubbed his hand wearily over his face. "You can't reduce constant terror to a political abstraction. I've been authorized to resume counterstrikes on terrorist leaders, and this operation of yours, this 'Red Desert,' drains my resources."

Dado leaned across the desk and in a voice strained by fatigue said, "I'm not concerned with terrorists and their Soviet popguns. The sun is about to fall in our streets. Professor Newman has stated that Tel Aviv could be destroyed by a single Hiroshima-size bomb—six hundred thousand people vaporized in a matter of seconds. And history says no one will care. The only dead Jew the world ever cared about was Christ. Now, understand me, Yanush, no one is going to interfere with this operation."

The General's eyes were ice blue and menacing. Berger knew he had pushed a little too far. His sources had confirmed that the Prime Minister had indeed authorized "Red Desert." But whether that authority extended to whatever Dado had in mind for Kahuta was an open question.

Lighting a fresh cigarette, Berger said, "I have always done my best for you. Why do you make me out to be an adversary?"

"I'm tired, Yanush. . . . Let's get on with it."

Berger opened a thick file and read in a dutiful, official manner. "'Farheed Shah, Director of the Kahuta Nuclear Research Center, arrives at the Madelaine Hotel in Paris, Thursday the 20th.'" Berger glanced at Dado. "The choice of the Madelaine helps. We've used it ourselves in the past. It's one of those small, private, discreet Parisian hotels. A quiet location. Four floors with twelve suites, most of which are owned by individuals and used for sexual liaisons." Berger resumed reading. "'At some point during that weekend a Swedish businessman will meet with Shah and deliver the operating manuals for Flash X-ray machines in return for three million Swiss francs.'" Berger closed the file. "This information is from Salim Bashira. I regard it as absolutely reliable."

Bashira was known to Dado. They had met in London in the summer of '88. Bashira had produced documents revealing the Saudi Arabian purchase of Chinese CSS-2 long-range missiles. Bashira had also presented evidence of Syrian poison-gas installations at Tibrisk. The Pakistani shipping tycoon had performed magnificently at great personal risk, and was a classic example of the dedication and quality of Berger's extraordinary global network of agents. While Dado mistrusted Berger, he nevertheless admired the intelligence chief's organizational brilliance.

"We have to prevent those X-ray manuals from being transferred," Dado said, rising. "We have to move quickly. Is Penelope back from Hamburg?"

"Yes."

"I want her and Kishon to organize Paris."

"I can't give you Kishon."

"Why not?"

"He was shot to death in Nicosia."

"When?"

"A month ago. As you know, the death of an agent is never acknowledged. My people are not honored with televised military funerals."

Berger suddenly looked very old, and Dado felt a fleeting sympathy for him.

The window rattled and the racket of helicopter rotors filled the room. Berger waited for the noise to subside and said, "I can give you Ben Landau. You worked with him in the past."

"Yes. Beirut, seventy-eight. We took out Ali Hasan, the last of the Munich planners. Penelope was the key, but Landau was good. Very good."

"So. He's acceptable for Paris?"

Dado nodded. "Any news from Erika?"

"It looks promising. Dr. Kleiser is anxious to meet Lawford. The elimination of Brunner was persuasive."

"What about Heinrich Mueller?"

"Very difficult. Brunner was careless—preoccupied with some teenage student. But Mueller is a different matter."

"He must be hit," Dado insisted. "He's lived too long and too well."

Berger was familiar with the rocket scientist's history as a primary supplier of Jewish slaves who died in the V-2 assembly tunnels at Nordhausen. "Let me think about Mueller," he said.

"You'll organize Paris?"

"Of course. I suppose you intend to go . . ."

"Once things are in place."

"If we stop the transfer of those manuals, we'll buy some time," Berger said, "but we have to find that Libyan launch site, and fast."

"We will," Dado replied with assurance. "Lawford will do the job."

Berger rose and they shook hands.

"There is something unrelated to Red Desert that you can help me with," Dado said.

"Yes?"

"Have Bashira locate a freighter—some old hulk with Panamanian registry; but its engines must be totally reliable. A vessel of, say, twenty thousand tons. And after a final voyage, Bashira must cause the ship to disappear."

Berger's owlish eyes blinked, and a spill of cigarette ash fell across his rumpled shirt.

"Take care with your cigarettes, Yanush. You'll set fire to the office."

At the window, Berger watched the Bell Ranger warming up on the pad, and saw Dado climb into the waiting helicopter. The rotor blades accelerated, beating the air furiously before rising, gaining altitude, and veering sharply north. Berger stared after the helicopter until it became a speck in the sky. Where was the General off to? With whom would he scheme? Where would he strike? To what apocalyptic brink would this child of the ovens take them? Dado had the confidence of the Prime Minister, and that made him extremely dangerous. Berger shook his head in dismay. The Prime Minister was a reasonable man, but the terrible truth of history demonstrated that the reasonable mind could not comprehend fanaticism. Dado was a legend, and the purple numerals tattooed on his forearm were a calculus forged in hell—the same hellfire from which the state itself had emerged. And after fifty years of continuous war, the national perception of fanaticism had blurred; in the pursuit of security, extreme ideologies were accepted as normal. The General was regarded as a symbol of strength in the face of endless hostility. Berger sighed heavily, thinking that if the Germans hadn't created Dado, the Arabs would have invented him. And like it or not, he, Berger, the chess player, the weary intellectual, was part of an inexorable force edging its way toward Armageddon.

CHAPTER SIXTEEN

Tom Lawford increased the water temperature until the skin at the nape of his neck burned. The sharp needle spray of the shower head was directed at the point of the arthritic nerve pain. Six days had passed since his encounter with the blinding headlights under the S-Bahn, and Erika Sperling had not yet contacted him. He shut the water taps, stepped out of the shower, and stared at his image in the mirror. Dark circles rimmed his gray eyes and an intricate web of wrinkles nestled at their corners. He had no Faustian need to remain young, but the relentless surge of time was making its point in a hell of a hurry. Staring at himself in the mirror, he thought how vulnerable he was: unarmed, operating in a foreign country without official sanction, digging into matters that concerned the Nazi past. The surviving scientists of Nordhausen were men without conscience, obsessed by a consuming technical arrogance. They would, if it suited their purpose, kill him without a second's thought. As he lathered his face, he tried to find comfort in Narda Simone's parting words, *"I'm trying to tell you that you're not alone."*

He shaved, brushed his teeth, swallowed two vitamin-C pills, and slipped into a terry-cloth robe.

He entered the sitting room and parted the window drapes. It was almost noon and the color of the sky promised more snow. Pedestrians scurried along, their heads bowed against the raw wind. Curbside piles of dirty snow were crystallizing into chunks of black ice. It was impossible to believe that this grim, walled-up city had once been the cultural center of Europe. The phone rang sharply, startling him.

"Mr. Lawford?"

"Yes."

"Erika Sperling. Can you meet me in fifteen minutes downstairs in the Bristol Bar?"

The Bristol Bar was beginning to fill up with German businessmen and foreign tourists enjoying a pre-lunch drink in the elegant room. The piano player wore a bemused smile and played a mechanical rendition of "Moonglow."

Nursing a spicy Bloody Mary, Lawford took in the panoramic view of the room reflected in the long mirror over the bar. His thoughts were focused on the enigmatic Erika Sperling. She had to be a tough case, working for Kleiser and doubling as a Mossad agent. She had probably been planted in STS years ago and was by now above suspicion. But people in Fräulein Sperling's profession were not famous for their longevity. He stared into his drink and swirled the perfectly cut ice cubes.

"Mr. Lawford?"

She was tall and slim, with sparkling blue-gray eyes, and the German accent lent a certain allure to her voice. Her cheekbones were sharp and dramatic, and curved symmetrically down to a full mouth. A spill of straight blond hair framed her oval face. He nodded and smiled. "Please, sit down."

She slid gracefully onto the bar stool, and ordered a vodka martini. He caught the subtle scent of a familiar, expensive perfume as her eyes boldly worked him over.

"Is there something wrong?" he asked genially.

She shook her head slightly. "No. It's just that you're much better-looking than I had supposed." She paused and her voice dropped. "For the record, I told Kleiser you were, at the moment, finishing a story about the rebirth of the German cinema."

"Why? He knows I'm here."

"We'll need some time together before I bring you to him."

"Time for what?"

"I believe the Agency calls it 'briefing.'"

"How do you explain the time spent with me to Kleiser?"

"There's nothing to explain. He asked me to sound you out, get friendly." She paused. "So to speak."

The bartender served her drink, and she raised the glass. "Cheers."

"Cheers." He nodded.

"It must have been boring for you, hanging around this hellish city for almost a week."

"Not entirely."

"Ah, you met a woman."

"No . . . no women." He sipped the Bloody Mary and described the episode under the S-Bahn.

"The drug trade in Berlin is enormous and violent. You were fortunate that it was the police who stopped you."

"I must admit, for a second or two I saw the shark."

"The shark?"

"An Americanism for danger. Why did it take you so long to contact me?"

"These are very cautious people. The entire STS operation is under the protection and security of Libyan Counterintelligence. Ever since the poison-gas scandal in eightynine, Qaddafi has been paranoid in his dealings with all European companies—especially STS. We have a Libyan control officer permanently assigned to oversee our security."

"Is that officer's name Abu Hasi?"

She seemed surprised. "Yes . . . how did you know?"

"He was apparently the security control officer in Washington. Hasi ordered the murder of a friend of mine."

There was no "I'm sorry" or even an "Oh." She went right past it and said, "Once Kleiser agreed to the proposed interview, he had me check every recent published article you've written. I was not given permission to contact you until late Tuesday."

"Does this obsession with security extend to all STS employees?"

"What do you mean?"

"I read where one of Kleiser's colleagues—a man named Brunner—had a fatal accident in Hamburg."

"It was Brunner's sudden death that convinced Kleiser to grant you an interview."

The pianist played a pretty version of "Memory."

She opened her purse and took out a pack of Gauloise cigarettes. Her fingers touched his hand as he held the flaming match to her cigarette. A secretive, sensual current ran between them. In that instant they both knew it was there, coursing beneath their words.

"What were you doing prowling around the ruins of those prewar embassies at midnight?" she asked.

"Morbid curiosity. Years ago, I interviewed Albert Speer and became interested in the Third Reich. I wondered what made a cultured, civilized society follow a lunatic into oblivion."

"It's not very complicated. We're a nation that periodically reverts to its primitive, barbaric origins. After all, one can hear Auschwitz in the last hundred bars of Wagner's *Götterdämmerung*."

"I never made that connection, but then, I'm not a fan of Wagner's and I'm not German."

"Well, you simply have to trust me. I *am* German. Pure. *Herrenvolk*. Dr. Goebbels would have considered me the perfect Aryan woman."

"But you work for Mossad."

"Yes."

"Why?"

"Is that important?"

"I'm in your hands. I'd like to know."

"You have things conveniently reversed. My life is in *your* hands, and I can't allow you to stumble into a situation about which you know nothing."

"Look, I've been stuck in this graveyard of a city waiting patiently for your call. Now, you may have an edge on information, but don't treat me as if I'm some goddamn blundering American. I've seen the shark more than once. Just be nice, Fräulein Sperling."

"Erika." She smiled at him. "And I'm sorry if I offended you. But believe me when I tell you that neither of us is allowed a single mistake." She crushed her cigarette out and said, "There is almost a billion dollars at stake for Kleiser and his STS group in Libya. So nothing is sacred. Everything and everyone is expendable. You have a critical role to play, and if you succeed, we may locate that base. Now, please sign the check. We must go."

"Where to?"

"I've taken another room in your name. On the remote chance that a bug may have been planted in your suite. You'll order some lunch and we'll rehearse. I'll play Dr. Kleiser and you'll play the cynical but objective American journalist."

CHAPTER SEVENTEEN

Narda Simone came out of the Métro and stepped into the bright winter sunlight. She had a profound affection for Paris. The city was a unique bastion of architectural beauty that had, for the most part, resisted the persistent spread of cubelike steel and glass. In Paris one could still imagine life before the two great wars.

She strolled across the Pont de la Concorde, stopping for a moment to watch the men fishing along the banks of the sluggish Seine.

A glass-enclosed *bâteau mouche* passed under the bridge and a small child standing on the prow waved to her. She waved back, thinking of how simply a woman was reminded of the biological clock. There was still time. She was only twenty-eight. But Dado had declared with finality that he could never again bear the burden of raising a child. And she understood. No man should suffer the pain of burying his son. Besides, there was still Avital—the pretty wraith who had retreated into the timeless abyss of the Hakala Ortho- dox sect. And she could only guess at the midnight ghosts that haunted Dado's sweat-soaked nightmares.

Her situation was probably hopeless, but she had burned her bridges long ago and had learned to accept the temporal nature of her relationship. Her life was a mirror of the nation she served. She was a victim of endless intrigues, lost dreams, and cemeteries filled with her contemporaries. She had performed unspeakable acts in the name of national security. And those violent and sometimes degrading missions had punched a hole in her soul. The older she became, the more desperately she needed moral reassurance.

And in Dado she had found a spiritual pillar. He was her lover, her religion, her cause. And she accepted the relationship as it was, savoring those rare moments of beauty and love.

As she entered the Tuileries Gardens, a gust of wind blew fallen leaves across her boots. Au pairs pushed baby carriages, and children raced along the hard dirt paths. Lovers strolled by, oblivious of the cold. Joggers circled the gardens, their breaths vaporizing in the air. A group of proud old men in shabby black coats decorated with W.W. I medals was gathered in a circle, reminiscing about battles long forgotten by their fellow citizens. None of the people in the park evinced any interest in the striking Israeli girl.

Dado was sitting on a bench close to the abandoned Jeu de Paume Museum, reading a newspaper. She approached him discreetly and asked for directions to the Ritz Hotel. Speaking French, he gave her directions, but she appeared to be confused. He folded the paper and offered to accompany her.

As they left the park, safely out of anyone's earshot, Narda switched to English. "Farheed Shah is in suite 347. Penelope and Landau are in 332. The Swede is named Olaf Nillsen. His arrival is confirmed for six P.M."

She went on to say that Berger's Paris agent had bribed the concierge at the Madelaine Hotel and that a tap had been installed on Shah's phone.

"And the protection?"

"The Libyan in charge of security remains with Shah in his suite. One man is stationed in the lobby, another is positioned diagonally across from the hotel entrance at the alley on Rue Boccador."

"And the police?"

"The mobile unit passes every two hours, on the odd hour."

As they approached the Place de la Concorde, he asked, "What time do you have?"

"Two-fifteen."

He adjusted his watch to conform to her setting. "It must happen fast," he said. "Very fast."

She smiled as if thanking him for directions and said, "I'm not new to this business."

Turning abruptly, she crossed the magnificent square that had witnessed the bloodbath of a noble revolution gone mad.

Walking in the opposite direction, Dado headed toward Pont Alexandre and the Left Bank. He'd go to the Select, have a brandy, and watch the students and the pretty girls, and think of the time when he and Avital lived in Paris, when he had taken special postgraduate courses at St. Cyr Military Academy. The Select Bar was a good place to reminisce for an hour or two before the killing began.

In the quiet elegance of his third-floor suite, Farheed Shah sipped Dom Perignon and spooned Iranian caviar onto a triangle of toast. The director of the Kahuta nuclear facility could not help but luxuriate in the moment. The small private hotel was an ideal place to do business, and after months of waiting and scheming, of disappointments and betrayal, the Flash X-ray manuals would finally be in his hands.

The test detonation would be undertaken immediately by Dr. Tukhali, and shortly thereafter, the first nuclear warheads would be transferred to Qaddafi.

He popped the savory fish eggs on his tongue, washing them down with champagne, thinking with pleasure that he would soon be the recipient of Pakistan's highest civilian award for meritorious service.

Shah's Libyan chief of security, Anwar Kaladi, was standing at the street-side window of the sitting room, peering through infrared binoculars, checking the intersecting alley. His point man was at his post, diagonally across the street from the hotel entrance. Another security man was on duty in the lobby. Kaladi raised the antenna on his walkie-talkie and quickly checked with his team, sending the password "Habibi" and receiving the word "Shukran"—meaning all was well.

Kaladi lit a cigarette and blew the smoke against the windowpane. He wished the Swede would arrive and the assignment over with. Kaladi had hated this mission from its inception in Washington—from the moment Hasi had ordered him to slit the American's throat in that Georgetown café. He had no objection to protecting the STS Germans; it was the Pakistanis he despised. He considered Pakistan to be a bastard state comprising tribal droppings, supported by American largess. Pakistan had lost every war it had ever fought except the terror campaign against its own people in the province of Baluchistan. That the pure desert people of Libya required Pakistani assistance in achieving the bomb was offensive to Kaladi, but the annihilation of the Zionist state was a political necessity fulfilling all Islamic aspirations. Kaladi did not understand the technical importance of the X-ray manuals the Swede was bringing, only that they were critical to the completion of the bomb.

Shah refilled his champagne glass and glanced at the frosted bottle of aquavit awaiting the arrival of Olaf Nillsen. Shah had nurtured his contact with Nillsen for almost two years before convincing the Swede to smuggle the restricted operating manuals. In the end, the three million Swiss francs had helped convince the reluctant Swedish scientist that the risk was worth the enterprise.

Shah opened the attaché case containing the neat stacks of Swiss francs and said, "Look, Anwar, how beautiful is this money."

Kaladi nodded perfunctorily but remained at the window, peering at the dark street through a slit in the drapery.

"Relax, my friend. Have a glass of champagne." Shah caught himself immediately. Kaladi was a strict Islamic fundamentalist; alcoholic beverages were forbidden. "What I mean is," Shah said reflexively, "have some food, get some fresh air. We are in no trouble here."

"After the transfer you'll be rid of me." Kaladi spoke with

104

undisguised disdain. "You can have as many whores as you wish."

The Libyan's blunt reference was to the beautiful and expensive French call girls from Madame Nicole's collection. Shah had been buying the services of a particularly striking dark-haired girl whom Kaladi mistrusted. The girl spoke fluent French but with a curious foreign accent. Using the walkie-talkie, Kaladi again checked with his team. The Swede was due any moment.

The night chambermaid pushed her cart wearily down the hall and knocked on the door of suite 332. A stocky, bespectacled man flashing a friendly smile opened the door. As the maid entered the suite Landau kicked the door shut, clasped his hand over her mouth, and shouted, "Penelope!"

A pleasant-looking middle-aged blond woman wearing an identical chambermaid's uniform came out of the bedroom, crossed the salon, and quickly, expertly, taped the maid's lips. She proceeded to tie the maid's wrists behind her back while speaking quietly in French to the terrified woman, telling her to remain calm and no harm would come to her. Landau removed a wicked-looking 9mm Uzi machine pistol from a suitcase and quickly screwed a tubular silencer to its muzzle. Taking the stockless Uzi, Penelope stepped out into the hall and hid the weapon under the towels atop the chambermaid's cart.

Across the street from the hotel, Saudiq Karim stamped his feet against the bitter cold. He had been on station for over an hour. The Swede had just entered the hotel, and according to plan, Karim would leave his post in five minutes and join his teammate in the lobby.

Glancing toward the corner, Karim noticed an attractive young woman pushing a baby carriage on Rue Marot. She was coming toward him, and as she drew close he openly admired her. Narda returned his smile, remarked about the cold, and fired a short burst from a silenced Ingram Mac-10 automatic. The hollow-head bullets tore into Karim's chest, exploding internally. The force of the slugs lifted him off the ground and slammed him against the wall, where he collapsed in a gathering pool of blood. Narda quickly pulled him into the alley, shoving his body behind the garbage cans. She then pushed the baby carriage into the dark alley.

Catching her breath, she reentered Rue Marot and strolled casually halfway up the street to a parked Simca. She unlocked the door, got behind the wheel, and turned the engine over. After a moment, she saw Dado walking briskly toward the service entrance of the Madelaine.

In the salon of his suite, Farheed Shah raised his champagne glass and toasted the tall broad-shouldered Swede. Returning the toast, Nillsen said, "Prosit," and downed the aquavit.

Some of the X-ray manuals were spread atop the coffee table in three piles of consecutively numbered printouts. The bulk of them were still inside an open suitcase.

The doorbell sounded. Kaladi turned from the window, crossed the salon, and peered through the peephole at the night maid.

In the small, deserted lobby, the Libyan bodyguard glanced up from his newspaper at the bespectacled, professorial-looking man who came out of the self-service elevator and walked to the front desk. After speaking briefly to the elderly concierge, Landau turned as if to enter the bar, then, remembering it was closed, took out a cigarette and searched his pockets for a match. Finding none, he approached the Libyan and politely asked for a light. As the Libyan reached into his pocket, Landau fired a silenced .22-caliber automatic into the man's forehead. A small hole appeared between the Libyan's eyes and a crimson spume splashed up against the patterned wallpaper. Seeing the blood-splattered Libyan slump to the floor, the horrified concierge came out from behind the desk, but Landau motioned him back.

Only after the chambermaid rang the bell repeatedly did Kaladi finally open the door. Employing a mixture of halting French and sign language, he tried to explain that this was not a good time for her to turn down the beds or change towels. Undaunted, the maid complained vociferously in rapid French, demanding entry, protesting that it was impossible for her to return later. Her duty was clear. She had to proceed suite by suite. She had to abide by the routine fixed by management.

Olaf Nillsen and Farheed Shah were startled when Kaladi slammed the door in the maid's face. Using her key, the persistent maid reopened the door and continued to complain bitterly.

"For God's sake, Kaladi," Shah said, "this woman will wake the dead. Let her in and be done with it."

Kaladi stepped back warily as the maid entered, carrying a pile of thick white towels and fresh pillow slips.

Shah and Nillsen returned to their blueprints.

Kaladi went back to the window and glanced across the street.

After a moment, Penelope came out of the bedroom, leveled the Uzi at Kaladi, and fired a short burst. His face disintegrated in pulpy red pieces, and he tumbled over the phone table. Penelope swung the Uzi at Nillsen and Shah; a hail of bullets shredded both men as if they were made of papier-mâché. Lowering the smoking Uzi, she rushed across the room and opened the door.

Shoving the chambermaid's cart ahead of him, Dado entered the suite and locked the door. Kneeling beside the cart, he slid open a compartment and removed a coil of electric wire, a detonator cap, and a glob of plastic explosive. He stepped over the bloody bodies of Shah and Nillsen, and proceeded to wire the suitcase containing the Flash X-ray manuals. Penelope stripped off her maid's uniform, removed her gray wig, shook out her blond hair, and straightened her wool skirt. "Quick! Move!" Dado snapped. "Take the money!"

Downstairs in the lobby, Landau handcuffed the elderly concierge to a steam pipe behind the counter. He then dragged the dead Libyan behind the front desk, dumping the body at the feet of the old man. Landau placed his finger to his lips, cautioning the chalky-faced concierge to silence.

* * *

Behind the wheel of the Simca, Narda saw Penelope come out of the Madelaine. She shifted into gear, eased away from the curb, and pulled up at the hotel's entrance.

Penelope tossed the attaché case containing the Swiss francs into the rear seat and got in alongside Narda. The door slammed shut. Narda gunned the Simca, turning at the corner into Avenue Montaigne.

Dado came out of the hotel and walked up Rue Marot toward the nearby Métro station at Place de l'Alma.

A moment later, Ben Landau left the side entrance and strolled toward the corner of Rue Boccador.

A taxi that Nillsen had called to collect him at 6:30 P.M. pulled up and parked at the entrance of the Madelaine.

The driver got out and was immediately slammed to the ground, stunned by the concussion of an ear-splitting explosion. Thirty feet of the hotel's facade was blown away. Bells rang loudly as the blast set off alarms in private dwellings lining Rue Marot.

In a matter of minutes the area was sealed off by motorcycles and patrol cars of the Metropolitan Police. It took the better part of an hour for intelligence officers attached to the Deuxième Bureau to arrive and begin the painstaking job of sifting through the debris.

CHAPTER EIGHTEEN

Switching the high beams on and off, Erika Sperling drove the BMW aggressively along the wide street paralleling the Berlin Wall.

"What's the rush?" Lawford asked.

"Kleiser believes punctuality demonstrates an orderly mind. He has no patience with tardiness."

For the better part of the last two days, she had drilled him on Kleiser's personal history and on the background of the STS organization.

During the briefing sessions she had paced like a jittery colt, tossing her pale hair, gesturing with her slender fingers. Stopping. Turning. Staring at him to make a point. Asking questions out of context, she had played the role of inquisitor. Her seductive perfume lingered in the air long after she left, and he had begun to create certain fantasies around the assertive Fräulein Sperling. At times, when he would answer questions too quickly, without thinking his response through, she would make caustic comments. At one point he shouted at her with unbridled anger, ordering her to be civil.

Unperturbed, she said, "Being civil is a luxury. I'm concerned with staying alive."

She continued the relentless assault until she was convinced that he could handle anything Fritz Kleiser would throw at him. Finally she said, "Whatever you do, don't patronize him. He needs you more than you need him."

She downshifted, double-clutched, and swung around a truck just as a pair of oncoming headlights blurred past. She cursed the truck driver brilliantly, using American expletives. Turning into Heerstrasse, they entered the snow-draped Grunewald forest. Glancing at Lawford, she said, "Remember, Kleiser's father was a member of the original Peenemünde rocket group and connected to the old SS Kameradschaft, which makes Fritz Kleiser an honorary—"

"I'm tuned in," Tom interrupted. "You're going to have to trust me. I've interviewed some tricky people."

She turned right at a fork and took a single-lane road that wound its way around the frozen Lake Havel. "I was reluctant to tell you about this because it didn't seem relevant. But Kleiser does have a weakness that may be worth mentioning. His sexual appetites are bizarre. He requires opium and the spectacle of two women making love in order to achieve sexual gratification."

"How would you know?"

She shrugged. "What does it matter?"

The road ended at a pair of tall iron grille gates complete with revolving TV cameras. Opening her window, Erika leaned out and pressed a button on a speaker.

"Ja?"

"Fräulein Sperling."

After a moment, the gates swung open.

Wearing a navy blazer and pale blue turtleneck, Dr. Fritz Kleiser stood at the picture window and watched the distant lights of the BMW flashing through the pines on the lower road. He sipped a brandy and smoked a thin cigar. Behind him, a fire crackled in the huge flagstone fireplace.

The study was lined with leather-bound editions of Goethe, Stendhal, Dickens, Turgenev, and Baudelaire. Covering one wall was an enormous antique Flemish tapestry in perfect condition. A grouping of Breughel paintings hung on the opposite wall. The furniture was dark oak, heavy and ornate. Like Kleiser himself, the vaulted baronial study belonged to Imperial Germany.

Upstairs, in the softly lit mirrored bedroom equipped with several large TV monitors, a pair of Swiss girls awaited him. He knew that Erika selected the girls through a modeling agency run by a Fräulein Hauser, but he never asked any questions. Erika took care of the details, including the opium and the pornographic videos that he enjoyed.

Using the phone on the exquisitely inlaid desk, he dialed Heinrich Mueller in Munich. From time to time the old man required reassurance. The subservience of the veteran rocket scientists never ceased to amaze Kleiser. These were his childhood heroes, and yet he was their leader.

"Ja?" Mueller's voice was reedy and hoarse with age.

"Good evening, my dear doctor," Kleiser said warmly.

"Good evening, Herr Oberst."

The Killer of Nordhausen—the man who had unleashed a reign of terror over the skies of London a half-century ago—addressed him as *"Oberst."* The Superior.

"I'm about to meet with the American journalist. Everything seems to be in order."

"A favorable article in the world press would be timely," Mueller agreed, but then nervously added, "It's not simply the press—there are dangerous elements closing in on us. I'm concerned with Farheed Shah's killing in Paris."

"The incident in Paris is no concern of yours. Concentrate on your work. Leave these matters with me," Kleiser replied, and abruptly dismissed Mueller. *"Auf wiedersehen, Herr Doktor."*

Kleiser hung up, hoping that Mueller and his colleagues would remain calm, despite the violent demise of Farheed Shah in Paris. He disliked reproving Mueller, but he had to maintain order, they were nearing the culmination of ten years' work. Walter Diehl had just returned from the Libyan base and was supervising the V-5 assembly at the Munich plant. Mueller's nervousness was contagious and potentially destructive; perhaps the old man needed a holiday.

Kleiser swirled the cognac and studied the magnificent Flemish tapestry, but his thoughts were focused on the recent terrorist action in Paris. With the killing of Shah, the Pakistanis had again been denied access to the Flash X-ray manuals and would now be forced to field-test their nuclear detonator and risk detection. He wondered if the Paris assassination had been a Mossad operation. He doubted it. It lacked the usual order and discretion employed by the Israeli counterterror squads. It was either an Indian Secret Service operation or, more likely, the KGB. The Supreme Soviet had officially protested STS activities in Libya to the West German government.

The enlistment of Lawford's journalistic skills was now critical. He would throw all the doors open to the prizewinning journalist. Let him write his article. Let him visit the launch site. The world must be made to believe that STS was indeed a peaceful commercial enterprise.

The butler ushered Erika Sperling and Tom Lawford into the vaulted study. Although he'd seen pictures of Kleiser, Tom was immediately struck by his military bearing and stern, aristocratic features.

"Leave us, Erika," Kleiser said curtly.

Once she was gone, his voice assumed a congenial warmth. "Care for a cognac, Mr. Lawford?"

"Sounds good to me."

Kleiser poured a drink and said, "Erika has the beauty of the North—Hanover. *Herrenvolk.* It's a reluctant beauty, as if it was beaten into her. Skol!"

"Cheers."

"Sit down, please," Kleiser said, indicating a sofa.

"You have quite a view of the lake from here," Tom noted.

"Just across there"—Kleiser indicated the opposite side of Lake Havel—"is the villa where Heydrich conducted his 'Final Solution' Wanasee Conference in January of forty-two."

"Does it bother you?"

"In what way?"

"Well, you could say that Germany gave birth to the Holocaust in that villa."

"Yes . . . the presence of that villa does at times cause me to think of that fateful meeting. But not especially of the Jews. Ironically and perhaps more importantly it causes me to wonder about the German psyche, and what monstrous force possessed the German nation. . . . I was quite young, of course, but to this day, I'll never understand why the German Jews were singled out. They were, after all, a loyal and industrious segment of German society. It was a terrible abuse of power."

"'Abuse' is hardly synonymous with 'genocide.'"

"I'm not excusing the Holocaust. On the contrary, I think it's an indelible national scar which will never disappear. But one must remember that in the twenties and thirties Germany was a lost nation, seeking a savior. Hitler was a psychopath, but he understood the tribal force of German mythology. He invoked our ancient mortal gods of fire and ice. He resurrected the Superman theory and appealed to the most violent and ignorant segment of our society, and finally he and his gang of thugs succeeded in corrupting the entire nation."

"Whom do you blame the corruption on now?"

"I'm afraid I don't understand the question."

"It's not very complicated," Tom said. "I'm not referring to past German sins. I'm talking about present-day sins. Your colleagues have built huge poison-gas factories in Libya and Iraq. In eighty-seven the Iraqi dictator gassed five thousand Kurdish people to death and tens of thousands of Iranian soldiers. This lethal gas was supplied by West German companies. Libya, too, has used poison gas in Qaddafi's simmering war with Chad. These are *current* events. German consortiums are supplying third-world countries with cataclysmic chemical and biological weapons. There's no Hitler around to blame this moral corruption on."

Kleiser studied Lawford for a moment, then smiled a small sardonic smile. "You certainly live up to your reputation for cynicism."

"Objective cynicism is an occupational hazard, but not as dangerous as manufacturing poison gas or long-range rockets."

"I resent being included in your group of misguided and greedy profiteers. I have never used my company in a dishonorable fashion."

"I never said you had. I'm sorry if you got that impression."

"You did mention long-range rockets, or am I hearing things?"

"I did indeed, but only in the context of a theoretical discussion."

The room fell silent except for the crackling fireplace, and Tom wondered whether he had gone too far.

Kleiser rose and slowly paced the Oriental rug. "I'm familiar with almost every important article you're written in the past decade. I've also viewed your periodic segments of *Nightside*. That's why I delayed our meeting. I don't give a damn what you think about Germany, past or present. I simply want to be certain you do not have preconceived ideas—or any innate prejudice—against my company's Libyan operations."

"I accepted this assignment because it interested me," Tom replied. "I'll never write anything but the truth as I see it. I don't ascribe to the theory that Germans are an aberrational people, fated to be villains. I may be a tough audience, but I'll print what I see and what I hear. You have my word."

Kleiser stared at Tom for a long beat. "I'm prepared to show you my entire operation. Everything. No holds barred, as they say."

"Including the launch site?"

"Ah"—Kleiser smiled—"you come right to the point."

"You're busy. I'm busy. Why waste our time? The launch site is the linchpin of the story."

"How so?"

"Your company's activities in Libya have frightened a lot of people, and that fear interests me. What the hell are you up to, Doctor?"

"I'm a businessman, nothing more."

"I certainly hope so. Because I'm going to dig hard, and I won't file a story that I consider to be incomplete. I never have. But I can give you my word to stay off the record with anything that we agree upon before I get started."

"I appreciate your forthrightness, but there are no restrictions. You are free to write and photograph exactly what you see. The launch site, the improved V-5, my assembly plant in Munich, the engine factory in Stuttgart, whatever you wish. The V-5 is designed to orbit the earth and place communications satellites into space. We are building an international rocket company that will service the third world and hopefully become the Federal Express of Space."

"Is it your position that the V-5 rocket has no military application?"

"Everything has a military application. One can say a telephone has military application. One can use a truck to transport either milk or high explosives. One can take a pen and set down a lethal equation, or one can take the same pen and create a magnificent poem."

"But isn't Libya a dangerous choice for this third-world enterprise? Long-range rockets are a far cry from telephones and fountain pens. You will admit that, to be generous, Qaddafi is an erratic mystic. A man capable of almost any irrational act."

Kleiser shrugged. "One man's fanatic is the next man's revolutionary. Another drink?"

"No, thanks."

"There are perhaps a hundred men who run the world. I'm not one of them," Kleiser said, and swallowed some cognac. "Our intention in Libya is peaceful. STS is a private commercial enterprise. A modest first step into a third-world market. We wish to provide technically deficient nations with an opportunity to enjoy modern telecommunications by launching inexpensive satellites for which we can turn a modest profit."

"But still, you must be aware of the rumored Libyan-Pakistani alliance. Those rumors imply that Pakistan will supply nuclear warheads to Qaddafi. And those warheads will be fitted to and launched by your V-5's."

"I'm glad you used the word 'rumors.' Because that's what this is all about—'rumors.' I'm not interested in making Colonel Qaddafi a superpower. But I would take money from the Vatican or the Kremlin or the Saudi royal family in order to continue my work. But as you will see, our V-5's are primitive compared to the solid-state missiles belonging to the superpowers. There is no complicated countdown with a solid-state missile, one only has to push a button. I'm not in the ICBM business. There is no money in building doomsday missiles that sit in underground silos. I'm interested in the scientific exploration of space."

"Your father and his colleagues—Mueller, Diehl, Von Braun, and the late Alois Brunner—killed a lot of people developing their science."

"Let us leave philosophical disagreements for another time, Mr. Lawford. Morality is largely in the eye of the beholder. The only nation in the world to have dropped the bomb is your country—not once, but twice, and largely as an experiment on a defeated enemy. I think you will agree that technology and morality are unfortunately mutually exclusive." Kleiser paused and said, "I know you've been to Israel. I read your interview of October 1973 with an Israeli general named Harel. I've also read your articles on Chairman Arafat and Abu Nidal, Castro, and the mafiosi of the Medellín cocaine cartel. I concluded that in each case you showed dispassionate fairness. A quality sorely missing in the German press. I don't consider messengers of truth to be troublemakers. I despise propagandists and sensationalists. I respect objective journalism, and that's all I ask for—objectivity."

"I can promise you that."

"You can write or think whatever you wish, but remember these words: I believe that peace will be achieved only when we live in a world without secrets, and space satellites will eliminate secrecy from the universe."

Tom thought that Erika had understated Kleiser's cunning and charm. He was a superb salesman.

"STS is in the forefront of peaceful space technology," Kleiser continued. "And you, Mr. Lawford, are in a unique position to calm international fears regarding my company's activities. I frankly admit I need your help, and I will withhold nothing from you."

"I appreciate your trust, and I can assure you that if I'm given all the facts, the article will appear in every important print and broadcast situation in the world. But I'm not a propagandist. Everything depends on content and the unfiltered truth behind STS activities in Libya."

"As it should be," Kleiser agreed.

He pressed a button on the intercom console. "I think we

understand one another. I apologize for not inviting you to stay for dinner, but I've been forced to deal with unexpected commitments."

"Before I go, can you tell me anything about Alois Brunner?"

"Ah . . . poor Brunner." Kleiser shook his head sadly. "He was a lovesick old man. In my opinion his death was unrelated to his position with STS. When a man plays forbidden games with a teenage girl, he's asking for trouble: parents become enraged, former boyfriends—it's a dangerous business."

"You don't connect Brunner's death with the recent terrorist action in Paris?"

Kleiser's eyes widened. "Paris?"

"The killing of Farheed Shah—the director of Pakistan's Kahuta nuclear facility."

"These things have nothing to do with STS. You should speak with an Indian official or the Soviets. They have reason to fear Pakistan's nuclear program."

The door opened and Erika entered.

"We have finished our business," Kleiser said to her. "Why not take our American friend to that wonderful restaurant on Perlbergerstrasse? Do you like Hungarian food, Mr. Lawford?"

"I don't think I've ever tried it."

Kleiser's voice was warm and friendly as he ushered them to the foyer. "One should try everything in his life, at least once. Don't you agree, Erika?"

"Absolutely."

"Ah. You see, Fräulein Sperling is that rare guileless woman. Loyal. Dedicated. And"—he kissed her cheek—"almost always agreeable."

Tom waited until they were at the door to ask a final question. "How would I get to see the tunnels at Nordhausen?"

Kleiser's easy smile vanished. "What does Nordhausen have to do with your story?"

"Nordhausen and its adjacent concentration camp, Dora, are critical to the story. The STS story begins at Nordhausen."

"But you can see these things on old newsreels."

"I have. I want to see those tunnels for myself."

"That may not be possible. Nordhausen is in the East. Besides, the tunnels may have been sealed and—"

"I will see to it," Erika interjected, and quickly added, "Your guests are waiting."

Kleiser extended his hand and Tom grasped it. "We are in business, Mr. Lawford. You have my word. Our entire operation is open to you. Once you return from Nordhausen, Erika will arrange for you to inspect our engine and rocket-assembly plants in Munich and Stuttgart—and finally we'll visit the Libyan V-5 launch site." Kleiser grinned. "I hope you enjoy the Hungarian food."

Reclining on the huge bed, the Swiss girls watched the blue movie on the large TV screen. They were both very young. One was blond with delicate features; the other was plain-looking, with large sad eyes and long shapely legs. They wore white formal tuxedo shirts with black bow ties and nothing else. Kleiser sat opposite them, staring intently and smoking a pipe full of opium. The blond girl turned from the TV set and kissed the dark-haired girl deeply. She undid the bow tie, opened the sad-eyed girl's shirt, and began to nurse her. The girl moaned and crushed the blond girl's head to her breast. Kleiser felt himself drifting off into a sensual dream, but for a millisecond he thought how vulnerable he was at times like this. These girls could be anyone—anyone at all.

The Hungarian restaurant was small and crowded with well-dressed upscale Berliners. The food was rich, spicy, and served with glasses of strong red wine. Erika critiqued certain details of Tom's meeting with Kleiser.

"Enough," Tom sighed. "Don't you ever take yes for an answer? The man said he'd open the doors."

"You should not have mentioned Nordhausen."

"Why not?"

"Anything to do with the Nazi past sets off alarms. Still . . ." She sipped the wine. "Overall I think you did quite well. I'll know for certain in the morning."

"How?"

"One of the girls entertaining Kleiser will report to me."

"You're really something."

"No. I'm nothing. My father was something. But that's a long, sad story." She tossed the wine down and he refilled her glass. "You can tell I trust you," she said, "because I'm getting drunk. But don't for a moment believe that Fritz Kleiser will take you to that launch site. Although, if by then the rockets are armed and ready, the location will no longer be relevant."

She signaled the waiter for a check.

"What's the rush?"

"I'm very tired. And I'm quite drunk. You'll drive me home, won't you?"

That mysterious, subtle, sensual current that had been there from the moment they met underscored her words. "You're really very handsome," she said, "for someone of advanced years."

Her pale hair glowed in the candlelight, and her eyes sparkled with promises.

"How old do you think I am?"

"Old enough to pay the bill and take me home."

The sharp cold air felt refreshing as they walked up the street and got into the BMW. Tom took a minute to familiarize himself with the dashboard while Erika fiddled with the radio before settling on a station. "American Armed Forces Network," she explained. "They play American jazz at this hour."

He shifted smoothly, going through the gears as she directed him toward Charlottenburg, a residential neighborhood in the British sector, not far from the Tiergarten Park. A silky voice came through the stereo speakers and Ella Fitzgerald sang: *"How long has this been going on?"*

"That's what Americans call a 'torch song,' isn't it?"

He nodded. "I would guess a lot of people fell in and out of love to that one."

"And you? Whom did you fall out of love with?"

"That's an unanswerable question."

"Why?"

"It's impossible to remember how and why certain relationships drifted and died. I find myself spending too much time doing that. It's a lousy business."

"Yes, it's quite futile trying to relive events one can't change."

She directed him to a snow-covered residential street. "The house is just up there. Park anywhere you see a place."

Feeling heady, he followed her up the worn wooden stairs, admiring her pretty legs. She tripped suddenly and fell backward. He caught her and held her for a moment before she smiled. "I've been climbing these stairs for years, and that's never happened before."

"Must be the goulash."

"Yes, of course, the goulash."

Inside the apartment, she turned the stereo on and poured some red wine into two crystal goblets. "Take your jacket off. Relax—I'll only be a moment."

"Where do you keep the cigarettes?"

"Behind you, on the shelf."

He lit a cigarette, dimmed the lights, and carried the goblet with him as he walked to the window. Joan Jett sang a childlike lyric of unrequited love.

Tom blew the cigarette smoke against the windowpane and thought about Erika and the seductive promise that danced in her eyes. She was an enigma wrapped in an arcane secret that dictated her emotions. But none of that mattered. What mattered now was very basic. She was alluring and totally desirable.

Erika stared at herself in the bathroom mirror. Perhaps it was the tension and the red wine, perhaps it was the hours she had spent with him rehearsing, or that she hadn't slept with a man in a long time. It was all of that and more. They were alike, haunted by memories and missed chances, burning out. She knew all about him. Mossad had been very thorough.

She brushed her hair rapidly and hard until it shone, then touched a fingertip of perfume to her throat and went out.

As she entered the living room, he turned from the window and said, "It's a charming apartment."

She walked to him. Her face was flushed and her eyes

challenging. "For Berlin, it's quite nice," she said. "I prefer the British sector. It's close to the Tiergarten, and—"

He kissed her lightly, once, twice, their lips brushing softly. She curved herself into him and his arms went around her. The force of their passion carried with it the loss of reason and reserve. She was, for him, the promissory note, and they made love until there were no more secrets.

CHAPTER NINETEEN

The sand-colored Bell Ranger helicopter flew north, following the foaming Mediterranean shoreline. Far below, the shadow of the rotor blades flashed across the Herodian ruins of Caesarea. They left the coastline at Acco, and veering inland, passed over a dazzling green-and-gold carpet of cultivated fields.

The pilot's face was stolid and his eyes impenetrable as he checked his gauges and instruments, making minor adjustments for the stiff westerly winds. Dado tugged at his arm and motioned below to the sprawling Hadera Air Force base where F-16's, F-15's, and Huey helicopters were parked under camouflage nets. They could see fuel trucks racing across the tarmac and maintenance men tending to C-130 tankers. Hawk ground-to-air missiles ringed the base and a huge radar scoop revolved atop the control tower.

The Soviet Soyuz-TM-6 satellite orbited the Hadera air base daily, and its pictures were passed on to Syrian Intelligence. The northern air base would be a prime first-strike target in the next war, a fact that pleased Israeli Air Force chief Arik Carmil because Hadera was an illusion.

With the exception of the men, trucks, and occasional jet arrivals and takeoffs, nothing was real. Hadera existed solely for the cameras in the Soviet satellite. The actual northern Air Force command center was not visible from the air. Illusions played a critical role in Israel's military strategy.

The Bell Ranger soared over Mount Carmel, revealing a spectacular view of the mountainous city with its pastel dwellings and palm-lined streets that sloped gently down to the sea. Speaking briefly to ground control at the Technion heliport, the pilot climbed up and to the east, heading toward a complex of glass-and-steel buildings draped across a hillside.

Minutes later, the chopper landed precisely in the center of the helipad at the rear of Technion's administration building. Crouching reflexively, Dado disembarked and was greeted by a balding man of medium height with puckish features and lively, humorous eyes.

Dr. Yuval Newman was a founding member of Technion. The research-and-development institute and its staff comprised the most gifted scientific minds in the nation. Newman's specialty was nuclear physics, but he had also pioneered advanced studies of electromagnetic superconductor microchips that had made the creation of the Yuval-15 supercomputer possible. He had recently turned his efforts to the largely uncharted field of nuclear-powered lasers.

The men shook hands.

"Come, Dado. I have reserved a choice table."

The garden terrace faced the sea, and they could see the distant gray silhouette of an American aircraft carrier docked at the Haifa Naval Base.

A dark-skinned Yemenite woman served them coffee and sweet rolls.

"I noted in the press that you visited Paris," Newman said. "The loss of the Flash X-ray manuals will force the Pakistanis into an open test."

"On the other hand," Dado offered, "Qaddafi might accept the warheads and gamble that they'll detonate."

"Perhaps . . ." Newman said, his lively eyes suddenly

cheerless and contemplative. "I've run the problem you posed to me. It's very chancy."

"But is it possible?"

"The question is relative; of course it's possible, but the price could be too steep. I'm talking about a political price. If an eight-hundred-megawatt reactor suffers significant structural damage, you can have a radioactive fallout ten times greater than that of Chernobyl. There is also the problem of plutonium at Kahuta." Newman paused and sighed. "Should the stored plutonium casings burst open, the monster is loose. Plutonium is the most lethal of all isotopes. It will kill every living creature—human, animal, plant, vegetable—within a twenty-five-mile radius. The site and surrounding area will be uninhabitable forever." Newman paused and sipped his coffee. "There is, however, a possibility—I say *possibility*—of carrying out this operation with minimal risk to life, if the damage can be confined to the facility itself. We must know at precisely what depth to detonate and the per-square-inch pressure of the cement separating the various levels. And since the Kahuta reactor is the type that must be shut down periodically for refueling, it would be prudent to find out when the core reactor is cold."

"What about the plutonium?"

"The implosion must be designed to cause the cupola to collapse onto the reactor. The lower levels will open like a drawbridge and the heavy water reservoir will boil, burst, and flood, pouring down and, in a sense, sealing the plutonium casings."

"What's the outside danger to Islamabad and Rawalpindi?"

"Minimal. Both cities are twenty-five miles upwind of Kahuta. But"—Newman shrugged—"if there is plutonium leakage, the entire northern province will be uninhabitable."

Dado shifted his long legs and said, "Let's walk back."

They strolled across the lawn, passing young people who greeted Newman.

As they approached the helipad, Dado asked, "What's your conclusion, Yuval?"

"I believe it can be done. But it requires meticulous planning. Absolute secrecy. Faultless intelligence. And perfect execution. Still, it remains a terrifying decision: the unexpected, the weather, the tides, a navigational miscalculation, a technical malfunction. What Heisenberg called 'The Uncertainty Principle.'"

"Above and beyond the risks," Dado reminded Newman, "the strike on Kahuta must have the unmistakable appearance of an accident."

"If we're successful and lucky, it will. The destruction of Kahuta will be attributed to the unpredictable savagery of nature. The northeast rim of Pakistan sits on an earthquake fault. A catastrophic quake leveled nearby cities in Afghanistan and India some years ago, and devastated Armenia in eighty-eight. But nature aside, nuclear accidents are not uncommon. Disastrous nuclear accidents have occurred in America, Britain, France, Italy, Sweden, and Russia. Sooner or later, the liberated atom bites us all. So why not Kahuta? No one is immune to nuclear jeopardy."

They stopped at the helipad, and Newman sighed. "Having said all that, Dado—it's still a desperate enterprise."

"But you're with me?"

Newman nodded. "I take fanatics at their word. I believe they intend to annihilate us."

"At some point I'll need your support with the Prime Minister."

"You have it," Newman said. "I assume you spoke to Berger about the ship?"

"Before Paris."

"And?"

"He's working on it. Once we have it, how much time do you need?"

"Three weeks. But if you don't locate that Libyan rocket base, the fate of Kahuta becomes academic—we will have ceased to exist."

Dado nodded. "We'll find it."

The men shook hands and Newman asked, "Where are you off to now?"

"Lunch with a bedouin chief."

Newman smiled and his playful eyes twinkled. "Only in

this hellish land can a man go from coffee with a nuclear physicist to lunch with a bedouin chief in less than thirty minutes."

Professor Newman watched the small two-seat helicopter rise, gain altitude, and veer sharply southeast.

Walking back toward the main building, he exchanged perfunctory words with his colleagues, but his brain whirled with doomsday thoughts of blast implosion, delayed mercury detonators, ascent propulsion, concentric gnomonic charts, meteorology, and a twenty-thousand-ton freighter that would have to vanish.

Brown-and-white goatskin tents were pitched in the shade of a limestone cliff at the edge of a stark, exquisite expanse of desert. The mud-colored hills of Jordan were off to the east. And to the north, the Dead Sea shimmered like a vast reflective mirror. A line of braying camels spit in protest as the sinuous bedouins slung crates over their flanks.

Inside the chief's tent, Dado and Sheik Oweidi were seated on a fine tribal Oriental rug covering the sand floor. Oweidi's face was severely lined and creased by years of exposure to wind and sun, but his black eyes were bright and alert.

Dado admired the bedouins' fierce independence. They had resisted the encroachment of alien cultures by using the desert to immunize themselves against the surrounding "civilized" world. The Awassi bedouins adhered to ancient codes that had governed their lives for five thousand years without benefit of a single written document. Their law was based on a single ethic: Life without honor is nothing.

As was the custom, the General and the sheik ate with their right hands, scooping rice and lamb out of a deep kettle and drinking strong palm wine. After the main course, veiled women brought vases of rose-scented water from which the men washed their hands.

Oweidi had a long-standing favor to repay the Israeli general. After the return of Sinai to Egypt, Israel had been forced to build new air bases in the Negev that encroached on bedouin land. Dado had intervened with the southern military command and made the case that the Awassi's long history of loyalty to the state demanded reciprocity. Dado's request was approved and Oweidi's tribe was not displaced by the new bases. While F-16's and F-15's howled across the desert, the land itself was still a bedouin preserve. The General also made certain that the hospital in nearby Hezeva opened its doors and services to the Awassi.

The sheik was delighted that now the opportunity to honor the debt had come to pass.

Over a dessert of sweet cakes and thick coffee, Oweidi handed Dado a letter of introduction to a Taureg bedouin chief in Libya. "My brother, Sheik Saleh, has seen the fire in the sky."

"You understand this favor may not be necessary."

"Yes, but I pray it is. What else is there for man to do but repay the kindness of a friend?"

Outside the tent, Oweidi kissed Dado on both cheeks and blessed him: "May God strengthen you."

"According to his will," Dado replied.

The helicopter rose, kicking up a cloud of swirling sand. The animals brayed nervously and the women cowered, but the old chief watched the disappearing flying machine until it was the size of a small bird.

The bright winter sun shone down out of an endless azure sky, illuminating the domes and spires of Jerusalem. The bay window in the Prime Minister's office afforded a splendid panoramic view of both the new and the old city, and beyond to the dark Judean Hills. The Prime Minister was the first member of his generation to hold the nation's highest office. He had served under Dado with the legendary Seventh Brigade in October 1973, and the men regarded each other as comrades in arms. The usual formalities of the office were dismissed when they were alone.

The Prime Minister listened intently as Dado outlined Operation Red Desert and briefly sketched the proposed elimination of Kahuta. When the General concluded, the Prime Minister rose and stared out of the picture window. "As of this moment, you still do not have the location of the German launch site in Libya."

"We will."

The Prime Minister turned from the view. "If not?"

"We go anyway. We're planning to hit the entire coast of Libya."

"But how do you stop the V-5 from being launched?"

"If Red Desert fails, we're lost; but Kahuta will also cease to exist."

"So, in effect, the Libyan strike is a cover for the Kahuta raid?"

"Exactly."

The Prime Minister grimaced slightly and rubbed the pit of his stomach. "We have no political problem with Washington as far as Libya is concerned, although the Europeans will join the rest of the UN in condemning us. So be it. Pakistan is another matter. Since the death of Zia, Washington has shut its eyes to their nuclear program. A strike on Kahuta can mean political suicide."

"We have no choice, Zvikah." Dado used the Prime Minister's nickname. "To do nothing is *certain* suicide. Pakistan is providing the ultimate terror weapon to Qaddafi. Had we not taken out the Baghdad reactor in eighty-one, Sadam Hussein would not have bothered using poison gas in his war with Iran; he would have dropped the bomb. Our strike on the Osirak reactor probably saved five million Iranians from nuclear incineration."

The Prime Minister poured a glass of heavy white liquid from a decanter and swallowed the thick brew. "Buttermilk." He grimaced. "What the Arabs failed to do, the Jews have succeeded in doing. This job has punched a hole in my stomach." He touched a napkin to his lips. "So Newman believes there is a chance to make Kahuta appear to be another nuclear accident."

"With reservations."

"Yes, of course, the Heisenberg Principle. Newman never fails to quote the Heisenberg Principle," the Prime Minister sighed. "Tell me, what the hell were you doing in Paris?"

"It was a complicated operation. I remained in the background."

"I know very well what you call 'background.'" The Prime Minister stared thoughtfully at his former commander, thinking that some men were ordained to ride the wild horse to their graves. "Keep me informed, Dado," he said with finality.

The Café Firenze was located on a side street, in the bustling commercial center of West Jerusalem. A favorite haunt of college students from the nearby university, the Firenze was famous for pizza and its superb collection of taped Italian operas. Only tourists bothered with the sidewalk tables and people-watching. The local clientele sat inside, conversed, and listened to Puccini.

Seated at a rear table, his back to the wall as always, Berger saw Dado enter and, for a fleeting moment, envied the General his Aryan good looks.

"Ah, Dado." Berger smiled, removing his glasses. "Just in time for some pizza."

"No, thanks. I had lunch in the desert."

"How is Sheik Oweidi?"

"A man of his word."

"You look pale."

"It's the light," Dado said, and ordered an Italian beer.

Watching Berger devour a sizzling slice of cheese pizza, he wondered if the intelligence chief's tongue was made of steel. "Take care, Yanush. That's hot."

"I cool it with the wine," Berger replied, swallowing the Chianti.

"My compliments to you," Dado said. "Paris was perfect."

Berger touched the napkin to his lips. "You had two of my best people."

"That's some Penelope," Dado said with admiration. "The woman is fifty-seven and dauntless. She handled the Uzi like a one-armed paratrooper."

The Ethiopian waitress who served Dado's beer was coal black, with fine, delicate features. Speaking Hebrew with biblical grammar, she asked if he cared for anything else.

Dado shook his head and thanked her politely. After she left, he sipped the cold beer and said, "Tell me about Berlin."

"Lawford met with Kleiser. The STS doors are apparently open to him."

"Including the launch site?"

"According to Erika, yes."

"I have a letter from Sheik Oweidi for Erika. Can you arrange delivery?"

"Of course."

"How?"

"In the usual manner, by a trusted courier. We've had no trouble over the years in maintaining contact. Leave it to me."

"With Abu Hasi on the case, Erika may be under surveillance."

"The letter will be delivered, Dado. You can sleep on it."

The men fell silent as two attractive blond girls sat down at an adjacent table. The girls struggled in Hebrew and Russian, but finally managed to order cappuccinos from the Ethiopian waitress.

"Moscow has come to Jerusalem," Berger remarked.

"Not enough. They're a strong people. I wish we had ten divisions of Soviet émigrés, but their parents prefer to go to America."

"Who can blame them? Israel cannot compete with the American dream."

"But what a mixture we've become—just like America. Black, white, Slavic, Yemenites, secular, religious, native-born kibbutzniks, settlers with skullcaps and Uzis. Yahweh's soup kitchen. Himmler's racial laundry. We're the lost tribe, Yanush—a nation of madmen, burned out by history." Dado paused. "One of Carmil's pilots claims he saw a lion in the Wadi Musa."

"Pilots hallucinate under G-forces."

"This pilot was throttled down."

"Maybe he saw a mountain lion. There are a few in the Arava."

"Perhaps," Dado said. He swallowed some beer and with his forefinger traced a crescent-shaped scar on his right cheek and asked casually, "Any news from Salim Bashira?"

"He's in the process of acquiring a twenty-year-old Greek freighter."

"What about the disappearance of the ship?"

"Bashira will send precise instructions when he knows the details of the voyage." Berger paused and shook his head. "Ah, listen to that woman sing."

A rich soprano aria from *Madame Butterfly* filled the café. Even the gossiping Russian girls halted their conversation to listen.

"The Italian opera company is scheduled to perform at Caesarea this summer," Berger commented.

"We have to make sure there will be a summer," Dado replied. "I'll need either photographs or accurate scale drawings of the Kahuta facility."

"That's a difficult proposition. We have a dedicated man inside Kahuta, but after our Paris action, I would think Pakistan Counterintelligence will be especially vigilant."

"See what you can do. Newman requires those pictures. I also need to know when the reactor is cold."

"All right." Berger nodded.

Dado sipped some beer and asked, "Anything on Mueller?"

"He will be attending a reunion of the old SS Kameradschaft next week in a village near Salzburg. They drink heavily, celebrating old atrocities. Mueller may get careless. I'm thinking of sending Landau and Penelope to Salzburg." Berger paused, and decided to take a chance. "Tell me, Dado, how do you propose to destroy Kahuta?"

"With great difficulty." Dado sighed, and rose. "Thanks for the beer, Yanush."

Watching the General leave, one of the Russian girls said, "The best are the older ones. I have decided to have an affair with my biology professor."

Unable to resist, Berger turned to the girls, smiled, and in perfect Russian said, "That's one way to ensure a passing grade."

Dado watched the blood-red sunset from the terrace of his seaside Jaffa home. A balmy sea breeze carried the musky scent of Africa, and seemed to belong to another season. The General's two-story house had been restored to its original graceful Moorish style. Jaffa's population was a balanced mixture of Arabs and Jews, most of whom were writers and artists, and in what might have been a testament to the creative spirit, it was probably the only city in the Middle East where Arabs and Jews lived together with some degree of tranquillity.

Fingering the geranium plants atop the terrace wall, Dado thought of Avital and how she had loved her garden—and the starry-eyed pleasure she displayed at the bloom of a rose. He hadn't seen her for weeks, and it bothered him. He would have to reclaim her from the Zealots. He could not allow her to bear a life of eternal penance, but for the moment he could do nothing. His mind reeled under the weight of detail surrounding Red Desert and the still-unresolved Kahuta operation.

"The sunset is magnificent," Narda exclaimed as she stepped out onto the terrace. "They say beauty is the last refuge of the hopeless."

"Who says?"

"I don't remember," she sighed. "Tell me, Dado—will the killing ever end?"

"Never. It's become an avocation, like collecting stamps. We kill them. They kill us. It's lasted too long. It's lost its rage. It's what we do."

Streaks of moonlight pierced the shutters, painting zebra stripes across their bodies. She had made love to him with a desperate defiance, as if challenging the unforgiving reality of the past.

He watched her, now breathing evenly—her silky black hair draped around her heart-shaped face. A light wind wafted into the bedroom, stirring her perfume, and he reflected on the sad irony that bound them together.

They had met in the spring of '81, between wars, on the manicured Lawn of Remembrance. Her brother's grave was located in the same line as Dado's son, Dani. He'd seen her lying prone on the gray slab of stone and pulled her to her feet. She had curled into him, and his khaki shirt was wet with her tears. And from that moment, she became one of his soldiers. They shared their ghosts. Their bodies. And their dark memories.

CHAPTER TWENTY

The BMW crawled around S-curves studded with slabs of concrete teeth and rolled across the White Line into the eastern sector of Checkpoint Charlie. Erika flashed her most engaging "dawn" smile at a grim-faced East German border guard. Unimpressed with her charms, the officer snapped, "Passports!" She handed him two passports and a letter bearing the seal of the East German Democratic Republic and the signature of the Minister of Tourism. The content of the letter urged all Federal Police to cooperate with Herr Lawford on his motor trip from Berlin to Nordhausen.

The Reuters bureau chief in East Berlin had arranged a meeting between Lawford and Minister Kladen. Tom had explained that Nordhausen was part of an exposé he was writing concerning Fritz Kleiser's STS rocket group. The East German Minister had readily agreed it was time that someone from the West revealed the criminal activities of the former Nazi rocket scientists.

After careful study of the documents, the border guard stamped their passports and advised Erika to take the

Potsdammer entrance to the autobahn. The barrier rose and the BMW entered East Berlin.

They drove south on Route 97 for two hours before leaving the autobahn at Magdeburg and stopping at a roadside café.

"Shouldn't we keep on going?" Tom asked. "Our pass is valid for only twelve hours."

"We're fine. Nordhausen is very close."

There were a few truck drivers and motorists in the café reading newspapers and speaking in hushed tones.

"Why are they all whispering?" Tom asked.

"It's always this way in the East," Erika said, sipping her coffee. "Excruciatingly quiet. It makes you want to scream. Look at them," she added, "the way they stare, as if we're from outer space."

"They're wondering what Miss East Germany is doing with an aging American tourist. I must look like a Roman ruin sitting alongside you."

"You're not bad for a Roman ruin. Not good. But not bad."

"You mean 'adequate'?"

"I mean not bad. Come, let's go."

The car heater dispelled the damp cold, and the fragrance of Erika's perfume laced the warm air. The single-lane country road climbed gradually toward distant snow-capped mountains, and patches of morning fog clung to the dips and hollows.

"The Minister said that Camp Dora has become a memorial museum," Erika said, "and most of the tunnels have been sealed for years. What do you expect to find?"

"I don't know, but I have to see it. Besides, I want Kleiser to understand that I consider Nordhausen to be a significant part of the story and that I don't intend to withhold anything."

"About what?"

"The fact that two of the surviving Nordhausen killers, Mueller and Diehl, are current members of STS."

* * *

They rolled through the small red-gabled village of Weigen and passed a sign that said "Nordhausen—8 kilometers."

"Look!" Erika exclaimed, pointing toward a wooden barrier up ahead.

"What is it?"

"A Federal Police checkpoint."

She downshifted, slowed, and rolled to a stop at the wooden barricade. A uniformed policeman, accompanied by a pleasant-looking middle-aged civilian, walked to the front of the car. The men conversed for a moment before the civilian came around to the passenger side.

"Mr. Lawford?"

"Yes."

"My name is Dieter Eckers. I'm with the Ministry of Tourism." He flashed a red-black-and-yellow card. "Minister Kladen selected me to be your guide at Nordhausen/ Dora."

Eckers climbed into the rear seat and exchanged greetings in German with Erika. He then indicated an upcoming fork in the road and said, "Take a right onto the asphalt road."

The rutted country lane was lined by leafless trees, and ground fog clung to barren fields plowed under for the winter.

Eckers said, "On this road, in April 1945, a fierce two-day battle took place between units of the American First Army and a brigade of Waffen SS. Many died on both sides. Some are buried just off this road. You can see the stones."

The road curved sharply right and snaked through scruffy hills for another five miles before ending in a cul-de-sac at the foot of the slate-gray mountain.

An enclosure of low wooden barracks sat on a flat plateau adjacent to the mountain. Watchtowers loomed over a barbed-wire fence surrounding the barracks, and in the center of the camp a red brick smokestack marked the spot of the crematorium. Less than a hundred yards from the camp, granite steps led up to the iron gates at the face of the mountain. Two Federal Policemen in gray coats and fur hats guarded the entrance.

Using his motorized Nikon, Tom quickly ran a series of

exposures from a variety of angles, encompassing the grim complex.

"Here you see Camp Dora," Eckers said. "Sixty thousand slave laborers passed through these gates from 1943 to 1945. Forty thousand died and were cremated."

Tom remembered it all from the archival newsreel footage he had seen; but film could not convey the stark reality.

"Would you care to enter the camp?" Eckers inquired.

Tom shook his head. "No. Our time is limited."

"Very well. Follow me please—and take care, these steps are worn."

Erika drew her long cashmere scarf around her throat, and Tom turned up his coat collar. Lowering their heads against the raw wind, they made their way up the granite steps to the tunnel's entrance.

Pulling hard on the iron rings, the Federal Policeman opened the steel gates. A malodorous stench of decay and an acrid odor of ammonia rushed out of the entrance. The policemen picked up powerful battery-lamps and entered the dark mouth of the tunnel.

"We must wait for a moment," Eckers said, and turned, pointing toward the Camp Dora entrance. "Down there, close by the camp's gates, was Heinrich Mueller's office. A large crane would be stationed there. As many as sixty slave laborers would be wired to the crane by their necks. The crane would then slowly rise, hanging all sixty. They were not only Jews. Many were captured French technicians pressed into service by the SS."

Erika stared down at the frozen mud. Tom said nothing, but he remembered the newsreels of the hangings, and shots of Mueller and Von Braun smiling as they watched the legs of the victims pedaling insanely in the air as they choked to death.

A policeman came out of the tunnel and nodded at Eckers.

"Follow me, please."

A bank of scoop-shaped lights cast an eerie light into what appeared to be a vast granite cathedral eighty feet high and sixty feet wide. Narrow-gauge steel tracks bisected the tunnel's length, and a single flatbed iron carriage remained on the tracks.

"There were over thirty tunnels," Eckers explained, "but this was the principal rocket-assembly hall, and the only remaining tunnel not sealed."

Using the flash attachment and shooting wide open, Tom snapped several shots of the flatbed iron carriage.

"That stench of ammonia comes from an old mine below this level," Eckers continued. "Even in this damp cold, the ammonia seared the workers' lungs. One can only imagine what it was like in the heat of summer with hundreds of people working in this tunnel without fresh air. They had to push these iron carriages five hundred yards to an inner chamber, where warheads were fitted to the rockets."

As they followed Eckers into the blackness, a second bank of lights flashed on.

"This tunnel was carved out of the mountain by hand, with pickaxes. The rubble was removed in sacks carried out on the backs of slaves."

Finding it impossible to comment or ask questions, they walked silently into the dark, foul-smelling belly of the Nazi past.

"The slaves worked twelve-hour shifts and were fed rations of two pieces of bread and a cup of soup." Eckers' voice echoed off the granite walls. "It was calculated that each man would last six months. There were no toilet facilities, no medical facilities. They worked and they died. The defiant ones committed acts of sabotage, which meant instant death on the crane. Two thousand V-2 rockets were assembled here. Fifteen hundred were launched. The Allies captured the remaining rockets, along with the criminals who designed them."

"Can we have a moment alone?" Tom asked.

"Yes . . . yes, of course. But please do not wander beyond the light," Eckers cautioned. "There are numerous bisecting tunnels. One can lose the way quite easily."

Following the steel tracks, Tom proceeded deeper into the tunnel. Erika walked beside him, her boots crunching on the fallen stones. A sudden draft of cold dank air whipped from a hidden crevice and carried with it the squealing sound of rats.

In the spectral darkness, they sensed the presence of ghosts—SS guards beating half-naked workers—and the grating sound of steel on steel and the groans of skeletal men straining under the weight of rubble-filled sacks in the terrible heat of summer. They stood silently for a long time, trying to understand what had happened here. It was beyond human conception that this dank tunnel had been the gateway to the space age and that man had taken his first step onto the moon from this foul-smelling granite tomb.

They drove back along the country road in haunted silence, their thoughts shadowed by the lingering ghosts of Nordhausen's sepulchral tunnels.

It was dark by the time they reached the autobahn at Magdeburg. Erika paid the toll, gunned the BMW, and sped past a long line of green Soviet military trucks.

Tom watched the speedometer needle move through the amber into the red zone and hover at 180 kilometers.

"You're doing over a hundred miles an hour," he cautioned. "What's the rush?"

"I need a drink and a bathroom."

"You make a mistake at this speed and you won't need anything."

"Sorry . . ." she sighed. "Sorry."

She eased off the accelerator and they cruised at a moderate speed for fifteen minutes before entering the roadside restaurant and gas station at Tucheim.

Erika went to the bathroom and Tom ordered two double cognacs. The bartender poured the drinks and asked, "American?"

Tom nodded.

"But the lady is German, yes?"

The bartender's English was halting, but too good for a man working a freeway road stop. Tom guessed the man was an informer for the East German Secret Police.

"The lady is Swiss," he replied.

"Ja . . . Ja." The bartender smiled knowingly. *"Die ganze Welt ist Schweizer."*

"I'm sorry—I don't understand."

"The whole world is Swiss. It's nothing. Just a joke."

Erika joined him at the bar and Tom carried their drinks to a window table.

Passing headlights flared into her eyes as she stared at the blur of traffic speeding north on the autobahn. She sipped some cognac and in a hoarse, throaty voice said, "My father was part of that horror at Nordhausen." She lit a cigarette, inhaled deeply, and blew the smoke up toward the ceiling. "He was a brilliant chemist. He had just received his doctorate from Hanover University when he was assigned to the V-2 project as a specialist in liquid fuels."

"What year was that?"

"The summer of 1943. He was then only twenty-two. It was at Nordhausen that my father first met Fritz Kleiser's father. He had something to do with rocket propulsion. In any case, when the Reich collapsed, my father escaped to Switzerland."

"Escaped from whom?"

She shrugged. "The Americans . . . the British . . . the Soviets; my father was not important enough to be considered a prize catch like Von Braun, but he was insignificant enough to be charged with war crimes. Having embraced the real criminals, the Allies required scapegoats." She crisscrossed the glowing end of her cigarette in the ashtray. "My father remained in Zurich for five years before returning to Hanover, where he met my mother."

"Did he ever see Kleiser's father again?"

"Often. They both worked for I.G. Farben." She crushed the cigarette out. "My father was soon dismissed."

"Why?"

"He suffered a breakdown. He would scream in his sleep. He would suddenly sob in the middle of the day. He was in and out of mental institutions. And finally he put a gun in his mouth. I found him."

She drained the cognac. "When I was old enough to understand, my mother explained to me about Nordhausen and the Holocaust. From that day on, I learned everything I possibly could about Hitler's Reich and the 'final solution.' When I was fifteen, I spent a summer in Israel and worked on a communal farm. I made friends with an Israeli girl whose parents were very kind and loving to me. I returned every summer."

"Doing penance for your father."

"Perhaps." She shrugged. "Perhaps for myself. Perhaps for Germany. I don't know. In any case, one summer a woman came to the farm and asked to meet me. The woman was from Mossad."

"And you were planted as a deep-cover agent inside STS."

"It wasn't difficult. After all, Fritz Kleiser knew my family. He told me to get in touch with him the moment I graduated from university. He said there would always be a place for me with him. The rest you know."

"Christ, it must have been hell for you in that tunnel. Why didn't you say something?"

"I've always wanted to see it. Without you, I wouldn't have gone. I couldn't face it alone, but it was something I had to do."

"Is your mother still alive?"

Erika nodded. "She lives in Hanover."

"What happened to Kleiser's father?"

"He died peacefully in his sleep."

CHAPTER TWENTY-ONE

Tom drove the last leg of the trip, and Erika directed him from the autobahn exit into East Berlin.

A frigid Siberian air mass had enveloped the city, and shivering pedestrians huddled together at bus stops.

"Make a left at the corner," she said, "and follow the street to the canal."

"Where are we going?"

"I've decided to take you to dinner."

They passed stately town houses that lined the left bank of the canal. "What happened over there?" Tom asked, indicating the empty silhouette of the opposite bank.

"Incendiary bombs. They say it was a firestorm—an inferno. Miraculously, this side was untouched. Slow down, and park wherever you can."

"I don't see any restaurants."

"This is a private house that became a restaurant," she explained. "Very old and very famous. A favorite of the elite since the days of the Weimar Republic. They say Marlene

Dietrich drank her first glass of champagne here. The owner is Magda Reimeck. She's quite old but still runs the place."

The sharp bite of arctic air took their breath away as they walked briskly toward a three-story brownstone ablaze with lights.

The maître d' greeted Erika warmly. She explained it was a last-minute decision and apologized for not having phoned to reserve a table. They followed him to a small elevator and rode up to the third floor.

The softly lit oak-paneled room was crowded with well-dressed men and women. The Slavic accents of Russian and Hungarian mixed with the familiar German. Incongruously, a vintage Louis Armstrong tape played "West End Blues." The candlelit tables were dressed with fine linen, silver service, and crystal glasses.

They were seated at a table overlooking the canal.

Without being asked, a waiter served them iced Polish vodka and a tin of Russian caviar.

"Look," Erika said, indicating the canal.

A tugboat sliced through the inky canal water, spreading ripples of yellow moonlight. Wispy white smoke curled out of its smokestack and rose up against the starlit blue-black night, hanging there, frozen in place by the cold.

"You could put a frame around that," Tom said, and lifted his glass. "Cheers."

"Cheers," she replied, touching glasses.

The straight vodka was strong and made them heady.

"You really could be 'Miss East Germany,'" he said.

"With this bent nose?"

"What bent nose?"

"Right here." She touched a small indentation on the bridge of her nose.

"Especially with your bent nose." He smiled.

They ordered more vodka and he proceeded to tell her about Hickey and Laos.

"And your family?" she asked. "I mean your marriage."

He studied the veins of vodka curling around the ice. "My marriage is in a state of evolution."

"Is that good or bad?"

"Probably good."

"Mossad told me your twin brother died recently."

"Six months ago." Tom nodded. "He died of AIDS. He had a long, obsessive love affair with a part-time actress who became a full-time junkie. She caught a bad needle and infected them both."

"I'm sorry," she whispered.

"We were twins, but not as close as we should have been. I always loved him, but never let him know it—until . . . the monster had him. I do that. I do that a lot."

"Do what?"

"Love people and keep it a secret."

"You don't have to send messages—one knows when one's loved."

"Only with animals. I had a cat that loved me. No words—but she let me know. I'd walk into a room and you could hear her purr." He poured another vodka and shrugged. "Who the hell knows about these things? I know less about myself now than I did years ago. Christ. I'm getting smashed. You'll have to drive us through Checkpoint Charlie."

"What makes you think I'm sober?"

"All you have to do is smile at those goons."

The tape changed to Benny Goodman's original recording of "Here's That Rainy Day."

"Why the American jazz?" he asked.

"It's a tradition. Even the hierarchy of the Reich had to tolerate American jazz when they dined at Magda's."

They ordered grilled veal sausages and a bottle of Laurent Perrier champagne.

A sudden hush fell over the patrons as a regal-looking white-haired woman made her way across the room.

"You're about to meet a legend," Erika said.

Magda Reimeck's face was etched with the lines of age, but her large dark eyes were remarkably young. She had the kind of commanding presence that surrounds timeless celebrity. Erika performed the introductions and Fräulein Reimeck decided to spend a moment at their table.

"What brings you to the East, Mr. Lawford?" she asked.

"We visited Nordhausen."

"Nordhausen . . . Nordhausen." The old woman repeated the name incredulously, as if he had mentioned a remote Tibetan village.

"It's quite close to Leipzig," Erika said.

"Ah, yes . . . farming country."

"Erika tells me that you opened this place in the twenties," Tom said.

"My father did. I was a child—but I have vivid memories of those days. Dietrich, Fritz Lang, Emil Jannings, Kurt Weill, Brecht, George Grosz. We served the princes and princesses of the arts. In the thirties the barons of commerce arrived. The power brokers of Europe. They all came here. Berlin was an exciting city in those days. But once that hysterical Austrian rose to power with his drug addicts and thugs . . ." She shrugged. "We were doomed. Still, who could imagine it would all end in flames? In March of forty-five a great Allied air raid created a firestorm that swept across the city. I went up on the roof and watched Berlin burn. There was a sad grandeur to it all. I was still a young woman, but on that night I understood the meaning of vengeance. But," she sighed, "we Berliners have a saying: *Berlin hat verstanden, und so habe ich.*"

Erika translated: "Berlin still stands, and so do I."

"How did you survive the Soviet occupation?"

Fräulein Reimeck smiled. "Some people waved white flags. I waved money." She kissed Erika's cheek and rose. "Give my love to your mother. A pleasure meeting you, Mr. Lawford."

The place fell silent as six decades of Berlin history crossed the elegant dining room.

Despite the biting cold, they decided to walk alongside the canal. A thin sheet of ice had begun to spread across the black water like white frosting on a dark cake. The moonlight filtered through a layer of low clouds, painting their faces in a chiaroscuro light. Their breaths vaporized in the air, and the events of the day seemed distant.

"It's almost beyond imagining," she said, "this city in flames."

"Fräulein Reimeck takes a very nationalistic view of aerial bombardment," Tom said. "But I suppose from her limited perception, the destruction of Berlin was somehow unique."

"Her perception may be limited, but she knows how to survive."

"That she does," Tom agreed.

Erika leaned on the railing and stared pensively at the freezing water. He put his arm around her waist and pulled her to him. "I think I'm in trouble with you, kiddo." He stared at her a moment, then kissed her deeply.

They crossed the cobblestoned street just as a police van careened around the corner, its blue light flashing, its siren wailing.

"That's the drug van," Erika explained. "They're raiding Turkish hashish dealers."

They cleared Checkpoint Charlie without difficulty and arrived at her apartment in less than fifteen minutes.

There was no preamble. No invitation. No prologue. She unbuttoned her coat and tossed it over a chair, and he followed her into the bedroom. Their arms went around each other, and reality slipped away as their lips fused and body heat coursed between them. Wordlessly they shed their clothes. Her eyes locked on his as she stretched out on the bed.

His lips brushed the fine line of her cheekbone and the soft curve of her lips. He cupped her small, firm breasts, and his lips moved over her flat belly and kissed the indentation of her waist.

Feeling her eyes on him, he pressed his mouth into the very core of her. She spread her legs wide apart, and her hips moved rhythmically, thrusting against his mouth. He lost all sense of time and place, aware only of a pulsing, consuming, sensual heat spreading throughout his body.

A moan escaped her lips. Her hips undulated. She trembled and dug her nails into his shoulders. She bruised his lips as her body arched, and she cried out, shuddering in a long series of climaxes.

He moved up and slipped inside her. He kissed her eyes, lips, throat, and soaked up the sweet scent of her perfume.

"Don't move," she whispered. "Not yet."

They remained fused together until the throbbing connection forced them to move. She wrapped her legs around his waist and they rocked together with a rising fury. They were like sweating, panting savages, experiencing a sensual exorcism of ghosts and a frenzied affirmation of life.

Her head was cradled against his shoulder, and the moonlight edging through the windowpane created a halo around her pale hair. They had showered and she fixed them tall vodka tonics. The stereo played a tape of Billy Taylor performing vintage Rodgers and Hart.

"You know," she said, "the other night was, for me, the first time in months. I was too aggressive. I wanted it to happen quickly. It wasn't . . . like this. I had forgotten what it can be like." She propped herself up against the pillows and sipped her drink. "I've had only one recent affair—with a young student from Berlin University. We hit it off. He made me laugh and feel alive—and for a while forget the reality of my situation. But I projected more into the relationship than was actually there." She paused. "I knew the precise moment it was over. We were here. In this bed. It was very late. He was curled up, asleep. His mouth pursed, like that of a child. He seemed to be my child, and in that instant I knew it was over. It's always been that way for me. I know the moment things begin, and the moment they're over."

"That kind of clarity comes with a driving singleness of purpose," Tom said. "Obsessions have a way of illuminating everything around that specific need."

"So there is something to be said for obsessions," she said.

"You pay a price, but I think so. When I was a kid just out of college, I was on an obsessive, single track. I wanted to be part of larger-than-life events. I might even have been a star-crossed patriot. And I achieved it all. But something happened—something went out of me. I think it began that morning in the jungle when Hickey saved me. I realized we had risked our lives in someone else's insane scenario. We were selling dope and running guns to primitive people, asking them to die in a war even we didn't understand. After that, I chased a byline—ran around the world recording terror. I won awards and lost my identity. Nothing touched me. I saw life through a lens. The people I loved got bursts of affection—spurts of attention—Claudia, my brother . . ." Tom shook his head sadly and lit a cigarette.

"Let me have a puff, please."

He held the cigarette to her lips and watched the hot end glow as she inhaled. "Seeing a twin brother die must be like witnessing your own death," she said.

"I tried everything to keep him alive. I wouldn't let him die. I used all my connections to get him unlicensed drugs. I took him to Karolinska Institute in Stockholm, and to the most advanced AIDS treatment center in Paris—and finally to Sloan-Kettering in New York. I wanted time to make up for the lost years and those huge gaps in our relationship. But in a sense, you're right. I was an observer—watching and trying to understand my own death.

"After Jack died, I made an effort with Claudia, another rush of affection. But I couldn't define our relationship. I had emptied myself of purpose, of truth. How the hell could I expect to keep a marriage together? I was using her and the past to keep going. And the irony is that at my lowest point, I had reached the height of professional success. I was totally lost—and famous. People admired me, envied me, looked up to me. And there I was, wandering around in a Kafkaesque nightmare."

"And now?"

"It's different. It's changed. I'm not sure why. Maybe Hickey . . . maybe you . . . maybe those tunnels at Nordhausen. Or . . ." He sighed. "Maybe it's just the shark."

Her arm encircled his neck and she pulled him down and whispered, "This is a moment, Tom. Let's use it. But for both our sakes, don't make too much of it."

The phone rang, startling them. After four rings Erika answered, and listened for a few seconds before saying, "I understand," and hanging up.

"I forgot to tell you," she said. "At some point during our flight to Munich tomorrow, a girlfriend of mine will greet me. A very attractive girl—a well-known fashion model. Her name is Elke Hauser. She will pass a letter to me that I must deliver to someone in Tripoli."

"Who is this Elke Hauser?"

"A Mossad courier and an old friend. Her modeling agency supplies the girls for Kleiser's opium parties."

"Nice touch. But if she's known and a friend, why the cloak-and-dagger stuff on the plane?"

"I've been instructed to take extraordinary precautions. Since I leaked the story of the V-5 rocket test, the Libyan security-control officer has placed all key STS employees under surveillance. I must assume I'm being watched by Hasi's people."

"Now, there's someone I'd like to spend a few minutes with."

"You can't touch him. Hasi has been on Mossad's hit list for years, but even with all their resources, they've been unable to reach him."

"Sometimes conditions change. Everyone makes mistakes."

"Don't even think about it. You have to put your emotions aside. You have to play the neutral, objective journalist. The possibility of a favorable article written by you is our life-insurance policy."

CHAPTER TWENTY-TWO

"You were right about Fräulein Hauser," Tom said. "She was not only attractive, she passed that letter like a magician making a coin disappear."

Erika squeezed Tom's hand and whispered, "Be careful with this driver. I don't think he speaks English, but I'm not sure. I haven't seen him before."

The STS limousine rolled under the Memorial Arch and entered Marienplatz, in the heart of Munich. A light snow was falling and the sidewalk tables had been taken inside the cafés.

Erika tugged at Tom's coat sleeve. "You see that dark three-story building?"

"The beer hall?"

"That's where Hitler delivered his first important political speech in 1923. He harangued a crowd of unemployed middle-class Bavarians and whipped them into a frenzy."

"Speaking of middle-class Supermen, tell me about Walter Diehl."

"He and Mueller are the last of the old-line scientists employed by Kleiser. And like most surviving Nazis, Diehl is angry at the fates; but he's a highly regarded rocket scientist. Just ask NASA, Diehl worked on the Saturn-5."

They crossed the Ludwigsbrücke Bridge, and continued on for three miles before turning into a secondary road that wound its way up to a set of iron-grille gates. Beyond the gates a two-story glass building with an enclosed walkway connected to a hangarlike structure. A parking lot held a scattering of expensive cars and one huge flatbed tractor trailer.

Walter Diehl was a stoop-shouldered balding man in his seventies. His features were delicate, almost feminine, and his nervous eyes darted from object to object. The cut of his ill-fitting dark blue suit belonged to another time. His desk was cluttered, and the office furniture was worn and obsolete. Tom thought everything about Diehl seemed leased— he had the look of a man whose bags were always packed. It was difficult to believe that this shabby relic had been a key player in the original V-2-rocket group at Peenemünde and Nordhausen.

Diehl kissed Erika on both cheeks and shook hands with Lawford.

"I'm pleased that you could come to Munich, Mr. Lawford."

"I wouldn't have missed it."

Diehl offered Tom a cigarette.

"No, thanks. I'm trying to quit."

"I've tried all my life without success."

"At your age, Walter," Erika remarked, "it doesn't matter anymore."

"On the contrary. The older one becomes, the more dearly one embraces life. I don't know if I said that correctly. My English is . . ."

"Your English is excellent, Mr. Diehl," Lawford said.

"Well, I lived for many years in America. I worked for NASA and Fairchild Aviation. One had to learn English." He paused. "Dr. Kleiser tells me you are about to write an in-depth piece about STS."

"Yes."

"Favorable, I hope."

"I'm a journalist, Mr. Diehl, not a propagandist."

"Of course."

"After you show us around, I would appreciate an interview with your colleague, Heinrich Mueller."

"I'm afraid it's not possible. Mueller is on holiday at Innsbruck. Perhaps after you return from Libya we can arrange something. Come. Please. I know you are anxious to see our assembly plant."

Indicating his Nikon, Tom asked, "Is it all right if I take a few pictures?"

"My instructions are very clear," Diehl replied. "You are free to photograph anything you like—and ask any questions you wish."

They followed the old man through a long corridor that paralleled a large room where men and women studied drawing boards and blueprints.

At the end of the hall Diehl opened a steel door and they entered the huge hangar-shaped assembly plant. Overhead tubular fluorescents bathed the vast interior in a harsh bright light.

In the center of the factory were flatbed carriages upon which technicians assembled rocket casings. The carriages rode on steel tracks in precisely the same manner as had the rusted iron relic in the tunnel at Nordhausen. In a separate section, computer specialists monitored their pale green display screens.

The motorized Nikon whirred and clicked as Tom ran off a series of exposures.

Diehl led them through the various stages of assembly to an enclosure where technicians wired color-coded circuitry into the rocket's nose cone.

"There are over one hundred and sixty patents in the V-5 rocket," Diehl explained, "although, I must confess, the basic technology is not dissimilar to that of the old V-2's."

"The technology may be old," Tom observed, "but those nose cones have a deadly look to me."

"They may resemble warheads, but I assure you they are designed for the sole purpose of launching a communication satellite into orbit."

"So there is no military application to the V-5?"

"Absolutely not. The V-5 is liquid-fueled with a mixture

of concentrated nitric acid and ordinary diesel oil. Our launch procedure is long and complex, hardly suited for military purposes."

"Then why all the secrecy?"

"We live in a competitive world. The Soviets are into commercial satellites, so are the French, Japanese, and Americans. We must take certain prudent precautions."

"Why the base in Libya?"

"Money and space. The V-5 can be ground-tested, but sooner or later, as with any missile, it must be fired over a test range. Colonel Qaddafi provides the land and facilities."

"In return for what?"

"For putting Libya in the space-satellite business. Dr. Kleiser has had to overcome many political difficulties."

"Political difficulties . . ." Tom smiled derisively. "You're doing business with the most dangerous and unpredictable dictator in the world."

Diehl's response was calm, immediate, and followed the party line. "We are a consortium of scientists engaged in a commercial enterprise. Our goal is to place a two-ton payload into a geo-orbit of three hundred kilometers. We hope to provide third-world countries with satellite communications at a reasonable cost. Your insinuation of a sinister purpose is totally unfounded."

"Can we have some coffee?" Erika asked, breaking the tension.

The cafeteria was a dark, low-ceilinged room with a small kitchen and a dozen Formica-topped tables. A beefy woman served them coffee.

Diehl lit a cigarette and said, "I have no wish to create a personal problem with you, Mr. Lawford, but it should be obvious that this is not a huge operation. In the course of a year, we assemble perhaps thirty rockets—hardly significant for military purposes."

"That depends on one's definition of military purposes. The V-5 nose cones are in fact no different from warheads capable of carrying a nuclear bomb."

"In matters of exploratory science, all things must be considered possible," Diehl replied curtly. "German technology shocked the world fifty years ago. Our V-2's flew two hundred and fifty miles on target. We developed the world's first ground-to-air heat-seeking missile. We flew the world's first jet fighters. We designed the first avionic wind tunnel. Despite incredible odds and the monumental stupidity of the Nazi hierarchy, we scientists achieved miracles."

"There's no doubt about the superiority of German technology, but it was in large part due to the use of slave labor."

"I think, Mr. Lawford, we are leaving the field of technology."

"Are you denying that these scientific miracles you described were achieved without the use of slave labor?"

"It's a matter of historic record that Nordhausen's workers were recruited from concentration camps and housed at Camp Dora. That recruitment program was initiated by Rudolph and Von Braun, through Himmler's SS section. I was not involved. Neither was Mueller or any current STS executives. We were members of a scientific team assigned to Nordhausen. We carried out our tasks. We were not criminals."

"My father thought he was a criminal," Erika countered.

"Your father's torment was self-inflicted and totally unwarranted. He was politically naive. He never fully understood our situation. In 1943 Nordhausen and the V-2 program represented the last hope to save the German nation. Nothing else mattered. We committed no atrocities. We followed orders. Nothing more!"

"That's bullshit," Tom snapped. "I've seen the film."

"Film? What film?"

"German documentary film that shows you, Mueller, and Rudolph watching a mass hanging at Nordhausen."

Diehl's birdlike eyes narrowed and his face reddened. *"Ich wiegere nicht, diese Unterhaltung weiter zu führen!"*

"Aber der Mann tut ja nur seine pflicht," Erica replied, then turned to Tom and translated. "He said he refuses to continue the conversation. I told him that you were simply doing your job."

"That's right," Tom agreed. "Just following orders. The origins of STS go back in time. These are questions I have to ask. Please don't take them personally, Mr. Diehl."

"My understanding is that you're interested in current STS activities in Libya, not matters that concern the Nazi past."

"To me they're inseparable."

"Not to your government, they weren't," Diehl replied smugly. "Your military experts treated us like royalty. The Pentagon awarded us lucrative contracts and the Department of State welcomed us to America. There was no mention of war crimes. We, the survivors of Peenemünde and Nordhausen, carried out President Kennedy's greatest propaganda coup. We put an American on the moon. We were young men obsessed by the dream of space travel. We were not monsters. As you well know, Mr. Lawford, every war has its atrocities."

Diehl crushed his cigarette out and rose. "My colleague, Mueller, returns tomorrow from his holiday. Perhaps he can show you the Stuttgart engine plant. Now, if you'll excuse me, I must return to my work."

CHAPTER TWENTY-THREE

Heinrich Mueller had decided to stop at Innsbruck on his return from the SS reunion. The alpine resort was only three hours from Munich, and should an emergency arise in the Stuttgart assembly plant, they knew where to reach him.

He had spent a pleasant afternoon at the university with his former colleague Professor Rolf Mannheim. After a relaxed lunch in the faculty dining room, they strolled the grounds and reminisced about the old days. Mannheim recalled a summer holiday at the 1935 Festival of Arts in Innsbruck. In those days, both Mueller and Mannheim had been part of a group of young academicians who joined Hitler's National Socialist movement, and almost sixty years later they still cherished the tenets of the Third Reich. The loss of the war to inferior races could be directly traced to the treachery of international Jewry. The German nation had fought magnificently against incredible odds, and it did not take long for the victors to recognize Germany's sacrifice.

The brutal truth of history had been illuminated in the flames that devoured the Third Reich. Immediately after the war, the Allies embraced and rebuilt Germany. The American President had recently placed a wreath at the Victory Column Memorial in Berlin. The generation of German youth that perished in World War Two had been honored by their former conquerors.

The sky had begun to darken when Mueller left the administration building and crossed the snow-covered campus. His gaunt figure seemed out of place among the students in their designer ski clothes and mirrored sunglasses. He noticed a tall, vivacious girl with thick auburn hair that tumbled over her shoulders, and for a second the flash of her face reminded him of a young woman with whom he had shared a memorable weekend at Innsbruck many years ago.

Turning into Karlsruhestrasse, he marveled at the majestic Alps, whose creamy peaks towered over the village.

The lights of shops suddenly blinked on, and old-fashioned streetlamps glowed softly in the suffused twilight.

Feeling chilled, he entered the Café Winkler and ordered a hot rum toddy. The popular café was crowded with young people. Their skis were stacked along the walls and they snapped their fingers in time to American rock music.

Mueller watched with fascination as a young girl slowly, seductively licked the whipped cream from atop her pastry. He felt a sensual stirring and decided not to return to Shoenfeldhaus. He would instead take Fräulein Beckman to dinner. The attractive STS bookkeeper was on holiday in Innsbruck, and she had, in her way, flirted with him. Yes. Why not? There was no need to be paranoid about one's safety. He would take the tram to Fräulein Beckman's hotel. Why not, indeed? A man must seize the moment—a simple fact that took most people a lifetime to appreciate.

He walked briskly, spurred by a buoyant sense of adventure. His Libyan bodyguards would be upset, but so be it. He was embarrassed to be seen in public with Arab *untermenschen.* The fact that such awesome oil wealth had been endowed upon these filthy Semitic Muslims was, in itself, an abomination. The Libyans could no more protect him than they had poor Brunner. Mueller took supreme comfort in the bulge of the Mauser automatic in his shoulder holster—self-reliance kept a man alive and prosperous.

He passed by the column of St. Anne with her marble halo and crossed the cobblestone plaza to the tram stop and waited patiently amidst a group of boisterous tourists. He noticed a petite woman who seemed lost in an oversize mink coat. Her male companion wore a green Austrian hunting outfit. Amused by the contrasting wardrobes of the couple, Mueller took no notice of the middle-aged blond woman carrying a vinyl tote bag standing a few feet behind him.

Just as the red-and-yellow tram clanged toward them, the blond woman took out a specially honed ice pick and thrust the needle-sharp point into the base of Mueller's spine. He fell from the platform and disappeared under the wheels of the tram.

Penelope heard the screams as she crossed the street and entered a waiting Opel driven by Ben Landau.

CHAPTER TWENTY-FOUR

It was close to midnight when Fritz Kleiser concluded his conversation with Diehl. He had informed Diehl of Mueller's death but had doctored the circumstances, saying that Mueller had lost his footing on an icy curb and fallen into the path of a tram. Kleiser went on to say that while it was a senseless and tragic end to a great man, Mueller's memory would best be served by the successful culmination of their Libyan enterprise; and he, Walter Diehl, would now supervise the launching of the V-5.

Once the shock of the news had worn off, Diehl described his meeting with Lawford. Kleiser assuaged the old man's concerns regarding the American journalist's interest in Nordhausen, and reminded Diehl that what truly counted was Lawford's perception of current STS activities. Kleiser exercised patience and persuasion with Diehl, and by the time he hung up, the old man was determined to carry out his sacred task in the name of all their dead comrades. He would proceed to Libya and make certain the V-5 launch went forward as planned.

Kleiser hung up, poured some brandy, leaned back in his chair, and studied the flames crackling in the huge fireplace. Events were now racing along on a momentum of their own creation. He would have to keep a strong hand on the controls.

Lawford's aggressive attitude with Diehl was reassuring and confirmed the fact that the American was not patronizing STS for some ulterior motive, but rather attacking the story in an objective, professional manner. Anything less from a veteran journalist would be suspect.

Kleiser's thoughts then turned to Mueller. The police had discovered a small hole at the base of Mueller's spine. Mossad. No question. Well, no matter. Time was on his side. The Pakistanis had decided to field-test their bomb and risk the political fallout. Once tested, the warhead would be shipped to Libya. Only a few more weeks remained to flash point.

The console buzzer sounded and Kleiser pressed the intercom button. *"Ja?"*

"Abu Hasi."

The wiry, hawk-faced Libyan entered the vaulted study and placed three black-and-white photos of Erika and an attractive brunette on Kleiser's desk.

"This is the young woman with whom Fräulein Sperling lunched here . . ."—Hasi indicated one of the photos— ". . . at the Europa Restaurant the same day we tested the V-5. And this photo of the two of them strolling through the shopping mall was taken the evening of Brunner's murder. And this, the most recent, shows this same woman arriving in Munich on the flight taken by Fräulein Sperling and Lawford."

"Meaning what?" Kleiser asked with undisguised annoyance.

"In my view, this woman is a courier—for either Mossad or German Intelligence—the BND."

"And how do you arrive at that conclusion?"

"We've identified this woman as Elke Hauser. She was born in Holland. She maintains a residence in Zurich and travels throughout Europe. She is, in our opinion, a courier."

"For whom?"

"As I said, either Mossad or BND."

Kleiser rose and relit his cigar, and in a calm but derisive tone said, "Why not include the CIA, the KGB, the Chinese, the Cubans, and the Bulgarians?" He paused, and his words were cold and clipped. "You disappoint me, Hasi. I know this woman. She happens to be a rather famous fashion model. There is nothing sinister about her. I've been to social affairs with her. Her modeling agency is in my office building. Elke Hauser and Fräulein Sperling attended Hanover University together and happen to be old friends."

"You find nothing suspicious about the coincidence of their meetings?"

"I find your insinuations and surveillance of my key people to be intrusive and insulting. You come here with your absurd conjecture and expect me to give my time and attention to this paranoia?"

Hasi remained silent as Kleiser walked to the huge picture window overlooking the frozen lake.

"You're supposed to be a seasoned professional," Kleiser said, with his back to Hasi. "Alois Brunner was murdered in his home. Farheed Shah and the Swede were murdered in that Paris hotel. And now, Mueller stabbed and thrown under the wheels of a train." He turned and faced Hasi. "So much for your security."

"I was not personally involved with the security of Brunner. I assume responsibility for Paris. I had one of my most reliable officers in charge, but no operation can be totally secure. In the case of Mueller, he left his guards and went off on his own. There is only so much one can do. I must also say that I have never fully agreed with the need for this American journalist. In my view, his presence increases our security problems."

"Your government is planning to incinerate Tel Aviv and Haifa. My company must be in business after that cataclysmic event. Between now and then, the image we project to the world is critical. If handled properly, Lawford becomes an instrument of corporate policy. I might remind you that your leader, my good friend, Colonel Qaddafi, permitted a third-rate American TV journalist to interview him on many sensitive subjects. Lawford's article will camouflage not only STS but also Libya and Pakistan."

"I will admit that I have no reason to suspect Lawford. He's just another presence to deal with. It's Fräulein Sperling who worries me. Someone inside STS leaked the story of the V-5 test flight conducted by Brunner. How many people here in Berlin knew of the results that same day?"

"Perhaps three or four."

"Including Erika Sperling?"

"I may have mentioned it to her."

"And she may have passed that information to Elke Hauser, who in turn passed it to either Mossad or BND. I want your approval to question Fräulein Sperling."

"You'll do nothing of the sort," Kleiser replied firmly. "You answer to Allah, but I answer to the world. Erika Sperling will not be subjected to any interrogation. She remains in place, without a trace of suspicion. I want her to accompany Lawford to Tripoli. Once his article appears in the world press, then, and only then, can you question her."

"It will be too late. We will have been compromised."

"How? By whom? Examine what you've said. A girlfriend of Erika's, a well-known fashion model, is a courier, and Erika Sperling, whom I've known since she was a small child, is a Mossad agent—all because they shared a few social engagements and a plane ride. Did it ever occur to you that perhaps Erika wanted to introduce Lawford to her girlfriend? After all, he's a man, and he's been alone for some time."

"Not quite. He's spent several nights in Fräulein Sperling's apartment."

"Proving only that Lawford is what he purports to be. A professional agent would not become involved with a fellow case officer. To me, your suspicions are founded in syllogistic nonsense. We will do nothing until Lawford files his piece."

"I'm afraid I must insist."

"You're in no position to insist on anything!" Kleiser roared. "You will do precisely what I order you to do. I will not tolerate any further unilateral action from you. Should you disobey me, I will be forced to take the matter up with Colonel Qaddafi. Are you willing to obstruct the launch of the V-5? Is that a risk you're willing to take? Answer me, Hasi!"

The Libyan control officer fell silent. Kleiser had all the cards. Colonel Qaddafi had absolute faith in the German. Kleiser's history had been checked and rechecked by Libyan Intelligence. He was under constant surveillance, and there was no denying his dedication to the Libyan missile program. Kleiser was also trusted by Pakistani Counterintelligence Chief Ayub Murrani. It would be prudent not to challenge him—for the moment.

"My instructions are quite clear," Hasi said. "I am to serve you and ensure your safety. I have no wish to quarrel with you. I will, of course, abide by your decision. You have my word. I will not confront Fräulein Sperling."

"I appreciate your concern with security," Kleiser replied in a conciliatory tone. "Let's hope that in a few weeks the entire matter will be irrelevant and there will be no Mossad and no Israel."

"Allah Inshallah," Hasi intoned, and left.

Kleiser stared at the photograph of the wide-eyed, striking Elke Hauser. She was a fine model, a good businesswoman, and a superb pimp. Her modeling agency had provided him with numerous inventive young girls. It was safe to assume that he was not Fräulein Hauser's only client. She ran a very lucrative but illegal enterprise. She would never involve herself with either the German Federal Police or the BND. Fräulein Hauser's modeling agency was not a cover for intelligence activities; it was a front for illicit sexual transactions.

Hasi's accusations lacked substance and logic. His suspicions were nothing more than the eclectic, flawed reasoning of a fanatical mind. Hasi's skills were exclusive to the acts of torture and murder. Well, for now there could be only one focus of attention—the American journalist's article.

Lawford was, at the moment, inspecting the rocket-engine plant in Stuttgart. Erika said that he had finished taping the first section of his article. The timing of the piece would fall in perfectly. Once Lawford reported that the operational base in Libya was strictly commercial, it would be ludicrous for the Western powers to level suspicion at STS. The entire Middle East could go up in smoke, and he, Kleiser, would be unaffected . . . neutral . . . an innocent bystander.

If Qaddafi had somehow acquired a nuclear warhead and affixed it to the V-5, it was not Kleiser's problem. The supplier was not responsible for the misuse of his product by a client.

Kleiser pressed the intercom button and instructed his secretary to notify Libyan Intelligence that he'd be arriving with the American, Tom Lawford, sometime Thursday.

CHAPTER TWENTY-FIVE

Three thousand miles south of Bombay, and thirty-five hundred miles east of Cape Town, the Pakistani research vessel bobbed and rolled in the vast, empty stretch of the Indian Ocean.

The tall, urbane godfather of the Pakistani bomb, Dr. I. Q. Khan, trained his infrared binoculars toward the horizon. The first rays of dawn lightened the eastern sky, and the outline of the barge and detonation tower were clearly visible. Two destroyers that had towed and anchored the barge to its impact point were now steaming back to their Karachi base at flank speed.

Dr. Jamil Tukhali, the young physicist and former protégé of the late Farheed Shah, stood alongside Khan on the command ship's bridge. Tukhali lowered his binoculars, checked his watch, and said, "Sixteen minutes."

Khan nodded. "One can almost sense the spirit of our martyred colleague Farheed Shah."

"In my view, those X-ray manuals were irrelevant. We should have field-tested months ago."

"Not so simple, my dear Tukhali. A zero-yield lab test

would have concealed the fact that our nuclear arsenal was operational. We now risk detection by American and Soviet satellites. The political fallout can be more dangerous than the radioactive fallout. We have so far managed to maintain the fiction of peaceful nuclear development."

"This must be a great moment for you, sir. A dream of twenty years only minutes away."

"We'll soon see."

Glancing skyward, they saw the flashing red wingtip lights of an Orion C-3 patrol craft equipped with magnetic high-frequency beams that would detonate the bomb.

In the wheelhouse, the captain ordered a speed correction. A radioman operating the ultrahigh-frequency transmitter spoke in hushed tones to the pilot of the circling Orion. Hunched over the phosphorescent screen, the radar man watched the green line as it constantly swept a fifty-mile radius. A sonar man transmitted underwater beams, guarding against the possibility of prowling submarines.

Addressing the radioman, Dr. Khan said, "Direct the pilot to flash point and maintain an altitude of ten thousand feet."

The radar man transmitted the message, and the pilot requested permission to speak to Dr. Khan.

"Yes, Captain," Khan said.

"Will we be safe at an altitude of only ten thousand feet?"

"We do not intend to blow up the Indian Ocean," Khan replied. "This is merely a detonator. Our explosion will produce a significant flash of light, but less than .02 kilotons of blast power. The radiation will be minor, and concussion rings will be lateral, not vertical. Do not be fearful, Captain. Be joyous. Your cameras are about to record the birth of the Islamic bomb." Khan paused. "Let's time-check. I have seven minutes, thirty seconds to detonation."

"Check," the pilot replied, and banked sharply, heading toward the distant barge.

The ship's captain said, "The American KH-11 satellite passed this latitude and longitude thirty-five minutes ago."

"One can never be certain," Khan cautioned. "The orbital paths of these satellites are often changed. But at this particular position there are several nations for the superpowers to blame. We have a certain plausible deniability. Let's devote our minds, our hearts, to silent prayer."

After a moment, the pilot's voice crackled over the radio. "Two minutes to flash point."

Stepping out onto the flying bridge, Khan and Tukhali trained their flash-filtered binoculars toward the distant outline of the barge.

"One minute!" The pilot's amplified voice boomed from exterior speakers.

"Colonel Qaddafi will soon have his warheads," Tukhali remarked. "Curious that it fell to him to liberate the Arab nations."

"He financed us, my boy," Dr. Khan replied. "Let him have the glory."

"Fifteen seconds!" The pilot's voice carried ominously across the bridge.

Inside the wheelhouse, the technicians fitted infrared dark-lensed glasses to their eyes and stepped out onto the flying bridge.

"Flash point!" the pilot's voice exclaimed. "All cameras go! All telemetry go! Five, four, three. Frequency beam activated. Two, one, zero!"

A great blinding yellow flash lit up the sea from horizon to horizon and transformed itself into a fiery red circle. Like a sudden sunrise it glowed brilliantly, then dimmed and brightened again for a few seconds before growing evanescent and dying.

Sounding like rolling thunder, the concussion ring swept across the water and flung the men against the wheelhouse.

Despite the searing, wind-whipped shock waves, Khan and Tukhali embraced. The captain opened a bottle of foaming champagne. "Allah will forgive us this transgression." He smiled and each man drank from the bottle.

"Gentlemen, Pakistan is a superpower," Khan said joyously. "We have fulfilled our sacred task."

"May God grant Farheed Shah his place of honor in Paradise," Tukhali replied with reverence. But the physicist was already thinking how and when he would inform Salim Bashira. The successful test meant that the warhead would be shipped to Libya on, or during the week of, March 13, when the Kahuta reactor was shut down.

CHAPTER TWENTY-SIX

The brilliant flash of light eluded the orbiting KH-11, the most sophisticated of all American spy satellites. Ironically, the detonation was detected by an aging, obsolete Vela satellite whose infrared sensors recorded the intensity of the light.

Technicians at Edwards Air Force Base analyzed the Vela's telemetry and determined that a low-yield nuclear explosion had occurred in the southern reaches of the Indian Ocean.

Secretary of State Harold Lukens was awakened, and immediately notified the President. An emergency meeting was hastily convened in the crisis room at the National Security Agency in Fort Meade, Maryland.

The men seated around the conference table included: Chief of Staff General Ray Martens; CIA Director Admiral Clarke Dwinell; Secretary of Defense Walter Gilford; and the director of nuclear research at Los Alamos, Dr. Carlton Summers.

Secretary of State Lukens called the meeting to order and in precise, measured words addressed the group. "Quantitative analysis pinpoints the blast area to be in the Indian Ocean, four hundred nautical miles south of the Prince Edward chain and some three thousand nautical miles east of Cape Town. The President is standing by waiting for our conclusions. The Soviets, the Chinese, the Indians, and our NATO allies are conducting individual analyses based on our initial findings. The explosion has rippled across the world, and the geopolitical ramifications are predictably obvious. The Indians have already officially accused Pakistan. We expect the Soviets to follow at any moment."

"Well, the sons of bitches asked for it," Chief of Staff Martens said.

"Let's not rush to judgment," Lukens cautioned. "We can't rule out South Africa or Israel."

Defense Secretary Gilford shook his head. "The Israelis have long ago achieved a laser-lab, zero-yield test. The South Africans would not bother towing a barge thousands of miles into the Indian Ocean when they have the emptiness of the Kalahari Desert in which to conduct an underground test. Everything points to Pakistan."

"Let's not be precipitous," Lukens warned again. "Pakistan's an ally of sorts on the subcontinent. We have to do what we can to protect them politically."

Admiral Dwinell then spoke in a cold, officious voice. "We're not here to engage in a geopolitical discussion. We're here to determine who set this thing off, and I have to agree with General Martens. We know Pakistan has been developing a nuclear-weapons capability since 1972. The Kahuta center was financed by Qaddafi. All of you, with the exception of Dr. Summers, are aware of the nuclear alliance between Libya and Pakistan. Several weeks ago, the director of Kahuta, Farheed Shah, and a Swedish businessman, Olaf Nillsen, were shot to death in Paris and their hotel suite destroyed. French Intelligence agents identified bits and pieces of the debris as remnants of technical manuals for Flash X-ray machines."

"Meaning what?" Lukens asked.

"I'll let Dr. Summers explain."

The tall, laconic nuclear physicist spoke calmly and clinically, as if diagnosing an illness. "The loss of those X-ray manuals made it impossible for the Pakistanis to

conduct a nuclear-detonation test in laboratory conditions.
It requires a very sophisticated sequence of critical elements
to set off the chain reaction inside a warhead. The X-ray
machines photograph that process in the laboratory. Without the Flash machine, you have to conduct an open field
detonation. The Pakistanis were obviously forced into just
such a test. The risk of detection was minimized by the
choice of location, but given all the facts, I agree with the
Admiral—Pakistan is the logical suspect."

Lukens rubbed his hand wearily across his eyes. "Christ,
this will create a hellish situation for the President. How can
we ask Congress for billions in Pakistani aid when they're
testing the bomb?"

There was a momentary silence, broken by Secretary of
Defense Gilford. "We've received reports of Soviet Echo
II-class submarines in the general area. Suppose they had a
nuclear accident—an explosion at sea?"

"An accident on a nuclear-powered submarine would
generate a meltdown, not a nuclear explosion," Dr. Summers explained. "And if that were the case, our SR-71 spy
plane and surface vessels would have detected a huge
radioactive mess out there."

"Could the Vela's sensors have malfunctioned?" Lukens
asked. "After all, that satellite has been up there a long time,
and its equipment isn't nearly as sophisticated as the
KH-11."

Admiral Dwinell shook his head. "The Vela may be
getting old, but it's never missed. Its sensors have correctly
identified thirty-five nuclear explosions."

"Well, I suppose we've got to face it." Lukens sighed. "I'll
tell the President that our collective opinion clearly points
to Pakistan, but we're still examining the data, and it may
require weeks or even months to arrive at any definitive
conclusions."

"Wait a minute," Chief of Staff Martens said, turning to
Dr. Summers. "Could the flash of light have been the result
of a natural phenomenon—an undersea volcano?"

Summers shook his head. "No single natural event can
simulate the intensity and instantaneous burst of light
recorded by the Vela's sensors. Besides, the shock waves and
radiation are very revealing. The usual nuclear test equals

ten kilotons of explosive energy. Hiroshima was twenty kilotons. This test yielded less than one kiloton. It's a telltale signature of a fusion trigger. The bomb makers wanted to be certain they've mastered the detonation device before assembling warheads."

"I can tell you, gentlemen," the Admiral said, "that our information indicates Pakistan was only a screwdriver away from assembling an array of nuclear warheads."

"But it's our understanding they have no missile-delivery systems," Defense Secretary Gilford replied.

"That's not true," Martens disagreed. "We've sold them two hundred F-16's with bomb racks capable of transporting a nuclear bomb."

"But the F-16's range is limited," Gilford persisted. "A nuclear-armed Pakistan is a threat only to India."

"Or the Soviet Union," Martens added.

"All right," Lukens said, "but to the best of our knowledge, the Pakistanis do not have ICBM's."

"No—but Qaddafi does," the Admiral noted ominously.

A hush fell across the table as the men stared at Admiral Dwinell, who proceeded to relate the details of the STS operation in Libya.

"Let me get this straight, Clarke," General Martens said. "You're telling us that Pakistan will provide nuclear warheads to Qaddafi, and those warheads will be fitted to the V-5 ICBM's."

"That's right."

There was a brief silence, broken by Dr. Summers. "Since I have nothing to contribute in the political arena," the physicist said, getting to his feet, "I'm sure you won't object if I go back to the hotel and get some sleep. I'm dog-tired. I will, of course, stay in Washington until additional reports come in from our SR-71."

"Thank you, Doctor," Lukens said. "It was kind of you to come on such short notice."

The Admiral waited for the door to close before addressing the group. "All of you had better be aware that the Israelis will not be fooled by any evasiveness on our part. We can, for public consumption, cast about for villains: South Africa, North Korea, Brazil, or even Argentina. Almost anyone could tow a barge into the deep southern reaches of the Indian Ocean and conduct a low-yield test. But the Israelis will not be misled. They have an agent inside Kahuta and have penetrated Pakistan Intelligence. I have reason to believe that agents of Mossad took out Farheed Shah and Nillsen in Paris."

"Are you suggesting that Israel is planning to attack Kahuta?" Lukens asked.

"They lack the technical capability. Kahuta is over five thousand miles round-trip from Tel Aviv. But anything or any place can be sabotaged. I'm sure you remember the munitions depot in Islamabad that was blown up in eighty-eight, and Islamabad is only twenty-five kilometers from Kahuta."

"But, Clarke," Defense Secretary Gilford interjected, "you assured us that you've planted an agent inside Mossad—a man who is in a position to alert us to any Israeli plans to strike at Kahuta. I assume that situation is still viable."

"We have a man in Berlin who has penetrated Mossad. But the agent and the circumstances are tenuous."

"That's double-speak," Lukens said testily.

"Not at all, Harold. Our man in Berlin is not a seasoned field agent. He's a deep-cover operative, and by definition, seldom used. However, he had, in my view, the proper credentials and motivation to carry out this operation. But in all candor, he may not succeed—or survive. He's largely dependent on his own intuitive talents and those of a Mossad operative."

"Forgive me, Admiral, but I sense a little tap-dancing here. Exactly what is it you're telling us?"

"I'm advising you not to take the Israelis for granted. We do have considerable political clout with them, but when their existence is threatened, there is no limit to what they will do in order to survive. They will employ any and all weapons at their command. You can count on it." The Admiral paused. "If I were you, Harold, I would prepare the President for a firestorm, a possible nuclear holocaust that could engulf all of the Middle East and the subcontinent of Asia. We're standing at the edge of a nuclear abyss."

BOOK II

PILLARS OF FIRE

CHAPTER TWENTY-SEVEN

Wishing his wife would stop baking, Zev Berger brushed crumbs of honey cake from his desktop. The woman was not a baker. She was an accomplished pianist, but she was definitely not a baker. Berger lit his first cigarette of the morning and offered a glass of tea to Narda.

She shook her head. "No, thanks."

Berger dipped a sugar cube in his tea glass and sucked the cube. "So, my beauty, how go things? I haven't seen you since Paris."

"Paris was cold."

"Yes, I imagine it was."

"I shot a young Libyan agent. He was not much older than a boy. I shot him the moment he smiled at me." She bit her lower lip. "Paris was very cold."

Berger stared at her while a tragic thought flashed in his mind: *What have we done to our children?*

"You're certain about the tea?" he asked hoarsely.

She nodded and tossed her long, gleaming hair.

"I have news from Bashira. You better take some notes."

Narda took a pen and notepad out of her handbag and propped the pad on her knee.

Berger rose and paced as he spoke. "The Pakistani nuclear test has caused the Indian government to warm up their relationship with us. They have assigned Pandit Sinde to work with Bashira. The two will meet in or near Karachi in a matter of days. The ship Dado requires will be purchased by Sinde's Indian agent in Amsterdam. Dado must arrange for a crew and a dry-dock berth at Eilat. Time is running out and—"

"Wait!" Narda interrupted. "Slow down. I'm not a god-damn secretary!"

Surprised at her angry outburst, Berger asked, "What's wrong?"

"I'm sorry. I'll . . . I'm tired."

Berger felt a flood of sympathy for her. Narda had performed clandestine missions that carried her to the brink of human endurance and yet she could not make sense out of her personal life. She was hopelessly in love with Dado, but the General would never abandon Avital.

Holding the pen poised over the pad, she said again, "I'm sorry. Go ahead."

"Bashira has determined that Kahuta's reactor will be shut down between March 13 and March 21 for spent fuel rods to be replaced."

"That's only two weeks off," she replied nervously. "What of the interior Kahuta photographs?"

"Bashira is aware of the urgency, and will do his best, but I can't pressure him. Pakistani security is on full alert. That's all I have."

She dropped the tablet in her bag and uncrossed her legs.

"Oh . . . there is one other item," Berger added. "Tell Dado that Sheik Oweidi's letter has been delivered to Erika."

"I'm worried about her," Narda said. "The closer she and Lawford get to Libya, the greater the risks."

"Even if Kleiser suspects her, he will not move against her until Lawford has filed his story. If anything happens to Erika, Kleiser loses Lawford."

"She must be protected," Narda insisted.

Berger pushed his glasses atop his head and nodded. "Leave it with me."

"Thank you, Zev." She paused. "By the way, Dado wanted me to congratulate you on Mueller's accident."

"He was careless and we were lucky." Berger came around the desk and took her arm. "Take a weekend. Go down to Eilat for a few days. Get some sun. Swim."

Narda walked to the grimy window and, as if to herself, asked, "With whom shall I swim?"

After she left, Berger sat at his desk, overwhelmed by the same grievous thought: What have we done to our children? We've stolen their youth and made them blind to beauty. We've become a nation of paratroopers and soothsayers clinging to ancient myths. Our pilots see African lions in the desert. We've lost our way, trying to cope with the madness of eternal hostility.

He sighed, thinking his own generation had long since surrendered their youthful idealism. They could only hope to grow old and suffer the death of romance. But the children bore the tragedy of the failed dream. And now it was too late for recriminations, too late for second-guessing. There was only one choice left—to survive at any price.

The General entered the old quarter of East Jerusalem through the Damascus Gate. The helicopter had whisked him from naval headquarters in Haifa to Jerusalem. He had been either at sea or in the air since four A.M. He had worked tirelessly since the Pakistani bomb test and had accelerated both operations: the Libyan strike and the assault against Kahuta.

Dado crossed the Street of Chain and entered the Mea Shearim Orthodox quarter. Two soldiers in their purple berets followed him at the usual twenty-five paces—one man on each side of the narrow street, their fingers curled around the triggers of their automatic rifles, their eyes tracing windows and rooftops. He glanced back at them and thought: Good boys. Brave boys. His boys. The elite. The best. Dani, too, had been the best—and the thousands who had been killed in the endless wars, they too were the best. All the technological brilliance in all the laboratories and computer rooms could not replace the value of a single soldier.

The winter sunshine warmed him and he unzipped his parka and rolled up his shirt sleeves. The small purple numbers on his forearm triggered the recurring image of his darkest dreams. It was a face . . . a woman's face, with the same color eyes and hair as his own. Was he subconsciously trying to visualize his mother? Or perhaps a sister? What did it matter now? Dreams were like smoke. Chimney smoke.

Across the street, the temple doors opened. The afternoon services had concluded and the faithful in their black suits and black fur hats poured out into the bright sunshine. The women followed, wearing their ankle-length cloaks with long sleeves.

Avital came out, and for a moment stood motionless in the sunlight, trying to adjust her eyes to the light. Dado shook his head sadly, remembering the vivacious beauty, now pale and wan, but still bearing the face of their fallen son. Crossing the street, he shoved his way through a gaggle of Zealots and took her gently by the arm.

"Have you been waiting long?" she asked.

"No."

"The holy man and his children have gone to Ashkelon. Come home with me. I'll make some lunch for you."

She placed an omelet and slices of freshly baked bread in front of him and poured two glasses of milk. They ate in silence for a moment before she said, "I went to the prophet of Kabala. He saw a vision of you running with the Torah. The holy scrolls were on fire. Jerusalem was burning, but you saved the scrolls. The prophet saw it very clearly."

"There are no prophets, Avital."

"Elijah will appear and raise all the dead children."

"Elijah will not appear. No one will rise. Not Dani. Not anyone."

"No. No . . . It's written, Dado. The Messiah will come and open the gates of Paradise."

"The Messiah will come when he's no longer needed."

"You mustn't carry your anger to God. Only love, Dado

. . . only love . . . and think of it—you're chosen, blessed. You will save the city and the holy scrolls. The prophet has seen the vision."

He slammed his fist on the table and his eyes blazed. "The prophet is a fake! A false prophet! I saw a soldier run from that synagogue in 1948 with burning scrolls. You knew that and you probably mentioned it to the mystic."

"Elijah will bless Israel, and the dead children will rise. It is written, Dado. It is—"

He pulled her to her feet and hugged her. "I want you to leave this place."

Her eyes were wide and shining with an inner fervor. "Will you go with me to the temple?"

"No."

"You must, Dado. One day you must—or the scrolls will burn."

"Yes. I know," he said gently, as if humoring a child.

"I love you," she said. "I pray for your soul and Dani's. I pray for your redemption."

He took her face in his hands and kissed her.

Huge waves exploded against the breakwater, hurling geysers of sea spray over the embankment.

They were seated in the enclosed terrace of the Jaffa restaurant. A few soldiers and some neighborhood families were enjoying platters of grilled St. Peter's fish caught daily in the Sea of Galilee.

The waiter served appetizers of fried sardines and smoked cod, then opened a second bottle of Ashkelon wine and refilled their glasses.

"Why does he bring these goddamn sardines?" Narda asked testily.

"It's a custom." Dado shrugged. "You don't have to eat them."

"Where the hell is Zichroni?"

"The man's working day and night. He'll be here. You're drinking too much."

"You look awful, Dado."

"You sound like Berger. He says I don't look well."

"And you always say it's the light," she replied, pouring some more wine.

179

"Easy with the wine, Narda."

"Why? I feel like drinking. Do I need your permission to drink?"

"What the hell is wrong with you?"

"Nothing. Nothing is wrong."

Far out at sea, they noticed the running lights of patrol boats crisscrossing the Tel Aviv–Jaffa coastline, guarding against seaborne terrorist infiltrators.

"What is it?" Dado asked.

"I was thinking of that Libyan. He smiled just before I shot him."

"What the hell does it matter? He was there to protect Farheed Shah."

"I know," she sighed. "Still, he was young and he smiled."

She twirled the stem of the glass and crushed the cigarette out. "You really should go with Avital to the temple. What are you afraid of? You once defended that same temple."

"It was a strongpoint—not a temple."

"What about the prophecy?"

"What about it?"

"Aren't you curious? I mean the city burning. You running with the Torah. That's quite a vision."

"It's not a vision. Avital knows that incident very well. She probably mentioned it to the prophet. It was in forty-eight. The soldier ran out of the temple with a Torah that was in flames."

"What happened to him?"

"He was shot dead. I tried to pull his body out of the way of a Jordanian tank. A column of armor had broken through our lines. A few hours later the rabbi negotiated the surrender of the Jewish Quarter. If the soldier had let the Torah burn, he'd be alive."

"To these Orthodox people the Torah is more important than life."

"That's the mystery. This soldier was not Orthodox. He was not religious. He was a survivor of the Treblinka uprising. He was tough. Very tough. He went up from the basement and saw the scrolls burning. He managed to carry them to the Damascus Gate before he fell."

"But isn't it curious that the prophet saw this vision, and told Avital it was you who carried the scrolls?"

"These mystics take advantage of disturbed minds. They should be forbidden to practice their witchcraft."

"It gives Avital comfort. Why get upset?"

"She belongs in therapy."

"You can say that about the whole country."

Dado's eyes brightened as he saw a thin, sad-eyed man coming toward him.

Adam Zichroni sat down alongside Narda and poured himself a glass of wine. He took a sip and said, "Ah . . . that's a fine wine."

"It's awful," Narda blurted.

"She prefers foreign wine," Dado said quickly.

"What do you know about things that I prefer?"

"She's slightly drunk."

"I'm becoming drunk. And it's none of your fucking business."

Zichroni shifted nervously in his chair.

"Excuse me," Narda said, and rose. "I've got to relieve myself of this camel piss they call wine."

They watched her stride off toward the rest rooms.

"What's wrong with her?" Zichroni asked.

"She had to kill a Libyan assassin. He was young, and he smiled."

"She's burning out, Dado."

"She's a strong girl. She'll be all right. Now, tell me, how does it go?"

"Air Force Chief Carmil and Matty's sea commandos and our own boys under Barzani's command are in perfect concert on the Libyan raid. Red Desert will consist of five wing groups, one of which will take out the desert launch site; obviously the target data is critical."

"We'll have it."

Zichroni lit a cigarette and swallowed some wine. "What's our time frame?"

"Between March 13 and 21. We have nine days from which to choose. Both attacks: Libya and Pakistan must be close together."

"What is the code name for the Kahuta strike?"

"There is none—we're still not certain that it can be done. Everything depends on accurate intelligence and Yuval Newman's genius."

"And the ship?"

"In process."

"Can we prepare to receive it?"

Dado nodded. "Professor Newman will personally select the specialists. But you can reserve a berth at Eilat to handle a twenty-thousand-ton freighter."

"The Jordanians keep watch on Eilat."

"Let them watch. The work will be done inside the aft hold."

"Has Berger confirmed the Pakistani test?"

"One of his agents witnessed the detonation."

"And Newman?"

"Working around the clock with his best people."

Narda was back and Zichroni rose.

"Sit down, please," she said.

"I have to leave," Zichroni replied, and kissed her cheek.

"Aren't you going to eat?" Dado asked.

"At home. I haven't seen my son in two weeks. You don't look well, Dado."

"It's the light," Narda said.

The moonlight streaked through the shutters and the boom of crashing waves echoed in the bedroom. Narda's arm was flung across Dado's shoulder and she could hear the rise and fall of his breathing. She had felt him stirring from time to time, but now his restlessness was accompanied by low moans, and he thrashed suddenly and bolted upright, hands flailing as if trying to grab something that had disappeared. His eyes were wide open, and beads of sweat oozed out of his forehead. It took a moment for him to catch his breath.

"I saw a face. A woman's face. She spoke to me in German, but I couldn't hear her. We were standing in a great crowd of people—men, women, children, infants, cats, dogs, suitcases. There was a sound of a train coming. And clouds of steam. And the people moved. There were screams. The woman's hand slipped away from mine, and she disappeared into the steam. The screams died. I was in a warehouse full of shoes, piles of shoes and stacks of human hair, and dolls. The door opened and a dark figure in an SS uniform was silhouetted in a blinding light. It was the Oven

Commander. I was the only one left, and he had come for me. But his face . . ." Dado's chest heaved as he sighed. "His face was the face of the dead soldier who saved the scrolls. Blood-tears came out of his eyes and ran down his cheeks. He held his hand out to me. Then everything burst into flames—the shoes, the hair, the dolls—and we stood in the center of the flames, and the screams began again: they were very close."

Narda put her arms around him and felt the cold sweat coming out of his pores. "It's nothing—images out of the past. It's all over."

"It's not over," he said quietly. "It will never be over."

CHAPTER TWENTY-EIGHT

The octagon-shaped glass-paneled restaurant sat on a bluff above the jutting sandspit at Gadani Beach. Salim Bashira hosted lunch for his Indian colleague Pandit Sinde. Sinde was a coffee-colored, slight man with bony, chiseled features. The diminutive Indian was an experienced shipping agent and a ranking officer of India's Central Bureau of Intelligence.

The men were eating a savory dish of shrimp and crab, sautéed in mustard oil, spiced with garlic and hot chilies.

Gadani was twenty-five miles east of Pakistan's port city of Karachi, and although blessed with a wide powdery beach, it was off limits to swimmers and sun worshipers. The sandspit served as a graveyard for oceangoing vessels and constituted a unique pig-iron mine for the blast furnaces of nearby state-owned steel mills. The seaside restaurant was crowded with marine engineers and plant managers from the Gadani steel mill.

Pandit Sinde had heard of Gadani, but nothing had prepared him for the sight he beheld. A twenty-thousand-ton freighter was beached on the sandspit, and held fast by steel cables attached to a winch. Like a sad, defenseless Goliath, the ship tilted to its port side as swarms of half-naked workers armed with cutting torches, sledgehammers, bolt cutters, screwdrivers, and crowbars swarmed over her, tearing her apart piece by piece. The Pathan tribesmen worked by hand, dissecting the huge propellers and crankshaft, draining oil from her engines and lifeboats, removing compasses, chairs, toilets, ornaments, railings, pipes, and cables.

"In six days there will be no sign of the ship," Bashira said, touching a napkin to his lips. "Everything is devoured."

Sinde saw the orange spray of sparks from blowtorches as welders, standing high up on the crane cable, cut a seam in the superstructure. A large hook was then fitted into the seam, and the crane cable grew taut. The cracking, wrenching sound of the hull being pulled apart pierced the open windows of the restaurant. Ragtag workers standing on the ship's railing leapt off, falling twenty feet down to the muddy bank, as a huge section of superstructure began to give way.

"My God . . ." Sinde whispered. "Those men. What can it be worth to do that work?"

"Sometimes their lives. They're Pathan tribesmen from the north. They travel a thousand miles to earn twenty dollars a week, working twelve-hour days. Many are crippled and some killed." Bashira shrugged. "A cable snaps or a chunk of iron comes loose. Every piece of metal is fed into the steel mills up the road. One can sit here at lunch and see ships literally disappear."

"But where is the profit?"

"A few investors buy an outdated ship or perhaps a fairly new ship that's been damaged. If it can limp into Gadani, an experienced harbor pilot using the tide, a bit of power, and considerable skill will place the ship upright on that sandspit. A twenty-year-old ship can be purchased for roughly a hundred dollars a ton. It costs next to nothing to demolish the ship, and the salvage price is three hundred dollars a ton—a profit of more than two hundred percent."

"Where do those worker-ants live?"

"Just over that rise is a collection of mud huts, driftwood, and cardboard boxes."

The waiter served a dessert of soft cheese dipped in sugar syrup, and small cups of thick black coffee spiced with cinnamon.

Once the waiter left, Bashira removed his green-tinted glasses and spoke in a hushed tone as he nonchalantly cleaned the lenses. "Our friends require photographs of Kahuta from the Soviet Soyuz-TM-6. The satellite's cameras provide a zero-resolution view of the Kahuta complex. And since India's relations with the Soviets are very close, this request should not be difficult to achieve."

"Consider it done," Sinde quietly replied. "How and to whom do I deliver the pictures?"

"When will you have them?"

"A day or two."

"Phone me from Moscow," Bashira said, and signaled the waiter for a check. "I don't mean to rush, but I have an appointment in Karachi and you have a three-o'clock plane to catch."

"Why did we come way out here for lunch?"

"Because I require a ship exactly like that beached whale out there."

"When?"

"The ship must sail in forty-eight hours for Eilat, Israel."

Seated alongside his chauffeur-bodyguard, Bashira peered out of the Jaguar's tinted window at the squalor of downtown Karachi. The streets were filthy and jammed with a raucous mixture of camel and donkey carts, Toyotas, and buses belching foul clouds of diesel fumes. The drivers relied on their horns, not brakes. Traffic lights were ignored and pedestrians crossed the streets at their own peril. Beggars, pimps, and drug dealers openly worked the corners. The city had been abandoned by the police and was governed by drug barons and the fanatical Muslim Brotherhood.

Karachi was a teeming metropolis without the basic amenities of civilized life. Garbage piled high in the alleys, raw sewage fouled the gutters, power failed, and water ran out. Parks and playgrounds were controlled by thugs. The very rich lived in the elegant seaside suburb of Clifton, and hired their own police, and provided their own power and water and garbage collectors. Bashira thought that the nation's capital of Islamabad, a thousand miles to the north, might as well have been on the moon. Karachi survived on opium and rage.

The Jaguar turned into the roundabout at the Farroq Hotel just off Zaibun-Nisa Road. Bashira tipped the doorman generously, but nevertheless ordered his chauffeur to remain with the car.

Walking deliberately, Bashira ignored the cries of beggars and peddlers and the outstretched hands of half-naked children. He shook his head sadly, thinking of the military's puppet president, Ghazi, and his pledge to revitalize the nation's economy. That pompous strutting rooster had armed the country to the teeth and cleverly played the Americans, who supplied an endless stream of sophisticated weaponry. If not for the opium trade and the continued financial support of Qaddafi, the country would be bankrupt. President Ghazi and his military patrons continued to pour hundreds of millions of dollars into the Kahuta nuclear facility while the people were being driven mad by poverty and hopelessness. The citizens of Pakistan were no different from those of India, the Philippines, Honduras, or Ethiopia. The superpowers pumped money and arms into the hands of petty racketeers, who governed while the people starved. Time was running out, and no one was listening.

The Kongori Café was dark and cavernous. Clouds of incense drifted up into gleaming brass lamps, and Oriental rugs were spread over the floor. Opium was smoked openly, and one could obtain alcoholic beverages. Since the Kongori was jointly owned by an Army general and a drug overlord, no one was anxious to disturb its tranquillity.

Weaving his way through the semidarkness, Bashira sat down opposite Dr. Tukhali and signaled the red-fezzed waiter, who took his order for Bell's Scotch. Glancing around cautiously, Bashira handed the young physicist a deposit slip from the secret bank account in Luxembourg.

"Your balance is impressive. My friends were pleased

with your information regarding the reactor shutdown. You're fast becoming a rich young man."

"The money is not for me."

"Yes. Yes. I know . . . the Cause."

"There will be civil war," Tukhali said gravely.

"Of that, my boy, I have no doubts. One can smell revolution in the streets."

Bashira leaned over the table. "My friends require photographs of Kahuta's infrastructure. Something to do with pressure per square inch of floor-level dividers."

"Pictures are not possible. The security is very tight since Director Shah was killed."

"Scale drawings will do."

Tukhali nodded. "I can take care of that. I can reduce the drawings to microfilm, but I'll need a special camera."

"You'll have it."

The waiter served a tall Scotch and soda and left. "To you, my boy," Bashira toasted.

Sipping his palm wine, Tukhali scanned the vast café, trying to penetrate the gloom. Satisfied that Bashira had not been followed, he leaned over the table and quietly said, "It's obvious that whatever your friends have in mind for Kahuta will take place between March 13 and 21, when the reactor vessel is cold. I want you to get me out."

Bashira knew it wasn't just his personal jeopardy that concerned Tukhali; it was the growing nest egg in the Luxembourg account. The young physicist wanted to lay his hands on the money.

"I wish to go to America until the time is right for my return to Pakistan," Tukhali said.

"I understand, and I guarantee a payment of one hundred thousand dollars upon delivery of those Kahuta specifications."

"The drawings will cost you a quarter of a million."

Bashira was not surprised by the demand, but rather by its bluntness. Tukhali's greed had heretofore been cloaked in revolutionary rhetoric.

"All right. I'll see to the money. But you must deliver quickly. We have only two weeks left in which to prepare."

CHAPTER TWENTY-NINE

The gleaming Lear jet left Italian airspace south of Ischia and descended to fifteen thousand feet over the Mediterranean on the last leg of its flight to Tripoli. Visiting the flight deck, Erika watched intently as the copilot punched a new course into the mini-computer and the plane automatically banked southwest.

Inside the luxuriously furnished cabin, Tom Lawford and Fritz Kleiser were seated opposite each other—Kleiser on the phone, and Tom busy revising his handwritten notes.

After a moment, Kleiser wound up his phone conversation and smiled, indicating Tom's notes. "You seem to be well into it."

"Just refining the structure."

"Where do you propose to begin the article?"

"Nordhausen."

"Ah—the past. What is it about the past that fascinates writers?"

"It's not a matter of fascination. Nordhausen seems a logical place to start."

"Well, you're the expert. When do you plan to submit the story?"

"I'll finish in Berlin and file in Rome."

Kleiser seemed surprised. "Rome? Why Rome?"

"Rome's AP bureau chief, Marco Bonini, hired me to write this piece."

"Yes—of course, Bonini. He was the man who originally contacted me about this proposed article."

"He's also a good friend," Tom added, "and all things being equal, we may get a Sunday-feature pickup in Europe and North America."

"Sounds impressive."

"You can't buy that kind of space."

In reality, the trip to Rome had nothing to do with the bureau chief or the article. Berger had advised him to invent an excuse that would logically permit his leaving Berlin for Rome.

"When will you be going?" Kleiser asked.

"I would guess the day after I return to Berlin."

Lawford gathered his notes and placed them in a manila folder. He then took out his Nikon and asked Kleiser to pose as if speaking on the phone. Positioning himself toward the aft section, and using a wide-angle lens, he ran off eight exposures.

As he stored the camera, Tom said, "Catching you in this environment makes a hell of an interesting shot. It's the kind of photograph editors feed on."

"Ah," Kleiser said, "wait until you see the launch site. The desert alone is a photographer's dream—desolate, but magnificent."

Erika came down the aisle and joined them. "Did either of you notice how smooth our descent has been?" She smiled and buckled her seat belt. "I was at the controls."

"You see," Kleiser told Tom, "this is a woman of many talents. I'd be lost without her."

The plane banked sharply and a beam of sunlight struck Kleiser's eyes. He pulled the window shade down and said, "You can see the coast of Libya."

Glancing out the oval window, Tom saw the dark curving smudge of coastline.

"By this time tomorrow," Kleiser said, "you'll have seen the launch site."

The Lear jet's wheels kissed the runway and its twin engines screamed in protest as they were thrust into reverse. The sleek aircraft slowed, swung sharply right, and taxied toward a maintenance man beckoning to them with upraised arms. Close by, a uniformed chauffeur lounged against a black Citroën, and two Libyan Army officers of the Al Mathaba Intelligence Unit stood beside a sand-colored Mercedes.

Kleiser collected his personal items and addressed Tom. "The driver will take you to the hotel. You're free to shop, sightsee, whatever you wish. Tomorrow morning at five-forty-five you must be ready to leave the hotel. I won't be joining you for dinner, but Erika knows the city and speaks fluent Arabic. She'll take good care of you."

Peering out the Citroën's windows, they saw a flotilla of tankers and freighters anchored in Tripoli harbor waiting for berths. And in the distance, to the west, orange flames flared from the stacks of petrochemical refineries and the long arms of construction cranes towered over unfinished seaside skyscrapers.

The broad two-lane highway ended abruptly in a traffic circle that funneled into single-lane spokes. The chauffeur said something in Arabic and Erika answered him.

"He says the highway is like Libya," she explained. "Incomplete."

Traversing the traffic circle, they found themselves hopelessly stuck behind a dilapidated truck belching black clouds of exhaust fumes.

She sighed. "I hate this city."

"How well do you know it?"

"Well enough. I've played tour guide to some of Kleiser's associates. By the way, be careful at the hotel. The rooms are bugged, and the hotel employees are members of the Anti-Imperialist Central Committee and report to the secret police."

* * *

They passed truckloads of hollow-eyed, unshaven soldiers and entered the old city at Al Mamun Street. Long lines of women, variously dressed in jeans and robes, queued up at supermarkets. Street hawkers sold dried fish and dates, and transistor radios played melancholy, reedy Arabic songs. Teenage girl soldiers in camouflage uniforms and white gloves directed traffic. Men dressed in black robes and red fezzes played backgammon in coffeehouses. And plastered everywhere were huge posters of Colonel Qaddafi wearing mirrored glasses and gold-braided military cap. His right fist was raised and clenched, and a slogan in green Arabic letters appeared beneath the portrait.

"What do the words mean?" Tom asked.

"It used to say, 'Revolution Forever.' This one is new. It's a quotation from one of Qaddafi's speeches. It says, 'I will die liberating the Galilee like a common soldier.'"

"Well, there have been five wars between the Arabs and Israelis," Tom noted. "So far, he's managed to miss them all."

"Careful," Erika cautioned, indicating the driver.

Their fifth-floor suites faced the sea and overlooked verdant, palm-lined gardens surrounding an exquisitely tiled but empty swimming pool.

Watching the sun slip into the sea, Tom felt the arthritic pain curve out of his neck and run down his left arm. He had taken two codeine and Empirin, which had the effect of speed, triggering a stream of introspective thoughts. He reflected on the ingeniousness of the STS-Libyan-Pakistani enterprise. The V-5 missile could be launched against Tel Aviv without directly implicating any of the perpetrators. It defied logic that anyone would supply Qaddafi with nuclear warheads and an ICBM delivery system. Qaddafi could not only deny his involvement, but might even suggest that a suicidal terrorist group had smuggled the bomb into Tel Aviv and detonated it. Suitcase atomic weapons existed and were functional. Accusatory fingers could also be pointed at the ruling dictators in Syria, Iran, and Iraq, all sworn to eradicate Israel. The bomb was no longer exclusive to the superpowers.

Tom felt as though he were riding the crest of a nuclear tidal wave rushing toward Armageddon. If by some miracle Israel survived the first strike, a thermonuclear holocaust could envelop every Arab capital city from Riyadh to Tehran. Half the world could be vaporized, and the surviving half faced with a radioactive fallout that would destroy crops, water, cattle, and the basic life-support systems. Mankind would have finally stumbled into the nuclear abyss.

A swelling moon rose in the dark blue sky, and the ageless precision of nature calmed his apocalyptic vision. He lit a cigarette and watched the balmy sea breeze grab the smoke. There was time, he thought—there was still time.

After a moment, Erika joined him on the terrace. She had changed from her slacks outfit to a stark, classic black dress. Her pale hair was swept up, and a strand of pearls circled her throat. The seductive aroma of her perfume laced the gentle breeze.

"I dismissed the chauffeur," she said. "He's picking us up at five-forty-five A.M. We're going to the oasis at Abu Najayim."

"The launch site?"

"Apparently."

"How far is it?"

"About two hundred miles south. Kleiser leaves tonight by helicopter."

She shivered suddenly and his arms went around her.

"What is it?"

"I feel as though I'm under a glass. Elke Hauser believes she's being watched as well. Hasi may be onto me."

"Kleiser has no reason to suspect you."

"He doesn't control the Libyan Secret Service."

They ate dinner at a small seaside restaurant and afterward took a cab to the Suq Al Jinnah. Fighting off peddlers and offers of whiskey and drugs, they walked through a claustrophobic maze of spidery streets. A smoky haze hung over the ancient quarter, and one street seemed to dissolve into another.

"You sure you know where you're going?" Tom asked.

"The letter was very specific. Number 67, Al Hamra Street. It should be right at . . ." They walked to the corner. "This corner."

But it wasn't.

Retracing their steps, they saw the numbers 67–74 painted over the curved arch of an arcade.

Number 67 was a jewelry store, and the owner's name, Abbas Jalloud, was embossed in gold leaf on the door. A dazzling array of gold filigree items and semiprecious stones was displayed in the window.

Two men playing dominoes in the alley stared at the blond German girl and the tall American as they entered the jewelry store.

Jalloud was a handsome man with light blue eyes and a thick shock of blue-black hair. Fine-lined tribal scars decorated the skin above his cheekbones. Jalloud was a Taureg of the Awassi tribe.

"Salaam Alakum," Jalloud greeted them.

"Salaam Alakum," Erika replied.

Glancing at the men playing dominoes, Jalloud whispered, "It's better if we speak in English."

"My husband and I are interested in purchasing a charm for our daughter," Erika said.

"A gold charm?"

"Yes."

"Solid or filigree?"

"It's a special charm. I have a description."

She handed him the letter Elke Hauser had given her. "A moment, please," he said, and went into the back room.

Outside the shop, parked across Al Hamra Street, was a Toyota pickup truck belonging to Libyan Counterintelligence. Seated on the passenger side, Abu Hasi angled the sideview mirror so that he had an unobstructed view of the arcade.

Jalloud came out of the back room and returned the letter to Erika. "I will have to order this particular item. Where can I reach you?"

"At Abu Najayim."

"We will do our best to find what you're looking for."

"Thank you."

Indicating an item in the showcase, Tom said, "Can I see that gold chain and charm?"

"With pleasure. Brazilian," Jalloud explained. "It's called a 'figa' in Portuguese. The fist with protruding thumb is thought to bring good fortune."

"How much is it?"

"To the world, three hundred fifty American dollars. But to you it is free."

"No. I insist on paying."

"You already have, sir."

"I have?"

"Yes—by permitting me to help you."

CHAPTER THIRTY

A white-hot sun blazed out of a cerulean sky and creamy puffs of cumulus clouds embroidered the distant mountains.

The dark ribbon of asphalt sliced through trackless sands and shimmering heat waves danced above the highway as if bonfires raged beneath the black tar.

The Citroën was air-conditioned and its tinted windows cut the desert glare. Erika wore a tailored khaki outfit and the gold chain with its lucky Brazilian talisman circled her throat.

The driver slid the divider glass open and in halting English said, "Military checkpoint—soon—crossroad to Abu Najayim. Papers please."

They handed him their passports and special visas signed by the chief of the Counterintelligence Bureau.

Indicating the undulating rose-colored dunes, Tom said, "Kleiser was right—the desert is magnificent."

"And dangerous," she said. "The Sahara is moving from Chad to Libya to Sudan to Egypt. Half the arable land in Africa has been swallowed up by the desert." She paused and her eyes narrowed. "Look there." She pointed to the top of a telephone pole protruding from a high dune.

The Citroën slowed and bumped over the dried carcass of a six-foot-long horned viper.

Erika wrinkled her nose. "Ugh."

"Checkpoint," the driver blurted.

A sand-colored Soviet-made T-72 battle tank blocked the road, and a few olive-green tents were pitched off to the right. An officer wearing reflective sunglasses motioned them to the shoulder of the road. A ragged-looking squad of soldiers lounged in the shade of the tank.

The officer examined their passports, leaned in the window, and spoke to Erika slowly in Arabic.

"He would like us to get out for a moment," she translated.

The contrast of the air-conditioned interior of the car to the furnace-like exterior was overwhelming. Tom turned the collar of his safari jacket up and put on his Australian bush hat. The soldiers grinned and made whispered comments about the two Westerners. The officer asked them to turn their pockets inside out, then frisked them quickly and efficiently. He then barked an order and one of the soldiers came forward, beckoning Tom and Erika to the shade of a tent. The driver raised the hood, then opened the trunk and the soldiers swarmed over the Citroën. A few knelt at the wheels and removed the hubcaps, while others entered the vehicle, pulled up the carpeting, and searched the seats. The officer and his adjutant inspected the trunk and its contents.

Walking toward the tent, Tom asked, "What are they looking for?"

"Special radios, miniature cameras, recording machines," Erika said. "This checkpoint marks the beginning of a military zone."

Inside the tent, they were shown to a makeshift toilet and washroom. Afterward the soldier offered them bottles of iced Coca-Cola. In return, Erika handed the soldier a pack of Gauloise cigarettes. *"Shikran, shikran."* The youthful soldier smiled, thanking her.

The officer entered the tent, and his penetrating black eyes were now friendly. He returned their documents and spoke softly in Arabic to Erika.

"He thanks us for our patience and regrets the inconvenience," she translated.

The captain saluted as they rolled past the checkpoint.

They drove at high speed for another twenty kilometers before slowing down and taking a secondary road that paralleled a deep wadi.

"Tell him to stop," Tom snapped.

"What is it?"

"Just tell him to stop and back up!"

She relayed Tom's request, and the driver stopped and reversed slowly.

"Hold it. Right here."

Tom started to get out but the driver shouted excitedly in Arabic.

"He says this is a restricted military zone and it's forbidden to get out," Erika explained.

Lowering the window, Tom pointed to a caked road that bisected a wadi. The impression of six-foot-wide tractor treads was clearly baked into the parched sand.

"You remember that enormous tractor trailer at the STS assembly plant in Munich?" he asked.

Erika nodded.

"Ask the driver if this depression through the wadi is a passable road."

Erika and the driver spoke in Arabic, after which she translated, "It's a Taureg caravan track. He thinks those treadmarks were made by tanks on maneuver."

"No tank in the world has a track that wide. Ask him where the wadi-road leads."

After a brief exchange with the chauffeur, Erika said, "It's a camel track to Jarmah—far to the south."

Tom slid the window closed. The driver shifted gears and picked up speed.

They rolled through a large village of mud-brick houses with TV antennas sprouting from the roofs. Bedouin tribesmen wearing blue robes with white cloths over their mouths stared at the passing Citroën. There was a pink mosque with gold-leaf domes and graceful minarets, and everywhere, posters of the sunglassed Qaddafi.

Upon leaving the village, the road widened into four lanes and appeared to be freshly paved. They sped past abandoned hulks of trucks, cars, oil drums, and huge wooden crates with Russian markings.

Thirty minutes later, they saw a deep wadi covered by camouflage netting, hiding the unmistakable silhouette of SAM-5 ground-to-air missiles.

"What could they be protecting out here?" Tom asked.

She shrugged. "I guess it makes Qaddafi feel secure to know that he has missiles in the desert."

Suddenly and magically, like a liquid mirage, a vast green belt circled by tall date palms shimmered up ahead.

"Oasis. Abu Najayim," the driver said.

Pools of blue water fed orange trees and acacias. Black-robed veiled women carried jugs of water atop their heads, and burnoosed tribesmen tended a line of braying camels. Children herded flocks of sheep and climbed palm trees, cutting down bunches of ripe dates.

The southern perimeter of the oasis opened onto the launch site. Tents and Quonset huts were grouped together at the edge of an orange grove. A rough landing strip, hewn out of a deep wadi, sliced through high dunes. Two Soviet-made MI-8 helicopters with green Libyan Air Force markings were parked in the shade of a camouflage netting. A sixty-foot-tall gantry arm held a V-5 rocket in vertical launch position.

The Citroën followed the perimeter road to a cluster of tents and parked in the shade of date palms.

They got out of the car and entered a large field tent where veiled women served food to German technicians and Libyan soldiers.

Smiling broadly, Fritz Kleiser, dressed in a safari suit and an old Afrika Corps cap, greeted them.

"Welcome to Abu Najayim," he said. "You're just in time for a snack."

They were served cold orange juice and a light lunch of goat cheese, pita bread, and scrambled eggs. Kleiser inquired about their hotel, the trip through the desert, and apologized for having been unable to share the previous evening with them.

After lunch, he chauffeured them around camp in a jeep. He spoke slowly, allowing sufficient time for note-taking, and stopping occasionally as Tom ran off multiple exposures on his Nikon.

"We miss nothing here," Kleiser said. "We have a doctor, a dentist, schoolteacher, cinema, and videocassettes of the latest American and European films. We are as self-sufficient as are those great oil platforms in the North Sea, but not as dangerous. The men work for six months at a stretch before being rotated back to Germany."

"I'm surprised you can get quality technicians to live in this environment," Tom said.

"All it takes is money."

"You're also a father figure to them, Fritz," Erika said.

"It's true, I suppose. These talented young men are being romanced by giants of West German industry, and yet they choose STS. With me, they have the freedom to explore, to create, and to dream; and curiously enough, the desert seems to instill a certain camaraderie."

"I would think after a few weeks of sand flies and heat blisters, even Berlin would look good," Tom commented.

"Perhaps, but as you see, the mood here is not one of depression. Come, we're about to run a full-thrust engine test."

Kleiser drove the jeep up onto a high ridge overlooking the camp and they trained their field glasses on the V-5 poised atop its launch platform.

Kleiser handed them each a wad of cotton. "You had better stuff this in your ears."

They felt the searing blast of heat before the ominous growl rumbled across the desert floor and hammered at their eardrums. A tongue of bright, smokeless orange flame shot out of the rocket's base. Shock waves whipped their clothes and stung their eyes. The test lasted eighteen seconds before the bright flames and thunderous roars receded.

Kleiser lowered his binoculars. "There you have it," he said proudly. "A perfect test. The liquid-fuel combination is our own formula—nitric acid and diesel oil."

"When do you actually launch?"

"As soon as we get official clearance. It can't be soon enough for me," Kleiser said, "and neither can the publication of your story—it's time the superpowers acknowledged that STS is a commercial enterprise."

They climbed into the jeep and Kleiser downshifted, saying, "I don't give a damn what you write or show about Nordhausen and the past. My concern is with the present and the future. Have you seen anything of a military intent?"

"No."

"Have you seen any attempt to conceal anything?"

Tom shook his head. "You've been as good as your word."

The sun was setting as they reached a trio of large canvas tents. "The one on the left is yours," Kleiser said affably. "The attendant inside will be at your service. Erika and I have a few routine items of business to discuss. Dinner will be served in the commissary shortly after sundown. Please feel free to wander about, talk to anyone you like, or shower and rest. Suit yourself. But take care—night comes quickly, without warning. The desert cools off rapidly, so dress accordingly. And wear boots, not sneakers; the night brings out vipers and scorpions."

Standing under the shower, cooling off in the spring-fed water, Tom thought that Kleiser had indeed kept his word. The entire STS operation had been revealed in detail; even Mueller's supposed accident hadn't slowed the process. Still, there was something amiss gnawing at him, something vaguely connected to the rocket-engine test. He soaped himself, searching his mind, replaying the test—but whatever it was that troubled him remained elusive. He shaved, dressed, put on his sheepskin jacket, and left the tent.

Kleiser had been right. Night had fallen in a hurry. A westerly breeze had risen and the sky was lustrous with stars. Pinpoints of light flickered throughout the camp as though a swarm of fireflies had descended on the base.

Glancing off at the palm grove, Tom noticed the smoke of cooking fires billowing up into the night lights. He started to turn away, then whirled around and stared at the luminous smoke as if he'd seen a revelation. That which had been troublesome and elusive about the rocket test suddenly became startlingly clear. The V-5 engine had produced no ignition smoke. He had witnessed many space shots and rocket tests, but never one that was smokeless.

He zipped up his jacket and strolled toward the V-5

gantry pad, where German technicians moved around, fiddling with connecting fuel lines.

Standing at the base of the V-5, Tom was struck by the absence of residual fuel vapors. No fuel. No smoke. And yet he had seen the flames and heard the roar of the engines. He shifted his attention to the nest of lines running from below ground up into the coaxial engines, and instantly understood the simplistic but ingenious nature of Kleiser's trick. A pilot light had ignited a massive flow of odorless, smokeless natural gas. The test firing had been a magnificent special effect—a brilliant illusion.

Leaving the gantry pad, Tom walked slowly past open tents and, peering inside, saw no luggage—only overnight duffel bags.

He entered a Quonset hut piled high with large wooden crates stamped in German with well-known brand names. Between the nests of crates an enormous spider was weaving a large, intricately laced web. The crates had obviously been undisturbed. He pressed his palm against a pile of crates and they tumbled, empty, to the dirt floor—another illusion.

Inside the Quonset hut that served as an elementary schoolroom for the German children, Tom inspected drawings of animals, ships, dolls, and zany faces, but there were no drawings of rockets. If children had been living in this place for six months, it was inconceivable that not one of their drawings would depict a rocket.

Lawford did not mention any of his observations at dinner, and while not patronizing, was friendly and gracious with Kleiser, thanking him again for his openness and truthfulness. It wasn't until coffee and sweet cakes were served that Tom casually asked about the absence of fuel-storage tanks.

Kleiser's brooding eyes narrowed, but he handled the question deftly. "The storage tanks are in a fenced-in area atop a wadi. The fuel travels through underground pipes to the launch pad."

After several brandies, Kleiser's mood became warm and expansive. He spoke of his achievements and the brilliance of German technology, and at one point he rose and toasted his employees, to enthusiastic applause.

After dessert Kleiser explained that he would not be returning to Berlin with them in the morning, but would instead be flying back to Tripoli by helicopter that night.

After a nightcap in Kleiser's tent, they accompanied him to the airstrip. He kissed Erika on both cheeks, shook hands with Tom, and boarded the Soviet-made chopper.

Once the flashing red lights of the MI-8 helicopter disappeared to the north, Tom and Erika walked across the compound toward the high dunes. He told her about the absence of ignition smoke and petrol fumes at the launch pad, and the spiderwebs on the empty equipment crates, and the imported children's drawings, and the absence of power generators and baggage.

"Are you saying that all of this is simply an elaborate stage setting?" she asked in disbelief.

"It may actually be used for rocket-engine tests, but it's too open and too impermanent to be the launch site. I want to see those so-called fuel tanks behind that fence."

Climbing up a high dune, they stared at the desolate, moonlit beauty of the undulating desert. Whirling sand blew off the crests of dunes like sea spray, and wadis snaked through the desert floor as if they were deep troughs—it was as though a great surging sea had been frozen in a limitless universe.

"God . . . it's beautiful," Erika whispered.

They stood silently, silhouetted atop the dune, mesmerized by the vast starlit stillness.

The wind shifted suddenly and carried with it an eerie, mournful cry. "Jackals," Erika said. "They sometimes follow bedouin caravans."

Tom glanced across the deep wadi to the fenced-in area surrounding the circular tops of sunken fuel tanks.

"Let me know if anyone comes out of the camp."

Sliding down the dune, he crossed the floor of the trenchlike wadi to the opposite side and began climbing the steep dune. Grabbing fistfuls of tamarisk shrubs for support, he pulled himself up foot by foot until he reached the top of the trench.

A dilapidated mesh fence enclosed a cluster of disks that appeared a few feet above the ground and could very well have been the tops of fuel-storage tanks. The distinct sharp odor of diesel fuel permeated the enclosure.

Slipping through a torn section of fence, Tom knelt at the base of a protruding disk, gripped the handle, and pulled. The lid opened and the profound odor of diesel fuel rose up. He took off his sheepskin jacket, rolled up his shirt sleeve, and plunged his right arm into the oily black liquid. The thick fuel reached his shoulder before his fingers struck a metallic seal. The "tanks" were only two feet deep, with dummy tops filled by a few jerricans of diesel. He moved quickly from disk to disk; the result was the same, except in two instances, where the tanks were empty all the way to the false metal bottom—and nowhere was there any evidence of nitric-acid fumes, the key ingredient in the V-5 rocket fuel.

He recrossed the deep wadi trench and hauled himself up the opposite dune, where Erika helped him to his feet. Catching his breath, he said, ". . . All dummy tops. Two feet of diesel trapped by a false bottom. This whole place is phony. They set that rocket test up for me. You were right, Kleiser never intended for me to see the launch site."

"He had me fooled," she said.

"The question is, where the hell is the actual site?"

"What about those huge tracks we saw on the way down here?"

"I would guess they were made by a trailer with tank treads hauling a V-5."

The wind stirred and the cry of jackals was close.

"Perhaps with certain calculations we can narrow the possibilities," she suggested. "We saw the tank treads about forty kilometers south of the military roadblock."

Tom nodded. "The KH-11 satellite could sweep that area. But if it's an underground silo . . ." His voice trailed off.

The sudden startling sound of braying camels spun them around.

Atop the adjacent dune, sitting astride their camels, silhouetted in the moonlight, was a line of blue-robed Taureg bedouins. White turbans with slitted eye holes covered their faces. Their rifle butts rested on their saddles, muzzles pointing skyward. Strung out in single file, they were like a vision out of the Arabian Nights.

The camels quieted and the wind again carried the wail of jackals. The leader shouted, *"Asfal!"* and his camel obediently folded its legs and assumed a sitting position. Followed by two of his men, the chief strode toward them, gliding across the dunes. His eyes shone through the slits in the cloth covering his face.

"Salaamat," he said.

"Marhaba," Erika replied.

"Ana akh ash-shaikh oweidi Ana ash Jalloud." He spoke with quiet authority, pausing between sentences. *"Mahal awamid alnaar fissama huwa Jarmah. Yakhtafi an-nar nahwa ash-sharq ind al-kufra."* He bowed. *"Salaam Alakum."*

"Salaam. Gayid har." She bowed in return.

The leader and his two subchiefs strode back to the waiting line of Tauregs and remounted their camels. The chief wheeled around and trotted up to the head of the column. Whipping their camels into a fast loping stride, they vanished into the shifting desert landscape like ghostly shadows in billowing robes.

"I'm sorry, but I couldn't interrupt him," Erika said. "They have very formal customs, and he was stretching matters to even speak with a woman. He's the brother of Sheik Oweidi, the Israeli bedouin chief who wrote the letter. He was contacted by the jeweler, Mr. Jalloud. He claims to have seen pillars of fire in the sky over Jarmah."

CHAPTER THIRTY-ONE

The jeweler, Abbas Jalloud, was naked and spread-eagled on a wet marble slab. Electric wires were attached to his testicles. A technician operated a voltage regulator and another man held a stick between Jalloud's teeth.

Hasi slid off the high stool, crossed the interrogation room, and opened the window. The gray dawn light dispelled the darkness on Al Jumaa Road. They had been at it for several hours, and Jalloud, like all bedouins, was tough and proud, but Hasi had begun to detect signs of surrender. He would crack this bedouin son of a bitch within the hour.

After taking a few breaths of fresh air, Hasi walked back to the stool, sat down, and nodded at the technician, who turned the voltage-meter knob. Jalloud screamed and his body arced against the restraining straps. His face was chalk white and his blue-black hair stood on end. The voltage was lowered and Jalloud's body fell back onto the marble slab and the wooden stick was removed from his mouth.

Hasi placed his lips to Jalloud's ear. "You have broken no laws. You have done nothing wrong. We will release you at once. Tell me about the letter the German woman gave you—to whom was the letter addressed?"

Jalloud remained defiantly silent. His lips blue. His chest cavity rising and falling.

"All right," Hasi said calmly. "We will try again."

The bearded technician clasped electrodes to Jalloud's nipples and two wires were wound into his ears. The stick was placed between his teeth and the voltage meter was raised to the limit. Jalloud screamed and his body arced against the restraining straps. His eyes rolled up into his head and he blacked out. His body slammed down against the wet marble.

"Wake him up," Hasi ordered.

The technician inserted a hypodermic needle of caffeine into Jalloud's arm and pushed the plunger to the incremental half. Jalloud's eyes fluttered and opened.

"You know where you are?" Hasi asked.

Jalloud nodded.

"Now, what must you tell me?"

Jalloud's eyes darted to the man operating the voltage meter.

"You'll be released immediately," Hasi assured him.

"The letter . . ." Jalloud rasped, "the letter was sent . . . to . . . to . . . Sheik Al Hatab."

"And its message?"

"That the bearer . . . might seek help."

"What kind of help?"

"I don't know."

The voltage hurled Jalloud against the straps. The current coursed through his nipples, testicles, and eardrums in four-second cycles until he lost consciousness. The hypo of caffeine was emptied into his arm and a few seconds later his blood-red eyes opened.

"What help was the German woman seeking?" Hasi asked.

"She . . . she . . . was going to Abu Najayim and . . . she wants to see the place of fire in the sky."

"Who sent the letter?"

"Sheik Oweidi."

"From what tribe?"

"Awassi."

"Where do the Awassi live?"

"Israel."

Back at his desk, Hasi sipped strong black coffee and tried to organize his thoughts. He knew the Tauregs moved freely from oasis to oasis and had undoubtedly seen a test firing of the V-5. If the Taureg chieftain met the Sperling woman, everything might have been compromised. He could still prevent Kleiser's private Lear jet from taking off, but he would be detaining Lawford, as well as Fräulein Sperling. He would have to proceed carefully.

Dr. Kleiser was staying on in Tripoli for high-level conferences. This was not the time to upset the German, besides which his evidence would be regarded as manufactured. Hasi's section chief envied him and feared him; it was pointless to bring this matter to Kassim's attention. If he could only get his hands on the German girl for a few minutes . . .

He lit a cigarette and dialed communications and ordered a seat on the eleven-A.M. Libyan Airways flight to Frankfurt and Berlin. He had certain resources in the divided city and the regulations governing field work were quite clear: if an agent deemed himself to be in an emergency situation, he could undertake unilateral action.

Hasi leaned back and watched the smoke curl up to the ceiling, wondering what Fräulein Sperling would look like after a few hours of interrogation.

CHAPTER THIRTY-TWO

Staring out of the taxi's windows, they felt disoriented and tense. The snow flurries and garish neon of the Kurfürstendamm seemed surreal after the sun-scorched Libyan desert.

They hadn't mentioned their shared secret since leaving Abu Najayim at five A.M. for Tripoli International Airport. The chauffeur's knowledge of English precluded any discussion of their discovery, and assuming the Lear jet was bugged, they hadn't spoken of Jarmah during the five-hour return flight. Adding to the tension was their anxiety to inform their respective agencies of the Jarmah launch site.

As they turned into Fasanenstrasse, Tom said, "I'll hold off phoning Washington until you speak with Mossad."

"It doesn't matter."

The taxi pulled up in front of the Kempinski Hotel. "I'll pick you up in about an hour," Tom said.

"Make it an hour and a half, and I'll pick you up."

Ten minutes later, Erika got out of the cab and shuddered in the bone-chilling night air as she walked from the curb to the door of her apartment building. Glancing back at the darkened street, she saw no one loitering or sitting in parked cars.

She entered the dimly lit foyer and started up the three flights of wooden stairs. Reaching the second floor, she stopped to put her heavy canvas bag down. The landing was unusually quiet; not a sound could be heard from any of the apartments. No babies cried. No domestic quarrels raged. No dogs barked.

Unbuttoning her coat, she froze as a shadow suddenly crossed the wall on the floor above. Holding her breath, she listened for the sound of footsteps, but heard nothing. Had she seen the shadow or imagined it? Fatigue and tension played curious games with the senses. Sighing audibly, she picked up her bag and trudged up the last flight to the third-floor landing.

Standing at the door, she heard a faint stirring sound from inside her apartment. Again she wondered—imagined or real? Placing her ear to the door, she strained, trying to identify the sound on the other side. Then she heard it. Sharp. Defined. But not from inside her apartment—a wooden planking creaked on the landing below. Someone was coming up the stairs.

One way or the other, she was trapped, and decided to gamble that the sound she heard coming from inside her apartment was imagined.

Taking a deep breath, she turned the key, entered the dark apartment, slammed the door shut, and leaned against it, hyperventilating.

She snapped the light on, and gasped.

"My name is Landau." The bespectacled middle-aged man smiled. "Ben Landau. I'm with Mossad. I was instructed to contact you. I'm sorry to have frightened you." He crossed to the bar and poured some cognac. "Here. Come. Take this. You're in no danger."

"I want a code," she said hoarsely.

"Jericho-Three."

She sighed in relief, shuddered reflexively, and took the brandy. As she raised the glass, she sensed another presence and whirled around. A plain-looking blond woman stood in the alcove.

"This is Penelope," Landau said.

The woman nodded, said something in Hebrew to Landau, then brushed past Erika and went out. Erika's hand trembled as she lit a cigarette. "How did you get in here?"

"That lock is rather simple. I suggest you have a dead bolt installed. You must also take care with the phone."

"What do you mean?"

"We saw phone repairmen enter the building, and while there are many apartments in this building, we thought it prudent to check yours."

"And?"

"The apartment is clean, but the phone has been bugged."

Landau lifted the phone receiver, undid the cap, and, using a small screwdriver, unscrewed two wires and extracted what appeared to be a miniature fuse.

"A micro-sensor. Primitive. But effective."

He replaced the bug and screwed the receiver cap back on. "We won't let them know that you've found the bug."

"When were these so-called phone men here?"

"The day you left for Munich with Lawford. We think that Hasi's agents followed you to the airport and had people at the Munich end who may have seen Elke Hauser coming out of the terminal. Hasi is probably suspicious of your relationship with Fräulein Hauser. We can only hope that Kleiser doesn't share those same suspicions."

"I was with Kleiser for five hours on the flight to Tripoli, and spent time with him in the desert at Abu Najayim. He never once displayed any distrust."

"Were you ever alone with him?"

She nodded. "For several hours before dinner. We went over some . . ." Her face reddened. "Some personal business of his."

Landau picked up the bottle of cognac. "Do you mind?"

"Help yourself."

He poured a hefty shot of brandy into a snifter and drained it. "You must be very careful these next few days. We intend to get you out by the thirteenth."

"Where will I go?"

"Out of harm's way. Zev Berger will see to all your needs." Landau took a Pan Am folder out of his jacket. "Lawford's ticket to Rome. Please see that he gets it without delay."

She glanced at the itinerary on the folder. Flight 203, Pan Am at nine A.M. from Berlin to Frankfurt, connecting with Lufthansa 154, departing Frankfurt at 10:50 A.M., arriving in Rome at 12:35 P.M.

"This is for tomorrow morning," she said with some surprise.

"Yes. General Harel will meet Lawford at the Excelsior Hotel." Landau tossed the cognac down and said, "Now, please tell me, where is this Nazi missile base?"

Erika stared at the scholarly-looking Mossad agent.

"Is something wrong?" he asked.

"No . . . I . . . You just . . ."

"Don't look the part?"

"Yes."

"If you only knew, Fräulein Sperling, how, when I was very young, I prayed that by the time I grew up I would look like Paul Newman. But"—he shrugged—"Yahweh, in his infinite wisdom, stuck me with this bland face."

"I only meant that you—"

"Show me the launch site, please," Landau interrupted.

Erika spread the detailed map of Libya on the coffee table and pointed out the various sites as she spoke. "This is Abu Najayim. The place Kleiser took us to."

"But that was not the base?"

She shook her head. "It was a well-designed camouflage. Tom thinks—"

"Tom?"

"Lawford."

"Ah . . . yes, of course. Go on, please."

"He was justifiably suspicious of it. The actual launch site is here—at Jarmah, three hundred and fifty miles or so south of Abu Najayim, and five hundred miles southeast of Tripoli."

"The V-5's are launched from Jarmah?"

"According to the Taureg chieftain. He described Jarmah as the place of fire in the sky—'pillars of fire,' to be literal. And the test range extends east almost to Egypt—here—to Al Kufra."

Landau folded the map in precise quarters.

"You're very efficient," Erika noted.

"One day I'll make a mistake," he sighed, "but that's the

nature of things. You were very brave and very bright. This information will buy us sufficient time to deal with Kahuta."

"It's Lawford who deserves the credit."

"I'm sure General Harel will let him know how grateful we are."

Landau took a small automatic out of his coat pocket and handed it to Erika. "You know how to use this?"

"Yes."

"Keep it with you. It's effective only inside ten meters, but it will deliver a message up to twenty meters. Now, let me have your car keys."

"Why?"

"Your car has been in the basement garage for almost a week. I want to be certain it's not bugged or wired with explosives. I don't want to lose you on the turn of a key."

She handed him the keys, and he opened the door and smiled. "If you hear a loud noise, you'll know I made a mistake."

Over dinner at a small candlelit restaurant in the Tiergarten, Erika briefed Tom on her unexpected Mossad visitors.

"Well, it's comforting to know that somebody's looking out for us," he said, refilling their wineglasses.

"You haven't said anything about your phone call to Washington."

"There's nothing to say. The Admiral seemed pleased with the Jarmah information—well, maybe 'relieved' is more accurate. I got the distinct impression that they have no problems with an Israeli strike on Jarmah and other Libyan targets. But they're still schizophrenic on the subject of Kahuta."

"In what way?"

"The Admiral wants details on the Kahuta plant and how close the Pakistanis are to nuclear warheads; but he made it clear the Agency will do everything in its power to prevent any Israeli action against Kahuta."

"How do they know that Israel is planning a strike?"

"They don't. They're counting on me to inform them."

"What will you do?"

"I don't know." Tom shrugged and sipped some wine. "But one way or the other, I'll have to betray someone."

"But isn't the whole question academic?"

"What do you mean?"

"From what I understand, the Israelis have no means to attack Kahuta."

"True . . . at least no way that we know of." Tom paused, then asked, "What was this woman Penelope like?"

"Nondescript. She reminded me of my mother's house-maid."

"Maybe you ought to go up to Hanover, to your mother's, until Mossad gets you out."

"Why? I'm not alone."

Her remark carried a curious symmetry. He remembered the night at Chadwick's when Narda had said, 'You're not alone.' "

They entered the Kempinski lobby and Tom stopped at the front desk and asked for his key. "I'll be checking out in the morning."

"Very good, sir," the concierge said, and handed him the key. "The bill is always ready."

Still dressed, they lounged on the bed, sipping brandy and listening to classical music on the stereo. The glow of neon through the windows lent a hazy definition to the dark bedroom.

Erika's eyes were misty, and she said, "You'll have to forgive me this moment of self-pity."

She rolled over and propped herself up on her elbows, her chin resting on her closed fists. Her eyes were fixed, pene-trating, as if she were X-raying his thoughts. She kissed him deeply and whispered, "I promise not to miss you."

"I'll wait for you in Rome."

"I'm not free to go anywhere on my own; neither are you. Once you get on that plane tomorrow, we'll never see each other again, so . . . just let it go—and make love to me."

CHAPTER THIRTY-THREE

Shortly after eight o'clock the next morning, Erika eased the BMW away from the hotel and turned north on the Kurfürstendamm, heading toward the autobahn.

She fingered the gold Brazilian charm that fell across her wine-colored turtleneck sweater. "Jalloud was right—this charm turned out to be lucky."

Tom nodded. "We smoked out Jarmah. Now it's up to the Israeli Air Force."

"They'll deal with it."

"If there's still time. . . ."

She glanced at him for a brief moment, then turned her attention back to the traffic.

They reached the autobahn and Erika gunned the BMW up the steep ramp, double-shifted, and accelerated, gaining the fast outside lane.

Her eyes flashed from the road to the sideview mirror. "I may be wrong, but I think we're being followed by a white VW van."

Tom turned and peered out the rear window.

"About six cars back," she said. "See it?"

"No . . . Wait! Yeah, I see him."

Reaching into her bag, Erika took out the 9mm Browning automatic.

"Take it," she said urgently.

Gripping the automatic, he switched the safety off and lowered his window as a blast of cold air rushed into the car.

Holding the wheel steady and maintaining speed, Erika glanced up at the rearview mirror. Tom held the automatic just below the window, while his eyes remained fixed on the sideview mirror.

"When did you first notice it?" he asked.

"At the Spandau ramp."

"What makes you think he's following us?"

"I've changed lanes twice, and so has he. He's also maintained the same distance and speed."

They traveled that way for another eight minutes—Tom staring into, and occasionally adjusting, the sideview mirror, and Erika's eyes constantly flicking up to the rearview.

As they sped under the first airport sign, she shouted, "They're changing lanes!"

In the sideview mirror Tom saw the van duck behind a small blue Opel and, with its right blinker flashing, head for the exit.

He closed the window and sighed. "I think we're both overtrained."

"Perhaps," she said, "but Landau and the woman, Penelope, weren't taking any chances."

"I hate leaving you here alone."

"Until your article runs, I'm in no danger from Kleiser—and since there will be no article, I should be fine."

"Why the hell doesn't Mossad get you out now?"

"I can't do anything to arouse suspicion until the Jarmah strike is under way."

The white VW van descended the exit ramp and the driver nodded to the woman alongside. She picked up a microphone attached to a high-frequency radio unit.

"Tripoli Blue. This is Tripoli Red."

In the blue Opel, Abu Hasi was seated next to a stocky Palestinian who drove the small car with casual expertise.

They were tailing Erika Sperling's BMW at a distance of ten car-lengths.

"Tripoli Blue. This is Tripoli Red," the woman's voice came in over a layer of static.

Hasi picked up the microphone and depressed a yellow button. "This is Tripoli Blue. Go ahead."

"We're on the airport road."

"Did she detect you?"

"No. But we thought it best to get off the autobahn."

"Take a position at the Tegel access road."

"The one that precedes the airport?"

"Yes. They must be making the nine-A.M. Pan Am to Frankfurt. There's nothing else going out. We'll rendezvous as planned. Over."

"Received. Over and out."

Hasi disliked the woman who had just spoken to him from the van. She was a sport killer, and he wanted Fräulein Sperling alive—if possible.

Tegel Airport was in the French section of West Berlin, and in a testament to the ironies of history, the French tricolor flew side by side with the flag of its traditional German enemy.

Erika parked at the Pan Am departure terminal, and as they got out of the car, a red-faced porter came over and shouted, "Frankfurt?"

Tom nodded and gave the porter his ticket and ten marks.

"That's too much," Erika said.

"Look at his gloves."

The porter wore old GI wool mittens that had for the most part unraveled.

"He can afford new gloves—they wear those to arouse sympathy from tourists."

"Ich glaube Sie sind ein bischen spät," the porter growled.

"Ja, ja." Erika nodded. *"Beeilen Sie sich bitte."*

Hefting Tom's bag onto the dolly, the porter indicated his watch and hurried off.

"He's afraid you'll miss your plane."

"It's not such a bad idea."

They stood very close, as if alone in the midst of arriving and departing traffic. Their breaths vaporized in sunlit puffs. Her face was tilted to the side and a small smile played on her lips—in the same way as when they had first met. She curled against him, folding herself into his arms. He kissed her hair and inhaled the sweet scent of her perfume.

"I'll phone you tonight."

"My phone's bugged, remember?"

"I'll make an obscene call. We'll turn Kleiser on."

Their eyes met for a final moment. She kissed him lightly and whispered, "Be careful."

Driving back into the city, she decided to take the lightly traveled Zimmerstrasse and avoid the congestion on Kurfürstendamm. The wide cobblestoned street ran parallel to the grim Berlin Wall.

The Browning automatic rested on the seat beside her. The radio was tuned to the classical-music station and a cigarette burned in the ashtray.

She tried not to think about Lawford's departure. She had to regard him as history. There was no other way. It was painful and difficult to shut down one's emotions, but experience had taught her the difference between the short run and the long run. In her business, one had to take the moment and regret nothing.

She stopped for a light at the Friedrichstrasse intersection, rolled her window down, and tossed out the cigarette. The light changed from amber to green and she turned into Strasse des 17 Juni and entered the Tiergarten Park.

The trees were bare and their branches were layered with snow. On the hillrise, a thick stand of pines bristled in the icy wind. The great park was silent and deserted, abandoned to the brutal Berlin winter. She passed the 240-foot-tall "Siegessäule," the ornate Victory Column commemorating the Franco-Prussian War. Many years ago, her father had taken her to the observation deck atop the column, and she had never forgotten that magnificent panoramic view of Berlin—it was an indelible childhood memory.

She fiddled with the radio, trying to get the news station, and by chance noticed the white top of a van speeding down a lateral road toward her. She grabbed the automatic and started to U-turn, when she saw a blue Opel slip out of a bicycle path and close in from the rear. The VW van turned into the road and was speeding toward her. Both vehicles braked and swerved broadside—the van in front of her, the Opel behind her, effectively trapping the BMW between them.

Her temples throbbed and her heart raced wildly.

The driver of the van held a silenced machine pistol, and a dark-skinned woman, similarly armed, came out of the passenger side.

Behind her, Erika saw two men get out of the blue Opel. A rush of adrenaline, like a charge of high voltage, kicked and jolted her into action. Flooring the accelerator, she steered directly toward the dark-skinned woman, who raised the machine pistol and fired. The windshield spiderwebbed, and slivers of glass sliced into Erika's forehead. Rivulets of blood seeped into her eyes. But she held the wheel steady and the gas pedal pressed to the floor. The BMW crashed into the woman, tossing her broken body onto the hood. For a split second the woman's face pressed against the shattered windshield before a stream of blood burst from her mouth and she slid off the hood.

Frantically Erika spun the wheel and sped toward the embankment, hoping to cut through the pines and come out on the other side, close to the Russian Memorial, where military police were always on duty. She was suddenly slammed forward against the wheel, and felt a searing pain knife through her left shoulder. The rear window had disintegrated under a hail of slugs. Blood ran down her arm and oozed out of her coat sleeve. The driver of the van and the men out of the Opel were closing in from different angles. She was soaked with blood, sweat, and urine. Her body trembled uncontrollably. She shifted desperately up and down, trying to gain traction, hoping the front wheels would grab the base of the embankment. But the wheels spun in the snow-softened earth. She reversed and stepped on the gas. The BMW kicked and bucked. They had shot out the tires. She was riding on the rims, and sparks flew from the steel grinding against the pavement.

The men raked the BMW with low-trajectory fire. She raised the automatic and pulled the trigger twice before screaming in pain as a ricocheting slug pierced her thigh. She collapsed on the seat and, as if in a dream, saw the door handle turn, and she tumbled out of the car at Abu Hasi's feet.

"Take her!" he commanded.

The tall man grabbed Erika's legs, and the stocky one hooked his hands under her arms.

Hasi's eyes opened wide in surprise as he saw the yellow blur of a taxi hurtling directly toward them. He raised the AK-47 assault rifle, but held his fire as the Mercedes taxi jumped the curb and careened up the opposite embankment, sliding sideways to a halt.

A man jumped out of the driver's side, and a woman got out of the passenger side. They crouched, took dead aim, and fired their automatic weapons.

Ducking behind the BMW, Hasi watched helplessly as a hail of slugs slammed into the two men carrying Erika. The tall man's legs buckled like pipe cleaners as he was cut in half. The stocky man's hands flew up as his face exploded. Erika fell to the ground, lying motionless between her dead and dying abductors.

Surprised by the sudden silence, Penelope raised herself above the boulder to signal Landau, who was positioned behind the taxi.

Scanning the embankment, Hasi saw the blond head appear and he squeezed the AK-47 trigger. Penelope's face vanished in a crimson spray. Landau saw her body hurled backward from the impact. Swearing, he tore through the woods, running full-out, coming at Hasi from his blind side.

The Parabellum automatic shivered in Landau's gloved hands as sixty hollow-point slugs streamed into Hasi, who was still crouched behind the hood of the BMW. His body jerked and danced as bits of clothes, bone, and blood splashed across the BMW's fender.

Landau quickly searched Hasi's jacket, removing his wallet and passport. The cold air smelled of gunsmoke and graphite as he knelt over Erika. Her eyes were half-open, and she was bloodstained from head to toe. Dark arterial blood pumped out of her left thigh. Using her scarf, Landau quickly tied a tourniquet above the wound and pulled the knot tight.

He carried her up the embankment and gently draped her across the rear seat of the taxi. He then covered her with his overcoat and hurried over to where Penelope lay. He picked up the Uzi machine pistol and flung it down the embankment. Penelope carried an Austrian passport in the name of Helga Honecker. The police would not connect her to Mossad.

Landau heard the wail of a distant siren as he got back behind the wheel of the Mercedes taxi. He carefully guided the taxi down the embankment, onto the roadway, and gunned the sedan toward Zimmerstrasse. He knew Berlin well. The nearest hospital was Charité, in the British sector, not more than eight minutes from the Tiergarten. The critically wounded German girl in the back seat was his responsibility and he had failed. And Penelope . . . she had committed that fatal but inevitable mistake that sooner or later befell them all.

Blasting the horn, Landau raced through red lights, spreading the panicked, cursing drivers in front of him. His hands and feet were steady, but his mind whirled with details. He would first phone Berger, then Erika's mother in Hanover. As to the police, he would plant the story of a drug dealer's shoot-out. Since Erika had provided Kleiser with opium, he might believe that she had been involved in a firefight while negotiating a buy; at the very least, the drug angle would screen Mossad's involvement.

As to Penelope, she was simply an Austrian tourist who had taken a brisk walk in the park and had the bad luck to be struck by stray bullets. Ultimately a Mossad agent identifying himself as her grieving Austrian husband would claim the body, and Penelope would be buried in the Galilee.

Landau kept the horn lever depressed as he careened into the hospital's emergency receiving compound. The blaring horn, screech of brakes, and Landau's frantic hand motions alerted a team of paramedics, one of whom dashed inside the admitting room while the others wheeled a gurney down the ramp.

"Multiple gunshots, but she's alive," Landau shouted in German.

Shoving Landau aside, they lifted Erika's broken body onto the cart. A doctor and two nurses came running down the ramp, wheeling an oxygen infuser and a D5W-dextrose bottle.

Landau watched with admiration the harmony and speed with which the emergency unit worked.

A nurse using large shears cut the clothes and underwear away from Erika. The doctor checked her nasal passages and ordered the oxygen hookup. The nurse inserted the dextrose IV. An AKG monitor was hooked up to assess vital signs: blood pressure, pulse, respiration. The doctor pinched Erika's nails to see if the color returned. He shook his head negatively at the blue line around her mouth. He ordered blood type and cross-matching for replacement. A second nurse removed Landau's makeshift tourniquet and applied pressure to the artery to staunch the blood flow. Her colleague prepared a fresh dressing and swabbed the wound with peroxide. The doctor examined Erika's pupils with a pencil flashlight to see if they were equal in size and whether she had suffered brain damage. He quickly checked the reflex action in her extremities, then rubbed his knuckles along her sternum to determine whether the pain registered on her brain. She moved slightly and the doctor sighed gratefully; she was not yet in terminal coma.

"Assemble the team," the doctor said. "I want transfusion. The blood loss is severe, and get Dr. Theisen. She may have collarbone implosion, rib-cage splinters in her lungs. The left thigh and shoulder need cleaning for bullet remnants and temporary reconstruction. The facial glass shards must also be removed and stitched. We have no personal history, but we can't wait for ID's—prepare to inject three million units of penicillin. Now, let's move!"

Pushing the gurney bearing Erika's battered body before them, the team disappeared through the emergency admittance doors.

A duty police officer of the Kriminalampt Volkspolizei came down the ramp and motioned to Landau. "Come with me, please."

They entered the small administration office, and the officer handed Landau a clipboard with an attached emergency information form. "Fill in the details. Name, badge number, address, license, where you picked up the woman, and so on. After which, you'll tell me exactly what happened before my bureau chief arrives, yes?"

"Yes, yes," Landau said, trembling, "but I must relieve myself. I'm going to be sick. I've never—"

"Through those doors. All the way down the corridor."

Landau nodded, backed away, and walked through swinging doors that opened to a long hallway.

The men's room was located at the far end of the corridor. Once inside the tiled bathroom, Landau checked the stalls to be sure they were unoccupied. He then tossed his taxi driver's cap and gloves in a wastebasket, lit a cigarette, walked to the urinal, and relieved himself. He washed his hands and face, cleaned his glasses, straightened his tie, and stepped out into the hallway.

He looked back but saw no one. He had been gone only a few minutes. He strolled calmly toward the exit door and left the building.

His mind raced as he walked toward the corner. He would make his calls from the safe house on Meineckestrasse. First Berger . . . then an anonymous tip to the police of the drug deal that had turned into a bloodbath . . . and finally, using the cover name of Klaus Anhalt, he would notify Erika's mother.

He hailed a taxi at the corner and told the driver to drop him off at the Am-Zoo U-Bahn station.

Settling back in the leather seat, Landau thumbed through the Libyan's wallet and papers. He was particularly interested in the green Tripoli driver's license, complete with photo—the cover name was Assad Akhdar, but the face was Abu Hasi's. It was a piece of news that would please Berger. Hasi had been on Mossad's hit list for many years. Berger would also see to it that a protective screen was placed around Erika Sperling. If she survived, she was marked, and would have to be safely tucked away.

As to Lawford, he was the wild card. General Harel would soon find out the extent of the American journalist's commitment. He sighed, thinking these matters were not his concern. He, Landau, was just a soldier.

CHAPTER THIRTY-FOUR

The sun was warm for early March and the sidewalk tables at the Café de Paris were busy with a lively crowd of Romans enjoying the springlike weather.

General Dado Harel was seated opposite the wiry Indian intelligence agent Pandit Sinde. Their table afforded an unobstructed view of the Excelsior Hotel directly across the Via Veneto.

The men sipped their espressos and watched the action on the legendary boulevard.

Dado tapped the thick manila envelope Sinde had placed on the table. "So, this is from Russia with love."

"Without question." Sinde nodded. "Minister Levechenko was well aware that these photographs taken by the Soyuz-TM-6 cameras were ordered for a very specific reason. You have three perspectives of the Kahuta Nuclear Research Center from an altitude of two hundred thousand feet down to zero resolution—one can see the textured concrete of the cupola."

"We're very grateful for your help."

"It's not totally altruistic." Sinde smiled. "Kahuta casts a long shadow over India. Levechenko asked if we intended to transfer these photographs to telemetric tape for insertion into the eyes of 'smart bombs.' He is, I think, convinced that my government has finally decided to take out the Kahuta facility."

"That's our hope," Dado said. "Politically speaking, it's crucial that Israel be distanced from this proposed operation."

"You needn't be concerned, General. Even if the Kremlin knew that Israel was the recipient of these photos, I doubt they would betray you. Levechenko and his superiors despise Pakistan for having harbored and armed the Afghan guerrillas. The Soviets have not forgotten their fifteen thousand dead soldiers, and the savage manner in which their bodies were mutilated. There is a photograph on Levechenko's wall of Mujahadeen fighters wearing gray fur caps taken from dead Russian soldiers. The Soviets will not shed any tears over the destruction of Kahuta."

"I understand, but in all your discussions you never once mentioned the State of Israel."

"Never. I'm certain Levechenko believes that India is preparing something."

Sinde did not mention the fact that in a unique display of appreciation at the prospect of India's attacking the Kahuta facility, Levechenko had sent a smashing blond KGB prostitute to Sinde's room at the Metropole Hotel. Between the vodka and the energetic prostitute, he had managed to keep warm in the otherwise unheated room.

Sinde glanced at a homely Italian woman seated at a nearby table. The woman seemed vaguely familiar; her huge breasts and garish makeup reminded him of one of those grotesque women that appeared in most of Fellini's pictures. Yes . . . that's probably where he'd seen her—in one of those surreal circus films. Looking away from the woman, Sinde asked, "I trust the freighter was satisfactory?"

Dado nodded. "The work has already begun at Eilat."

"Bashira cautions that the captain must speak Greek and carry Greek papers."

"Yes, we know," Dado replied, and leaning forward, said, "My government has one more favor to ask of you . . ." His voice trailed off as a waiter hovered at an adjacent table.

Sinde began to feel apprehensive; only Buddha knew what apocalyptic madness the Israeli general had in mind. The Indian agent lit a cigarette and inhaled deeply. He was in a difficult position. He'd been ordered by his superiors to cooperate with Mossad, but he knew something of General Harel's history, and Sinde's instincts told him to exert extreme caution.

Once the waiter left, Dado said, "There's a strip of microfilm that Bashira will pass to you."

"No . . . no . . . not to me," Sinde replied firmly. "My bureau has determined that chief of Pakistan Counterintelligence General Murrani has placed his entire section on high alert."

"What has this to do with you meeting Bashira?"

"I will not enter Pakistan again." Sinde puffed nervously on the cigarette. "I have taken enough risks for ten lifetimes. Bashira will inevitably be discovered and betrayed. General Murrani is no fool, and I'm not going to tempt fate. I'm sorry, but you'll have to find some other way to pass the microfilm."

"The possibility of being found out exists for all of us," Dado pressed. "You're a professional intelligence agent."

"Yes, but I'm also an Indian. I represent Pakistan's historic enemy. I'm too visible. And frankly, I'm fearful. I don't relish a public hanging in Islamabad."

"But your government, perhaps even more than mine, will be relieved once Kahuta is dealt with."

"I understand, and I intend to cooperate with you in every way possible, but I will not meet with Bashira inside Pakistan."

Dado rose and picked up the thick manila envelope containing the Soviet satellite pictures of Kahuta. "I'll be in touch."

Sinde sighed in relief as he watched the broad-shouldered Israeli cross the Via Veneto and head toward the Excelsior Hotel. There was something fatal about the General, Sinde thought—he was doubtless brilliant, but there was madness in those implacable blue eyes. The General probed relentlessly, but studiously avoided answering questions. And Sinde had many questions. Why the satellite photos of Kahuta, when internal sabotage was the only possible course of action? And why the twenty-year-old freighter? What was on the microfilm that Bashira needed to transmit?

Ah, to hell with it, Sinde thought. The answers did not concern him. He would, of course, cooperate—but to a degree.

He glanced at the homely Italian actress with the deep cleavage. Ah . . . these Western women had tits—not like bony Indian women swathed in saris. The painted woman smiled at Sinde and he returned her smile, thinking that a KGB prostitute and an Italian grotesquerie on the same trip would enliven late-night conversation at the Delhi Polo Club.

The concierge handed Dado his room key and two message slips: using the code name "Yanush," Berger had phoned a few minutes ago, and Amos Gideon was waiting in the bar.

"Would you please phone Mr. Gideon and tell him that I'll be there in five minutes?"

"Certainly, sir."

"Where can I have a document copied?"

"Just beyond the elevators, to the left."

Dado handed the manila envelope to the young woman who operated the Siemens copying machine.

"Can you run off a set of these photographs and charge it to room 504?"

"Your name?"

"Steifell," he said. "Victor Steifell."

A computer instantly verified the name and room number and she proceeded to feed the Soyuz photographs of Kahuta into the copier. The last photo came out of the slot, and she placed the originals and duplicates in separate envelopes. He thanked her and gave her a five-thousand-lire tip.

Amos Gideon was seated on a high stool at the long mahogany bar, reading the *International Herald Tribune*. His El Al flight captain's jacket was draped over his shoulders. He smoked and sipped an Italian beer. Gideon was a slim, wiry man with a puckish face that seemed at odds with his moody black eyes. He had been an ace combat pilot credited with downing eight Syrian MIG-25's in the summer of '82 over Lebanon. Gideon had also led the first wave of fighter bombers on the strike against PLO headquarters in Tunis. He had resigned from active duty in 1990 and had spent the past two years flying commercial 747's.

Dado clamped his big right hand on Gideon's shoulder. "Good to see you, Amos."

Gideon tapped the *Tribune*. "We gave up territory for peace, but the killers keep coming. I know you were in favor of it. So was I. But look at this editorial—they attack us for defending ourselves."

"What does it matter? We could give them Tel Aviv, and the press would criticize us. We could resettle in Auschwitz and still be attacked—it's the way it is."

Dado handed him the manila envelope containing the original satellite photos of Kahuta. "Berger will be waiting for you on the tarmac at Ben-Gurion."

"And if he's not there?"

"Go up to Technion and put it in the hands of Professor Newman."

"Done."

"Have a safe flight, Amos."

Dado rode up the elevator with two Englishmen who were discussing a large transfer of gold bullion. Leaving the elevator on the fifth floor, Dado walked along the carpeted hallway to room 504.

After checking the corridor, he slipped a snub-nosed .38 revolver out of his shoulder holster and unlocked the door. Hearing no suspicious sounds from inside, he swung the door open and took a few tentative steps into the room before closing the door behind him. Gun in hand, he checked the bedroom, bathroom, and finally, the closets.

Satisfied the room was secure, he holstered the .38 and direct-dialed Zev Berger. They would speak in a prearranged Hebrew code, without reference to names or places.

Narda Simone drove the Fiat with uncommon assurance through the mad "dodg-'em-car" Roman traffic. She had picked Lawford up at Fiumicino and exchanged desultory conversation with him on the long ride into the city.

They circled the Arch of Constantine and passed the magnificent marble ruins of Emperor Caracalla's Baths.

Pointing to huge ocher walls sprawled across a distant hilltop, Tom said, "Nero's summer palace."

"Do you know Rome well?"

"Well enough." He nodded. "It's a city that still belongs to Caesar. A Sunday performance at the Colosseum would be a very hot ticket."

"Ticket to what?"

"Oh, I don't know, lions eating Christians, baboons urinating on vestal virgins, gladiators and tigers, Amazon women strangling dwarfs— you know, a well-rounded three-act play."

They stopped at a light close to the Colosseum and he casually asked, "What does the General have in mind?"

She tossed her long black hair and shrugged. "I was told to collect you at the airport; nothing more."

They passed the lively, sun-drenched sidewalk cafés along the Via Veneto and swung into the rotunda of the Excelsior Hotel. Narda tipped the uniformed doorman and instructed him to see that Lawford's suitcase was delivered to suite 507.

The suite was light and airy, and a wide balcony afforded a splendid view of the city.

"Satisfactory, I hope," she said.

"Perfect." He nodded. "I'm going to freshen up. I'll be only a few minutes—why don't you open a couple of beers?"

As she started to cross to the mini-bar, the doorbell sounded. "Yes?"

"Portiere," the muffled voice answered.

She peered through the eyepiece and opened the door. The stoop-shouldered porter came in carrying Lawford's suitcase. He followed Narda into the bedroom and hefted the bag onto the luggage rack. The porter stood there for a moment, distracted by the open bathroom door and the sound of a shower running. Narda tipped him generously and he beamed and doffed his cap. *"Grazie, grazie mille, signorina."*

* * *

Back in the salon, Narda dialed Dado's room and got a busy signal. Feeling apprehensive, she lit a cigarette and waited a moment before trying again. The line was still busy. She hung up, crossed to the mini-bar, and took out two bottles of beer. She poured the foaming brew into two tall, tapered glasses. Taking one, she stepped out onto the balcony.

The Eternal City glowed in the bright sunshine. The dome of St. Peter's reminded her of the Dome of the Rock in Jerusalem. She never understood why the ancient Romans had surrendered their gods so quickly and embraced the Christian revelation. Maybe it had something to do with the fact that the Romans had largely stolen their own gods from the Greeks, so accepted yet another theology without any sense of loss. Sipping the beer, she sighed and thought people were always seeking new gods. Her younger sister had recently returned to Tel Aviv after a pilgrimage to Tibet, where she consulted with a renowned lama. Narda shook her head, thinking that however Jews might appear to embrace and explore other theologies, in their hearts, despite themselves, they feared their terrible god, Yahweh.

"Nice view." Lawford's voice startled her.

"Your beer is on the table," she said, stepping back inside.

There was a soft knock at the door.

"Yes?" Narda called out.

"Dado," the voice answered.

She peered through the eyepiece and opened the door.

The General came into the room, stopped, and stared at Lawford. For a long moment neither man moved. They reminded Narda of two old lions who had once shared a moment of triumph, then wandered their separate ways through the jungle of time before once again coming face-to-face.

Dado walked quickly to Tom and they shook hands warmly.

"My God, man, you haven't picked up a single line," Dado lied. In truth, he thought the handsome American had aged badly.

"You too. You haven't changed at all," Tom lied with equal conviction, thinking the General had grown old in a rush; his once-blond hair was now gray, and his blue eyes had faded.

"How long has it been?" Dado asked.

"October seventy-three."

"Nineteen years," Dado murmured, then brightened. "Sit down. Sit down. Narda, order some chicken sandwiches and a bottle of good Scotch." He turned to Tom. "Is that okay for you?"

"Fine."

"How was the flight?"

"It seemed endless."

"After Libya, it's no wonder. That was a good piece of work."

"It was Erika—she carried the mail."

Dado shook a cigarette out of a pack and offered one to Tom.

"No, thanks."

Dado lit the cigarette, inhaled, and blew the smoke up toward the ceiling. "I have bad news for you," he said quietly. "Erika Sperling has been critically wounded."

Narda gasped and the color drained from her cheeks.

Lawford stared at the General in stunned silence.

"She has a chance," Dado said. "The concern at the moment is blood loss and infection."

"How did it happen?" Tom asked.

"After she left you at Tegel, she was followed back into the city and ambushed in the Tiergarten."

"By whom?"

"A Libyan hit team."

"Goddammit!" Tom exclaimed angrily. "You should have protected her! She deserved the best you had!"

Narda's eyes darted from one man to the other.

"Erika is a seasoned deep-cover agent," Dado calmly replied. "No one forced her to do anything. She has always acted out of her own conscience and her own free will. It's impossible to make any operation one-hundred-percent secure. She knew there was a risk of surveillance, and we did our best to protect her. None of us could predict that Abu Hasi would act unilaterally. I had my best field people watching her."

The doorbell rang and Narda admitted the waiter.

The young man pushed a serving cart to the center of the salon and began to arrange place settings. Narda quickly signed the check and hustled him out of the room. Dado opened the bottle of Scotch and poured two generous drinks.

"Make it three," Narda said.

They sipped their drinks in silence for a moment before Lawford turned to the General and said, "Tell me what happened."

"Landau and Penelope followed Erika from the airport back to the city, but lost her. The Libyans trapped her in the Tiergarten Park near the War Memorial. It was bitterly cold and the park was deserted. Erika managed to run one of them over—a woman. The men opened fire with automatic weapons. Landau and Penelope wiped them out, including Hasi. But Erika was badly wounded and Penelope was killed."

Narda bit her lip and poured herself another Scotch.

"Landau rushed Erika to Charité Hospital," Dado continued. "She's listed as critical, but stable. Her mother is with her, and she has the best possible care, but there are complications."

"What kind of complications?"

"As I said, the chief concern is infection. But if Landau had not acted decisively, she'd be gone."

"How do you know Abu Hasi was involved?"

"Landau took his ID. His picture matched those in our files. Hasi was security control for STS. He undoubtedly ordered Hickey's murder. We have reason to believe that one of the Libyans we hit in Paris was Hickey's killer."

Tom stared at the skyline of the city, then turned to Dado and in a flat, cold voice said, "You set Hickey up, didn't you?"

"I set things in motion and Berger made the arrangements with the Admiral."

"Arrangements? You call targeting an agent 'arrangements'?"

"Hickey was not targeted. The Admiral requested that Narda engage Hickey's company to place Mueller under surveillance."

"So a cover story was invented."

"That's right. We were anxious to know what Mueller was up to in Washington and why he was traveling on a Pakistani diplomatic passport and why he was staying at the Pakistani embassy. One of the answers was on Hickey's sound tape—the word 'maraging,' the special alloy needed for Kahuta's centrifuges. Mueller was trying to acquire that alloy from a company in Maryland—a connection he had from his NASA days. We also wanted the Admiral to realize just how tight the German-Pakistani relationship was."

"But in the general scheme of things, you regarded Hickey as a tool—an irrelevance—a means to further your ends."

"We never believed the Agency would leave Hickey out in the cold," Narda interjected. "I told you that in Washington. I personally warned Manfredi that we considered the Mueller surveillance to be a high-risk operation."

"You can color it purple," Tom sighed, "but in my book, you set Hickey up."

"We couldn't predict his murder," Dado said, "but yes, we did use him. And we used you. We'd use anyone in order to survive. What would you do if your country was facing nuclear annihilation?"

"Spare me the flag-waving—and the politics."

"Politics has nothing to do with this. I'm not a politician. I'm a soldier. And my position is very clear. The next time someone intends to make soap of us, we'll take the whole world into the bathtub with us."

"So everyone's expendable, right?"

"Now you're getting warm."

"Jesus Christ, you're some piece of work."

"Look, Tom . . . I'm not going to argue morality or ethics with you. You did your job. You discovered the location of the V-5 silo. The Admiral is delighted. You'll probably get a medal. The men responsible for killing Hickey have themselves been eliminated. You're in good shape—there's nothing more to be said."

"Why did you want me to come to Rome?"

"Once you located the Jarmah launch site, there was no point in risking your cover any longer. We wanted you out of Berlin."

"Why didn't you get Erika out?"

"She works for Kleiser. She couldn't suddenly disappear. We can't risk arousing Kleiser's suspicions until we're ready to hit Jarmah. And let me tell you, you're not the only one concerned with Erika's safety. One of my best people lost her life trying to save Erika. You can't replace a woman like Penelope. I recruited her years ago, after her husband was killed in the 1973 war. I didn't protect Penelope either. I can't protect anyone. I don't run an insurance company. There's no Blue Cross here—there's a blue star, and millions have died to preserve it." Dado's voice trembled. "My son included."

Tom eyed the General for a moment, then crossed the room and freshened his drink. "What happened to Landau?"

"He escaped undetected and planted the drug story with the police."

"For Kleiser's consumption?"

Dado nodded. "Erika provided opium for him, so it's conceivable that she was caught in a dealers' shoot-out while trying to make a buy."

"That won't work," Tom said emphatically. "The fact that Abu Hasi was killed with the others tells Kleiser the firefight had nothing to do with drugs. He has to know that Erika had outside protection. Maybe not Mossad, maybe CIA or West German Intelligence; but her cover is gone. She's marked."

"If you're Kleiser, at this moment Erika Sperling is history," Dado replied. "His entire operation is approaching zero hour. He's got a hell of a lot to attend to. He may assume that Erika was a plant, but there is absolutely no reason for him to think that she discovered the Jarmah launch site. What matters now is to maintain your own credibility with Kleiser."

"You mean the article?"

Dado nodded. "You have to phone Kleiser. You've heard the news about Erika. You never imagined she dealt with professional drug dealers, and you're shocked by the incident. He will commiserate with you, and after a polite note of concern for Erika, he'll inquire as to the status of your article."

"And I'll tell him it's finished and I'm about to file."

"Right. We need seven days. The warhead will leave Pakistan for Jarmah on the twelfth. We have to keep Kleiser calm and confident for seven days."

"What about Erika? How will she handle the German police? Once she's able to speak, they'll interrogate her."

"Berger's already taken care of that. He phoned Manfredi. The CIA informed Bonn that Erika Sperling was working on a highly classified project for the Agency. Inspector Lehmans of the Federal Police has thrown a protective screen around her. If she survives her wounds, she'll be taken care of for the rest of her life."

Tom sighed heavily. "I suppose if there's a hero in all this, it's Landau."

"He's not a hero. He did what he was supposed to do, what he was trained to do. You've done it yourself. If you had been in that car with Erika, you'd have died trying to save her."

"Well, I wasn't in that car. I'm here—and what the hell do I do now? Hang around Rome, fix things with Bonini at the AP bureau, and charm Kleiser while I wait for you to take out Jarmah?"

The General stared at Lawford for a moment, then drained his Scotch and said, "There is something else you can do."

They walked along the sluggish Tiber River in the late-afternoon sun, two men from opposite sides of the world, bonded by a shared week spent in the hell of combat. They had seen the elephant together. They had heard the ear-shattering roar of howitzers and the agonizing screams of the wounded. Their allegiances were different, but the underlying respect for one another remained undiminished by the rush of time and events.

"Your government wants inside data on Kahuta. So do we," the General said. "You can get it for us, Tom. The entire infrastructure, floor by floor."

"It's not just data you want. You're planning a strike on Kahuta, right?"

"You expect me to answer that?"

"Yes. I do,"

"How can I? Your orders are clear. You're to report any hint of an Israeli strike on Kahuta to the Admiral."

"You'll have to trust me. If I'm the point man, I want to know what's at stake."

Dado stared off at the Italian flag whipping in the breeze atop Castel Sant'Angelo across the Tiber. He was faced with a decision not unlike those instant critical choices taken in the midst of battle, when everything hung in the balance. His mind raced, filtering and sifting the pros and cons. Lawford's allegiance to the Agency was questionable. The Admiral had hung Hickey out to die. And Landau, a Mossad agent, had eliminated Hickey's killer—so maybe Lawford owed them one. And then there was Erika, clinging tenuously to life. Whether Lawford would betray the intended Kahuta strike was a calculated risk, but there wasn't much choice now that Sinde had backed away; besides, Lawford would fit right in with Pakistan's coming celebration of Army Day. He was an accredited journalist, above suspicion—a courier who could meet with Bashira and bring out the microfilm.

"I'm going to trust you, Tom," Dado finally said. "We are planning a strike against Kahuta."

"How?"

"The data that you can pass to us will probably determine the method of attack. As long as Kahuta exists, the jeopardy continues, and not only for Israel." Dado paused. "Suppose a warhead falls into the hands of theological fanatics like Hezbollah—what then? You remember the Shia zealot who drove that truckload of TNT into the Marine headquarters in Beirut?"

Tom nodded.

"If that fanatic had had a nuclear device, you think he'd have hesitated to use it? America itself can be a target of nuclear terror. What more can I say? I need your help."

Lawford woke up at noon after a fitful sleep haunted by the nightmarish imagery of being trapped in the dark maze of Nordhausen's tunnels.

Only in the light of day did he realize the deadly nature of the commitment he'd made to the General.

He had phoned Admiral Dwinell at midnight, Rome time—6:00 P.M. Washington time. Delighted at the prospect of obtaining the Kahuta microfilm, the Admiral immediately contacted the American ambassador in Rome, instructing him to provide Lawford with plane tickets and the necessary documentation to visit Pakistan. His name would be added to the list of Western journalists invited to attend Pakistan's celebration of Army Day.

At some point during the festivities, Salim Bashira would pass the microfilm to Lawford.

The Admiral had pressed again as to whether Tom had any evidence of a planned Israeli strike on Kahuta. He replied that he had not, and keeping faith with Dado's request, made no mention of March 12th—the date the Pakistani warhead would be delivered to Qaddafi.

Tom rose and went out onto the balcony and took deep breaths of air. Yesterday's springlike sunshine had been replaced by gray cloud cover and a cool northerly breeze. He checked his watch, walked back inside and direct-dialed Fritz Kleiser at his Berlin office. The call filtered through two secretaries before the deep, charming voice came on the line. "Ah. It's you, Mr. Lawford. I expect you've read about the incident in the Tiergarten."

"Yes. I was shocked. The story is carried on the front page of the *Tribune*. I had no idea that Erika was involved in drugs."

"Nor I."

"Do you have any late report on her condition?"

"No calls or visitors are permitted—except for her mother. But I did manage to speak with the floor nurse this morning. It appears that Erika's vital signs are stabilizing. She will require additional surgery, but for the moment she's out of danger. The police are guarding her—they're obviously anxious to talk to her."

"About the drugs?" Tom asked innocently.

"Apparently there's more to this than drugs. An Austrian woman, a tourist, walking in the park, was also killed in the firefight, and a taxi driver is being sought for questioning."

"That's curious," Tom said. "There's no mention of a taxi driver in the *Tribune* account."

"According to the German press, a taxi driver brought Erika to the hospital. The man apparently witnessed the entire incident and disappeared. The taxi company has no record of the car or driver."

There was a pause while Kleiser relit a cigar. "By the way, it was fortunate you decided to file the story in Rome. You might have been with her, had you stayed."

"Yes. That was a piece of luck."

"I realize that you're upset," Kleiser said tentatively, "and I don't mean to sound callous, but I'm rather anxious to know if you've contacted the AP bureau chief in Rome."

"As a matter of fact, I've just come from seeing him. It's going to take longer than I thought. Bonini wants me to expand the piece into a two-part story that will run on successive Sundays. It's a lot more work, but it's a hell of a break."

Kleiser blew some smoke up to the ceiling and asked, "When would the first section run?"

"Next Sunday, the eighth."

"Perfect," Kleiser said, and meant it. The article would precede the V-5 launch.

"As I said," Tom continued, "a two-part AP feature story will reach close to a billion readers. And I would think the article will be picked up by other media as well."

"I hope you treat me kindly."

"You'll find the story to be objective and truthful."

"I expected no less," Kleiser said affably, then asked, "How long will you be in Rome?"

"Probably a week. I'll be staying with a friend on the Via Margutta."

"Well, I'm here if you need me. Anything at all, just phone."

"I will. By the way, would you see to it that a bouquet of flowers is sent to Erika in my name?"

"With pleasure."

Tom hung up and dialed the front desk. "Will you prepare my bill. I'll be leaving today."

"Certainly, Mr. Lawford. A package just arrived for you from the American embassy. I'll send it right up."

CHAPTER THIRTY-FIVE

Kleiser rocked contentedly in his chair for a moment, then glanced at the front-page photograph of Abu Hasi's bloody face. Gripped by a sudden surge of anger, he crumpled the paper and tossed it into the basket. Hasi had almost wrecked everything. The Libyan agent had taken it upon himself to move against Erika.

Knocking some ash from the cigar, Kleiser thought: In absolute fairness, one had to conclude that there might have been a germ of truth in Hasi's accusations. When one sifted the facts of yesterday's shoot-out, one had to conclude that a team of professionals had been protecting Erika.

The drug angle was an obvious fabrication, a cover story released by the police. The ambush in the Tiergarten was the result of a clumsy attempt by Hasi to kidnap Erika. The Austrian woman who had been found shot to death was no tourist; both she and the missing taxi driver had undoubtedly been working for one of the intelligence agencies. Erika had been planted in his company years ago. She worked either for the BND, or the CIA, or Mossad. The facts pointed to West German Intelligence, but since all three agencies cooperated on certain matters, it was impossible to be certain.

No matter, he thought. Nothing of critical importance had been compromised. With the exception of himself, no one in the STS organization knew the exact location of the Jarmah silo. The site was, of course, known to Qaddafi and the chief of Pakistan Counterintelligence, as well as a small cadre of "on-site" engineers. There were, too, occasional bands of nomadic Tauregs who used the spring water at the Jarmah oasis. But it was inconceivable that Erika would have established contact with anyone in that tight circle. She might very well have leaked certain facts concerning STS operations to the press, or to the BND, but there wasn't a whisper of a chance that she had located the V-5 launch site. Even the well-schooled, seasoned American journalist had been duped by the rocket-engine test at Abu Najayim. Kleiser's real concern was Erika's knowledge of his bizarre proclivities for opium and women; but since she had provided both objects of his desire, it was unlikely that she would reveal his minor character flaws.

No. . . . All things considered, there was little reason to undertake any further action against Fräulein Sperling. If she had indeed betrayed his trust, it was a bitter personal disappointment, but pragmatically speaking, Fräulein Sperling was now irrelevant. Everything was moving forward—Lawford's article would soon appear. The assembled V-5 was en route to Jarmah, and Colonel Qaddafi had approved the initial payment of seven hundred million dollars.

Walter Diehl had arrived in Jarmah to supervise the fueling and arming of the rocket. The old man had the experience and credentials to direct the launch procedures, and zero hour was almost upon them.

Kleiser swung around in his chair, noticed a light snow beginning to fall, and thought it would be prudent to be seen on the ski slopes of St. Moritz on the morning of the thirteenth. It was the height of the winter season and he would be very visible at the Swiss resort. One had to accept the fact that in certain quarters suspicion would be leveled at STS, but if Lawford's article was indeed objective, if he had written a truthful account of that which he had seen, heard, and photographed, it would be difficult for anyone to make a factual connection between STS and the nuclear destruction of Tel Aviv and Haifa. There were twenty-five well-financed terrorist organizations that could conceivably have acquired nuclear warheads. The nuclear club had greatly expanded during the last decade, and the acquisition of the bomb by fanatical enemies of the Zionist state was not an illogical assumption.

Kleiser rocked contentedly in his chair. He had covered his tracks brilliantly, and he owed himself a little diversion —an entertainment. He picked up his personal phone directory and thumbed through the pages. Perhaps the Swiss girls, the twins . . . What had he done with their number? He opened the desk drawer and saw one of Hasi's photographs of Erika strolling through the Tiergarten with Elke Hauser. The striking fashion model's face triggered a sudden pervasive sense of foreboding. Staring at the photograph, Kleiser thought that if Hasi had been right, if Fräulein Hauser had been more than a high-fashion pimp, if she had indeed been a courier, then perhaps the infiltration of STS was more extensive than he perceived.

He slammed the drawer shut, angered by his growing paranoia. He was slipping into the same conjectural quicksand that Hasi had fallen victim to. He had to get a grip on his nerves. He had covered everything, and nothing of significance had gone wrong. His meeting with Qaddafi, the shooting in the park, and the approaching V-5 launch had unnerved him. He desperately needed a night of relaxation, of escape—the kind of escape that only opium and compliant young girls could provide.

CHAPTER THIRTY-SIX

Five hundred and fifty miles south of Tripoli, close to the oasis of Jarmah, a huge C-17 McDonnell Douglas transport landed on the hard-packed desert strip. The mammoth aircraft used most of the twenty-thousand-foot runway before coming to a stop and shutting down its outboard engines. Then it turned and taxied slowly toward a waiting crane-rigged flatbed trailer truck.

A group of khaki-clad men wearing reflective sunglasses stood at the rear of the truck, waiting for the aircraft to halt.

The aft section of the plane opened and a ramp was lowered to the desert floor. Walter Diehl strode out of the plane and shook hands with the waiting crew chief. The men exchanged a few words, and with Diehl supervising, the crew chief organized the transfer of a gleaming sixty-foot-tall multistage V-5 rocket from the plane's cargo bay to the flatbed trailer.

Once the transfer was made, Diehl motioned thumbs-up to the C-17 pilot. The ramp folded back into the aft section, and the two inboard engines whined into life.

The huge cargo plane taxied to the head end of the desert

strip, revving up all four engines as the cockpit crew checked the four sets of gauges. Once the critical needle points were in the green, the pilot released the brakes and shoved the throttles forward, and the aircraft thundered down the runway.

Standing alongside the trailer truck, Diehl watched the C-17 disappear into the cloudless pale sky. The old man felt the hot sun baking into his shoulders and for a brief moment luxuriated in the dry heat. The arthritic aches and pains he had suffered in Munich had disappeared in the desert. He thought it ironic that this dimensionless rose-colored wasteland would be the scene of his greatest triumph.

The multiple nuclear warhead would be arriving from Islamabad in five days. The liquid fueling and countdown would commence as soon as the warhead was attached. The V-5's flight from Jarmah to the Israeli targets would take eighteen minutes. Once the rocket reached a stratospheric apex of forty miles, the warheads would separate and descend, directed to their targets by a preprogrammed inertial-guidance system. Tel Aviv and Haifa would vanish in a radioactive mushroom cloud eight seconds after the initial blast.

He got into the cab of the trailer and motioned ahead to the Libyan driver. The flatbed truck traveled three hundred yards before coming to a stop at the edge of a circular outline that appeared to be baked into the desert floor.

Diehl spoke briefly into a high-frequency radio-mike, and a moment later the wail of a siren pierced the desert stillness.

The circle opened, sliding apart in two concave halves that receded into hidden apertures. Standing on the launch pad, the crew rose up from the underground silo into the dazzling sunlight. The crane operator raised the V-5 from the truck bed, and the launch crew swiftly and expertly affixed the V-5 to the gantry platform.

Diehl climbed aboard the platform and signaled the chief engineer, who spoke into a walkie-talkie. The siren sounded, and the gantry platform slowly descended into the dark, air-cooled silo. The concave halves came together, sealing the parched desert floor.

CHAPTER THIRTY-SEVEN

Major General Ayub Murrani, chief of Pakistan's Counterintelligence Bureau, insisted the meeting be held in the Defense Ministry in the city of Lahore. Murrani despised the characterless northern cities of Islamabad and Rawalpindi and equally loathed the squalid southern seaport of Karachi. In order to think, to meditate, to weigh complex problems, a man required an aesthetic setting. Lahore combined the stately dignity of the British raj with the architectural opulence of the Mogul Empire. It was the jewel city of Pakistan, and had it not been situated on the border with India, Lahore would have certainly been the nation's capital.

The Intelligence Section was situated in a sixteenth-century Mogul palace complete with marble halls and spacious, airy offices. Murrani often thought the complex of offices would have been ideally suited for scholars and poets.

Murrani was a delicate-looking man with thin, patrician features, but his aesthetic looks were deceptive. People who crossed swords with the intelligence chief had a way of disappearing. Murrani had survived and outwitted the elder Bhutto, and his successor, the fanatic Zia, and afterward, Bhutto's ambitious daughter. He was the true power behind the throne, and the tentacles of his bureau reached out into the military-industrial complex that ruled the nation. Murrani was not a backstage bureaucrat; he had served with distinction in all three of Pakistan's wars with India. His agents had infiltrated the Baluchistani Revolutionary Council when that province was in revolt, and by selective assassination managed to decimate its leadership.

Murrani had graduated from Cambridge with a doctorate in political science, but he also had an artistic side. He'd written and published three volumes of poetry while still a student. Paradoxically, over the course of years he had ordered and directed numerous killings of political opponents, but Murrani took no satisfaction in murder, and regarded violence as an act of intellectual bankruptcy. In truth, he would have preferred to stroll in the Shalimar Gardens and meditate on the poetic harmony of nature, but the meeting at hand was centered on matters far removed from the transcendental bliss of nature. The subject of this morning's agenda was apocalyptic, and demanded a certain barbaric pragmatism.

Murrani had only contempt for Qaddafi, but considered Pakistan's long-standing nuclear agreement with the Libyan dictator to be a psychological and fiscal national imperative. The arrangement provided billions of dollars, and assured the inevitable emergence of Pakistan as a superpower on a par with India.

Seated behind his marble-topped desk, Murrani waited for the servant to finish pouring tea for the three men seated before him.

Dr. I. Q. Khan, director of Pakistan's Nuclear Research Center, was a brilliant physicist and a dedicated patriot. There was not a doubt in Murrani's mind about Dr. Khan's sterling character.

S. M. Abassi, the diminutive chief of Special Branch Internal Security, was also an individual of impeccable character.

Chief of Staff General Afzal Rahman was a huge man whose long career served as a testament to courage and patriotism. There were, however, unconfirmed reports of Rahman's use of opium.

Murrani fitted an American cigarette into his ivory holder. "Gentlemen," he said, opening the meeting, "the centrifugal forces acting on Pakistan are numerous and distressing." He lit the cigarette and continued. "Our four provinces are held together in uneasy alliance. We have the misfortune of being surrounded by powerful neighbors, and internally . . ." Murrani's eyes flicked to Internal Security Chief Abassi. "We suffer from a vast, cancerous criminal network growing rich on opium; and since the Afghan truce of eighty-eight, we have been victimized by Afghani terrorists trained and financed by the Soviets. Elements of these leftist guerrillas have settled in the northwest province, dangerously close to Kahuta, and frankly, I believe we are vulnerable to sabotage."

"I assure you," Abassi said, "the security at Kahuta is flawless. Our nuclear-research center is impregnable."

Murrani stared at Abassi for a moment, then shifted his attention to Dr. Khan. "When do you intend to transfer the warhead to our Libyan brothers?"

"The Kahuta reactor will be shut down at midnight on the twelfth for fuel-rod replacement. A multiple warhead will be ready for shipment that afternoon."

"By what means?"

"An Air Force cargo plane will fly directly from Islamabad to the Jarmah landing strip."

"What are the chances of this flight being intercepted?"

"None," General Rahman interjected. "We've been flying that route for years."

"So, the security in and around Kahuta is flawless, and the shipment of warheads is equally secure." Murrani shrugged. "Well, then, we have nothing to worry about."

Dr. Khan shifted nervously in his chair and said, "I should point out that security cannot ensure against an accident."

"What sort of accident did you have in mind, Doctor?"

"Once a nuclear chain reaction is set in motion, there is a certain irreducible risk of a meltdown."

"Are all the proper safeguards employed at Kahuta?"

"Absolutely."

"Well, then we run no greater risks than any other nation employing nuclear power, is that correct?"

"Yes, of course."

"So we can conclude that while accidents are in the hands of Allah, security remains in our hands."

"Let me assure you once again," Abassi said, "nothing has been left to chance."

Murrani flicked some ash from his cigarette, and glanced at the bright sunshine flooding the veranda. The men studied him in wary silence, knowing that the wily intelligence chief had not summoned them from their duties for assurances that could have been delivered by phone.

After what seemed an interminable passage of time, Murrani rose and faced them. "I have no wish to cast aspersions, but I recall hearing similar assurances of security several years ago, in February of 1988, to be exact, with respect to the Islamabad munitions depot. Two months later, the entire dump exploded, killing three hundred soldiers and injuring thousands of civilians. The loss in matériel was in excess of two hundred million dollars."

General Rahman cleared his throat and said, "After an exhaustive investigation, we determined the blast was caused by a flash fire while soldiers were transferring mortar shells."

"Yes." Murrani nodded. "I saw the report. And in that same summer of eighty-eight, President Zia and most of the general staff were blown to bits when their plane exploded. Was that too an accident?"

The question hung in the air like an accusation. Murrani knew that the late President's death was no accident because he had arranged for the time bomb to be placed aboard the aircraft. In the late fall of 1991, Murrani had engineered the election of President Ahmad Ghazi, over whom he exerted total control.

Clearing his throat, Abassi broke the tense silence. "There has never been any conclusive proof of sabotage with respect to that incident."

"Perhaps, but we seem to be plagued by accidents. Two weeks ago, eighteen workers burned to death at the small-

247

arms factory in Rana—another accident." Murrani glanced out at the formal gardens below, then turned and in a cold, clipped voice said, "Do you gentlemen think that our late colleague Farheed Shah met with an accident in his Paris hotel? Was the German rocket specialist Brunner also the victim of an accident while in his own house in Hamburg? Was Heinrich Mueller killed accidentally by a tram?" Murrani's eyes darted from General Rahman to Abassi. "These 'accidents' are interconnected," he continued, "and are directly related to the imminent delivery of our nuclear warhead to Qaddafi. As the date of the launch approaches, the danger to Kahuta and to the Libyan launch site increases."

"Danger from whom?" Abassi asked.

Murrani waved his hand. "The KHAD, Mossad, KGB, CIA, Indian Bureau, what does it matter? The object of the exercise is to protect ourselves from a catastrophic strike on Kahuta."

"Well," General Rahman said quietly, "there is one external threat we can dismiss. The Israelis cannot launch an air strike from Tel Aviv to Kahuta; it's beyond the capability of their F-16's and F-15's."

"They could take off from India," Murrani countered. "It's only a matter of minutes from the Indian frontier to Kahuta."

"The Indian government will never permit Israeli jets to use their airfields," Rahman argued. "India does not even maintain formal diplomatic relations with Israel. The Indians know very well we can counterstrike their nuclear facility at Delhi."

Murrani nodded, then addressed Security Chief Abassi. "I want you to supply me with a computerized readout on all employees at Kahuta, from broom pushers to physicists —complete data: education, ethnicity, family, birthplace, salary, homes, apartments, married, single, and aberrational behavior, drugs, sexual appetites, any arrests, however minor."

"Foreign technicians as well?"

"Everyone."

There was a momentary silence. Then Murrani said

warmly, "I thank you, gentlemen, for your vigilance and your fraternity."

Dr. Khan rose, hesitated, then finally asked, "Do you actually suspect an Israeli strike on Kahuta?"

"Any people who have managed to survive five thousand years of relentless persecution have my respect."

CHAPTER THIRTY-EIGHT

Five days . . ." the Prime Minister murmured, his face ashen in the pale light.

Dado Harel and Zev Berger were seated at the large circular desk in the Prime Minister's office. Berger smoked, and Dado sipped sweet Turkish coffee—the caffeine helped keep him alert. He had managed only a few catnaps since returning from Rome—dark circles rimmed his eyes, and gray stubble covered his cheeks. He had been dividing his time between Air Force Command Headquarters in the Negev Desert and the Naval Command Center in Haifa, while consulting periodically with Professor Yuval Newman at the Red Sea port of Eilat. Newman was supervising the installation of supersecret equipment in a rusty twenty-five-year-old Greek freighter.

"Five days . . ." the Prime Minister repeated solemnly.

"We'll manage," Dado said. "We owe a great debt to Erika Sperling."

"What's the prognosis for her recovery?" the Prime Minister asked.

"The operating team believes there is a chance she can regain use of her left leg," Berger replied. "Her face requires further cosmetic surgery, but she's young and strong, and that's in her favor."

"We owe no less a debt to Tom Lawford," Dado added. "At the moment he's en route to Pakistan."

"Am I right in assuming that the Admiral is still unaware of our intentions to move against Kahuta?"

"All he knows is that Lawford will be passed precise data on Kahuta's infrastructure."

The Prime Minister sipped some buttermilk and asked Berger, "What is Admiral Dwinell's attitude toward our Libyan strike?"

"Totally cooperative. The Agency has supplied our Air Command with digital photographs of all principal Libyan targets. These photographs were taken by the American KH-11 satellite."

"How does one photograph an underground silo?"

"The KH-11's cameras captured the imprint of a circle in the sand adjacent to the Jarmah oasis," Dado explained. "This circle is actually a cover that slides open like any other underground missile silo."

"Can we penetrate this silo?"

"Our F-16's will be fitted with video-guided bombs. The explosive charge is designed to punch through the silo cover. The second wave will drop iron bombs with delayed fuses. Once the underground fuel-storage tanks ignite, the silo will become an inferno."

"Won't the V-5's warhead detonate?"

"Professor Newman doubts it."

"I have it here," Berger said, shuffling some papers. "This is from Newman. 'Implosion of a nuclear mass relies on precise detonation of conventional explosives within the warhead in order to compress a uranium core into a supercritical explosive mass . . .' "—Berger glanced up from the document—"which means that external concussion or fire will not in itself cause nuclear detonation."

"Why do you propose to hit the entire Libyan coast?" the Prime Minister asked Dado. "Why not a swift single, surgical strike at Jarmah?"

"For several reasons: this raid will balance the scales for

twenty years of Libyan-sponsored terrorism, and the size of the operation will send a warning message to Baghdad, Damascus, and Riyadh. And, hopefully, the Libyan raid will, in a sense, act as a cover for the Kahuta strike, which will take place five days later, just about the time the UN Security Council will be condemning us for attacking Libya."

"I have to say something here," Berger interjected. "I have no problem with the Libyan strike, but I want to go on record as being opposed to the Kahuta operation. Once Jarmah has been wiped out, why must we concern ourselves with Pakistan?"

"That's a bullshit, self-serving political question!" Dado snapped, his eyes blazing with anger. "You were the one who described Kahuta as the head of the snake, or am I wrong?"

"No," Berger said quietly, "but that was some time ago. I think the Libyan raid will be sufficient warning to the Pakistanis. On reflection, I find a strike on Kahuta political-ly unacceptable."

"You find? Who the hell are you to make that judgment? Even if we overlooked Pakistan's long-standing commit-ment to supply Qaddafi with nuclear warheads, there is nothing to prevent them from supplying Iraq or Syria with warheads. As long as Kahuta exists, Israel is only minutes from nuclear incineration."

"In any case," the Prime Minister addressed Berger, "Dado has assured me that the destruction of Kahuta will have the appearance of an internal accident, on the order of Chernobyl."

"How can you guarantee that?" Berger asked Dado.

"I believe the plan will succeed."

"And if you're wrong," Berger persisted, "the world will brand us as a gangster state."

"The world? The world?" Dado slammed his fist on the desk. "What fucking world? The same world that shut its eyes to the slaughter of two million Jewish children? In all the great Allied air raids, not one bomb was dropped on any of the thirteen Nazi killing centers. Not one rail hub was destroyed. The trains kept running. Day and night. Rain. Snow. The war raging all around. The trains kept running from all over Europe straight into the gas chambers. Stalin knew. Churchill knew. Roosevelt knew. They all knew. But no one cared. Not then. Not now. To whom shall we apologize for our survival? To the self-loathing Jews? To our home-grown theological fascists? To those frightened Israelis who deserted us to drive taxis in New York? To the Arabists in the news media? To those self-proclaimed intellectuals who characterize us as Nazis? To those oil-rich sheiks? To whom do we owe our destruction? Is your memory bank empty, Berger? Have you closed the book on history? The same Nazis who kept the trains running are at this moment five days away from achieving our destruction. When the Pakistanis tested their bomb, were they worried about world opinion? The sun is about to fall in our streets and you're concerned with a world that barely tolerates us. What the hell is there to think about?"

The General caught his breath and turned to the Prime Minister. "I have no time left, Zvikah. I'll bring Yuval Newman to explain the Kahuta operation in scientific detail." Dado left, slamming the door behind him.

Berger lit a fresh cigarette and coughed violently for a moment. The Prime Minister handed him a glass of water. "You smoke too much, Yanush."

Berger gulped the water and caught his breath. "I'm sorry. I should know better than to challenge him. He's a brilliant soldier, and a patriot. But he's motivated by a Holocaust mentality, and he's taking us to the edge of the abyss."

"No. You're wrong. Others are," the Prime Minister said, and sat down wearily. "I want your word that you will cooperate with him in every possible way."

"You have it. But I must go on record: Dado is dangerous, and consumed with vengeance for the Six Million. He goes his own way and he trusts no one."

"What do you expect? Any child who witnessed an endless stream of human beings gassed and burned in orderly fashion by a presumably civilized nation, will never again trust man or God. You and I can never understand his rage." The Prime Minister poured some buttermilk. "I don't disagree with your concerns over the Kahuta operation. If we fail, world opinion will bury us. I know that. But a nation makes choices. And men make choices: difficult, critical choices. But I can tell you this much: the plan that

Dado conceived is ingenious, and if successful, Kahuta will appear to have been destroyed by an internal accident—and there is no reason for the world to assume that Pakistan is immune to a nuclear accident. At one time or another, every nation employing nuclear power has suffered an accident."

Berger rose and shrugged. "Maybe this mission can be carried out without significant loss of life, without a hitch, without a mistake. But the chance of failure is there, and the abyss opens and the wild horse breaks loose. And even if this operation succeeds, the truth will eventually come out. Someone always talks."

"You're probably right. But what can we do? It's the way we live. This isn't the time for bickering. A decision has been taken, and I want you to give Dado all the help you can. We have five days . . . five days before the silo at Jarmah opens. And if the Libyan strike fails, Kahuta becomes academic, because we will no longer exist."

CHAPTER THIRTY-NINE

The Israeli port of Eilat and the Jordanian port of Aqaba were divided by less than fifteen miles of azure water. Although both nations were still technically in a state of war, they nevertheless respected the sanctity of each other's seaports. Their "hands-across-the-strait policy" was governed by mutual commercial interests. The Gulf of Aqaba flowed into the Red Sea and represented a gateway to the Far Eastern markets for both nations, and the powdery beaches, iridescent waters, and tropical climate provided both with a year-round tourist attraction producing millions in hard currency.

On the Israeli side of the gulf, Eilat was divided into three distinct enclaves: the Southern Naval Command, with its own piers and facilities; commercial cargo and shipping piers; and the resort area of marinas, beaches, and hotels.

The *Athenian Queen* was in dry dock in the commercial section of the port. The twenty-five-year-old freighter was dwarfed on either side by mammoth tankers unloading fuel purchased in Amsterdam's spot market by Israel's Ministry of Energy. The nation's underground storage tanks were strategically placed and always filled to capacity, ready to service a war machine that might be called upon at any moment.

Displacing twenty-five thousand tons, the *Athenian Queen* was six hundred feet long and sixty-eight feet abeam. Her paint was peeling, and her decks were stained with the residue of long-forgotten cargoes. A cacophony of jackhammers, hissing acetylene torches, bolt cutters, and amplified voices barking orders rose from her aft hold and foredeck. The obsolete Greek-registered freighter was fast acquiring a sophisticated lethality.

Its hull was being coated with a chemically treated nonreflective substance, making the ship difficult to pick up on long-range radar. State-of-the-art AN-TPD-37 radar dishes had been bolted to a steel post high above the bridge. Doppler digital electronic scanners and jammers had been installed and rigged alongside the stack. Global Positioning System, the most precise radio navigation ever developed, had been incorporated into the ship's electronic gyro systems. The freighter's ancient fire-tube boilers had been replaced with Mercedes-Benz turbines, permitting a flank speed of thirty nautical knots. The bridge was equipped with loran, sonar, and a supersolid Mitrek high-frequency radio console.

General Dado Harel shoved his sunglasses atop his head as he entered the bridge and joined the group surrounding Matty Alon. The square-jawed, dark-skinned Alon held the rank of commander in the Israeli Navy and had volunteered to captain this voyage. He was a decorated hero of three wars and had served in Dado's elite SOD unit. Alon had carefully selected the crew—the men were not only highly skilled seamen, but also spoke Greek and Arabic.

Alon and his chief navigator, Yossi, bent over an angled board on which a trace slide covered their planned route from Eilat to an interdict point forty miles southeast of Karachi in the Arabian Sea.

They discussed azimuths, longitudes, latitudes, minutes, degrees, moontides, currents, and seasonal wind direction. They would have a final meteorological profile on the night they sailed.

Alon tossed his pencil down and nodded to Dado, who followed him out onto the flying bridge.

Alon's eyes crinkled at the corners and he scratched the stubble on his cheeks. His voice was deep and authoritative. "At the southern tip of the Red Sea we pass into the Strait of Bab al-Mandab. You can spit into Yemen from the bridge. We have to appear totally innocent. East German pilots fly MIG-25's for Yemen. We have to be careful there and at Ras Rumera."

"Why would they bother with us? We're a Greek freighter riding high in the water, having unloaded a cargo of aluminum in Aqaba. We'll have the Jordanian manifests to prove it."

"The documentation is only helpful once the mission is completed. But you know very well we can never permit an inspection at sea."

"I understand, Matty. But I don't think South Yemen MIG's are going to be interested in this ancient freighter."

"Maybe so, but once we enter the Arabian Sea and pass Oman, there's the British naval base at Al Masirah—the Royal Navy supplements Omani coastal patrols."

"We'll be in international waters."

"They can still challenge us."

"So, we'll say hello." Dado squeezed Alon's shoulder. "We're a tired Greek freighter on our way to Calcutta."

The spiderweb lines at Alon's eyes sharpened as he frowned. "I'd feel better if we installed a battery of Quad-40's."

"No. It means more men, more camouflage, and if we're stopped by a frigate, the Quads won't help; besides, we'll have the *Dolphin* with us."

Alon stared at Dado with some surprise. "For sure?"

"It's arranged. Zichroni took care of it. The *Dolphin* will rendezvous with us at Juwara, south of the British base."

"We have to sail between two and three in the morning in order to be off Karachi in predawn light and avoid satellite detection."

"How many days do you calculate between departure and arrival?"

"No surprises . . . calm seas . . . five and a half days," he said, glancing at the nearby scruffy hills of Jordan. "What about the documents?"

"In process. Greek passports, ID cards, driver's licenses, inoculation certificates, letters from home, family photos, currency."

"When do we sail?"

"As soon as the pictures arrive."

"And if Lawford fails?"

"We go without them. Newman will have to make adjustments."

Alon stared off at the wide sweep of beach a half-mile away. "Look, Dado, the Swedish girls sunbathing, water-skiing, windsailing . . ."

"They help maintain our image of desperate tranquillity."

"Desperate or not, I'd like to be on the beach with those Swedes."

"What would you do?"

"What can I do at this stage of my life? I'd look and I'd fantasize." Alon grinned and slapped Dado's shoulder. "All right. Let's run the personnel down once more. We have Professor Newman and three of his staff. We have two pilots and a navigator for the Osprey, and my crew of eighteen men. Twenty-five in all."

"Twenty-six. You forgot about me."

"Does the Prime Minister know you're planning to be on board?"

"He will," Dado said. "How much more time do you need?"

"Seventy-two hours."

Dado walked aft and climbed down the ladder into the cavernous hold. It took a moment for his eyes to adjust to the work lights running off a small generator. As he crossed the gymnasium-size hold, his eardrums reverberated with the staccato rat-tat-tat of jackhammers cutting squares in the concrete base of a hydraulic platform.

Professor Yuval Newman supervised a team of aeronautical engineers who were seated at a computer console operating a maze of dials and multicolored luminous buttons. A projection screen displayed a concentric global spiderweb of grid lines, with Kahuta at its center. A digital readout flashed at the base of the screen: "Latitude 33.38 North/ longitude 73.27 East."

"A gnomonic map," Newman explained to Dado. "What you see is target data. Now, watch this." He gave an order to the computer technician, and the gnomonic map vanished, replaced instantly by a series of photographs of Kahuta, commencing at an altitude of 150,000 feet and descending in 10,000-foot increments, all the way down to a resolution of three feet, so that the concrete chips on the reactor's cupola stood out in bold relief.

"We transposed the satellite photographs from Soyuz-TM-6 to geometric modules and inserted the images into Jericho's brain," Newman explained. "Once the guidance system locks on target, nothing can deflect it from its programmed course."

Taking Dado by the arm, Newman walked the General over to a huge steel-plated hydraulic platform.

"The gantry will be welded to those bolted plates."

"And Jericho?"

"When it's assembled, I'll give you a guided tour." Newman paused. "When do I receive my Kahuta infrastructure pictures?"

"With luck, perhaps by tomorrow night. I must admit that I've never fully understood their importance. My understanding is that Jericho will do the job no matter how Kahuta lays out."

"That's technically correct. But in order to achieve target destruction and radioactive containment, I require precise structural intelligence. I have no desire to blow up northeast Pakistan. This has to be a surgical strike. Those photographs are critical. The idea is to create an implosion that will bury Kahuta under its own debris. If I'm forced to guess, Jericho could unleash the monster." He checked his watch. "Come, let's go up—it's almost time."

Their eyes narrowed against the bright sunlight as they stared off toward the beating sound of a helicopter's rotor blades coming in from the north.

"What about the Libyan strike?" Newman asked.

"0400 hours Thursday."

"That's cutting it too close. Suppose the Pakistanis ship the warhead a day or so early. Then what?"

"We still have a safety margin. A three-stage liquid-propelled rocket requires a forty-eight-hour countdown."

"Who told you that?"

"You did."

"I could be mistaken. My propulsion engineers could be mistaken. The Germans may have accelerated the V-5 fueling procedure."

"Well, what do you suggest?"

"Move it up. Hit Jarmah on Tuesday. Can you do that?"

Dado nodded. "Arik's boys have been set to go for weeks."

The chopper landed on the pier and its rotor blade decelerated.

"Come. Our taxi has arrived," Newman said. "What are we going to tell the Prime Minister?"

"The truth."

"Pakistan is a far cry from the Libyan operation," Newman cautioned. "Kahuta can turn into a catastrophe beyond imagination."

"The Prime Minister is a strong man. He understands the risks."

As they started down the gangway, Dado's fingers closed on Newman's arm. "When I say tell him the truth, I mean within reason."

High up on the bridge, Captain Matty Alon raised his binoculars and scanned the Jordanian side of the gulf. He swung the glasses slowly, panning the brown hills—and stopped abruptly as he saw what appeared to be the sun glinting off a long-lens telescope trained on the *Athenian Queen.*

Alon held the glasses steady and adjusted focus, fine-tuning the powerful lenses to his eyes, but detected nothing on the mountainside except the constantly rotating radar dish whose beams were aimed at Eilat.

CHAPTER FORTY

Tom Lawford opened the window shutters and a cool breeze smelling faintly of rain entered the suite. He studied the lacy pattern of lights lining the walkways of the vast public park and zoo opposite the hotel. Beyond the park, to the east, he could see the amber glow illuminating the tower of Badashi Mosque and the maze of colored lights surrounding the rose-colored Lahore Fort. The points of interest were, at least from a distance, exactly as described in the guidebook he had picked up at the Rome airport. He wished that he was here as a tourist and Erika was— A sudden chorus of thunderous roars interrupted his thoughts, and he remembered the concierge saying that one could hear the lions in the zoo being fed at night.

The phone rang loudly in two-ring cycles.

"I'm sorry to be late, Mr. Lawford." The rich baritone voice carried a British accent. "I've taken a table in the piano lounge."

"You mean the bar?"

"No . . . I mean the lounge. There are no bars in Faletti's

Hotel or any other hotel in Pakistan. I'll be seated at a table set between marble elephants."

The lounge was decorated with an Eastern elegance that was not evident in the gloomy lobby. Magnificent tapestries hung from the walls, and expensive Oriental rugs covered the tiled floors, and in the center of the room an atrium containing live palms soared up to a stained-glass ceiling.

The patrons compensated for the lack of alcohol by overdosing on tobacco. Cigarettes and cigars glowed in the semidarkness, and clouds of smoke drifted up to slowly revolving fans.

Salim Bashira wore a gray pin-striped suit, a dark blue shirt, and a maroon tie. In contrast, Lawford was dressed casually, in a suede jacket over an open blue shirt. They seemed an odd couple sitting in the flickering candlelight, shadowed on either side by a pair of tall, handsomely carved marble elephants. A single candle burned on their table.

Bashira glanced around, and nonchalantly moved the cut-glass candle holder to a vacant adjacent table.

"The candle holder usually contains a bug. A favorite device of General Murrani's Bureau of Counterintelligence," he explained, smoothing his wavy silvery hair. "There could be a sound gun aimed at us from several different angles, but one must inevitably dive into the pool—so to speak. Have a taste of your tea; it's made with ginseng root."

"Isn't ginseng considered to be an aphrodisiac?"

"So they say." Bashira smiled. "I find that sensual arousal is probably man's most subjective emotion. One can watch the most graphic pornography and feel nothing. I myself have, on occasion, been blessed with a woman whose smile could stimulate a gauze-wrapped mummy to erection. These things are in the mind. Don't you agree?"

"I'm no authority on the subject. I've always had bad luck with smiling women."

"Are you married?"

"Yes."

"So far, I've managed to avoid that bond. It seems a hopeless and unnatural undertaking." Bashira paused. "Speaking of women, I have a message for you from mutual friends. A woman who met with a recent accident is now apparently out of danger. She is, however, undergoing complicated reconstructive surgery. I was told the message would be self-explanatory."

"It is."

"Can I ask you a personal question?"

"Of course."

"You're an American. A Christian. You have no particular affinity for Israel. Why do you put yourself at risk?"

"I'm a journalist. Things like this are supposed to interest me. . . . They haven't for a long time. Does that answer your question?"

"Succinctly," Bashira said, and opened a platinum cigarette case and offered Tom a thin dark brown cigarillo.

"I shouldn't, but I will."

Bashira took a slim flask out of his jacket. "Rémy-Martin," he said, and poured a hefty shot into both their teacups. "It would be best if you remain in the hotel tonight. The food is passable, but drink only tea—no tap water—and nothing that's iced . . . no raw fruit or uncooked vegetables. We can't have you falling victim to dysentery."

"Curious," Tom said. "Sitting in a bar where no one is allowed to drink, but people are smoking themselves to death."

"The vagaries of Islam," Bashira said and lowered his voice. "At the presidential reception you will find yourself in the midst of Pakistan's military and political elite—the cream of Punjab, gathered together to celebrate Army Day. There will also be a representative international group of journalists, a contingent of foreign ambassadors with their wives or mistresses; in the case of the Italian ambassador, both. The music will be native to Pakistan, as will the food. A certain congeniality will be at play, but keep in mind: you will not be the only intelligence operative at the reception. Be careful with your idle conversation. The best policy is to smile and nod."

Bashira paused as a tall, striking woman wearing a red-and-yellow sari walked by on the arm of a diminutive Saudi sheik.

"Ah, look there, Mr. Lawford. That woman—the face of a madonna and the walk of a fifty-rupee whore. Forgive the digression." He paused. "At the appropriate moment, I will ask you for a cigarette. You will search your pockets and ask me for a match; if I have the goods, I will hand you a matchbook. The microfilm will be glued inside its cover. If I haven't received the goods, I will say I'm sorry, but I have no matches."

"Assuming you pass the matchbook to me, how do I get out?"

Bashira placed two hundred rupees on the table and said, "Come, my boy, let's stroll around the park and work up a little dinner appetite."

"I thought you were busy for dinner."

"I am. I have to meet with Intelligence Chief Murrani. I'm to give him a progress report on a shipment of a critical alloy called maraging steel."

"Do you spell that m-a-r-a-g-i-n-g?"

"Yes. Why do you ask?"

"That word was on the tape of a murdered friend of mine."

CHAPTER FORTY-ONE

Seated at his desk, General Murrani studied the list of Kahuta employees with red checks beside their names. The French windows were open and the sweet fragrance of jasmine filled the office. From time to time the intelligence chief would ask his aide for the detailed personal history of one of the checked names. They had been at it all day and had sifted through a long list of foreign-born technicians. The various offenses committed by the red-checked foreigners were minor: drunk driving, recreational drug use, petty theft, and simple assault—all committed in their native countries. There was one unusual case that caused Murrani a rare moment of amusement. A Belgian physicist had marched the length of the crack Simplon Express from club car to tourist, exposing himself all the way. After several tours, the train master finally apprehended the flasher and confined him to his stateroom under threat of arrest. Murrani wondered if the Belgian kept his fly zipped while handling radioactive material at Kahuta.

Murrani's smile faded as he scanned the names of the Pakistani nationals employed at Kahuta. Five names had been red-lined: an electrical engineer had an arrest charge for molesting a sixteen-year-old boy. Only the intervention of former director Farheed Shah had prevented the engineer's arrest. A senior chemist had been photographed by the secret police in the company of a suspected Afghan agent. A thorough investigation had uncovered nothing more than a coincidence—the men had been introduced by an Afghan refugee, a former college professor. Two other employees had been charged with occasional opium use, an insignificant offense. There was nothing in their respective files to suggest any subversive activity.

The fifth name aroused Murrani's interest. It belonged to a young physicist whose credentials gave him the freedom to move about the entire Kahuta facility—from the first-level reactor hall to the fifth-level plutonium-reprocessing hall. The physicist in question had been Farheed Shah's immediate assistant, and now served Dr. I. Q. Khan in a similar capacity. This same young man had also witnessed the seaborne nuclear-detonation test. A red check had been placed opposite Dr. Jamil Tukhali's name solely because of his place of birth—a remote village in the rebellious Baluchistani district. It defied credibility that anyone born to primitive tribal people could rise to such heights of technological brilliance on talent alone. In Pakistan, Tukhali would have needed more than remarkable ability; he would have required connections—high-level connections.

Murrani leaned back and tapped a ruler contemplatively into his open palm. The Baluchistani people never produced anything but gunmen and opium. How could it be that such an extraordinary talent had risen from such a backward people? And while there was nothing criminal in Tukhali's file, his success was at odds with his roots. The central government had fought a long, bitter war against the fiercely independent Baluchistani tribesmen, and it was entirely possible that Tukhali's family had suffered at the hands of government troops.

"Captain Meidan," Murrani called out to his aide.

"Yes, sir?" The young officer looked up from his files.

"Did you personally red-line the Pakistani nationals employed at Kahuta?"

"Those were my orders, sir."

"You have those files handy?"

"Yes, sir."

"Find the one on Dr. Jamil Tukhali."

The captain's fingers flew over the alphabetized readouts and pulled a sheet. "I have it, sir."

"In what village was Tukhali born?"

"Bughti—a village close by Quetta. It was destroyed by artillery and aerial bombardment in November 1978—at the conclusion of the Baluch insurrection."

"You say destroyed?"

"Destroyed and abandoned, sir."

"Impossible," Murrani replied. "I've been to that village. I accompanied President Zia there some years ago, on one of his political trips to that district. The village of Bughti is a collection of pastel stucco homes, clean streets, a school, and, amazingly enough, a hospital managed by an Indian doctor."

"But, sir, according to our records, Bughti was one of eighteen villages burned to the ground by napalm."

"Well, unless my memory is playing tricks, the village has been rebuilt."

"There is no record of government restoration."

"Phone Khattak in the Interior Ministry. Find out who paid for the reconstruction of the village, and when the work was undertaken."

"What does it matter, sir? I mean, what does it have to do with Dr. Tukhali?"

"Perhaps nothing. Perhaps everything. Tiles remain tiles until they're pieced together to form a mosaic. When have you heard of a hospital in a small Baluch village? A *hospital,* Captain! I was curious when we passed through in the presidential caravan. But I thought the hospital was one of Zia's magnanimous gestures."

The young intelligence officer paused, cleared his throat. "Forgive me, sir. But I still don't see—"

"It's simple, Captain," Murrani interrupted. "If the government left that village in ruins and did not finance its reconstruction, then who did? And why? A hospital, Captain—a goddamn hospital in that fly-infested tribal shithole!"

The phone console buzzed, and Murrani pressed a speaker button.

"Salim Bashira," the secretary announced.

Murrani picked up the receiver. "Salim, my friend. We have a reservation at the Kowloon in fifteen minutes."

"I have a report on the maraging shipment," Bashira said.

"Save it for dinner, and I expect you to be well-behaved. A pair of ladies will be joining us for dessert."

"I look forward to it."

Murrani hung up and stepped out onto the veranda and watched the workmen in the formal gardens below stringing colorful lanterns and setting up a banquet table. Electricians angled colored spotlights to illuminate and enhance the numerous fountains and marble cascades. The Army Day reception was already assuming a festive air, but Murrani was disturbed by a pervasive feeling of impending disaster. Something was amiss, a tile out of place, the mosaic blurred. The Libyan assassin, Hasi, killed in a Berlin shoot-out involving Kleiser's executive secretary, Erika Sperling. According to West German police, an Austrian woman, a tourist, was also killed. There was a missing taxi driver. Farheed Shah and the Swede blown up in Paris. The German rocket scientists Brunner and Mueller both murdered. Now the hospital in Tukhali's flyspecked village. Murrani sighed, thinking that perhaps he was unduly concerned. The shipment of the multiple nuclear warhead from Kahuta to Jarmah was imminent. In less than forty-eight hours, Tel Aviv and Haifa would cease to exist. Pakistan's historic agreement with Qaddafi would finally be fulfilled. The Zionist state would be obliterated and yet no fingers could be pointed at Pakistan. Qaddafi would strut and preen and act out whatever role he believed Allah had written for him, but Pakistan would remain above world suspicion. After all, they had fired no missiles and set off no bombs.

The logical analysis of events calmed Murrani's nagging fears. He took deep lungfuls of the sweet jasmine air and cleared his mind. He would enjoy himself tonight. Bashira was good company, and Bengali women were always interesting.

CHAPTER FORTY-TWO

The high whine of fourteen thousand whirling centrifuges penetrated the plugged eardrums of white-clad technicians who checked the fuel rods bombarding the reactor pool with neutrons. Serpentine copper pipes carried the radioactive chain into the spinning centrifuges that separated the plutonium isotopes from the enriched uranium.

Above the floor, paratroopers patrolled the catwalk circling the great Kahuta cupola. Specially trained guard units fanned out through the first level and rode up and down the elevators, making their presence felt in all five levels. Plainclothes secret police kept watch over engineers, physicists, and computer technicians as they performed their sensitive chores.

Standing on the observation deck above the reactor hall, Dr. I. Q. Khan and Dr. Jamil Tukhali gazed down at the apocalyptic testament to Pakistani science.

"Three hundred centrifuges broke loose from their bearings at 3:13 A.M.," Tukhali said. "We have never maintained capacity output."

"As we speak, Salim Bashira is acquiring two thousand bearing molds of maraging steel," Dr. Khan replied.

"Forgive me, sir, but I've heard that many times during my tenure."

"Bashira has performed miracles for us in the past, and he will again."

"When do we expect to receive these casings?"

"We shut down in four days for refueling. The maraging bearings are due to arrive before we resume operations."

The wall phone lit up and blinked. Tukhali grabbed the receiver, spoke briefly, and hung up.

"That was Superintendent Mehta. He asks that you inspect the warhead before it's crated."

They got off the elevator at the fifth level and passed the storage rooms containing lead coffins of plutonium before entering a huge, harshly lit room. The walls, floor, and ceiling were made of burnished copper sufficiently thick to prevent plutonium seepage.

A tall man wearing a white apron, white gloves, and gauze mask stood alongside three other similarly dressed technicians. They stared at the six-by-three-foot conical nuclear warhead resting on a conveyor belt at the end of which was a large wooden crate waiting to receive its doomsday cargo. The warhead possessed sufficient blast power to obliterate a five-square-mile radius—more than twice the explosive force unleashed on Hiroshima.

The superintendent removed his face mask and turned to Dr. Khan. "I assume the inertial guidance and computer bearings will be fitted by the German technicians at the launch site."

"That is correct."

"With that in mind, I thought you might want to personally check the detonation package before we inserted it."

"It's all been checked, tested, and X-rayed. Proceed with assembly and shipment."

CHAPTER FORTY-THREE

A dark red ball rose up over the horizon, silhouetting the men and machines grouped around the Pakistani C-17. The huge transport plane had landed after an uneventful ten-hour flight from Rawalpindi to Jarmah. Sitting upright on the cargo ramp, the multinuclear warhead protruded from its wooden crate. At the opposite end of the desert strip, Kleiser's Lear jet stood waiting.

A detail of Libyan paratroopers wearing green uniforms and red berets eased the doomsday crate down the aircraft's conveyor belt. The unloading procedure was performed with reverential awe. The soldiers avoided touching the conical warhead as if the mere caress of a human hand would trigger a cataclysmic explosion. The trailer crane hoist was poised above the conveyor belt waiting for the soldiers to position the crate atop steel cables laid out on the desert floor.

Dr. Fritz Kleiser and a sunburned Walter Diehl observed the proceedings along with a team of young German technicians whose job it was to attach the warhead to the V-5 rocket.

An almost religious silence surrounded the men as they watched the burly paratroopers inch the crate down the conveyor rollers. The beatific stillness was suddenly broken by jarring radio static, followed by a burst of Arabic. A soldier operating a high-frequency transmitter motioned to the officer in charge, who jogged over, picked up the microphone, answered briefly in prearranged code, and signed off. The officer then issued an order and the detail came to attention.

A distant speck appeared in the northern sky, and drew closer, gradually assuming the shape of a grotesque grasshopper. The huge Soviet-made MI-24 helicopter came in low, banked eastward, and hovered in the crimson light, settling slowly, its giant rotors stirring up thick, swirling clouds of sand.

The cabin door opened and an accordionlike stepladder was lowered to the ground. Six women soldiers carrying automatic weapons and wearing leopard camouflage uniforms came down the stairs and stood at attention on either side.

Seconds later, a white-robed Qaddafi descended and strode past his German colleagues without a nod. The paratroop officer saluted, but Qaddafi ignored the respectful gesture. Removing his reflective glasses, he stared at the warhead protruding from the crate. He pressed his palms against its conical sides and bowed his head in prayer. A light wind moaned through the wadis and dunes, underscoring the palpable silence.

After a long moment, Qaddafi raised his head and stared off at a distant funnel of sand that had risen from the desert floor, obscuring the dawn light. The sand cloud was a good omen. The finger of God was obliterating the sun, just as this bomb would obliterate the Zionist predators.

Without a word or gesture of recognition to anyone, he reentered the helicopter. The female soldiers followed him, and the accordion steps withdrew. The cabin door closed and locked. The high whine of twin jets screamed and the rotor blades rotated and whirled, kicking up a cloud of dust. The MI-24, like some prehistoric flying bug, rose, gained altitude, veered sharply north, and disappeared.

Pointing off toward the gathering funnel of sand, the

Pakistani pilot of the C-17 leaned out of the cockpit window and shouted down to the Libyan ground crew. The paratroop officer waved his acknowledgment and his men quickly hooked the six-foot-tall wooden crate onto the crane cable. The warhead was raised and swung out over the flatbed truck and lowered into the waiting hands of the German technicians. The cables were released and the truck lumbered off toward the underground silo.

At the head end of the landing strip, Kleiser's Lear jet revved its engines.

Kleiser shouted over the noise and asked Diehl what time the launch was scheduled to lift off.

"Six-fifty-five A.M.," Diehl replied, "approximately forty-eight hours from now."

Kleiser nodded. "In case of emergency, you can reach me at the Palace Hotel in St. Moritz."

"And Lawford?"

"He's returned to New York. The article's been filed. I spoke with the AP bureau chief in Rome, and he gave me a brief capsule of the piece. In essence it makes the case for our seeking financial support from Qaddafi, and says that if the V-5 is misused, it's certainly no fault of ours. The initial segment breaks in the world press this Sunday."

"I'm worried about Fräulein Sperling's connection to Mossad."

Kleiser looked at the old man with fleeting disdain. "Erika was not Mossad. She was planted by West German Federal Police."

"How do you know that?"

"Inspector Lehmans closed the case. The police have thrown a wall around her. Erika worked for the Bundeswehr."

As Diehl started to speak, the Pakistani C-17 revved up, and the whalelike craft began to taxi.

"I must go!" Kleiser shouted.

The men embraced and Kleiser ran up the steps, which were immediately withdrawn and the Lear jet's door locked.

Diehl climbed into a jeep and followed the dust cloud raised by the flatbed truck carrying the warhead.

The Libyan paratroopers loaded into jeeps and headed back toward the shelter of the Jarmah oasis.

Kleiser's plane hurtled down the strip and arced up into the lightening sky. Seconds later, the C-17 roared down the makeshift runway with full power on all four engines. Reluctantly it broke free of gravity, and its huge head rose up into the sky.

A Taureg chieftain emerged from the Jarmah palm grove and stared off at the distant towering cloud of whirling sand. He motioned to a group of bedouin sweepers that their brooms would not be required to obscure the landing strip from the prying eyes of orbiting satellites. The imminent sandstorm would obliterate all marks left by aircraft and vehicles.

CHAPTER FORTY-FOUR

Two F-16's, camouflaged sand and green, howled across the desert floor, sliced through a narrow mountain ridge, and hurtled out over the Mediterranean.

"Group commanders," Air Force Chief Carmil explained to Dado. "Tomorrow the boys will pay Qaddafi a memorable visit."

They were standing on an observation deck below the control-tower radar dish. "We've launched fifty flights a day: F-15's flying aerial-combat exercises and the F-16's practicing low-level bombing runs. Come, Dado, before it gets dark, I want to show you something."

Descending the spiral steel steps, they walked to a waiting jeep in which Narda sat beside a young officer. They got into the rear seat and the officer gunned the jeep and sped off past ground crews working on a C-135 tanker. At the far end of the field they slowed down and turned into a huge hangar.

Inside the immense darkness, a single floodlit F-16 was being fitted with a vast array of missiles, flares, electronic pods, and bombs. Speaking in the elite and alien language of twenty-first-century combat pilots, General Carmil conducted Dado on a tour of the sleek aircraft. Narda listened, but did not understand the strange litany of Sparrows, Sidewinders, Popeyes, MK-82 Snakeyes, Amraam, Orpheus Recce Pods, SUU-25 flares, Wild Weasel radar-detector pods, inertial guidance, look-down radar display, fuel cells, and drop tanks.

Dado and Carmil studied the F-16 with the awed reverence reserved for a priceless work of art. In that instant, Narda perceived the true tragedy of the nation: an American jet fighter had become the treasured icon of Israel.

After dinner, Narda and Dado joined two hundred airmen in an underground theater, where General Carmil conducted his final briefing of Operation Red Desert. While each wing group had its own respective targets, all five attack squadrons were aware of the full scope and objectives of the mission. Each pilot was familiar with the full range of targets extending from Tripoli to Benghazi.

The Libyan coast was lit up on a huge screen behind Carmil. The various targets were color-coded and flashing: terrorist training camps, oil refineries, airfields, tank parks, poison-gas factories, radar installations, missile batteries, and the small nuclear-research reactor at Tajura—and, in vivid orange, the underground V-5 silo at Jarmah. Carmil reviewed the coordinated timing of the predawn attack by sea commandos and missile attack ships. After he concluded, Carmil introduced Dado.

The airmen were very young, but they knew the history of the man walking up to the stage. General Dado Harel was part of Israel's military mythology. The pilots saw in his imposing figure signposts of the state's violent history. It was the first time the chief of the supersecret Special Operations Division had come to address them, and they felt honored by his presence.

Dado waited for absolute silence before speaking. "All of you in this room represent a tradition of courage and excellence. You are the nation's silhouette in the sky. You are the front line of Israel. You are the best men we have. And we must call upon you once more. The survival of the state is at stake. The enemy is a practitioner of murder. A financier of murder. A killer of those who are defenseless. The Libyan dictator is a pathological terrorist who believes he has the ear of God. He has managed at last to realize his dream—the possession of nuclear warheads obtained from Pakistan. He has also acquired an ICBM delivery system from modern-day Nazi rocket scientists. We have an old score to settle with these murderers—an outstanding debt—and tomorrow morning you boys will be the collectors."

Dado paused. The upturned young faces reminded him of his son, Dani, and all the fallen in all the wars. They were the children of the lost tribes of Yahweh. The blood of Abraham, Isaac, Jacob, Moses, and Jesus coursed through their veins. They belonged to scriptures and testaments, inquisitions, pogroms, gas chambers, and G-forces. They saw lions and they were lions. What could one say to these boys? There could be no protective detachment, no optimistic allegories. He owed them nothing less than a diamond-hard truth.

In a subdued tone he said, "No matter how successful we are in carrying out this mission, our struggle will not end. The war is continuous. The tunnel is long, and there is no light. In this moment, you are the light of Israel. Tomorrow, the spirit of all our fallen comrades will fly with you."

The theater was silent as the General left the stage. Only Narda took notice of the fact that Dado had not invoked the name of God in his speech to the fliers.

Yahweh remained the demon in Dado's subconscious, an unforgiving, all-powerful trickster lurking in clouds of locomotive steam.

The General parked the jeep at the museum's hilltop entrance. Far below, the floodlit spires and domes of Jerusalem's Old City glowed in the moonless night. Dado tossed his cigarette away and motioned to his soldier bodyguards that he would be only a moment.

The doorman had been expecting him and the old man saluted as the General entered the Hall of Remembrance. The cavernous museum was illuminated by mirrors reflecting the surreal flickering light of countless candles. There were no exhibits. No sounds. No words. No statistical abstractions. Only photographs of Jewish children staring innocently at the camera moments before being gassed. In the trusting eyes of the condemned children, Dado perceived the raison d'être of Israel's existence.

CHAPTER FORTY-FIVE

F ifteen miles off the Libyan coast, due north of Tripoli, an Israeli "Reshef II" command frigate wallowed in the deep Mediterranean troughs. Forty miles to the east, two more frigates were poised off Misurata, their missiles targeted on Libyan SA-5 antiaircraft installations. One hundred miles farther east, an LCVP shrouded in a smoke screen laid down by an attack corvette chugged toward the Benghazi cove. The landing craft carried an elite Seaborne Commando Assault Team. Faces blackened, the men were seated in jeeps, waiting for the impact of the keel heaving up onto the beach.

Twenty-five thousand feet above the Israeli flotilla, an E-2C Hawkeye battle-command radar plane circled in a tight radius. The control center of the Hawkeye was illuminated in a pale green light cast by a computerized radar-image locator.

Standing just behind technicians seated at the glowing panel, General Arik Carmil checked the computer's digital clock. It read 4:16 A.M. Using a Mode 3 UMF-FM channel,

Carmil radioed the Reshef command frigate: "Aladdin to Seagull One. Over."

"This is Seagull One, Aladdin. Over."

"Time check—0416. Over."

"Affirmative. Sharks deployed. Over."

"Roger, stand by, Seagull One. Over."

"Seagull One—standing by. Over and out."

Carmil carefully studied the radar-warning scope scanning the Libyan coast. The luminous screen indicated no aircraft blips in or out of Tripoli International Airport or the adjacent military air base. Shifting his attention to the large circular three-hundred-mile-radius display screen, Carmil scrutinized the data transmitted by the disk-roto-dome suspended high above the E-2C's fuselage. The blips of light indicated no intruders in the air or at sea.

The navigator handed Carmil a steaming mug of coffee. "We should soon be picking up our F-15 cover."

The digital clock read 4:19 A.M. The LCVP would now be moving at flank speed toward the Benghazi cove. Once the ramp hit the beach, the assault team would race their jeeps along the coastal road and conduct a lightning strike against the Benghazi air-defense complex. Intelligence data gathered over a five-week period confirmed little or no traffic on the coast road between three and five A.M. The LCVP would hit the beach in twenty minutes. The jeeps would take ten minutes to traverse the sixteen kilometers from landing point to target. Carmil ordered the flight engineer to set the battle clock to thirty minutes.

"We have F-15's, sir!" the radar man shouted.

The engineer tuned the rotodome disk east-southeast ten degrees and Carmil saw the computer-enhanced image of the distinctive twin-dorsal combat craft. The F-15's were armed with state-of-the-art AIM-9, AIM-7, and AIM-120 missile systems, constituting a lethal array of aerial-combat weaponry. They would fly top-cover for the five separate F-16 bomber groups. Each F-16 carried three two-thousand-pound iron bombs, AGM-88 antiradar missiles, heat-deflector balloons, and pods of "Popeye" high-explosive rockets. The F-16 wing groups were code-named for their respective targets: Red Desert-1, Tripoli; Red Desert-2, Tajura and Misurata; Red Desert-3, Surt; Red Desert-4, Benghazi; and Red Desert-5, the V-5 silo at Jarmah.

At 0436 hours the LCVP's ramp splashed down onto the muddy beach at Benghazi cove. The commandos gunned their jeeps up the beach onto the coast road and sped along the two-lane highway unchallenged. At kilometer stone six they saw the amber lights of the SA-5 Communication Center. The column broke off into three groups.

Firing automatic weapons and grenade launchers, the lead formation charged through the main gate.

Group Two circled the base and broached the seaside gate.

Group Three blew a hole in the perimeter fence and raced toward the fire-control radar complex.

Sappers placed TNT satchels at missile bunkers.

Assault squads charged into barracks, spraying automatic fire at the startled Libyan soldiers.

At 0450 hours three munitions bunkers and six SAM-9 missile batteries blew up, turning the sprawling base into a blazing inferno.

Libyan soldiers stumbled out of their barracks and returned the fire, but caught unawares, they were no match for the precision of the attacking force.

Assault teams shot their way into the central-command bunker and set a three-minute-delay TNT charge in the radar-control dome.

Sapper teams blew up the fuel depot and a searing heat enveloped the base, accompanied by thunderous roars and shattering concussion rings.

Libyan antiaircraft gun crews trained a ZSV-23 multibarreled gun into the central compound, pouring a hailstorm of indiscriminate fire into the exploding inferno. Libyan soldiers as well as Israeli commandos fell under the relentless fire.

The delayed fuses on the TNT satchels and plastic disks detonated, and the entire complex erupted in a tidal wave of bright red flames.

The Israeli commandos hauled the bodies of their dead and wounded comrades into the jeeps and took off on the

Coast Highway, speeding back toward the cove. Eighteen minutes had elapsed from the time the LCVP ramp had splashed down on the muddy bank.

In the circling E-2C Hawkeye command center, General Carmil pressed the air-to-sea intercom button.

"Aladdin to Seagull One. Report on sharks. Over."

The command Reshef II's captain responded immediately. *"Seagull One to Aladdin. Sharks returning to mother. Mission achieved. Casualties moderate. Over."*

"Roger, Seagull One," Carmil replied. "Deploy 'Gabriels'! Over."

"Roger. Over and out."

A devastating salvo of "Gabriel" sea-to-land missiles was launched from the attacking flotilla. High-explosive warheads homed in on the preprogrammed targets at Tripoli, Misurata, Surt, Rabta, and the naval base at Benghazi.

The rotoscope operator at the E-2C console called out, "Red Desert on screen!"

Carmil saw the fast-approaching blips of the F-16 bomber groups. He grabbed the microphone and said, "Red Desert One. This is Aladdin. Over."

"Read you, Aladdin. Over."

"Deploy to target. Repeat. Deploy to target. Over."

"Roger. Over and out."

The Tripoli air-defense commander at Azziza Barracks ordered all coastal antiaircraft and missile batteries into action. Tracers, like slivers of neon, crisscrossed the dawn sky and salvos of SAM-9 ground-to-air missiles were fired without benefit of radar, the radar-control installations having been knocked out by the sea-launched Gabriels. Frantic reports from Benghazi indicated a seaborne invasion was under way.

The Azziza commander was certain that the entire coast was under attack from a large naval-air battle group attached to the U.S. Sixth Fleet.

The sea-launched missile barrage and commando assault had now been joined by massive aerial bombardment. Tons of high explosives rained down on military targets from

Tripoli to Benghazi: airfields, radar-control centers, SA-5 missile launchers, poison-gas factories, Army and Navy bases, tank parks, and guerrilla training camps. A late report confirmed the destruction of the small nuclear-research facility at Tajura.

The commander was losing his voice. For the last twenty minutes he'd been shouting orders above the cacophony: phones rang incessantly, radar operators called out location changes on fast-moving green blips, officers barked orders at their adjutants and immediately countermanded them.

The youthful Libyan commander pleaded in vain with Air Defense at Surt for MIG-27 jet-fighter groups to go up and challenge the attacking U.S. F-16's. The Air Force chief refused, saying it was impossible to launch flights while under bombardment.

Agonizing, the commander wished Colonel Qaddafi was present to assume charge, but the Leader was in Khartoum on a state visit to Sudan. His only option was to be certain that SAM-9 missile batteries and ZSV-23 antiaircraft guns remained in action.

He was about to ring up Tripoli Southern Air Command when his adjutant handed him a telex report from the naval base at Surt. The commander's breath whistled through his teeth, and his eyes widened in disbelief: four F-16's had been hit and gone down over the Mediterranean, and a piece of wing debris had been recovered bearing the solid blue Star of David. Momentarily speechless, the commander cleared his throat and said, "Try to reach Colonel Qaddafi at the Presidential Palace in Khartoum."

Far below the surface, at Military Command Center in Tel Aviv, General Dado Harel, Narda Simone, and Adam Zichroni were seated at the combat communication console, monitoring the incoming reports from General Arik Carmil.

The digital clock over the display screen read 5:25 A.M. The Prime Minister was at his home, anxiously awaiting Dado's report—only the Minister of Defense and Inner Cabinet had been advised of the strike. The nation and the world were still unaware of the raid.

"Aladdin to Lamplight!" Carmil's voice suddenly boomed over the communication speaker. *"Aladdin to Lamplight. Over!"*

"This is Lamplight. Over," Dado shouted.

"Seagull flotilla returning to base. All principal targets achieved. Four Red Desert falcons down—have beeper readings on two. Red Desert groups one through four refueling and returning. Red Desert Five en route to Jarmah target. Will advise. Over."

"Roger, Aladdin. Over and out."

Five hundred and fifty miles south of Tripoli, deep in the underground silo and unaware of the Israeli raid, Walter Diehl inspected the computer-readout screen. High-ranking Libyan officers were seated alongside the German ascent-systems engineers.

They were seven minutes from launch, and counting. The V-5 was fueled, the multiple warhead attached and programmed to target. The booster engines displayed no malfunction. Diehl addressed his chief engineer: "Retract silo covers at three minutes to launch."

The eight F-16's in the Red Desert-5 squadron swooped over the desert floor in arrow formation. The wing commander had the Jarmah oasis on his "look-down" radar screen and the circle-in-the-sand marking the underground silo was faintly discernible on the infrared TV screen. He flicked a toggle switch arming the Paveway laser-guided Smart Bombs that would punch through the silo's lid before the squadron unloaded their two-thousand-pound MK-84 iron bombs.

The wing commander pressed the intercom on his oxygen-feed line.

"Eagle to Red Desert Five. Climb and follow!"

The arrow formation climbed skyward, discharging an exploding array of orange heat-emitting missile-deflection balloons.

"Eagle to Red Desert . . ." The wing commander's voice was suddenly suspended in mid-sentence, interrupted by an incredible sight. The circle-in-the-sand was slowly opening in two equal halves.

* * *

Inside the silo, Diehl, his engineers, and Libyan officers blinked at the bright sunlight streaming in as the protective lid withdrew. The chief German engineer activated a hydraulic lever, and warning sirens wailed as the V-5 launch platform rose.

Flashing out of the sun, the F-16's peeled off and followed their wing commander down toward the opening crevice in the desert floor.

As the V-5's gleaming nose cone emerged from the open silo, the wing commander fired his Paveway bombs and banked sharply. A yellow sheet of flame shot skyward from the open silo.

The F-16's dived, dropping sixty thousand pounds of bombs into the flaming silo.

Palm trees in the Jarmah oasis were torn from their roots by concussion rings, and a searing, fiery-red column rose up from the silo and towered above the desert floor.

The Red Desert-5 group jettisoned their external fuel tanks, banked sharply, and hurtled north, climbing toward their rendezvous with KC-130 tankers.

Zichroni and Narda watched Dado pacing the carpet in the underground communication center.

"Either Red Desert Five achieved its mission," Dado said, "or in fourteen minutes Tel Aviv and Haifa are memories."

"How do you arrive at fourteen minutes?" Zichroni asked.

"They'd have to launch by . . ." Dado's voice trailed off as a burst of static sounded on the intercom.

"Aladdin to Lamplight! Aladdin to Lamplight! Over!"

Dado rushed to the console and pressed the intercom button. "Lamplight reads. Over!"

"Red Desert Five mission achieved," General Carmil reported. *"Target destroyed. Wing commander advised that the silo had already opened. Over."*

Wiping beads of perspiration from her forehead, Narda sighed in relief.

Zichroni whispered a thankful prayer.

"What are our losses, Aladdin?" Dado asked anxiously. "Over."

"The bodies of four pilots have been recovered from the sea. Two pilots were rescued by the Reshef II. Sea Commando Assault Group reports eight killed and fourteen wounded. Seagull flotilla and Red Desert groups returning to base. Over."

"Come home, Aladdin. Over."

"Roger, Lamplight. Over and out."

The communications room fell silent. There was no jubilation or handshaking. Dado dialed the Prime Minister. The call was answered instantly.

"Mr. Prime Minister, I'm pleased to report that Red Desert achieved all objectives. Considering the scope of the operation, our casualties were light."

Dado accepted the Prime Minister's congratulations and assured him that the Kahuta operation was proceeding on schedule. The *Athenian Queen* would sail at three o'clock the following morning.

The Prime Minister promptly briefed the Minister of Defense and five members of the Inner Cabinet on the results of Red Desert, but made no mention of the impending Kahuta operation. He ordered his press secretary to call a news conference for ten A.M.

Once alone, the Prime Minister dialed the American ambassador on a secure line.

The ambassador's voice was sleep-laden but he managed a polite, "Good morning, Mr. Prime Minister."

"Good morning to you, Kenneth. I'm sorry to have awakened you but I have urgent news for you."

"What is it?"

"I wish to inform you that at five A.M. our time, the Israeli Defense Forces carried out a preemptive strike against selected military targets in Libya."

After a moment of silence the American ambassador said, "You don't say . . ."

CHAPTER FORTY-SIX

The pressroom at the Ministry of Information in Jerusalem overflowed with the large contingent of foreign journalists. A babel of languages rose from the group of excited men and women awaiting the arrival of the Prime Minister. Rumors surrounding the early-morning Israeli raid were raging.

The UN Security Council had been called into emergency meeting.

Colonel Qaddafi was at the moment en route from Khartoum to Tripoli.

The Arab League had convened an extraordinary session in Algiers.

The People's Republic of China, the USSR, Italy, and France had already condemned the Israeli air strike.

The Royal Saudi Army and Air Force had been placed on full alert.

The Syrian Minister of Defense was en route to Tripoli.

The Iraqi strongman, Sadam Hussein, had placed his million-man army at the disposal of his Libyan brothers.

The American KH-11 satellite had detected a radioactive

cloud over the devastated Libyan reactor at Tajura. The degree of radioactivity was slight and drifting south over the uninhabited desert wastes. Cyanide and mustard-gas emissions were reported fifty miles south of Tripoli from the ruins of an immense poison-gas factory.

The U.S. destroyer *Kingman*, cruising inside the Gulf of Sidra, had rescued a downed Israeli pilot.

The tense, high-pitched gaggle of voices lowered abruptly as the Israeli Prime Minister, flanked by his press secretary and Minister of Defense, entered the pressroom.

The youthful press secretary stepped up to the lectern. "Prime Minister Shomron will issue a brief statement, after which he will take questions. Please be aware that certain military operational details will not be forthcoming at this time."

The Prime Minister adjusted the goosenecked lectern microphone and sipped some water. His eyes seemed sunken, and his skin was pallid. He studied the sea of faces before him—some were familiar, others not, some friendly, others hostile. He had to take care. The journalists were seasoned and clever. He would describe the missile silo at Jarmah without revealing the presence of nuclear warheads. He wanted to avoid any dialogue that would probe into how and from whom Qaddafi had acquired nuclear warheads. Such questions would inevitably lead to Pakistan and might compromise the impending Kahuta mission. Zev Berger had suggested that in his address the Prime Minister substitute "poison-gas warheads" in place of "nuclear warheads."

The Prime Minister cleared his throat and in a voice strained by fatigue and anxiety spoke slowly, deliberately.

"At five o'clock this morning, units of the Israeli Defense Forces launched a combined air-sea strike against selected military targets in Libya—a nation that has been in a state of war with Israel since 1948." He paused, giving the journalists an opportunity to keep pace with their hastily scribbled notes.

"Our forces scrupulously avoided civilian areas," the Prime Minister continued. "The action was preemptive in nature and undertaken to deter the terrorist leader of that state from launching a doomsday device against Tel Aviv and Haifa. Our Air Force located and destroyed a secret missile base in the western Libyan desert at the oasis of Jarmah. This base was financed by Colonel Qaddafi, but it was designed and staffed by rocket scientists under the direction of Dr. Fritz Kleiser and his colleague Walter Diehl. Kleiser and others are affiliated with a West German company known as Space Transportation Systems." The Prime Minister paused and sipped some water. "Intelligence reports confirmed the existence at Jarmah of advanced intercontinental rockets known as V-5's, armed with multiple warheads containing lethal Tabun poison gas. We have repeatedly warned not only Colonel Qaddafi but also Syria, Iraq, and Saudi Arabia that Israel will not hesitate to defend its citizens with every means at our disposal. We have wished for peace for almost fifty years, but that peace will not be made in exchange for our destruction and disappearance. We are an ancient people. We have survived five thousand years of persecution and unspeakable violence. We are still here. And we will remain here. Our enemies should make no mistake: the State of Israel will not perish." He paused. "Now, ladies and gentlemen, I will do my best to answer your questions."

An array of hands instantly shot up, and shouts for recognition filled the pressroom.

CHAPTER FORTY-SEVEN

Reclining naked in the brilliant sunshine flooding his sun deck, Dr. Fritz Kleiser surveyed the frozen lake and towering alpine peaks of St. Moritz. He had been skiing for three days, but his recreational activities had not been confined to the ski slopes. His Geneva banker had provided a very young, expensive Swiss call girl.

Kleiser sipped a vodka and fresh blood-orange juice and listened to a soccer game between West Germany and Italy. It was a diversion while he waited anxiously for the news bulletin announcing the nuclear destruction of Tel Aviv and Haifa.

The V-5 launch should have occurred an hour ago, unless there had been an engine malfunction and the launch postponed. But in that case, Diehl would have called. On the other hand, there might have been a minor delay and the countdown pushed back an hour or so. In any event, Diehl was a veteran of countless rocket launches and capable of addressing any technical problem.

The Italians scored a goal and perhaps that was a good omen; Kleiser had made a large bet on the Italian team. He sighed with satisfaction, thinking of the seven hundred million dollars Qaddafi had transferred to the STS account in Hamburg. He sipped his drink and flicked his sunglasses down over his eyes.

He had almost dozed off when an announcer's voice interrupted the game with a news bulletin. Kleiser bolted upright and listened in shocked disbelief.

"... *The Israeli force struck targets all along the Libyan coast. Included in the attack was an alleged rocket base in the deep Libyan desert at Jarmah. The combined air-sea assault was well-coordinated and designed to—*" Kleiser snapped the radio off. A knot of heat and pain balled up in his stomach. Erika, he thought. Erika! Abu Hasi had been right. She had somehow discovered the Jarmah site and betrayed him to Mossad. Her treachery had condemned him. His name would be placed at the top of Qaddafi's hit list. A team of assassins was probably combing Europe for him at this very moment. My God, he thought. My God ...

The Swiss girl came out onto the terrace. Her small white teeth were nibbling on a jam-laden piece of toast.

"Is something wrong, Putzi?" she asked demurely as she walked toward him, naked. "Have I upset my Putzi?"

His rage and terror fused and focused on the dumb peasant face smiling ingenuously at him.

He hit her twice. She fell backward, bouncing hard on the wooden decking. He straddled her and struck her repeatedly, cursing her with each blow, hammering at her until her face was unrecognizable.

CHAPTER FORTY-EIGHT

Beth-Zion Military Hospital was situated in a pine forest on a high bluff overlooking the Mediterranean. The sprawling medical complex was considered to be one of the finest orthopedic-reconstructive-surgery centers in the world. During Israel's fifty years of almost continuous warfare, the staff of surgeons and therapists had repaired shattered bodies and replaced lost limbs with a remarkable record of success.

As he came out of the hospital's administration building, Zev Berger squinted in the bright sunlight for a moment before spotting Erika Sperling. She wore a blue robe and huge dark glasses, and her wheelchair faced the sea.

Her face was scarred with purple stitches that ran from her right cheekbone down to the corner of her mouth. The doctors had assured her that cosmetic surgery would obscure the scarred tissue. An intramedullary rod had been inserted in her left leg, replacing the shattered thigh bone, and would eventually support her weight and permit mobility.

She removed her sunglasses as the portly intelligence chief kissed her forehead. "You'll find some flowers in your room and a box of cookies," he said, trying not to show his shock at seeing her scarred face. "The flowers I'm sure you'll enjoy. The cookies . . ." He shrugged. "Passable at best. My wife is not a baker."

"Don't ever tell her that." Erika smiled.

"Never," he agreed, and took an envelope out of his pocket and handed it to her. "The Prime Minister wants you to have this. Just a few lines to express his personal gratitude on behalf of the state."

Erika examined the state seal of the menurah for a moment before saying, "Narda told me that the rocket silo had already opened. Is it true?"

"The wing commander's cameras photographed it. We calculate that the rocket was only eight minutes from lift-off."

"Eight minutes . . ." she murmured.

"Apparently the nuclear warheads had been received forty-eight hours earlier than we anticipated. Fortunately we acted in time."

"And what of Kahuta?"

Berger shifted uncomfortably. "We're working on it. Lawford is at the moment in Lahore. He volunteered to help effect the transfer of a critical piece of intelligence."

"Promise me something." She chewed the corner of her lower lip. "I don't want to see him. Not now. Not like this."

"You have my word."

A nurse wearing a powder-blue uniform came toward them.

"It's whirlpool time," Erika sighed.

"I have to be going anyway."

"Tell me, Zev. Is Lawford in a high-risk situation?"

"Yes. I'd have to say it's high-risk."

"When is he due to return?"

"We should know something very soon."

"Let me know."

"Of course."

The nurse nodded at Berger and wheeled Erika off toward the west wing.

As he watched them go, Berger thought that all the grandiose schemes, with all their meticulous planning, in the end depended upon the courage and determination of a single human being.

CHAPTER FORTY-NINE

The festivities in the Defense Ministry gardens had begun at twilight. The spectacular fountains and marble cascades were illuminated by rose-colored spotlights, and Chinese lanterns were strung across the lawn. A military orchestra played a range of popular Western classics, interspersed with indigenous percussive Pakistani music.

The women wore ankle-length skirts with short silk jackets in brilliant colors, embroidered with gold sequins. The men wore tuxedos. A large table was set with steaming delicacies of grilled meat, chicken, and seafood. The drinks were soft, and the cigarette and cigar smoke was heavy.

There was a drumroll and cymbal crash, and President Ghazi stepped to the microphone. His voice was high-pitched and reedy as he expressed his gratitude to the foreign press and assembled dignitaries for joining him in celebration of Pakistan's Army Day. He alluded to Pakistan's growing military might, and condemned the unprovoked Israeli attack upon Libya.

Sipping his iced tea, Lawford thought that Ghazi lied with effortless brilliance. The fact that Pakistan had supplied

Qaddafi with nuclear warheads was conveniently forgotten. But then, President Ghazi was a figurehead, controlled by the ruling military clique.

Ghazi concluded his brief remarks and left, surrounded by a sea of uniforms. After his departure, the party livened noticeably, and the pungent odor of hashish laced the night air. Lawford and Bashira passed each other several times and greeted each other perfunctorily, well aware that sprinkled among the guests were agents of General Murrani's Counterintelligence Bureau.

The festive sounds floated up to the third-floor veranda and drifted into Murrani's office.

Seated at his desk, Murrani sipped a gin and tonic and chain-smoked. He was uneasy, burdened with intrigue. The succession of recent events was ominous.

His adjutant, Captain Meidan, was on the phone, concluding a conversation with the mobile unit following Dr. Tukhali. Bureaucrats at the Ministry of the Interior finally reported that Bughti, Tukhali's village of birth, had been rebuilt and the new hospital erected with funds provided by a Swiss holding company called Lizrose. Swiss law protected the true identities of Lizrose's officers, but Murrani's suspicions had been confirmed—the village of Bughti owed its restoration to nongovernmental financing. Why would a dummy Swiss corporation have any interest in rebuilding a ruined village in a primitive district of Baluchistan? There could be only one answer: Tukhali had coerced someone of importance, someone of means, into financing the reconstruction of his native village—in return for what? Kahuta's secrets? Had Tukhali betrayed his mentor, Farheed Shah? The young physicist had been Shah's assistant and might have been aware of the director's impending trip to Paris. It was a fair assumption that Tukhali despised the central government, whose forces had decimated his village and his people.

The tiles were falling into place at last. Tukhali had traded Kahuta's secrets to whoever it was that had financed the rebirth of his village. And that someone was undoubtedly the power behind the mysterious Lizrose Company.

Murrani sighed heavily, thinking that however valid his

suspicions, they were rooted in conjecture and supported only by a tenuous layer of facts. For the moment, the only logical course of action was to keep Dr. Tukhali under surveillance.

Captain Meidan hung up, cleared his throat, and said, "General . . ."

"Yes?"

"Tukhali left Pindi on the two-P.M. express. He arrived at Lahore station a half-hour ago and rented a Fiat sedan. He then—"

"Wait," Murrani interrupted. "According to our records, he owns a new Toyota, does he not?"

"Yes, sir." Meidan glanced at an open folder. "He purchased the car six weeks ago from a dealer in Pindi."

"And he left this new car home and took the train to Lahore and rented a Fiat?"

"There's more. May I proceed?"

"Yes. Yes, go on."

"Our trace unit followed him to a garage on Durand Road. After a few minutes he drove the Fiat out with new Indian license plates: GII-6852."

"Where is he now?"

"The Cathay Restaurant on Ravi Road in the old city."

"Indian plates . . ." Murrani mused. "All right, dispatch a unit to the frontier police at Amritsar. Have them deliver photographs of Tukhali to the duty officer, and alert them to the Fiat with the Indian plates."

"May I ask why?"

"The frontier is less than twenty minutes from downtown Lahore. I think our brilliant physicist is going to run."

"Shall I add a car to Kadhar's unit?"

"That would be prudent. If Tukhali runs, I want him detained. There's to be no shooting," Murrani cautioned. "The frontier police are not famous for their intelligence. Alive, Tukhali is an intelligence prize; dead, he's just another Baluchistani tribesman."

"But, sir, why don't we order Kadhar's unit to take him now?"

"Because, my boy, Tukhali may be taking someone else out."

"The director of Lizrose?"

"Perhaps." Murrani freshened his drink with a hefty shot of gin.

Captain Meidan issued a stream of orders to mobile intelligence units tailing Tukhali, and to the duty officer on the Pakistani side of the frontier at Amritsar.

Murrani fitted another cigarette into his ivory cigarette holder. The gin relaxed him and his anxiety was replaced by a growing feeling of anticipation. The net was closing on those who plotted the destruction of Kahuta. And he, General Ayub Murrani, would emerge as the great defender of the state. He would say nothing. He would remain in the shadows, abiding by his philosophy that true power was always invisible.

Meidan hung up. "Everything is in place."

"Have a gin and tonic, Captain."

"With pleasure, sir."

"You see, one small imperfection," Murrani said pointedly. "A new hospital in a dead village, and you have the missing tile. The mosaic is complete. A discernible pattern emerges. Think for a moment, Captain. The Israeli strike on Jarmah was timed perfectly, even though we had advanced the delivery date of the warhead. And why did the Israeli Prime Minister in his press conference make no mention of nuclear warheads?" Murrani rose and paced. "That, my boy, is a critical question."

"Perhaps they truly suspected poison-gas warheads rather than nuclear heads."

"That assumption fails when one looks at recent events," Murrani countered. "Mossad has been ahead of us all the way. They were aware of Mueller's trip to Washington. They knew about Director Shah's trip to Paris. The rocket scientist Brunner, blown up in Hamburg, was a warning to Kleiser, as was the killing of Mueller at Innsbruck. The Libyan agent Abu Hasi, shot to death in an ambush involving Kleiser's secretary—a German woman named Sperling. In my view, the missing taxi driver and the dead Austrian woman were Mossad agents protecting the German girl. Libyan Intelligence informs us that Kleiser took this same girl, Erika Sperling, to Tripoli in the company of an American journalist."

"You suspect Kleiser as well?"

"I think his STS company was infiltrated by Mossad."

"But how does this pattern connect with the Israeli Prime Minister's remarks?"

"Ask yourself, Captain: why does the Prime Minister substitute 'poison gas' for 'nuclear warheads'?"

Meidan shrugged. "I don't know."

"The reason should be obvious to you. If he mentions the fact that a nuclear warhead was poised atop the V-5 rocket in the Libyan desert, the press will inevitably ask: where and from whom did Qaddafi obtain such a sophisticated weapon? And since we are the only Islamic nation to possess the bomb, the Israeli Prime Minister's deception can mean only one thing—the Israelis are planning to attack Kahuta."

"I'm afraid I still don't see the—"

Murrani interrupted impatiently. "Put yourself in the Prime Minister's shoes. You're planning to destroy Kahuta —one way or another. If you mention nuclear warheads, the journalists' questions will inevitably lead to Pakistan. The very last thing you want is for the world to know that Kahuta exists even in your remote consciousness. I believe that Kahuta will be destroyed by an act of sabotage—and with the considerable help of Dr. Tukhali." Murrani drained his drink. "Order my car, Captain."

In the gardens below Murrani's office, the Army Day celebration was at its height. A group of Afghan dancers from Peshawar performed on the stage.

Leaning against a lattice gazebo, Lawford watched the festivities. It was close to eleven and he was tired. He turned to say something to an Italian journalist, but the man had disappeared.

"Were you looking for someone?" Salim Bashira suddenly asked.

Concealing his surprise, Tom said, "Yes. A colleague of mine."

"How long have you been here, sir?"

"You mean at the party?"

"I mean in Lahore."

"A few days."

"Have you been to the restaurant on Ravi Road?"

"Which one is that?"

"There is only one great restaurant on Ravi Road."

"The Cathay?"

"Yes, exactly."

"I'll have to try it."

The code had been used. Bashira had the microfilm. Tom took a pack of cigarettes out of his pocket and offered one to Bashira.

"Yes, thank you."

Tom searched in his pockets for a match. Bashira waited a moment before taking out a matchbook. "Here."

"Thanks. I must have left my lighter at the hotel."

"You can keep those."

After lighting both their cigarettes, Tom dropped the matchbook into his pocket.

"How long will you be staying in Pakistan?" Bashira inquired.

"Oh, I don't know . . . a few more days."

"Well, you've chosen the right city. You ought to take a leisurely walk through the old city; Lahore offers a superb blend of architecture, combining the Mogul Empire and the British raj." Bashira smiled. "Nice talking to you, sir."

The stocky silver-haired tycoon moved off through the crowd.

Lawford was eager to get away, but he forced himself to stroll back among the guests for a few minutes before saying good-bye to his journalist friend. He thanked his Pakistani host and took a taxi back to his hotel.

CHAPTER FIFTY

In his darkened hotel suite, Lawford nervously paced the worn rug. It was close to midnight, and he felt the tension rising. He had changed from his tuxedo into slacks, a turtleneck sweater, and sneakers. The matchbook Bashira had passed to him was tucked into the zippered pocket of his suede jacket.

The phone rang sharply in two-ring cycles.

"Hello," Tom answered.

"Ten minutes," Tukhali said, and hung up.

Tukhali paused as he left the Cathay Restaurant, his eyes scanning Ravi Road; seeing nothing suspicious, he walked quickly to his rented Fiat.

He got behind the wheel, turned the engine over, and checked the rearview mirror. Several cars were parked adjacent to the restaurant, but they appeared to be unoccupied. He waited another five minutes before heading out toward the Melaram intersection.

The black Volvo was parked at the access road just off the intersection. Captain Meidan was seated behind the wheel, with Murrani alongside. The two-way high-frequency radio hummed with power.

Murrani lit a cigarette and lowered the window.

"Perhaps he's not going to run," Meidan said.

"Why the rental car?"

"According to our data, Tukhali is something of a ladies' man. Perhaps he—"

The radio voice crackled through a smattering of static, interrupting Meidan. *"Unit One to Spider. Over."*

Murrani grabbed the microphone. "Spider reads. Over."

"Tukhali is heading your way. Over."

"Proceed to intercept positions. Over."

"Roger, Spider, and out."

Tukhali drove slowly, his eyes constantly glancing in the rearview mirror. He had noticed following headlights at Anarkali, near the museum, but they had quickly disappeared. Traffic was light at this hour, and a trailing car was easily spotted. He was beginning to feel less tense. Bashira's innovative plan was flawless. Taking the American journalist out was in itself a brilliant ruse. There was no reason to assume any problems. The frontier police exerted themselves only on vehicles entering Pakistan; those leaving were given only a cursory inspection.

Tukhali opened the window, and the cool night wind felt refreshing. He had the key to his Luxembourg account, and the final payment of $250,000 had been duly noted on his balance sheet. He patted his jacket, feeling the outline of his forged Indian passport and the packet of ten thousand dollars' worth of rupees, an adequate sum, should a bribe be necessary. Everything was proceeding smoothly. The Israeli raid on Libya had diverted attention from Kahuta. General Murrani's people would be poring over details of the Israeli strike, and in particular the bombing of the Jarmah silo. There was no cause for alarm. The frontier was only eighteen kilometers from Faletti's Hotel. In less than twenty minutes he would be safe in India. His whole life was ahead of him. The Cause would have to be taken up by the Baluchistani people themselves. He had done his share. His efforts had brought about the restoration of his native village, complete with a new hospital. He had risked his life passing Kahuta's secrets to Bashira. He had performed brilliantly and courageously. The money was irrelevant. Any man who had placed his life on the line deserved some small compensation.

As Tukhali turned into the Egerton intersection, Murrani's black Volvo, its headlights doused, slid behind him and followed at a distance of two hundred meters.

"Tukhali's dressed like a chauffeur," Captain Meidan said, hanging up the radio mike. "Black jacket, trousers, and black bow tie. Kadhar's unit believes he's posing as one of those Indian drivers from Amritsar who shuttle foreigners back and forth across the border."

"It will be interesting to see who his passenger is," Murrani replied.

Crossing the gloomy lobby, Lawford passed an English couple returning from the Army Day festivities. The woman was tall, red-haired, and angry. "Christ, what a fucking bore," she exclaimed. "Hasn't anyone in this charmless bloody country heard of champagne?"

"It's forbidden, dear," her companion reminded her.

Tom handed his room key to the concierge and walked outside. Bashira had shown him a photograph of Tukhali and told him the physicist would be driving a Fiat with Indian license plates.

A horse-drawn carriage pulled up at the hotel entrance; a young French-speaking couple got out and glanced suspiciously at Lawford before going inside. Tom was beginning to feel uneasy and vulnerable standing in the brilliantly lit hotel entrance. He was thinking about going back inside when the Fiat turned into the circular driveway.

Tukhali jumped out of the two-door coupé and obsequiously held the passenger door open for Lawford. Tom got in, and Tukhali hurried around to the other side and slid behind the wheel.

Shifting gears smoothly, he eased the Fiat out into the light traffic on Egerton Road. "We should arrive at the frontier in fifteen minutes."

As they took the sharp left on Sharah Road, Lawford turned and stared out of the rear window.

"I assure you, I was not followed."

"How would you know?"

"I have eyes, and I've been cautious."

"Can you spot a tail team?"

"Tail team?"

"Just drive." Tom sighed.

"Unit One to Spider," the car radio crackled.

General Murrani picked up the microphone. "Spider reads. Over."

"Fiat on Grand Trunk and passing signpost to frontier. Suggest intercept at Shaliam Cross. Over."

"Alert frontier duty officer and units one through four. We'll make initial contact. Over."

"We read. Over and out."

Murrani felt jubilant. The quarry was almost in hand. Unit One had checked with the concierge at Faletti's. Tukhali's passenger was an American journalist named Tom Lawford. Murrani would have wagered his life that Lawford was the same journalist who had accompanied Erika Sperling to Tripoli. There was no longer any doubt. They had been victimized by a CIA/Mossad operation—but the game was not yet over.

"Pick it up, Captain. Pick it up!" Murrani ordered. "When we get on Grand Trunk, turn off all running lights."

"Yes, sir," Meidan replied.

Murrani took a battery-powered red light out of the glove compartment, and reaching through the open window, placed its magnetic bottom on the Volvo's roof.

They turned onto Grand Trunk Road and traveled four kilometers before Murrani said, "Anyplace along here will do."

"Right, sir."

Meidan eased the sedan onto the shoulder of the road and set the hand brake, but kept the motor running. Murrani lit a fresh cigarette and felt his pulse quickening.

Tukhali geared down and reduced speed as the flashing arrows warned that the highway narrowed into two lanes.

"There he is!" Murrani exclaimed. "Let's go, Captain."

Releasing the brake, Captain Meidan engaged the gears,

and with the running lights out, swerved back onto the highway, following the Fiat at a distance of several hundred yards.

Tukhali slowed to a crawl as warning lights indicated the road narrowed once again, to a single lane each way.

They passed under a huge green sign that read: "Caution —25-kilometer limit here to frontier."

On the Indian side of the border, Pandit Sinde paced nervously behind the barrier. A detachment of tough Gurkha troops manned arc lights and heavy machine guns. Sinde was apprehensive. Tukhali and Lawford were late, and if the mission failed, his superiors would point an accusatory finger at him, and not without cause. He had been fearful of any further contacts with Bashira and refused to cross back inside Pakistan—and now everything depended upon the American and Tukhali.

Sinde shivered as beads of perspiration ran down his rib cage, chilling his body. Raising the infrared binoculars, he scanned the Pakistani side of the border. The activity appeared to be normal. Pakistani frontier police rarely checked the drivers of outgoing cars. The inspection of incoming cars was intense: trunks were opened, interiors searched for false compartments, and hubcaps removed. Those bloody Arabs, Sinde thought, what did they think would be smuggled into Pakistan from India? Ninety percent of the world's opium was harvested and refined in Pakistan. Sinde was about to lower the binoculars when he saw flashing red lights on the Pakistani side, and seconds later, heard the ominous wail of sirens.

The Fiat was trapped.

Murrani's command car and his mobile units were behind them, and jeeps of the frontier police blocked the road ahead.

The loudspeaker of a military sound truck thundered across the road: *"Fiat . . . India license GH-6852. Stop! Cut your engine! Come out of your vehicle—hands raised!"*

Tukhali's hands remained frozen to the wheel. His eyes were wide with fear and he gasped for breath. Pulling him aside forcefully, Tom quickly switched positions with the stricken man and slapped Tukhali's face back and forth. "Listen to me! We're going over that shoulder!"

"It's impossible," Tukhali whined fearfully. "The gully is fifty feet deep—and it's mined."

"Grip that door handle!" Tom ordered. "You either jump when I tell you to, or you're dead!"

From the darkness, the sound truck repeated its command, and up ahead a column of jeeps sped toward them. Behind them, Murrani and a group of armed men had their guns leveled at the Fiat.

Tom downshifted, floored the accelerator, and spun the wheel. The tires screeched and smoked as the Fiat zoomed across the shoulder of the road. The speedometer needle shot up into the red zone as they careened toward the precipice.

Tom's heart pounded wildly.

Tukhali mumbled a prayer.

"Get set!" Tom snapped.

They felt the release of tire-to-road gravity as they became airborne, catapulting out over the bluff.

"Jump!" Tom screamed, flinging his door open.

They hit the ground on a rocky slope fifteen feet below the precipice.

The Fiat sailed over their heads and slammed into a boulder at the base of the gully and burst into bright orange flames.

Tom struggled to his feet. A fiery, knifelike pain sliced into his right wrist, and his forearm began to swell. Gasping for breath, he peered through the flickering light thrown by the flaming wreck. Confused shouts from above echoed down into the gully, and searchlight beams stabbed through the darkness.

Some fifty feet off, in the dying light of car flames, he saw Tukhali darting along the boulder-strewn floor of the gully like a halfback weaving through the secondary.

"Son of a bitch . . ." Tom murmured in admiration as the diminutive figure hurdled a line of granite slabs, running full-out toward the incline leading up to the Indian side of the border.

A burst of yellow tracers suddenly stitched their way across the gully. Crouching, Tom ran between sharp, craggy rocks, his swollen right arm hanging limp. He called out to Tukhali, but the Pakistani never looked back.

On the Indian side, Pandit Sinde ordered his Gurkha troops to knock out the Pakistani searchlights probing the gully. There was nothing unusual about firefights and skirmishes at the frontier post. The heavy machine guns opened up and tracers like slivers of neon streaked toward the floodlights.

The arc lights exploded, and the electric cables shorted, snapping and spitting purple flames.

On Sinde's command, the Gurkha troops ceased firing. "I want a detail of six men!" Sinde ordered. "The rest of you hold positions and prepare to return hostile fire!"

Atop the highway bluff, General Murrani and his men peered into the dark gully. Their lights had been knocked out, and the dying flames of the wrecked Fiat provided only a faint flickering light.

"Captain Meidan!"

"Yes, sir!"

"Take a detail of frontier police down into that gully."

"But, sir, the fugitives must already be on the Indian side of the gully."

"Do as I say!" Murrani roared.

Gun in hand, Captain Meidan dashed past the flashing lights of staff cars, running hard toward a column of jeeps manned by frontier police.

In the beam of their headlights a hundred meters distant, an officer of the frontier-police contingent saw the armed figure running toward them, gun in hand. Reflexively the officer raised his M-16 automatic and fired a long burst. Captain Meidan's arms went skyward as a hail of lead cut him in half. The entire detail of frontier police jumped out of their jeeps, firing wildly.

Murrani's men waved their hands frantically, shouting to the police to hold their fire, but in the darkness, the intelligence officers posed a threatening presence, and the police continued to fire at the indistinct figures.

Murrani and his men took cover, cursing the frontier police and their ancestors. Murrani grabbed an intercom mike and ordered the sound truck into action. A moment later, amid the confused firing on the dark road, an amplified voice boomed, "Cease fire! Cease fire!"

His heart racing, his right wrist swollen to the size of an orange, Tom sprinted across the rocky gully floor some twenty yards behind Tukhali.

He heard the whine of bullets and felt the searing heat of near-misses, but kept going toward the steep incline leading to the Indian side. Up ahead, Tukhali had already started to scramble up the embankment.

Tom stumbled over a rock and sprawled facedown on the stony ground. Painfully he raised himself and regained his footing. Bleeding from cuts on both arms and his left knee, he staggered and lurched his way toward the incline.

There was a sudden loud crack, and Tom froze in horror as Tukhali burst into flames, his body glowing brightly like a struck match before collapsing in a dark ash. The concussion ring followed instantly, and shards of bone and flesh pelted Tom's face. Tukhali had stepped on a gelatin mine, and for a split second Tom wondered whether to go on or retrace his steps. But there was no choice—if he fell into Pakistani hands, he'd be a propaganda showpiece until they decided to hang him.

Expecting instant incineration with each step, he stumbled and groped his way up the steep incline. Grabbing clumps of weeds with his left hand, he slowly, breathlessly made his way up the embankment.

He was shrouded by a soaring sheet of dark shale some fifteen feet from the bluff when the sun came up. A blinding hot-white light thrown by carbon-arc lamps froze him in place like a stop-motion frame of film. Ghostly silhouetted figures of helmeted soldiers carrying automatic weapons moved out in front of the lights. In that moment Tom understood the panic and terror of a cornered animal flushed from its habitat. He simply stood there panting, gasping, caught in the lights. They had him. After all he'd been through, they had him. The Pakistan Intelligence Bureau had closed the net.

A slim, narrow-shouldered figure wearing civilian clothes picked his way down the incline.

Pandit Sinde drew close and extended his hand. "Welcome to India, Mr. Lawford."

CHAPTER FIFTY-ONE

The hum of electronic equipment underscored the palpable tension that enveloped the communications room at Technion.

"What the hell happened?" Dado asked in frustration. "We should have heard something two hours ago."

"It was a difficult operation," Berger replied, lighting a fresh cigarette. "Bashira organized it as best he could. But Tukhali is not a professional, and Lawford is out of his milieu. Anything is possible under those circumstances: a car doesn't start, a phone call is intercepted, something out of the past surfaces—"

"Spare me the lecture!" Dado snapped. "We're not at the Academy!"

"This isn't the time for short tempers," Professor Newman intervened, "and we do have alternate choices."

Dado shook his head. "Another ten minutes, Yuval, and your people must go ahead."

"Without those sketches I'll be forced to overcompensate. I prefer precision to exaggeration."

"So do I, but we're running out of time. It's going to take hours for your team to assemble the explosive."

"Not to assemble—to design."

"All right, to design," Dado sighed. "The *Athenian Queen* will be at the rendezvous point in eighteen hours. We can't risk holding her dead in the water off the Omani coast."

"I thought *Dolphin* was escorting her," Berger said.

"She is. But we can't start torpedoing Omani patrol frigates; besides, there's a British base at Masirah and the Soviet Soyuz-TM-6 orbits at dusk. We have to rendezvous with Matty at eighteen hundred hours tomorrow."

"I promise you," Newman said with calm assurance, "we can load the warhead by daybreak—barring a mechanical problem with the Osprey, we'll make it."

"The Security Council is in emergency session," Berger interjected. "The Chinese delegate spoke for over an hour, ranting about our unprovoked attack on the peace-loving nation of Libya."

"Fucking hypocrites!" Dado exclaimed. "The Chinese have supplied Iraq, Iran, Syria, and the Saudis with long- and short-range missiles."

"Perhaps the Libyan raid will tend to dissuade our neighbors from using them," Newman suggested.

"I doubt it," Berger said. "Our intelligence reports indicate that the Syrians have already armed their missiles with poison-gas warheads. When the next war breaks out, all our friends will use them—in tandem."

"Well, they may get a message from Kahuta," said Dado.

"Not if we're successful," Newman countered. "Hopefully, the destruction of Kahuta will appear to have been caused by a cruel whim of nature; an earthquake will have erupted along the northwest Himalayan fault—a quake of sufficient magnitude to reduce Kahuta to rubble. And if nature is not blamed, the evidence will indicate an internal accident—an explosion in the reactor chamber, not unlike Chernobyl. In any case, if Jericho works, Israel will be held blameless. And that, gentlemen, is the point of the exercise."

"Suppose Jericho fails?" Berger asked.

Newman shrugged. "I'll tell you what I told the Prime Minister. When one deals with state-of-the-art weaponry, we know only that we shall never know. While these weapon

311

systems are scientifically sound, we can't measure their emotions."

"Emotions?" Berger repeated incredulously.

"Yes. Emotions. Jericho has extraordinary sensory perception. Its brain is augmented by one hundred and seventy-five backup computerized targeting programmers. But"— he paused—"sometimes they go their own way. Remember the tragic flight of the Challenger space shuttle. These fantastic robotic machines, these incredible space-age vehicles, can develop viruses and mind-sets, causing erratic behavior."

"Well, I ask again, what happens if Jericho fails?"

The black phone rang suddenly, startling the men, who reacted with dread fascination. They stared transfixed, hoping for the best but expecting the worst.

It rang the prescribed six times and stopped. They rushed to the fax machine, which had begun to hum and tick. A length of paper rose from the cylinder with typed English letters in caps: "LAWFORD SAFE. TUKHALI DEAD. A SERIES OF PHOTOGRAPHIC SKETCHES FOLLOWS (15) REPEAT FIFTEEN."

In the third-floor analytical laboratory, Dado and Berger watched as Professor Newman and his team studied Tukhali's photographic sketches under a powerful magnifying lens. The men conversed in their exotic space-age language: target assessment, track formulation, Sinda thermal analysis code, interface homing, electro-optical sensors, computer fuse boosters, and delayed detonation. The chief systems engineer finally made his last notation and departed with his staff.

Professor Newman crossed the room and said, "We're in business. Tukhali's sketches pinpoint the exact location of the reactor core within the cupola and measure the cupola's size and strength, and, most important, the depth-per-square-inch pressure of floor-level separation."

"What makes that so important?" Dado asked.

"We have to penetrate and detonate at a depth of twenty meters, between the third and fourth levels. This will cause the forty-ton concrete cupola to collapse downward, and the lower level to erupt. The heat of the blast will weld them together and the site will seal itself, avoiding a heavy fallout."

"According to our information, the reactor is cold," Berger stated.

"Even so, the stored fuel rods will throw off radiation grads and generate a small amount of radioactivity."

"What sort of ordnance are we using?" Dado asked.

"A 'fuel-air' bomb. It triggers a non-nuclear chain reaction igniting and exploding the oxygen. These expanding air chambers are wrapped in beryllium and compressed into a hollow sphere layered with seven hundred kilos of plastic. The energy released will equal one thousand tons of TNT. Two square miles of the Kahuta complex will experience the force of a six-point-five earthquake. Power and communication lines in Rawalpindi and Islamabad will be knocked out. But if Jericho behaves, we will have avoided a Chernobyl syndrome. Meteorology is also in our favor; at this time of year the prevailing winds will carry any radioactivity over the tip of southern Iran and out over the Arabian Sea."

"What about the nuclear weapons already manufactured and stored at Kahuta?" Berger inquired.

"The bombs might be assembled, but certainly not armed. That would be suicidal—absolutely inconceivable. Nuclear weapons must go through a complex arming procedure before they can be launched. No sane physicist would permit the storage of armed nuclear weapons."

"Suppose you're wrong?"

"In that unlikely case," Newman sighed, "the Himalayan Mountains might decide to take a stroll across northeast Pakistan."

CHAPTER FIFTY-TWO

The Osprey CV-22-A long-range tilt-rotor aircraft sat on the tarmac, its twin tri-bladed propellers pointing skyward at right angles to the wing. Painted in the sand-and-green Israeli Air Force camouflage colors, the aircraft resembled a hybrid bird of prey resting in the predawn desert light.

The aircraft's unique wingtip-mounted propellers allowed it to take off and land vertically like a helicopter, and to cruise at high speeds over long distances as a turboprop aircraft. The American-made plane represented a remarkable achievement in aeronautical design, incorporating fixed-wing flight dynamics with the avionic capabilities of a helicopter.

Dado watched from a distance as Professor Newman and Air Force General Carmil supervised the transfer of the conical warhead from the UH-60 helicopter to the Osprey's cargo conveyor belt.

Standing beside Dado, Narda sipped some coffee and said, "It seems too ugly to fly."

"It's an incredible plane," Dado said with admiration. "The Americans concentrate on their scandals and overlook their genius."

"Speaking of Americans, Lawford did the job."

"He sure as hell did," Dado agreed. "When he arrives, I want you to have him checked by our doctors at Beth-Zion."

"He'll insist on seeing you."

"Tell him I'm at a secret commando base in the desert. I'll be returning before the week is out. One other thing: be certain that either you or Zichroni is at the communication console at zero hour. Notify the Prime Minister the instant Radio Islamabad goes dead."

"And if it doesn't?"

"You'll know we failed."

The warhead container rode up the Osprey's conveyor belt and disappeared inside the aircraft's cargo bay. General Carmil waved for Dado to come.

"Take care, Narda."

She nodded and slipped her dark glasses on against the opaque rising sun.

General Carmil accompanied Dado and Professor Newman to the passenger door. "You'll have F-15 escorts flying top-cover all the way around the Yemen peninsula—if any MIG's come up, they'll have their hands full. I have some of my best boys in that wing group."

"Your men have always performed, Arik. I meant what I said to them before Libya. Our pilots are the light of the nation."

The generals shook hands and Dado followed Newman into the cabin. The Osprey's door closed and the lock bolted.

The twin Allison engines coughed into life. Slowly the vertical rotor-prop blades revolved, then whirled and spun with a velocity that caused the aircraft to reverberate. The stubby plane rose hesitantly and hovered ten feet above the ground.

The pilot gave the thumbs-up signal and the Osprey zoomed skyward, its passengers and crew experiencing the smooth, swift ascent of a high-speed elevator.

General Carmil and the ground crew watched in awe as the hybrid craft reached an altitude of six hundred feet and hovered momentarily as its rotor-prop wing mounts tilted backward, changing its configuration into that of a conventional plane. Climbing to ten thousand feet, the Osprey turned gracefully southeast and disappeared into a cloud bank.

Forty thousand feet over the Red Sea, the F-15 wing commander led his escorting flight in a tight formation. His "look-down" radar displayed the computer-enhanced image of the Osprey fifteen thousand feet below.

The commander tuned the Mikron-UHF-FM to a prearranged frequency and spoke in a staccato burst. "Eagle One to Grasshopper. Over."

"Grasshopper reads," the Osprey pilot replied. *"Over."*

"We have you on LTI. Over."

"Roger, Eagle One. Over and out."

Inside the Osprey's pressurized cabin, Professor Newman unbuckled his seat belt, went into the galley, poured two vodkas over ice, and handed one to Dado.

"Cheers," Newman said.

"Cheers," Dado replied.

"This is a brand-new experience for me," Newman said, "flying in a hybrid plane with a thousand tons of TNT."

"It's just a number, Yuval."

"Yes, I know. But God help us if Jericho fails."

"If I were you, I wouldn't count on Yahweh for any help."

"But you're not me," Newman said, "and I do." He turned and walked back to the rear of the aircraft and sat down beside his chief ascent engineer.

Sipping the vodka, Dado shook his head in disbelief. Here was Yuval Newman, a brilliant alchemist whose genius could destroy the universe, and yet this implacable man of science still believed in the Magic Soap Trickster. Ah, well, what did it matter? Sooner or later, every man found a personal myth he settled for. The important thing was that Newman had been with him from the start, and the professor's precise scientific appraisal had persuaded the Prime Minister to approve the operation. If Newman had to call upon Yahweh for assistance, one could only hope the professor had the right area code.

Dado drained the vodka, pulled the window shade down, tilted the seat back, closed his eyes, and almost immediately fell asleep.

CHAPTER FIFTY-THREE

A gusting March wind rustled the tall pines surrounding the CIA Headquarters Building, causing the windows to rattle in Admiral Clarke Dwinell's corner office.

The Admiral blew rings of pipe smoke as he watched the UN Security Council debate on television. The American ambassador was speaking against the Chinese-sponsored motion to condemn Israel for its raid on Libya.

"Since the government of Libya deems itself to be in a state of war with Israel, it would seem prudent for Colonel Qaddafi to take his own bellicose threats seriously. And if the Libyan chief of state possessed long-range missiles equipped with deadly poison gas, targeted at Israel's population centers, then . . ."—The ambassador raised his arms in supplication— ". . . how can the Israeli action be considered anything but a legitimate preemptive act of self-defense?"

The Admiral's door opened and Manfredi entered. "I finally reached Dr. Summers at Los Alamos. He's studied the . . ." His voice trailed off as the Admiral motioned for silence and directed Manfredi's attention to the TV screen.

"No Libyan territory was occupied," the American ambassador continued, "nor was the political independence of that nation subverted. The Israeli raid was not only preemptive but also retaliatory. The members of this council must not forget the Libyan government's financial and logistical support of terrorists trained and equipped to conduct murderous raids against the citizens of Israel. I must remind this honorable forum that any civilized state has the right and duty to protect the lives and property of its citizens. Therefore, it is my government's view that . . ."

The Admiral snapped the TV set off. "We'll veto the resolution to condemn."

"Why not?" Manfredi said. "After all, we hit Libya in eighty-six for a lot less."

The Admiral tamped his pipe and asked, "What did Summers have to say?"

"The Kahuta photo sketches confirm that Pakistan is manufacturing plutonium-core nuclear weapons. The plant's enrichment centrifuges and U-239 separation equal anything in the West."

"Mossad was right on target," the Admiral said.

"We've got to inform the Congressional Oversight Committee," Manfredi cautioned. "We can't sit on this. Those photos will leak. You'll see them in the New York *Times* within ten days."

"I agree, but once we reveal this, congressional aid to Pakistan will be cut off." The Admiral relit his pipe and puffed thoughtfully. "Let's dump it in the President's lap. We're playing on a doomsday chessboard. The Islamic bomb opens the road to Armageddon. The Israeli raid on Libya bought a little time, but practically speaking, there's nothing to prevent Pakistan from shipping nuclear warheads to that lunatic in Baghdad, or to the Saudis, or Syria, or Iran, or some terrorist group, or again to Qaddafi. Kahuta is a universal time bomb ticking toward a nuclear midnight, and the Israelis know that."

"Lawford said he had no knowledge of any Mossad plans to hit Kahuta, but they would never confide in him."

"Why not?" the Admiral asked. "He's been tight with Mossad all the way. He's performed brilliantly for them. He located Jarmah, and he brought out those photos of Kahuta.

He's been in a high-risk mode for months. Berger may have mentioned something to Lawford about a possible Kahuta operation—not specifics, but something." The Admiral rose and paced for a moment before facing Manfredi. "Where is Lawford?"

"En route to Tel Aviv."

"I thought he was coming home."

"According to Indian Intelligence, he was patched up and put on an Air India flight to Rome with a connecting El Al flight to Tel Aviv."

"Why wouldn't he come straight home?"

"Berger thinks it's the girl."

"What girl?"

"Erika Sperling."

"You mean to say Lawford's become emotionally involved with a case agent?"

"It happens to the best of us."

The Admiral's face reddened. "No, not to the best of us, to the *worst* of us. I never demanded sainthood for my people. I never met a saint I liked or trusted. A man can have a recreational moment with a woman, but not an emotional involvement and *never* with a case agent." The Admiral shook his head in disgust. "Hickey warned us. Lawford was burned-out, empty, lost. You give a man like that, who's still got some cowboy in him, a sense of purpose, and you no longer have an agent—you have a goddamn missionary." The Admiral sighed heavily. "But it's my fault. It was expedient to use Lawford. I gambled and lost."

"We don't know that Lawford's been disloyal," Manfredi argued, "and you certainly can't quarrel with his performance."

"Lawford's performance is not at issue. It's his judgment." The Admiral sat down wearily. "Logic says the Israelis have opened a combat file on Kahuta, and if I'm right, the strike will be run by General Dado Harel's Special Operations Unit. We know Lawford met with Harel in Rome prior to his trip to Pakistan. The General must have convinced him of Kahuta's threat to the world."

"You just made the same case."

"But I'm not a goddamn missionary. We collect and we

analyze. We don't act out of emotion. I tell you, Al, the General appealed to the missionary in Lawford."

"I don't know . . ." Manfredi mused. "You think Harel would risk telling Lawford that they were planning to hit Kahuta?"

"If I were the General, it's a risk I would take. I wouldn't tell him how, but I would certainly try to enlist his services. Hell, there's no downside."

"I can't believe Lawford would withhold critical information from us."

"You better call Zev Berger. Tell him we want Lawford back. It's a matter of state security. We've got to find out what that son of a bitch knows before it's too late."

Manfredi rose and sighed heavily. "I have to admit, to my way of thinking, the planet would be a safer place without Kahuta."

"You miss the point, Al. If Kahuta is destroyed, Pakistan may blame India. The entire subcontinent could go up in a nuclear holocaust. And if the Russians and Chinese get into it"—the Admiral paused—"the monster is loose."

CHAPTER FIFTY-FOUR

The pilot throttled back, cutting their airspeed to three hundred knots as the Osprey began its descent from twenty-six thousand feet.

"Hold at eighteen thousand," the navigator said. "Bearing one-eight-five. If the ship's maintained speed and true bearing, we should see them when we break cloud cover."

"Red light on intercom," the copilot said.

The pilot flipped a switch, and an incoming radio voice sounded in the cockpit.

"Queen Bee to Grasshopper. Queen Bee to Grasshopper. Over."

The pilot replied at once, "Grasshopper reads. Over."

"We have you on loran. Over."

"Roger, we're coming down. Over and out."

"Nice going, Yaki," the pilot complimented the navigator. "Send our escort home."

The navigator tuned the UHF-FM, selecting Mode Three on the prearranged encrypted air-to-air channel.

"Grasshopper to Eagle One. Over."

"Eagle One reads. Over."

"We're at IP and descending to Queen Bee. Thanks for the company. Over."

"Roger, Grasshopper. We'll see you on the return trip. Good luck. Over and out."

The wing commander rolled his F-15, and the squadron followed their leader down to twenty-eight thousand feet, where they leveled off and, like a flock of migrating birds, formed an arrow formation, wheeled eastward, and streaked toward the Red Sea.

The last traces of daylight had faded and the sky turned gray-blue as night fell over the Arabian Sea. The *Athenian Queen* plowed slowly through the heavy swells, its bow pointed into the wind. Captain Matty Alon pressed the All Stations intercom button. "Turn on foredeck landing lights. Prepare to receive Grasshopper."

A display of blue and white lights formed a luminous oval outline on the foredeck. A crew of seamen stood by, anxiously awaiting eye contact with the descending Osprey.

Inside the bridge, the radar man noticed a glowing blip on his screen and pressed targeting and location buttons.

"We have Grasshopper, Captain," he called out. "She's at eight thousand and dropping in a tight circle."

"What's her heading?"

"One-eight-five."

"Alter course to bearing one-eight-five," Alon ordered.

The helmsman spun the wheel, lining up the new heading on the gyrocompass.

"What's your last reading on *Dolphin?*" Alon asked the radioman.

"Two miles to port at a depth of forty fathoms."

"Advise *Dolphin* that we have altered course to one-eight-five and are preparing to receive Grasshopper."

General Dado Harel stood in the open doorway of the Osprey's flight deck.

"Are we all right?" he asked the young pilot.

"So far we're fine, General. How is Professor Newman holding up?"

"Having placed his cares and woes on Yahweh's shoulders, he sleeps like a baby."

"Good. I must tell you we're going to be busy here."

"Don't pay any attention to me. I want to see how you turn this plane back into a helicopter."

The pilot nodded and slipped a clipboard out of a leather sleeve.

"Ready for check?"

"Ready," the copilot answered.

"Altimeter."

"Set."

"Cowl flaps."

"Closed."

"Power."

"One thousand rpm's, both engines."

"Mixture."

"Full rich."

"Booster pumps."

"On."

"Tilt-rotor switch."

"On approach."

"Prop-synch mode."

"Set for landing."

"Airspeed."

"One-five-five."

The pilot eased the throttle forward and the aircraft accelerated its descent in a tight radius.

The navigator called out altimeter readings. "Five thousand . . . four-eight . . ."

The pilot throttled back slightly as the navigator called, "Three thousand."

"There she is!" the copilot exclaimed.

In the darkness below, the lights on the ship's foredeck created the illusion of a luminous oblong shape floating in limbo on the surface of the sea.

"Stand by tilt-rotor lift," the pilot commanded.

"Amber on tilt-rotor lift," the copilot responded.

"Props to helicopter rotation."

The copilot's fingers moved deftly across a series of overhead relay switches. "Chopper rotation."

The Osprey's engine pitch changed abruptly from a steady hum to a high whine.

"Tilt rotor to upright."

The copilot pressed two red buttons. "Tilt rotor activated."

Dado watched the turboprops as they seemed to separate from their rear wing mounts, and with blades still whirling, tilt slowly up to a vertical rotor position.

The pilot's and copilot's fingers flicked expertly over a complex series of switches and buttons.

"Okay," the pilot said, "let's join the Navy."

The crewmen on the *Athenian Queen* heard the beating rotor blades and felt the rotor backwash before seeing the dark hybrid silhouette. On the flying bridge, Captain Matty Alon stroked his beard and watched the Osprey position itself directly above the foredeck. He had never seen such an aircraft, and he shook his head in wonderment. Never discount the Americans, he thought . . . the world should not yet be surrendered to the Japanese.

The pilot peered down at the illuminated foredeck and saw the silhouetted figures of seamen just outside the bright blue and white landing lights.

"Six hundred feet," the navigator called out.

"Wind direction and speed?" the pilot asked.

"West-to-east, fifteen knots."

"Left five degrees."

"Check," the copilot replied.

"Rate of descent, one hundred fpm."

"Check."

The Osprey descended to sixty feet and hovered above the foredeck.

"Steady now!" the pilot shouted.

On the foredeck, seamen clung to the ship's railing as the Osprey's turboprops whipped up a gale-force wind before the aircraft finally settled onto the deck.

The pilot and copilot shut down both engines and set the parking brakes. The whirling turboprops slowed, each blade becoming discernible as the rotations eased. The prop backwash died and the seamen quickly placed wheel chocks and ran steel cables from the strut loops to deck hooks.

The cabin door opened and Dado jumped down, then turned to assist Newman. Both men were given a bear hug by Matty Alon. They exchanged greetings as the crewmen covered the Osprey with a canvas tarpaulin. Captain Alon introduced Professor Newman to the chief engineer who would supervise the warhead's transfer from the Osprey to the aft hold.

It was 7:05 P.M. The *Athenian Queen* was thirty-three hours from flash point.

CHAPTER FIFTY-FIVE

Narda brought the jeep to a full stop at the guard post and presented her ID card to a young officer. He checked her name against Mossad's personnel roster and waved her through. She steered carefully around the concrete teeth and, once clear of the barrier, glanced at Lawford. His skin was pale and taut against his cheekbones, and his gray eyes were sullen. There was a plaster-of-paris cast on his right wrist and a small bandage over his left eye.

After stopping at a second checkpoint, she entered the vast Tel Aviv military compound.

The sun flared against the windshield, and Tom clenched his eyes and whispered, "Christ . . ."

"What is it?"

"Nothing."

"The General would like you to be checked by our orthopedic surgeon at Beth-Zion Military Hospital."

"It's just a broken wrist. Besides, there's nothing wrong with the Indian doctors . . . they took good care of me."

"Perhaps, but Beth-Zion is considered to be—"

"Don't be so goddamn chauvinistic," he interrupted angrily.

"I know you're tired and preoccupied, but I'm not speaking out of chauvinism. I never said we were better than anyone else. I never expressed the slightest bit of patriotic jingoism. From the day we first met, my only concern was—"

"Okay!" he snapped. "Okay."

"It's not okay. It would be wise to have your arm checked."

"I got the message. Now, tell me, where the hell is Dado?"

She knew that at this very moment the *Athenian Queen* was steaming toward the flash point off Karachi. Zichroni had confirmed the Osprey's touchdown. But she couldn't tell Lawford any of it.

"The General is at a desert base analyzing the results of the Libyan operation. He'll be back in a few days."

"Well, he should be feeling pretty good. The Libyan raid was a complete success."

"We've conducted many successful raids, but the war goes on."

She parked in the shade of a squat four-story mud-colored building.

Zev Berger extended his hand to Lawford but stopped abruptly when he saw the cast.

"It's okay. I can use my hand, not my wrist."

"Sit down, please. Narda, tell Shoshana to bring coffee." Berger turned to Lawford. "Cigarette?"

"No, thanks."

Lighting the cigarette, Berger spoke through the smoke. "Needless to say, we hold you in the greatest esteem. That was a high-risk operation, and you never wavered."

"How would you know?"

"I have a complete report from Pandit Sinde."

Narda helped the young secretary serve the coffee.

"Thank you, Shoshana," Berger said, dismissing the girl.

Sipping the strong Turkish coffee, Lawford asked, "What did you want to see me about?"

"I would like you to take me through the events from the time you left Rome until you crossed into India."

"What for?"

Berger exchanged a quick glance with Narda before saying, "It's now obvious that Pakistan Intelligence was onto Dr. Tukhali. Salim Bashira is still on station, and therefore in grave jeopardy. There may be some small, seemingly irrelevant piece of information you have that might save him."

"Nothing I know can save Bashira."

"You're a professional," Berger insisted. "You know very well that some innocuous piece of conversation, something you overheard at the party, something Tukhali may have said—a word, a comment, a gesture—might help. I admit I'm searching for straws but . . ."

"I'm all you have."

"Yes."

"All right." Tom sighed. "I'll walk you through it. But first there's something you can do for me. I want to see Erika Sperling."

"I'm sorry, but I have no idea where she is."

"That's a goddamn lie and you know it! She's in a hospital somewhere in the north."

"I told him," Narda said.

Berger sighed. "I can't help you, Mr. Lawford. I gave Erika my word that I would protect her from just such a visit. She made it very clear. She doesn't want to see you."

"That's her vanity talking."

"Perhaps, but I can't betray my promise to her."

"You owe me this favor."

"I owe Erika Sperling more."

"Why not wait and see the General?" Narda suggested to Lawford. "I'm sure Dado will arrange something. After all, he made no promises to Erika."

Tom stared at her for a moment, then nodded. "Okay, let's get started. I'm dead tired."

"We have a suite reserved for you at the Dan Hotel," Berger said, removing his glasses and holding them up to the light. "By the way, Manfredi phoned. They want you to return immediately."

"Fine. You told me."

"He said it was a matter of state security. What shall I tell him?"

"Tell him to go fuck himself. Now, get a tape recorder and I'll walk you through Pakistan."

CHAPTER FIFTY-SIX

A small army of experts from General Ayub Murrani's Bureau of Intelligence dissected Dr. Tukhali's apartment. Walls were combed by metal detectors, books torn apart, paintings ripped from their frames, furniture smashed, clothing slashed, toiletries and medicine bottles emptied, blankets, pillows, and carpets slit and peeled, floorboards pried up. The contents of the apartment looked as if they had been put through a Cuisinart. Murrani's team of intelligence agents worked methodically, in a silent fury.

Any employee at the Kahuta facility having had contact with Tukhali was being questioned by Special Branch Internal Security Police. A team of investigators had flown to the district of Baluchistan to interrogate the people in Tukhali's native village of Bughti.

Murrani was seated at Tukhali's desk. He'd spent the entire morning scrutinizing every notation, memo, letter, postcard, file, photograph, and handwritten note in the apartment. He was interrupted periodically by aides bringing scraps of bills or credit-card slips found in Tukhali's suit pockets. Phone calls had come in from Chief of Internal

Security Abassi and Chief of Staff General Rahman. Both men confirmed that security forces at Kahuta had been tripled, and all antiaircraft units and Crotale ground-to-air missile batteries surrounding the nuclear facility were on high alert. Fearing the landing of an Israeli sabotage team, Murrani had ordered increased naval and air patrols off Karachi on the Arabian Sea coast.

Several days earlier he'd met with President Ghazi and the director of Kahuta, Dr. I. Q. Khan, and informed them of the incident at the border. Khan had expressed concern over critical data that Tukhali might have passed to hostile forces during his long tenure at Kahuta. The President had cut Khan off, angrily stating that past damage was beyond repair, and in contrast he complimented Murrani on having exposed the treasonous Tukhali. Ghazi declared that he would summon the American ambassador and demand an accounting of Tom Lawford's involvement in the affair.

Murrani had been amused by the President's officious manner—a display of authority solely for Dr. Khan's benefit. In truth, Ghazi could not survive in office without the forbearance of General Murrani. The meeting had been a pro forma exercise.

Sifting through the maze of papers, Murrani recalled Dr. Khan's parting words: "The fate of our nuclear-research center and perhaps the state itself rests in your hands, General."

Murrani despised the urbane physicist's transparent attempt to remove himself from responsibility for the security breach at Kahuta. Khan, the President, General Rahman, and Abassi had dumped the burden on his shoulders. He would deal with them in time, but first things first. He had to crack the mystery surrounding Tukhali's defection and the role played by the American journalist. Murrani was convinced that Lawford was the same journalist who had accompanied Fritz Kleiser to Libya. He had phoned STS's Berlin office, but the secretary had no idea of Kleiser's whereabouts. He had also tried the chief of Libyan Intelligence, but the Libyans were still reeling from the devastating Israeli raid. Murrani's Swiss connection had promised to uncover the names behind the arcane Lizrose Company, the dummy corporation that had financed the reconstruction of Tukhali's village.

Shifting in his chair, he began to search through a stack of technical papers written by Tukhali, when an investigating officer saluted and handed him a small leather-bound address book. "We found this inside a dinner jacket."

Murrani put on his reading glasses and examined each page carefully. There were no addresses—only phone numbers and names, mostly of women—with the exception of a single page that had been carefully inscribed with dollar amounts in large increments. The last figure was $250,000. Alongside the final entry was a phone number without an area code. Murrani swiveled around and called to his new adjutant, "Captain!"

"Yes, sir!"

"Have Internal Security try this number, using every area code in every major city. When and if a connection is made, they are to hang up and give me the complete number."

CHAPTER FIFTY-SEVEN

The *Athenian Queen* plowed through the swelling sea forty nautical miles south-southeast of Karachi. It was 3:25 A.M., Pakistani time, and a heavy rain fell out of the reddish sky.

The ship's running lights were off, and the crew was on full alert. Three miles to port and fifty fathoms down, the *Dolphin* submarine shadowed the *Athenian Queen*.

The bridge was quiet except for the creaking sound of the ship as it rolled and pitched with the movement of the sea. General Harel and Captain Alon stood on either side of the helmsman. The faces of technicians manning the loran and radar systems were illuminated in the phosphorescent glow of their display screens.

"What's our present speed?" Dado asked.

"Twenty-eight knots," Alon replied. "We'll arrive at flash point by 4 A.M., as planned. That is, if all goes well."

"Why shouldn't it?"

"Anything can happen—Pakistani patrol planes, frigates, and we're not too far from the British naval base at Masirah."

"But we're a Greek freighter enjoying the right of free passage in international waters."

"Ships nearing the Persian Gulf border are frequently stopped by Pakistani patrol boats looking for opium smugglers."

The bridge phone rang and Alon answered. "Okay." He hung up and turned to Dado. "Newman wants you. Can you find your way aft?"

"I think so."

Dado left, and Alon went over to his radar man.

"Anything?"

"A few blips far to the south."

Alon then spoke to the radioman. "Advise *Dolphin* to slow to fifteen knots and maintain present bearing." He started to leave but had a second thought. "Have the *Dolphin*'s skipper load and arm his torpedoes."

Dado was about to step off the aft ladder when the ship rolled severely. Clinging to the bottom rung, he waited for the vessel to right itself before lowering his feet to the deck. It took a moment for his eyes to adjust to the streaky light in the vast, empty hold.

The "Jericho III" was upright on its platform, held fast by the circular steel bands of the gantry. Through a trick of light, the conical warhead perched atop the thirty-five-foot-tall missile glowed as if the incredible explosive force packed within its three-foot diameter generated its own fiery brilliance.

Dado crossed the huge cargo hold toward the computer console monitoring Jericho's telemetric systems.

Professor Newman whispered an order to the propulsion engineer and turned to greet the General.

"Look here, Dado. At one console, three men control ascent systems, thermodynamic fuel thrust, reentry-track formulations, and target assessment. You see this red button? Avi, here, presses that button and the solid fuel detonates. After a six-second burn, two hundred thousand pounds of thrust lifts Jericho into the stratosphere in less than two minutes."

"How long from lift-off to target?"

"Three minutes, forty-six seconds."

Dado glanced at the flashing telemetric numerals on the computer display screens and felt a sudden dread. "Let's go up on deck."

"Anything wrong?"

"No, no. It's the roll, my stomach. I'm not a good sailor, Yuval."

The wind and rain offered a refreshing relief from the dank gloom of the hold.

"Will this rain affect Jericho?" Dado asked.

"No, though if we hit a severe storm it's another matter," Newman replied. "But uncertainty is the soul of science—the Heisenberg theory, random particles, and all that. Anything can happen. Now, having said that, Jericho III is not a brilliant missile—it's a genius missile. Its brain has been preprogrammed to target; its computer inertial-guidance system constantly matches its TV eye with target profile. A multispectral sensor penetrates natural barriers. A laser-gyro beam transmits an electronic shield that confuses and avoids any missile sent against it. Jericho also carries one hundred and seventy-five backup computers. What I'm saying is: it's alive. It can think, it can feel, and it can see. Barring the unforeseen, it will do the job."

"I'm used to trusting men, not machines."

"You're trusting me, Dado. Now, relax. Have some coffee. I've got to get back to my children."

As the professor went below, Dado peered through the curtain of rain and recalled the eyes of the condemned children looking into the cameras held by SS men. There had been no Jerichos to save them. No F-16's. No tanks. No Uzis. Nothing. No one.

CHAPTER FIFTY-EIGHT

In the master bedroom of his seaside Clifton villa, Salim Bashira gazed pensively at the open attaché case containing his passport, bankbooks, keys to numbered accounts, and a Walther automatic that protruded from beneath a layer of rupees. He was struck by the incongruity of having spent a lifetime building an empire and collecting priceless objects of art, and in the end, having it all reduced to some documents, money, and a handgun.

He had, many years ago, given an oath to his mother on her deathbed, and he had never wavered, nor had any regrets. Not every man was granted the opportunity to help ensure the survival of his people. He had played a deadly game for many years, and now his own fate would be measured in the next few hours. So far, his luck was holding. But the terrifying question remained unanswered: how had General Murrani discovered Tukhali's espionage activities? Somewhere, somehow, a mistake had been made—a fatal mistake. Perhaps Tukhali had confided in the wrong person, or perhaps he himself had committed a blunder. But what? Not knowing was maddening.

Bashira shook his head in dismay and fingered the cyanide capsule in his pocket. No matter what happened, there would be no public hanging. He would not entertain the masses at the end of a rope.

He walked to the French windows and threw them open. The sea air smelled of rain, foghorns boomed ominously, and somewhere out there in the darkness, the *Athenian Queen* was closing in on the flash point.

CHAPTER FIFTY-NINE

In the dimly lit wheelhouse, the technicians were oblivious of everything but their glowing display screens.

Captain Alon and General Harel balanced themselves against the ship's roll and pitch. Alon chewed nervously on a dead cigar and asked the loran operator for a bearing check.

"Three nautical miles from IP, bearing one-eight-six."

"Speed?"

"Six knots."

On the foredeck, the canvas tarpaulin had been removed, and the Osprey was being refueled and a battery generator hooked up.

Alon pressed the intercom button connecting to his aft crew chief. "Raffy?"

There was a momentary pause and the chief responded, "Raffy here."

"Open aft hatch—and advise."

"We have only eighteen minutes, Matty," Dado said ominously.

"We'll make it."

The crew chief's voice came over the speaker. "Aft hatch open."

"Okay, Raffy. Test Jericho's hydraulic lift and advise."

In the semidarkness of the aft hold, Professor Yuval Newman felt his pulse quicken as the hydraulic-lift warning lights flashed and the thirty-six-foot-tall missile rose slowly on its steel-plated platform.

The crew chief and deckhands watched attentively as the Jericho's conical head protruded from the aft hold. The chief checked the hydraulic pump's pressure readings. Satisfied, he pressed the intercom button connecting to the bridge.

"Hydraulic lift, okay."

"Take her down, Raffy, and stand by."

Alon pressed the aft-hold intercom.

The flight-ascent engineer answered, "Yes, Captain . . ."

"Is Yuval close?"

"Right here."

"Put him on."

Feeling useless, Dado watched in silence. The command preparations belonged to Captain Alon.

"This is Newman."

"Countdown check," Alon ordered. "Eighteen minutes and fourteen seconds."

"Telemetry countdown is synchronous."

"Anything else I should know?" Alon asked.

"The detonation computers are calibrated for lift-off at precisely 0400 hours. We have only a slim variant margin. Any significant delay means a scrub."

"What do you consider significant?"

"Fifteen minutes."

"All right. Stand by."

Alon then called to his radioman, "Confirm our position with *Dolphin* and synchronize minutes to launch."

"Yes, sir."

"And, Avi, confirm that *Dolphin*'s fish are armed and ready."

The radioman nodded and proceeded to punch in the vertical marine communication channel.

"Why torpedoes?" Dado asked.

"Just a precaution."

"Against what?"

"Who knows?"

A tense, profound silence enveloped the bridge. The creaking sound of the ship underscored the ominous quiet.

The operational clock read 0344—sixteen minutes to lift-off.

In the gloom of the aft hold, Yuval Newman ran through a series of algorithmic target equations with the ascent-systems engineer.

On the foredeck, the Osprey's flight crew boarded the aircraft and began to run through the preflight checklist.

On the bridge, Alon handed Dado a cup of coffee. "This rain helps."

"How?"

"A heavy rain tends to calm the sea."

"Smoke?" Alon offered Dado a small cigar.

"No, thanks."

"I've got a sighting!" the radar man exclaimed.

"Speed and bearing!" Alon snapped.

"Bearing one-seven-six, closing fast, speed approximately thirty-five knots."

"Range?"

"I make it less than two miles."

"Christ . . ." Alon whispered. "It's got to be a Pakistani corvette. They carry Exocet missiles, quad-forty gun batteries, and sonar-wave antisubmarine depth charges."

"Can we jam its radar?"

"Too late. We'll see their lights any minute. We must have been spotted by an E2-C radar plane. I was afraid of this. Drifting almost dead in the water and showing no lights is good cause for suspicion." Alon turned to the radioman. "Avi, what frequency are you on?"

"Karachi Maritime."

"Kill it. Go dead."

"Why are they patrolling international waters?" Dado asked.

"They may think we're in trouble, or that we're running opium. Or, in view of the Libyan raid and the business with Tukhali, they may have increased their coastal patrols. Whatever it is, we've got to make a decision, and fast. We can kick in the turbines and run. We can order *Dolphin* to sink them on sight. But if that corvette disappears from its home-base radarscope, we'll have a fleet of planes and an armada of ships out here in a matter of minutes. We can still launch Jericho, but we're dead. The third option is to try to bluff our way through—and hope we don't have to use *Dolphin*'s torpedoes."

Dado stared off to port through the rain and nodded. "All right, try to bluff them. But if we have to, sink them. We can blow this ship up and take off on the Osprey. Without a cargo load, she'll handle all of us."

"Easier said than done. Keep in mind, once we sink that corvette, the Pakistani F-16's are only minutes away. The Osprey will be target practice."

"Can we launch Jericho, set explosives, and transfer everyone to *Dolphin*?"

Alon shook his head. "We're only forty miles from the air-sea naval base at Karachi. That's about six minutes for an F-16, a little more for helicopter gunships. Transferring everyone to the sub at night in a rolling sea is difficult and time-consuming. If we have to sink the Pakistani corvette, our only choice is the Osprey."

Alon activated the auxiliary vertical marine channel.

"*Dolphin,* this is Queen Bee. Over."

"*We read you. Over.*"

"Do you have the intruder on your loran? Over."

"*Affirmative. Bearing now one-eight-three and closing at thirty-four knots. Over.*"

"We're proceeding on course. Shadow us on port, and stand by to fire on my command. Over."

"*Roger, Queen Bee. Over and out.*"

Alon pressed the intercom connecting to the aft hold.

"Newman here."

"We have an intruder we believe to be a Pakistani corvette. But we are proceeding to flash point. Stand by to launch Jericho."

"Standing by."

Alon pressed the aft-deck intercom button. "Raffy!"

"Go ahead, Matty."

"We have an intruder."

"I see his lights."

"If I can't talk our way past them, *Dolphin* will sink them. We'll then launch Jericho, set explosive charges, and take everyone off on the Osprey. Have the boys stand by to open seacocks and plant TNT bundles below the waterline—but nothing is activated without my specific command."

"Right."

"And, Raffy, send a runner forward. I want the flight crew to maintain preflight mode but cover the aircraft."

"Done!"

Standing on the flying bridge of the Pakistani corvette, the captain and first officer had their infrared binoculars trained on the freighter's dark hulk.

"Searchlights!" the captain ordered.

Powerful carbon-arc beams stabbed through the darkness and rain. Six hundred yards ahead, the beams faintly illuminated the *Athenian Queen.*

"Gun crews to battle stations and boarding party stand by!" the captain commanded. He then called to the communications officer. "Lieutenant Hamidi . . ."

"Hamidi on line."

"Radio our position to base. Advise them that we have a freighter riding dead slow, showing no running lights, and transmitting no radio signals. We are proceeding to establish contact. Send that at once."

"Yes, sir!"

The captain then addressed his first officer.

"Activate loudspeaker."

"You have it, sir."

"Slow to fifteen knots, and come twenty degrees starboard. Stand by, all stations."

The captain waited for the message to be conveyed before raising his binoculars.

"What do you think?" the first officer asked.

"She's high in the water, no lights, barely turning her screws . . ." the captain murmured, the infrared binoculars fixed to his eyes. "Looks like she's flying a Greek flag; it might be an opium tub or a harmless freighter in trouble."

"But, sir, how can we board her? She's in international waters."

"For the record, we're offering emergency assistance."

In the *Athenian Queen*'s aft hold, Professor Newman checked the countdown telemetry and phoned the bridge.

"Matty?"

"Yes, go ahead."

"Eight minutes, twenty-six seconds, and counting."

"Check."

The rain-streaked windows surrounding the bridge flared in the arc lights of the oncoming frigate.

"The bastards are showing us their muscle," Alon said, and turned to the helmsman. "Ten degrees starboard."

"Coming ten degrees starboard."

Alon then called to the engine room, "Stand by for full standard."

"Standing by."

"Yossi!"

The loran radar operator swiveled around.

"Where's *Dolphin?*" Alon asked.

"Four hundred yards to port, at twenty fathoms."

The corvette's powerful searchlights flooded the bridge, and an amplified voice carried across the narrow stretch of sea separating the two vessels.

"Attention aboard! Attention aboard! Attention aboard! This is Captain Khadra, Pakistani Coastal Patrol number two-three-eight. We wish to speak with your captain."

Matty Alon picked up a battery-charged bullhorn and went out onto the flying bridge. The rain pelted his face as he raised the bullhorn to his lips. "I'm Captain Dimitri Minardos. Repeat, Dimitri Minardos. What can we do for you?"

"Identify your ship, Captain."

Alon's eyes narrowed against the searchlights and he saw the manned gun batteries and the silhouetted figures of a boarding party poised in the frigate's bow.

"*Athenian Queen*—out of Aqaba, bound for Calcutta."

"What is your home port?"

"Piraeus."

There was an ominous pause and Alon calculated how much time he'd need to fire *Dolphin*'s torpedoes.

"Do you require assistance?" The Pakistani captain's voice boomed across the narrow strip of water separating the two ships.

"Negative!" Alon replied. "Repeat, negative! We had a fire in the engine room. We're on auxiliary power, preparing to resume full power."

"Stand by, *Athenian Queen*," the Pakistani captain ordered.

Alon went quickly back inside the bridge.

"Four minutes," Dado said.

The *Dolphin*'s periscope poked above the black water and turned slowly, like the head of a cobra seeking a victim. The Pakistani corvette glowed in the submarine's scopefinder, the numbers 238 clearly visible in the cross hairs.

"Engines to All Stop," the sub's commander ordered.

"All Stop, sir."

"Range to target four hundred and fifty yards."

The chief officer repeated the message.

"Stand by, forward torpedo tubes."

In the aft hold, the Jericho launch team stared at the telemetric display screen—the digital countdown meter displayed three minutes and eighteen seconds. Newman could only guess at the drama being played up above, but his palms were sweating and he was hyperventilating. He glanced at Jericho III with its gleaming conical warhead. They were fast approaching a point of no return. Jericho's detonator-computers were already ticking down toward a zero conclusion.

On the foredeck, the pilot, copilot, and navigator were at their stations in the Osprey's cockpit. The hybrid craft was covered by a canvas tarpaulin. The air inside the cabin was close, and the movement of the ship made the flight crew queasy.

The pilot fought off the seasickness and concentrated on

completing takeoff preparations without activating the rotors. "Boost pumps, and try magneto," he said, "but don't engage."

The copilot flipped a toggle switch. "Magneto check."

"Advance mixture to full rich."

"Full rich."

The navigator punched his route home into the flight navigational computer.

Matty Alon paced the bridge. The digital clock read two and a half minutes to launch.

"We've got to make a decision, Matty," Dado said quietly.

Alon nodded. "Avi, switch on the Mitrek, and tune to frequency seven-one-three-six—Marine Emergency Allocation—and try to raise the corvette."

"Dado, hit those five toggle switches behind you. I want to light us up, show them we've restored power."

A hush fell over the bridge. Dado noticed that Alon's shirt was soaked with perspiration.

"I have contact!" the radioman shouted. Alon took the microphone and leaned over the operator. "Pakistan Two-three-eight, this is Captain Minardos, *Athenian Queen*. Over."

"This is Pakistan Two-three-eight. We read you. Over."

"We have full power—repeat, full power—and intend to proceed on course to Calcutta. Over."

"Hold position, Athenian Queen. Repeat, hold position."

"Shit," Alon hissed.

"You have to sink her," Dado said.

Alon activated the vertical marine channel. *"Dolphin, this is Queen Bee. Over."*

"Read you, Matty."

"Stand by to fire torpedoes on my count. Thirty seconds —mark!"

"Mark!"

Alon watched the sweep hand on his watch; beads of sweat oozed out of his forehead.

"Mark!" he called.

"Twenty-five," the submarine captain responded.

"Mark!"

"Twenty."

The corvette's powerful searchlights suddenly went out and the bridge radio crackled: *"Pakistan Two-three-eight calling* Athenian Queen. *Over."*

"Hold the count, *Dolphin!*" Alon shouted, and raced over to the Mitrek radio unit. "This is Minardos. We read. Over!"

"Proceed to your destination. Good luck. Over."

"Thank you for assistance, Two-three-eight. We are proceeding. Good luck to you. Over and out."

The sleek corvette heeled hard to starboard, its twin screws churning up a foaming wake.

"We're lucky, Dado! Goddamn lucky!" Alon exclaimed. "Our bluff worked. His base commander bought our story." Alon spoke to the radioman. "Avi, give me All Stations on this speaker."

Grabbing both knobs of the telegraph connection to the engine room, Alon set the arrow indicators to Full Ahead.

The ship shuddered as the giant screws bit into the sea.

"Hold course," Alon said to the helmsman.

"Avi, switch channels to Radio Islamabad."

"Switching channels."

"Raffy," Alon called into the speaker, "do you read me, Raffy?"

"I read you. Go ahead."

"Raise Jericho—and confirm when positioned."

"Zvikah. Do you read me?"

The forward crew chief replied, "I read you. Over."

"Remove tarp from Osprey. Disengage battery generator. Have pilot warm up rotors."

"Jericho in launch mode!" Newman's voice boomed over the speaker. "Fifty-five seconds and counting."

"Check!" Alon confirmed. "Avi, tell *Dolphin* to hold position and stand by. Joel, give me a loran reading."

"On station."

Alon grabbed the telegraph handles and moved indicators to Dead Slow.

The ship shuddered and settled.

Alon grabbed Dado's arm. "Let's go aft!"

* * *

They raced down the passageway to the aft deck and joined Raffy and his crew.

Jericho III was poised on its steel platform, beads of rain glistening off its warhead.

In the aft hold, the ascent engineer's index finger rested on the red firing button. The telemetric readout displayed ten seconds.

"Fire on six," Newman ordered.

They watched the spinning digital numbers: 00.09—00.08—00.07—00.06.

The engineer pressed the firing button.

On the aft deck, Dado, Alon, and the crew watched as a red glow appeared at the base of the missile and slowly transformed itself into a brilliant yellow-orange tail.

A thunderous roar rolled across the deck.

The six-second burn detonated the solid fuel, and two hundred thousand pounds of thrust hurled Jericho skyward.

CHAPTER SIXTY

Seven hundred and eighty miles north of Karachi, a crescent moon cast a faint, pale light over the Kahuta Nuclear Research Center. The security forces and missile batteries guarding the vast complex were on full alert.

Inside the reactor hall, a team of physicists and engineers initiated reactor-restart procedures. The vibrating hum of ten thousand whirling centrifuges echoed off the walls and rose up to the soaring concave cupola. Fresh uranium fuel rods, arranged in perfect symmetry, were submerged in the reservoir of heavy water. Technicians seated at computer banks checked and rechecked readouts analyzing the reactor's vital systems. It was 4:02 A.M. In less than eight hours, the reactor would be running at full power.

Close to the main gate, fifty feet below ground, two radar technicians drank coffee and chain-smoked, trying to fight off the hypnotic effects of monitoring the luminescent scope with its rotating green line. The Kahuta radar station was a sensitive but tedious assignment. Aircraft rarely entered the restricted twenty-mile radius, and radar operators sharpened their skills by tracking Pakistani Air Force F-16 jet fighters.

The bored duty officer yawned and glanced at his watch. Three more hours to go. He got to his feet, stretched, and poured a fresh cup of coffee.

"Coffee?" he asked his fellow officer.

"No, thanks. It's running through me."

"Take a break—relieve yourself."

"You won't fall asleep?"

"No. No, go ahead."

"I'll be right back."

"Take your time, Kasim. This alert is horseshit, routine nonsense."

The duty officer returned to his seat, glanced at the glowing radar screen, and reached for another cigarette. He shook one out of the pack, struck a match, raised it toward the cigarette, and froze. His hair bristled and goose bumps pimpled his arms. A large, pale green blip glowed in the wake of the sweep hand and grew in size with astonishing speed. The match burned the officer's fingers, galvanizing him into action. He quickly activated the computerized target vector. The numbers flashed instantly. The intruding object was at forty-seven thousand feet, descending at a rate of two hundred feet per second. The officer's fingers flew over the computer keys. The object would impact in three minutes and twenty-seven seconds. He turned on the radar computer-image enhancement. The intruder was wingless and conical. The panicked officer lost precious seconds as he frantically screamed, *"Warhead!"* to the empty room. Panting for breath, he pressed the base intercom P.A. button, and shouted, *"Red alert! Red alert! Incoming warhead! Incoming warhead! Launch heat-seekers! Launch missiles!"*

The cry of sirens pierced the night. Crotale missile batteries swung into action. Salvos of heat-seeking missiles were launched at the incoming warhead. Multibarreled AA guns opened up, crisscrossing the sky with luminous tracers. Troops poured out of their barracks and jumped into armored personnel carriers, driving madly in all directions. Pakistani Air Force F-16's scrambled skyward from their base adjacent to Kahuta.

The Jericho warhead smashed through the first level with the force of a wrecking ball before burying itself thirty-five feet down, between the third and fourth levels. The warhead's computerized brain triggered the detonator. The plastic blanket exploded inside the casing, crushing the beryllium sphere and expanding the air-lock chambers into a supercritical mass, instantaneously liberating an explosive force of one thousand tons of TNT.

The third and fourth levels erupted as a tornado of blistering heat and expanding shock waves spread vertically and horizontally.

In the reactor hall, the huge cupola collapsed in a shattering roar, sending tons of concrete crashing down into the heavy-water tank. The casing burst open, and a tidal wave of radioactive heavy water swept over the technicians, turning them into live, running X rays, iridescent shapes, dashing madly before glowing blue and vaporizing.

A whirlwind of orange-green flames flashed through the first level like a giant acetylene torch, consuming everything in its path. Miles of piping melted into puddles of molten copper. Electric cables shorted and coiled, spitting purple flames like nests of striking serpents.

In a matter of seconds, the Kahuta Nuclear Research Center was reduced to a roiling inferno of radioactive debris.

Twenty-five kilometers north of Kahuta, the earth rolled under the twin cities of Islamabad and Rawalpindi. Windows blew out. Water mains erupted. Power lines went down. People panicked and stumbled into the deserted streets, staring in horror at two great tongues of fire licking the dawn sky over Kahuta.

* * *

At 2:26 A.M., Tel Aviv time, Adam Zichroni notified the Prime Minister that Radio Islamabad had ceased broadcasting.

At 4:26 P.M., Pacific Time, the Caltech seismology lab in Pasadena registered an earthquake of 6.5 magnitude, centered in northeast Pakistan.

CHAPTER SIXTY-ONE

A heavy mist enveloped the *Athenian Queen* as she wallowed dead in the water.

Captain Matty Alon rechecked coordinates with his loran operator.

"The readings are identical," the operator said. "Trust me, Matty. We're forty miles east of Karachi and three miles off Gadani Beach. Look at the screen—you can see the curve of the beach."

"If we're in position, where's the guide boat?"

"How the hell would I know? I didn't plan this operation. I only volunteered for it."

Alon squeezed the man's shoulder. "All right, Yossi. All right."

The nerves of his crew were at the cutting edge, and the tension had not eased with the launching of Jericho. Minutes after the launch, the Osprey had taken off with Dado, Newman, and the Jericho team, while Alon's crew busied themselves dismantling the high-tech launch equipment and dumping it overboard.

For the past two hours they had been steaming inside

Pakistani territorial waters. All they knew for certain was that Radio Islamabad had gone off the air three and a half minutes after Jericho's lift-off. If the warhead had hit its intended target, the entire coast would be alive with patrols . . . unless the ruling military clique had withheld the devastating news from its Southern Naval Command.

"Let's give the pilot boat another fifteen minutes," Alon said to the exhausted bridge crew. With that, he picked up his binoculars and went out onto the flying bridge.

He could smell land, but the billowing mists had drawn an impenetrable curtain between the ship and the coast. The fathometer indicated shoals and shallow trenches, and they could not chance running aground three miles from shore.

Bashira's plan had to be followed explicitly or abandoned. Alon hoped the audacity of the plan would prove to be its strength—his previous work with Salim Bashira gave him confidence in the longtime Mossad operative.

As he scanned the sea, Alon heard, or thought he heard, the faint putt-putt of a small engine. Snapping on the forward searchlight, he directed it toward the sound, and through the silky mists he saw what appeared to be the silhouette of a motor launch. His pulse quickened as he discerned the hazy figure of a tall man standing in the launch's prow. Alon shouted into the intercom.

"Lower sea ladder, Raffy! Lower sea ladder!"

"Sea ladder down," the crew chief replied.

Alon picked up the battery-powered megaphone and called out to the approaching launch. "This is Captain Minardos. We've been waiting for you!"

"Sorry, Captain!" the harbor pilot shouted. "It's this damned fog!"

Swerving sharply hard to port, the launch hove to, alongside the freighter's starboard side. The pilot cupped his hands and called up to Alon, "Request permission to come aboard."

Thirty minutes later, the *Athenian Queen*'s keel knifed into the sandbank at full speed and slid to a stop one hundred feet from Gadani Beach.

"Now, Captain Minardos," the pilot said. "Now you will see something."

He pulled the lever, and the ship's horn boomed three times.

Wearing rags, a mass of shouting brown-skinned men materialized out of nowhere and raced across the mudbank. They clambered up the cargo nets slung over the ship's port side. Once aboard, they formed a chain, and, hand over hand, passed pickaxes, cutting torches, bolt cutters, and sledgehammers. Armed with tools, the Pathan tribesmen swarmed over the vessel like an army of warrior ants about to feed on a helpless animal.

Alon and his eighteen crew members disembarked and dutifully followed the harbor pilot up the embankment to the waiting immigration officer.

On the road, above the makeshift immigration booth, Salim Bashira leaned casually against his Jaguar. A dusty transport bus was parked alongside the gleaming sedan.

Alon and his crew produced their Greek passports and were waved through immigration.

The crewmen boarded the bus, and Alon got into the Jaguar with Bashira.

Moving at a leisurely speed, both vehicles took the coastal road west, toward Karachi.

"In a few days," Bashira said, indicating the smokestacks of the nearby steel mills, "the *Athenian Queen* will have disappeared into those blast furnaces without a trace. Open the glove compartment, Matty. You'll find an envelope with plane tickets for you and your crew. We leave Karachi for Athens at thirteen hundred hours on Olympic Airways."

"And then?"

"Small groups will depart from Athens for Tel Aviv over a discreet ten-day period. In case you haven't heard, there was a catastrophic earthquake in the north. Our nuclear-research center reportedly suffered grave damage."

CHAPTER SIXTY-TWO

Racing from the smoldering temple, the soldier cradled the burning scrolls in his arms. Dado chased him. A Jordanian tank lumbered into the Street of Chain. The soldier disappeared beneath the tank treads. Avital knelt over the bloody residue, picking the pieces of scroll from the matted corpse. The Prophet Elijah swayed in prayer over Avital. A very young Dado leveled his rifle and put a bullet through the Prophet's eye. The eye grew larger, ballooning, filling the street—thick veins of blood crisscrossed the white of the eye. The immense eye rose above the Old City. Dado raised his rifle, aimed at the eye, and fired. A deluge of blood poured down, sweeping Avital and the dead soldier's body from the Street of Chain. Only the young Dado remained. Yahweh, wearing striped death-camp pajamas, came toward him.

Dado bolted upright against the seat belt, caught his breath, and wiped some sweat from his forehead.

"What is it?" Newman asked.

"Nothing," Dado replied hoarsely, and peered out the oval window.

Far below, the azure waters of the Gulf of Aden shimmered in the sunlight. Dado unbuckled his seat belt, rose, and glanced at the Jericho technicians playing cards in the rear of the plane.

"Are you all right?" Newman asked.

"I'm fine," Dado replied, and walked forward to the flight deck.

"How much longer?" he asked the pilot.

"If this tailwind holds, four hours."

"Do we have top cover?"

"We rendezvoused with the F-15 escort group an hour ago." The pilot paused. "Are you all right, General?"

"Just tired."

"Your face is chalky."

"So is yours, son."

"It's the light," the navigator said.

CHAPTER SIXTY-THREE

The briefing theater in the Defense Ministry at Lahore overflowed with representatives of the international press. The air-conditioning system was turned up to counter the intense heat thrown by the lights and cameras. President Ghazi's address was being transmitted to the world, via satellite.

His black eyes were somber, and the tone of his voice was solemn.

"A monumental tragedy has befallen our nation. I regret to inform you that Pakistan's nuclear-research center at Kahuta has been destroyed by a devastating earthquake. One hundred and seventy-six of our technicians have perished in the disaster. The cities of Islamabad, Peshawar, and Rawalpindi have been temporarily evacuated. Army units of our Northern Command are attempting to seal the Kahuta site and contain radioactive fallout. I appeal to the world's scientific community for immediate assistance. The Islamic Republic of Pakistan harbored no ambitions to become a nuclear power. The Kahuta Nuclear Research Center was designed to provide cheap energy for our entire northwest province." He paused, waiting for the scribbling journalists to keep pace with his remarks.

Seated in the back row, General Ayub Murrani watched the President's performance with detached amusement. Although he despised the man, he nevertheless admired Ghazi's remarkable ability to conceal the truth behind a convincing facade of innocence.

The superpowers were aware that Kahuta had existed solely to produce nuclear weapons, and in reality, Ghazi's remarks were intended to mask the truth from the Pakistani people.

Murrani had earlier informed the President that the disaster at Kahuta had been caused by internal and external enemies. Murrani's Swiss connection had finally penetrated the maze of dummy corporations behind Lizrose—the trail led directly to Salim Bashira's Global Transport Systems. The phone number found in Dr. Tukhali's directory had been traced to Bashira's villa. The shipping tycoon's bank accounts had been emptied, his office closed, and Bashira himself gone.

Murrani was convinced that Bashira had fed the data supplied by Tukhali to the Indian Bureau of Intelligence. One had to keep in mind that the American journalist, Lawford, and Dr. Tukhali had made a run for the Indian border, and Bashira had numerous Indian business contacts. How the Indians had managed to destroy Kahuta remained a mystery.

In any case, the facts would not be revealed to the nation. The resulting rage would topple the regime. It had been Murrani's suggestion to blame the disaster on nature. No one could be held responsible for an earthquake. Fortunately, the radioactive fallout had been minimal. But it would cost hundreds of millions to concretize the Kahuta site. It would require a mountain of cement, but perhaps one day people would ski on it—there was always an upside.

The intelligence chief lit a cigarette and watched the President pause dramatically as he prepared to conclude his remarks on a pious note.

"We remain a bastion of Islamic faith on the subcontinent of Asia. We place our lives, and our fortunes, in the hands of the Prophet Muhammad and God Almighty—Allah."

CHAPTER SIXTY-FOUR

Admiral Clarke Dwinell snapped off the television set and slammed his fist down onto his polished oak desk. "How? How did those fucking Israelis do it?"

"We don't know that they did anything," Manfredi countered. "It may very well have been an earthquake. The entire region sits on a fault."

The Admiral picked up his coffee mug and glanced out at the dazzling morning sun filtering through the tall pines. "The Israelis hit Kahuta. There's not a doubt in my mind." He swiveled around and leaned forward. "The disaster at Kahuta wipes the Libyan air strike off the world stage. The Security Council's current debate to condemn Israel has been suspended. Teams of nuclear physicists from the Soviet Union, the U.S., Western Europe, and the International Atomic Energy Agency are converging on Kahuta. The entire world's attention is focused on the Pakistani nuclear debacle. I tell you that once Mossad received those pictures from Lawford, they acted. Their timing was perfect on all counts. The reactor was cold, and the fallout is Three Mile Island, not Chernobyl. Our KH-11 pictures confirm that an implosion occurred, sealing the site. It was swift and surgical."

"But how? It's five thousand miles round trip over hostile territory from Tel Aviv to Kahuta. And even if by some miracle a few F-16's got through, the pilots would be frozen to the stick."

"That's not how it was done." The Admiral rocked back and forth for a moment. "The Israelis successfully tested an advanced Jericho III missile over a year ago."

"It's still an IRBM with only a thousand-mile range. How does Jericho get from Israel to Pakistan?"

"They found a way."

"How can you be sure it wasn't an accident?" Manfredi persisted. "We know that an earthquake of 6.5 magnitude did in fact strike northeast Pakistan."

"The Richter scale does not distinguish earthquakes from underground nuclear explosions. We tested something in Nevada last week that registered 4.5 and blew out windows a hundred miles away in Las Vegas. This was no accident. Kahuta was in the doomsday business, and one way or the other, the Israelis took it out. I just hope to God the Pakistanis don't blame India, or the whole goddamn subcontinent will go up." The Admiral pressed a button on the intercom.

"Yes, sir?"

"Get Zev Berger, please."

Releasing the intercom, he asked Manfredi, "What's the latest on Lawford?"

"He's still in Tel Aviv."

"That missionary bastard is in bed with Mossad. The German girl turned him. If any of this ever leaks, if the Oversight Committee tumbles onto the fact that one of our own—"

"Zev Berger on line three," the secretary's voice interrupted.

"Get on the extension, Al."

Admiral Dwinell picked up the receiver and smiled warmly, as if Berger could see him. "Good evening, Zev."

"Good morning to you, Admiral."

"How are you?"

"Overweight and overworked, but holding up."

"Good. I called to remind you that we require Lawford's immediate return. I'm officially requesting that you take him into protective custody. We'll send an Air Force plane for him."

"Fortunately, that won't be necessary. He's booked on tonight's El Al flight to New York."

Seated behind his scarred desk, Berger glanced at Narda, who was listening on the extension. "Is there any message for Lawford?" he asked.

"No. Just make sure he's on that plane."

"I'll do my best. Is there anything else?"

"One small item."

"Yes?"

"How did you manage it?"

"Manage what?"

"Kahuta."

Berger sighed. "When the first case of AIDS is reported on the moon, Israel will be blamed."

"You're probably right, Zev." The Admiral chuckled. "You sound tired. Take a day off. Get some rest. We'll be speaking very soon . . . and please make sure Lawford gets on that plane."

"Not to worry. Take care, Admiral."

"You too, Zev."

There was a soft knock at the door and the secretary entered and handed the Admiral a red envelope. "From NSA." The Admiral read from a single sheet stamped "Top Secret": "RECORDED BY KH-11 SATT: 1640 HOURS OVER ARABIAN SEA."

"Take a look at this, Al."

Manfredi peered over the Admiral's shoulder.

> "Queen Bee to Grasshopper. Queen Bee to Grasshopper. Over."
> "Grasshopper reads. Over."
> "You're on loran. Over."
> "Roger, we're on the way. Over and out."

[Pause. New mode.]

> "Grasshopper to Eagle One. Over."
> "Eagle One reads. Over."

362

"We're at IP and descending to Queen Bee. Thanks for the company. Over."

"Roger, Grasshopper. Over and out."

The Admiral closed the file. "This was recorded Tuesday, approximately eighteen hours before Kahuta went up."

" 'Queen Bee' . . . " Manfredi mused. " 'Grasshopper'— sounds like codes used by the British. Probably air-sea maneuvers out of that limey base at Masirah."

"Call London and check with Saunders at MI-6. One thing is certain. Those voices belong to people who were operating very sophisticated stuff off the coast of Pakistan."

CHAPTER SIXTY-FIVE

*Z*ev Berger lit a cigarette and shook his head in feigned dismay. "Ah . . . the games we play."

"You think the Admiral knows?" Narda asked.

"Of course he knows."

"Still, he can't prove anything."

"For the moment. But they will. The Americans are unbelievable. They can listen to conversations on Pluto. In time, they'll know everything." Berger paused. "But I must admit, the operation was a geopolitical triumph. This time our friends will not be forced to condemn us."

"That's high praise considering you were always opposed to the operation."

"Not in theory; only in practice. I'm fearful of any operation which demands perfect planning and perfect execution. But sometimes, everything works. So you have an earthquake in northeast Pakistan, and the universe breathes a little easier with the Muslim bomb removed from the world stage. Have a cookie, Narda."

"No, thank you."

"These cookies are not my wife's. I bought these cookies this morning at Hertzberg's Bakery."

She eyed him suspiciously but bit into the cookie and sipped some coffee. "What did you want to see me about?"

"I'm offering you a post in the Cultural Affairs Section of our London embassy."

Narda stared at the intelligence chief's innocent brown eyes.

"Dado's orders?"

"No, mine. Go for a while, Narda. You've been through enough. You're still young. Dado will never leave Avital. He will never leave the Holocaust. He will never resolve his personal war with Yahweh. He will never forgive the past. Save yourself."

She studied him for a moment and said, "You're a decent man, Yanush, and I thank you for the offer, but London is too cold for me. I'm a Mediterranean person."

CHAPTER SIXTY-SIX

General Dado Harel and Tom Lawford walked through the dappled sunlight toward the circular floral garden. "There she is," Dado said. "I'll wait for you at the entrance. We don't have much time."

Erika wore large sunglasses, and her face was tilted up toward the sun. The gold Brazilian necklace circled her throat and the "Figa" talisman glinted in the sunlight.

As Lawford approached, she removed her glasses and glared at him. "Berger gave me his word. I didn't want to see you. He gave me his word."

"And he kept his word. The General brought me here. Besides, I'm an outpatient. The doctors here checked my arm."

"Please go."

Tom shook his head sadly. "For Chrissakes, Erika . . ."

She stared at him for a long moment. The angry light in her eyes dimmed, and she said, "I don't know where the nurse has gone. Would you please wheel me to the other side?"

He pushed the wheelchair along a palm-lined walkway toward a circular promontory overlooking the Mediterranean.

High above, a pair of hawks circled gracefully, riding the thermals, and far below, huge waves exploded against the long breakwater, sending up fountains of sea spray.

"What happened to your arm?" she asked.

"A car accident."

"Why did you do it? Why did you agree to go?"

"The General made a strong case."

"Is that all?"

"Maybe it was the tunnels at Nordhausen. Maybe a lot of things. Hell, I don't know."

She stared off at the gray silhouette of a corvette patrolling the coastline. "Not wanting to see you was not a matter of vanity," she said softly. "I don't care about my face. It's being so damned helpless, being unable to walk. Since Berlin I haven't even let my mother see me—only Narda. She visits me often."

"The doctor said your scars are healing, and you're going to be walking very soon. And as far as I'm concerned"—he smiled, "you're still a candidate for Miss Germany."

Ich glaube Sie sind.

"Meaning?"

"It's a little late."

He leaned over and kissed her.

"Don't do that, please." She smiled. "The last thing I need now is sexual frustration."

"I should never have left you alone."

"You couldn't have done anything. It happened fast, very fast. Landau saved my life, and Penelope lost hers."

"Have you heard about Kleiser?"

"No."

"He's been arrested by the Swiss police. It seems he almost killed a very young girl, beat her to a pulp."

"Probably some child he paid for."

Tom took out a small card-size envelope and placed it in her lap. "All my numbers. Phone me."

"Why should I?"

"I want to know that you're all right."

She stared at him and thought that his gray eyes seemed softer than she had remembered.

"Promise me you'll call."

She nodded. "All right, I promise."

He bent down and kissed her lightly. Her arm circled his neck and they embraced passionately. Memories flooded. Time and place slipped away.

"Mr. Lawford?"

Tom whirled around. A uniformed nurse stood at the garden entrance.

"Yes?" he answered, somewhat embarrassed.

"General Harel asked me to remind you that he's waiting."

"You better leave," Erika said.

Their eyes met and locked for the last time. She watched him go, and hoped he would remember her. Nothing more. . . .

Dado drove the sand-colored Volvo south along the Coastal Highway toward Ben-Gurion International Airport. Lawford stared vacantly out the window. They had not spoken since leaving the hospital.

Following closely behind was a military jeep driven by the General's personal bodyguards. It wasn't until they passed the first airport-approach sign that Dado said, "You have to let go of her."

"I was just thinking how well she's handled this. The doctor told me she has a steel rod in place of her thigh bone. He says she'll be ambulatory but will always suffer a degree of pain."

"She'll handle the pain. She's handled a more profound pain all her life."

"When she's walking, when she improves, I want to see her."

"Leave it alone, Tom. Erika Sperling is on a Libyan hit list. She can only be safe here. You want to settle down on a kibbutz and spend your days growing peaches?"

"I'm counting on you, Dado. I want you to put her in touch with me."

"Give it some time, and if you still want to see her, I'll arrange it. You have my word."

They entered the main gate, swung around the rotunda, and pulled up at the curbside departure terminal.

The jeep parked behind them. The soldiers got out and waited for the men to say their good-byes.

"My boys will take you to security, where Narda will be waiting. There is no way I can ever thank you. The Holy Land is yours."

They shook hands and Tom said, "Tell me, how did you manage Kahuta?"

The General stared at him for a long moment and thought: Why not? He had trusted Lawford all the way. "We used one of our aircraft carriers. Now, go on before you miss the plane."

Tom entered the noisy terminal and followed the soldiers through the milling crowd. He knew Dado was right, but the memory of those stolen, intimate moments with Erika were indelible, and would remain undiminished by time or place—and for that he was grateful.

He squared his shoulders and picked up his pace. He had seen the shark, and with one exception his debts had been paid in full. He still owed his marriage an honest resolution. Well, time would tell. It always did.

CHAPTER SIXTY-SEVEN

Like dark shadows risen from the mists of antiquity, the Zealots swayed and chanted before the floodlit Western Wall. As he watched them, Dado was struck by the realization that Avital's prophecy had come to pass. He had, in a sense, saved the Holy Scriptures from the fire. The nuclear sun had not fallen into this sacred place.

The Zealots would pray for Elijah to appear. The Arabs would kneel at the Dome of the Rock. The Christians would seek redemption in the Church of the Holy Sepulcher. Jerusalem would endure. And perhaps, Dado thought, that was Yahweh's greatest trick.

The General put his collar up against the night wind and walked toward the bullet-chipped Jaffa Gate. Tomorrow he would go down to the desert airbase and speak to the pilot who had seen the lion in the Arava. . . .